❧ THE ❧
QUEEN
and the
KNAVE

OTHER PROPER ROMANCES
BY SARAH M. EDEN

Ashes on the Moor

<u>Hope Springs</u>
Longing for Home
Longing for Home, vol. 2: Hope Springs

<u>Savage Wells</u>
The Sheriffs of Savage Wells
Healing Hearts
Wyoming Wild

<u>The Dread Penny Society</u>
The Lady and the Highwayman
The Gentleman and the Thief
The Merchant and the Rogue
The Bachelor and the Bride
The Dread Penny Society:
The Complete Penny Dreadful Collection

PROPER ROMANCE

THE QUEEN and the KNAVE

SARAH M. EDEN

SHADOW MOUNTAIN PUBLISHING

To Sammie Trinidad,
a light and a delight,
a woman I am honored to call my friend

Library of Congress Cataloging-in-Publication Data
Names: Eden, Sarah M., author.
Title: The queen and the knave / Sarah M. Eden.
Other titles: Proper romance.
Description: Salt Lake City: Shadow Mountain Publishing, [2023] | Series: Proper romance | Summary: "For Dread Penny Society leader Móirín Donnelly and Constable Detective Fitzgerald Parkington to enjoy the romance growing between them, they must team up to stop the Tempest once and for all"—Provided by publisher.
Identifiers: LCCN 2023005386 | ISBN 9781639931521 (trade paperback)
Subjects: LCSH: Penny dreadfuls—Fiction. | BISAC: FICTION / Romance / Historical / Victorian | FICTION / Romance / Clean & Wholesome | LCGFT: Romance fiction. | Novels.
Classification: LCC PS3605. D45365 Q44 2023 | DDC 813/.6—dc23/eng/20230313
LC record available at https://lccn.loc.gov/2023005386

Printed in the United States of America
Lake Book Manufacturing, LLC, Melrose Park, IL

10   9   8   7   6   5   4   3   2   1

CHAPTER 1

London, 1866

Móirín Donnelly had been called a great many things in her twenty-seven years, but "naive" was not one of them. She knew more than enough of the world to realize 'twas a cruel place, and she'd lived long enough in its harsher corners to know how to navigate its labyrinth of uncertainty.

On a dark, fearful night, mere hours after the funeral of two of her closest friends, and even merer hours after learning of the betrayal of a man she'd thought of as something near to family, she moved with silent footfall along the corridor of an unlit home on King Street, one she knew well, though no one would guess that she did. *Almost* no one.

For five years, this had been the headquarters of the Dread Penny Society, a group of penny dreadful authors who secretly fought for the good of the poor and the voiceless, who undertook dangerous missions to protect lives that most people considered unworthy of acknowledgment. In so doing, the DPS had earned themselves some extremely dangerous enemies.

'Twas Móirín who'd begun it all shortly after arriving in London from Dublin, along with a chance-met author named

Fletcher Walker and a philanthropic gentleman who'd wished to do good in the world without drawing attention. That gentleman had, shortly before his death, provided the funds for Móirín to purchase this house for use as the society's headquarters. He'd believed in what they did, though no one but Fletcher and Móirín had any idea of his connection to the organization's earliest days. Móirín had been the head of the Dread Penny Society over the years, but her role had been kept hidden even from the members. A lot was kept secret in the DPS.

Now those members were in hiding, and she, alone, tiptoed through this house to search out the mole who'd betrayed them all.

Holding aloft her shuttered lantern, she took hold of the door handle to the room Nolan Cook, the man who'd worked as butler and general caretaker, had called his own these past five years. He'd been a constant in the entryway, aware of all their comings and goings, privy to their membership and much of what they'd undertaken.

They'd trusted him with so very much. And he, in return, had offered their secrets to the most dangerous criminal London had ever known.

Móirín turned the handle and pushed the door open. Its hinges squealed as the door scraped against the floor. Her arrival would not go unnoticed by anyone who might be lurking inside. She pulled a long-bladed knife from her boot and held it at the ready.

No sound echoed from within the room. No movement. No breathing. No breeze from an open window.

Nolan had disappeared before his betrayal had been discovered. No one knew precisely when or where he'd gone. She'd searched the entire house, leaving this room to the last.

She stepped over the threshold, slowly sweeping the space with the focused light of her shuttered lantern. The small bureau to one side had no bits or baubles strewn atop it. The bed, up against the far wall, was neatly made. She raised the lantern higher and inspected the walls. Bare as a vulture's head.

Móirín set the lantern on the bureau, not loosening her grip on her knife. She flipped back the metal shutters on the four sides of the lantern, allowing the flame to illuminate the room more fully.

It was empty.

She'd known the chances of Nolan still being in the DPS headquarters were slim at best. He'd probably stepped out the front door right after the Dreadfuls had assembled earlier that night and been on his way. 'Tweren't likely that he'd've gone down to the belowstairs and cowered in the very first place he'd've been looked for. Still, she'd thought it best to be absolutely certain. Móirín hadn't survived all she had by being reckless.

What clues have you left me, then, Nolan?

She pulled open each drawer in the bureau. All were empty. Nothing sat beneath the bed. The washbasin was dry as a bone. He'd scampered off, for certain, but something in the pristinely vacant room wasn't right. 'Twas . . . *too* empty.

Nolan was forever reading newspapers, yet not a single one was in the room. He'd have certainly packed his things before running off, yet he'd left behind not so much as a stray thread or a bit of lint. Dust, yes. But nothing that'd lead anyone to believe this room had ever been lived in. 'Twas too thorough for Móirín's peace of mind.

Movement in the corridor heightened her senses even further.

She heard footsteps. Ones made cautiously, quietly. Someone was attempting to sneak up on her. She hadn't let anyone do that to her since she'd left Ireland; it certainly wouldn't happen now.

Móirín adjusted her hold on her knife, then moved behind the door, positioning herself so she could see the person entering the room before being seen herself.

Then she waited.

She'd left footprints in the dust. Any housebreaker or cutthroat worth his salt would notice and track her that way. She was ready for that possibility.

A shadow fell across the threshold. Not a sound. Not even a breath.

The Phantom Fox was this stealthy, being a legend among sneak thieves. She was also a friend of Móirín's. And she wouldn't have made any noise upon approach. This was someone else, for sure and certain.

The Tempest, London's criminal overlord and the person the DPS was currently hiding from, likely could have arrived relatively undetected, but her style was louder, bolder, more inclined to crowing than tiptoeing. So, 'twasn't her stepping into the room either.

The new arrival moved forward, revealing a man's boot and trouser leg.

"You're either Ana or Móirín, and I know Ana ain't here."

Móirín lowered her knife. "B'gor, Fletcher Walker. Why're you sneakin' about the place?" She stepped out from behind the door.

"B'gor?" he repeated with a smirk. "Leaning a bit heavily into your Irish roots."

"Anything else I might've said would've melted your ears." She met Fletcher in the middle of the room.

"My dainty ears thank you." Fletcher looked around the room. "Clean as a whistle, i'n'it?"

"Except for all the dust."

Fletcher nodded. "Something ain't right about it."

"I've been feeling the same since stepping inside." She shook her head. "It ain't so much that it's empty. It feels . . . abandoned. Dusty like no one's been caring for it, not for a long time."

"There ain't no personal belongings anywhere to be seen." Fletcher's eyes darted about. "And the only footprints in the dust are ours. It's been there quite some time, I'd guess."

"Months, at least." Móirín could see the truth clearly. "Nolan's not called this room home for a long time."

Fletcher met her gaze. "Then where *has* he been calling home?"

Móirín sheathed her knife. "'Tis a question we need an answer to."

"I suspect we ain't gonna like the answer we get."

"More likely than not, we'll full hate it."

Móirín picked up her lantern and crossed to the bed. The dust on the floor and bed was thick and undisturbed. Nolan hadn't moved his bed in ages. That was a helpful thing. The wall behind it hid one of many secret passages in this house, but Nolan hadn't tucked himself in there when he'd flown.

"How much of the ol' place have you searched?" Fletcher asked.

"All of it. He ain't here." She looked to Fletcher. "Did you send out your urchins?"

"Oi. Any Dreadfuls who weren't here tonight will know

the lay of things in no time." Fletcher looked out for the street urchins of London, having been one himself and knowing the nightmare they often lived. "The Dreadfuls are being told to keep themselves as safe as they can and await instructions from you."

"*I'll* send instructions?"

"The *Dread Master*'ll send instructions." Fletcher dipped his head. "I stand by what I said earlier: they need you now, Móirín. They need the confidence that comes from knowing who's leading us."

"And who's to say knowing 'tis me hiding behind the fearsome mask won't make them feel *less* safe?" She led the way out of the room.

"Because they know you—*Móirín Donnelly*—and not a one of them wouldn't trust you to lead them through purgatory itself and back."

"And if that's precisely where this path is leading us?" They climbed the servants' stairs, landing themselves on the ground level and the corridor leading back to the entryway.

"We've set ourselves up for a fight with the devil for years now," Fletcher said. "I'd've been shocked if we hadn't eventually found ourselves there."

They stopped in the entryway, dark except for her lantern. Shadows danced and mocked and hinted at things not seen, things meant to be noticed but hidden from view. This house held a great many secrets, many of which the Dreadfuls didn't know about, not even Fletcher.

Móirín wasn't entirely unlike the house. She knew the burden of secrets, knew the dangers that came with them.

The Tempest had killed before, and she'd do so again. Móirín hadn't a doubt in the world that the Dread Master was high on the Tempest's list of people she'd enjoy snuffing out. Keeping her identity a secret wasn't a matter of mere self-preservation. If the Dreadfuls didn't know the identity of their leader, and if the Tempest knew that information couldn't be tortured out of them, they would be safer. And that mattered to Móirín. It had always mattered.

"I'll send word around to all the Dreadfuls," she said. "But this secret needs keeping a touch longer. It'll keep the Dreadfuls safer, and it'll safeguard my network of informants. They only know me through this mask, and it's crucial it stays that way."

He nodded. "I'll trust you on this, Móirín. But I'll also warn you. This ain't the time for one of your stubborn stands. With the DPS scattered and the Tempest claiming victory, this ain't a war that can be won alone."

"I don't intend to be alone, just anonymous." She nodded to the front door. "Lock it up, Fletcher. No one'll be coming through that blue door any time soon."

He pulled a heavy iron key from his waistcoat pocket. "Cain't say I like doing this, knowing it might mean it never opens again—not to the DPS, leastwise."

"There're other doors," she said. "Other ways in."

"Why do I get the feeling you're being poetic and not just literal?" he said dryly.

"I ain't a poet."

"Most think you ain't a writer at all, but we both know that ain't true." He slid the key into the lock and turned. The bolt slung into place with a thud that felt far too final.

Móirín pushed forward the topic at hand to distract herself. "Members of the DPS have to write penny dreadfuls," she reminded him. "Couldn't've run a society I wasn't eligible to join, now could I?"

"We also all thought a person had to be male to join." He shot her a look as they walked toward the back of the house. Her lantern continued being their only source of light, but they knew their way around, she even better than he. "That put me in a bit of a bind with my Elizabeth, though she found a way around that, clever as she is."

"Clever enough that none of us knew she was the famous 'Mr. King' for quite a long time." Móirín's footsteps were slow and steady, but her mind raced ahead. "Make certain she closes down her school, and the two of you stash yourselves in my safe house on Riding House. The Tempest knows you're the acting head of this organization, which makes you a target. The Tempest also knows Elizabeth is Mr. King. I don't doubt she'd use that to blackmail Elizabeth."

"The school's already being emptied," Fletcher assured her.

"Have Barnabus and Gemma relocate to the Riding House safe house as well," she added. Those two were already in hiding, but having them in the same location as Fletcher and Elizabeth would simplify things.

"I will," he said.

"When you reach the back of headquarters," Móirín said, "take the hidden passageway from the cloakroom rather than the door. It'll be safer."

"And how do you mean to get out?"

"A secret passage behind the pub."

His brow hooked upward. "There's a secret passage behind the pub?"

"I chose this place for a reason," she said. "It's served us well. And if we don't all get murdered in our attempt to bring down the Tempest, it'll do so again."

"'If we don't get murdered . . . ' You never were one for mincing words."

Móirín motioned him down the servants' stairs once more. "You and Elizabeth get yourselves situated. I'll meet you at Riding House once I've seen to another bit of business."

"And what's that?"

"There's someone else who needs some information whispered in his ear, and I suspect he'll not be terribly pleased about it."

Indeed, were she to wager, she'd put every penny she had on her soon-to-be confidant disliking everything about their coming encounter, not because of what she would be telling him but because *she* was the one doing the telling.

CHAPTER 2

"The filchpurse dropped down on t' other side of t' wall!"

Fitzgerald Parkington acknowledged his colleague's shouted report by shifting his aim to that very wall and running at it, full tilt. On his last step, he sprang into a jump and flung his arms atop the stones, then pulled himself up and over the wall. He landed on the spongy ground and continued his pursuit.

The thief was well within view. In fact, the prattle-head had actually paused to look back. Fitz had chased him before, and Lanky Mack had slowed his escape on those occasions, too. This'n was a regular beef-head, he were.

With a flash of panic across his overly pale face, Lanky Mack took to a run once more, jumping over headstones and weaving around trees.

Why was it so many criminals thought he wouldn't chase them through a churchyard?

Fitz leapt over a precariously crooked stone slab, then dodged one lying newly on its side. This cemetery hadn't had a new burial in years, full to bursting as it was. Sometimes it seemed even the grave markers were being crowded out.

Mathers, his fellow constable, would make for the church-yard gate. That was what always happened when Fitz kept on the heels of a fleeing ruffian: his colleagues headed their quarry off at the next pass and then crowed over the capture.

Lanky Mack dodged to the right of a tree, but he'd have to double back seeing as a toppled stone cut off the path in the other direction.

Fitz set himself at the trunk, feet braced for collision.

Only a moment later, Lanky Mack and his pocket of plunder crashed into him. The man fell backward against the tree trunk.

With a grip as ironclad as he could manage, Fitz grabbed hold of the thief's collar and pulled him forward, spinning him around and pressing his chest against the tree. He grabbed the man's upper arms, pulling them toward each other behind Lanky Mack's back. He tightened his grip enough to make it too uncomfortable for wiggling overly much. That'd simplify things.

Unfortunately, it also put Fitz at an uncomfortably close distance to the man's stench, one that identified his newly adopted variety of thievery: toshing.

"Blimey, Lanky Mack," Fitz muttered. "You know scavenging in the sewers is against the law."

"Seems to me a bloke oughta be permitted to keep what he digs out of the dung heaps."

Fitz agreed, truth be told. The horridness of the job spoke to a desperation he hated punishing people for.

"You's a blue-bottle, not an alley cat. Seems to me you oughtn't be climbing walls." Lanky Mack was always full of complaints whenever Fitz caught him committing any of his specialty crimes: bobbing, gulling, pickpocketing, and now, it seemed, lowering himself into the perils of the sewers to dig out coins or whatever valuables he could find in the muck below. He weren't dangerous in the way many criminals were, but he certainly caused a heap of trouble.

"I saw you nip a watch off that cove on Baker Street," Fitz said. "Which is what I chased you down for. But you'll be searched at the station and lose whatever it is you dug from the sewers."

Lanky Mack muttered a frustrated oath.

Mathers walked leisurely over to them. "You'll be for t' prison this time, Lanky. Oughtn't be stealing."

The soon-to-be prisoner went along quite willingly—this was a familiar arrangement, after all. "Just tryin' to feed my children. Cain't blame a man for that."

"Shouldn't take much to feed them children," Fitz drawled, "seeing as they don't exist."

"Forgot you knew that," Lanky Mack grumbled.

"I think you also forgot I can scale a wall."

Lanky Mack grinned back at him as they made their way toward the station, marked by the distinctive blue lamp recently adopted as the means of identifying a police station. "Did forget for a minute there. You do it faster than you used to."

Lanky Mack weren't the only regular occupant of the station cell who treated Fitz with some degree of friendliness. He had an odd connection with the people of Marylebone.

It weren't the rummest part of London, and not everyone living there had much liking for the constabulary, so he and Mathers received a few side-eyes and looks of distrust as they went along. But most people knew Fitz and that he understood the difference between hardened criminals and those made desperate by poverty. He felt he'd earned some trust from the people he looked out for.

He had the faith of both his fellow officers and the chief of D Division as well. That meant a lot to him. He worked hard to be good at what he did.

Sergeant Ott looked up from his reading—the familiar red cover of Mr. King's latest penny dreadful offering—as they stepped inside the station.

"You look a bit worse for the wear, Parkington," he said.

"Had to climb a wall," Fitz explained.

"Wha'? Again?"

"Getting so a man cain't make an honest living," Lanky Mack said, putting on the same show for the sergeant as he had for Fitz.

"If you ever decide on an honest living, drop a word, mate," the sergeant tossed back.

"Oi," Fitz agreed. "We'll parade you about for all to cheer such a change in you." He locked the man in the cell that awaited him, one he'd spent many a day in. "Turn out your pockets. Off with your hat and shoes. Mathers'll be in to gather up all your ill-gotten items."

"Even them I dug out of the—" He seemed to suddenly remember that scavenging in the sewers was a crime. "Even them things?"

Fitz nodded. "Even them things, Lanky Mack. All of it."

With a grunt of annoyance, the man set to work.

Fitz made his way back to the sergeant's desk.

"Last night on patrol for you, i'n'it?" Ott said.

"Oi." Fitz managed not to preen, though he was well chuffed at the change he was making. "D Division's loss is the Detective Branch's gain, or so I'd like to think."

Ott gave a quick nod, which was as sentimental as he was likely to get about losing his best constable. Praise was sparse in the Metropolitan Police. Fitz hadn't embraced the role of constable to be admired, but he wanted to feel he was doing good and doing it well. It was sometimes blasted hard to tell.

"A detective, then." Ott shrugged. "Cain't deny you'll be well good at it. We might have a chance to call on your sniffing skills here in Marylebone now and then."

"I'd be glad to return and help," he said.

"Where'll you be doing your sniffing?" Ott asked.

"All over London. Maybe beyond, now and then." He liked the idea. He saw what crime did to people, and moving into the role of constable detective meant he could do a heap more good than he was now chasing thieves over walls and such.

And, for himself, having all of London open to him for sniffing out clues and mysteries meant he might finally manage to solve the one mystery that had driven him toward the Detective Department in the first place: the disappearance of the only family member he'd ever had.

"M Division's had their hands full of late, what with the Kincaids active again."

The Kincaids were London's most notorious family of grave robbers, though they didn't restrict their crimes to the no-longer-living. They hailed from Southwark—overseen by the Metropolitan Police's M Division—but they plied their various trades all over London. Fitz, himself, had reported evidence of their presence in Marylebone.

They were working alongside one so feared that even the police cowered at the mere mention of the violent criminal. Anyone with a whisper of sense was terrified of the Mastiff.

Cruelty to children. Exploitation of vulnerable women. Cardsharking. Blackmail. Arson. Grave robbery. Murder.

The Mastiff was guilty of it all—both the doing and the

planning. All the Metropolitan Police knew that their top-tier enemy was, without a doubt, guilty of even more than they knew. And mixed into it all was something or someone called the Tempest.

What the Force needed was a detective clever enough, tenacious enough, and eager to find the answers, no matter how dangerous.

They had one now.

Fitz was specifically being transferred to the Detective Branch at Scotland Yard to track down criminals in hiding and dismantle their networks.

The door to the station house opened, pulling Fitz's eyes in that direction. In walked a woman he knew immediately: Móirín Donnelly. She was proud, confident, and spitting daggers as usual when her eyes settled on him. She was also, without question, the most strikingly beautiful woman he'd ever known. Her fierceness added intrigue to her allure. He, who prided himself on maintaining his focus and resolve, never could seem to keep his attention away from her whenever their paths crossed.

But she'd never before crossed his path *here*.

"If you've no one you're hopin' to annoy at the minute, I'd be appreciative of a bit o' your time, Parky."

Whether Sergeant Ott was too shocked or too amused at the odd greeting, it mattered little. Móirín Donnelly enjoyed causing Fitz difficulty when she could, but she weren't one to do drastic things without a reason. If she'd come to Marylebone in the dead of night looking for him, something terrible was likely to have happened.

Or it was about to.

THE QUEEN AND THE KNAVE

by Mr. King

Installment I
in which a brave Queen plans a Celebration
but instead faces a grave Danger!

Long ago and far away, the proud and prosperous kingdom of Amesby lost its beloved king. With broken hearts,
they passed their period of national mourning, with no one
so sorrowful as his only child. The kingdom was now under
her rule: the very young, very grief-stricken Queen Eleanor.
Though she had been raised to one day ascend to her father's
throne, she did not feel herself at all prepared to do so at
merely twenty years of age.

Fate, in its oft-cruel sense of timing, set before her the
task of hosting the once-a-decade Unification Ceremony, in
which the country's ruling barons gathered at the royal palace
to declare their loyalty to the kingdom and confidence in its
monarch, who in turn pledged to hear the counsel of the barons and listen to the needs of the people.

Eleanor had been queen but a month! A month in which
she had grown *less* sure of herself, not more. A month in

which she had made more missteps than she felt herself able to ever forget or overcome.

Failure to complete the Unification Ceremony would send her kingdom into chaos and warfare.

Thus, summons were sent to all corners of the kingdom by way of the fastest messengers available. All the barons in the land—and there were a great many—were required to make their way to the royal palace. There would be a week of gatherings, contests of skill and strength, the ceremony itself, and, at the end, a grand ball.

All was predetermined. All was required.

In the afternoon of the day of the barons' arrivals, which the queen was required to *not* be present for—a tradition held over from the days when the monarch was often at odds with the barons—Her Majesty took to walking about her private garden, the only part of the palace, beyond her personal quarters, where no one was permitted to be but herself.

Oh, Father! she silently bemoaned. *I am not equal to this. I am not the leader or diplomat you were.*

Should the worst happen and the Unification Ceremony not be completed properly, her father's kingdom would fracture. Should that fracture widen and deepen, peace would be lost, and countless people would suffer. Horrifyingly many would die.

It was too much for her inexperienced shoulders to bear. But what choice did she have?

Her feet took her past the sentry box where a guardsman stood, keeping the monarch's private garden private. She knew this sentry. His father had also been a guardsman—the Captain of the Guard, in fact—and Eleanor had come to know Reynard Atteberry when they were both children. They had played together. They'd once even been friends, a rare thing for a princess. She was too often kept separated and isolated, and that meant she was often lonely.

"Good morning, Reynard," she said as she reached his post. "Thank you for watching over the garden."

"My pleasure, Your Majesty." He spoke without taking his eyes off the path beyond the gate he guarded, watching for anyone approaching. He had a duty to fulfill, after all. Duty always came before friendship, even before happiness at times.

Duty.

Always.

Eleanor continued onward, beginning a second circuit of her only place of solace. If she could find a bit of peace, she might feel less disheartened.

She'd only just stepped beyond the shadow of the sentry box when a new shadow fell across her path.

Amesby was home to a great many barons with a history of warring with one another and a peace brokered between them every ten years. But the kingdom was also home to those who possessed magic but not the right temperament for utilizing it without causing pain and suffering.

Dezmerina was one such sorceress.

Eleanor had seen her but twice before: shortly before her mother's death and shortly after.

The sorceress now stood on Eleanor's path, watching her with the hard and unyielding expression Eleanor had seen in her nightmares.

"They are all arriving today," Dezmerina said, her inflection flat but still sinister, calm but still threatening.

"You are not amongst those required to be here this

week." Eleanor attempted to sound like *Queen* Eleanor, but somehow managed to sound like a tiny child.

"I require myself to be here," Dezmerina said. "I am owed this moment."

"And what moment is that?" Eleanor tipped her chin, trying to hide her worry.

"Amesby has ignored me long enough, has withheld from me what I am entitled to. Your father refused to cede to me what was mine."

"And what is that?"

Dezmerina took a step closer to her. Eleanor stepped backward.

A smile slowly pulled at the sorceress's lips. "A throne. Mark my words, it will be mine."

The air around them began to stir, though not a single blade of grass moved. Dezmerina raised her arms at her side. Her eyes turned dark and sinister. Her voice pitched low, she intoned,

> *"Whene'er the sun lights Amesby skies,*
> *Her queen will see through pine marten's eyes.*
> *While battles rage and chaos reigns,*
> *Her life will ebb whilst mine remains."*

The swirl of air wrapped itself ever tighter around Queen Eleanor, squeezing and pressing her from all sides, and her body shrunk with it. She tried to call out, pleading for help from anyone who might be near enough to hear, but the transformation stole her voice.

Dezmerina cackled an evil laugh, pleased with herself and pleased with the pain her curse would cause the daughter of the man who had made himself her enemy. Throwing her arms downward, she disappeared in a crash of thunder.

Sentries were forbidden from leaving their post. The sentry box was to always be directly beside them, the gate to the garden ever behind them. Reynard Atteberry was not one for breaking rules nor doing things he oughtn't. He was honest, dependable, as steadfast as stone.

He'd seen and heard all that had happened, having been overlooked by Dezmerina, no doubt on account of his lowly birth and place of comparative unimportance. What, after all, mattered a single guardsman to one whose entire focus was on destroying a monarchy?

Reynard abandoned his post that day, violated every rule he'd been taught about being a sentry and a guard. He rushed toward the small creature, its dark fur glistening in the sunlight.

Her queen will see through pine marten's eyes.

And that was precisely what the ice-hearted, villainous sorceress had transformed Queen Eleanor into. No larger than a cat, but with the proportions of a weasel and the distinctive cream-colored fur "bib" about its throat. There was no mistaking that Queen Eleanor, only a month on the throne, had been transformed into a pine marten.

How the curse could be undone, Reynard knew not.

But he knew this: he had sworn to safeguard his queen, and he would do so at all costs.

CHAPTER 3

As a general rule, Móirín avoided the blue lanterns that illuminated London and the constables who plied their trades in the buildings those lanterns demarcated. But sometimes she couldn't avoid it. The DPS was scattered and in danger, and they needed help.

Fortunately for them all, they had long since claimed the friendship of a police constable who had proven himself both competent and discreet. She needed both traits at that moment—no matter the risk. So long as they weren't truly friends but also weren't actually enemies, he was unlikely to learn too much about her or dig too deeply into her past. And that was crucial.

Yet, there she was, stepping into the station where she knew he would be working that night, about to do something ridiculously dangerous: talk at length about criminals and crimes with a man who could ruin her life if he ever pieced together that her past touched on both topics.

There were two men in the room when she stepped through the door of the station. The one that wasn't Parkington was likely the sergeant in charge. He had his nose buried in Mr.

King's latest. Móirín herself was penning a serial story, something she'd done in secret for years. She was starting to see her newest, written under the name Chauncey Finnegan, in hands around the city. 'Twas a fine feeling, that.

"Hello there, miss," said the one she suspected was the sergeant. "What can we do for you?" His tone was congenial, but his gaze was a little warm. Not so much that she felt uncomfortable or threatened, though heaven knew a great many men managed to give that impression. His look was more a friendliness mixed with appreciation for a pretty face.

"I'd like to have a word with your constable, here." She nodded toward Parkington.

"Is that word going to be an appropriate one?" Parkington drawled, amusement in his eyes.

"That depends on whether or not you learn rather suddenly how to behave."

He was terribly fun to banter with. She looked forward to it every time she saw him. And, though she knew 'twas a fair risk, she sometimes went out of her way to gab with him when they were in company. A fool she was at times, no denying that.

A smile spread over the sergeant's face. "As this seems a personal matter more than a police one, I'll leave you to it, Parkington."

"Thank you." Móirín was tempted to correct him, to insist it *was* a police matter, but she was willing to let the sergeant think that she and Parkington were sweet on each other if it meant she could manage this business without drawing too much notice.

Parkington sauntered over. He had a way of moving sometimes that spoke of arrogance yet undermined it at the same time. He poked at her every chance he got, and he seemed to enjoy doing it. Heaven knew, he made sparring a great deal of fun.

"What is it you've come to tell me?" he asked. "I can't think of anything I've done to earn your ire, and I can't imagine you've come to say nice things about me."

"I'm not so vicious as all that," she insisted with a smile. "I can't remember the last time I tracked down someone specifically so I could say unflattering things about them. When they wander across my path, certainly. But only if they deserve it."

"And you seem to think I often deserve it," he said dryly, still not looking truly offended.

"That sounds like something you ought to work on," she said with a shrug.

Nearby, the sergeant laughed.

Móirín tossed him a smile. While policemen were best approached with a great deal of wariness, she had found it also helped to be on friendly terms with them. And the sergeant had, unknowingly, proven very helpful just then, reminding her that they could be overheard. It was crucial she relay her message privately.

"Is there a place we can talk?" she asked Parkington. "Won't take but a moment of your time, but I need to tell you something without ears hovering over us."

"I ought to call Sergeant Ott that from now on: Ears." He looked at his superior. "What do you think? Care for a new moniker?"

The sergeant shook his head, his grin not slipping. "Find a quiet spot so the woman can tell you what she's come to say."

"There's a room in the back," Parkington said. "You can say your piece there."

She followed him down the corridor, past the cell. There was only one prisoner being held, and he was sleeping. Sitting outside his cell was another police constable who looked as though he meant to follow the prisoner's lead at any moment. It was a quiet night at the police station, which served her purposes just fine.

The room they stepped into was small. A single narrow window high on the wall would have been the only source of light during the day, but, as it was quite late at night, there was no light in the room at all. Parkington left the door open, then struck a lucifer match and lit a lantern on one of the smallest tables she'd ever seen.

The cramped room likely wasn't used for much. Perhaps a constable would sit inside to read a report or jot down a note or two. Móirín had a hidden room at the DPS headquarters where she both did her work as the Dread Master and drafted the penny dreadfuls she wrote under her various pen names.

With the room now lit, Parkington closed the door. The bottom scraped the floor as it settled into the doorframe, a sign that the door fit tight. 'Twould be more soundproof than one with a large gap at the bottom. The glass window appeared to be without gaps or cracks. If they kept their voices quiet, they were unlikely to be overheard.

Parkington must have realized the same thing because when he spoke, he did so in a low voice. "What is it you needed to say to me?" He was handsome enough when there was amusement in his eyes, but when he'd intelligence there as well the man was a right distraction.

She needed to keep her focus. "I'm certain the Metropolitan Police is eager to capture the one known as the Mastiff."

Parkington's expression turned somber. "The whole of Scotland Yard is eager to capture him."

She'd suspected as much. "If you'll send a couple of

constables to the churchyard where Dr. and Mrs. Milligan were buried earlier today, you'll find him."

"He ain't likely to gad about anywhere for long," Parkington said.

"He will this time."

His eyes narrowed. "Why's that?"

"Because he's dead." As much as she enjoyed a dramatic reveal, she knew they hadn't a great deal of time to enjoy it. "He was discovered tonight by someone visiting the graves of the Milligans, and he had clearly been murdered. Unless someone has moved his body, which is entirely possible, you'll find him there."

Móirín didn't know if it would suit the purposes of the Tempest to keep the Mastiff's death a question mark in the minds of the police, which would justify the work of moving the body. She hated not knowing, not being able to predict what this newly revealed enemy meant to do next.

"I realize you're likely to think this a reason for relief and celebration," Móirín said, "but 'tisn't."

"Why not?" Parkington watched her closely but without the doubt many others in his profession held against the poor, especially when those poor were women.

"The ones that found his body were not the only ones there. Another person was hovering nearby, enjoying the sight. Have you come across, scrawled on walls, or falling from the lips of criminals, 'The Tempest is coming'?"

Parkington nodded. "Everywhere."

"Gemma Milligan was the first to suggest that the Tempest was a person, rather than a symbol of chaos. She was proven correct. The one who calls herself the Tempest has proudly confessed to killing the Mastiff. She indicated *she* has been directing his criminal network all this time. 'Twas, in fact, *hers*, and he was merely doing her bidding. The Mastiff is dead, but he was never the one London should have been most terrified of."

"Scotland Yard needs to be looking for a woman called the Tempest?" He repeated her words of warning.

"'Tis crucial that they do. She's slippery. We know of at least two names she's gone by: Serena, a woman who claimed to be held against her will by the Mastiff, and Clare, a woman who claimed to be working for a demanding and dangerous madam. There are likely other identities she has assumed over the years. Seems blasted good at it, in fact."

"That'll make her harder to identify."

"Fletcher Walker wants—needs—your help." She knew Parkington had worked with Fletcher quite a lot, so bringing up his name would redirect any suspicions Parkington might have about Móirín's involvement. "And the people I've looked after for years, the vulnerable and hurting, are being targeted by this network of criminals. Stopping the one running it is important to me."

"It is to me as well. Helping people is the whole reason I do what I do."

If only Móirín could truly trust that. She wanted to, but she didn't dare.

"And Fletcher sent you to deliver this message to me?" Parkington smiled a little. "That must be a lowering thing for you."

"You have no idea," she muttered dryly, pleased to see his grin grow. He really was a good sort: personable, intelligent, reasonable and, as his gorgeous green eyes continually reminded her, rather handsome. 'Twasn't his fault her past made him something of an enemy to her. Life was simply unfair like that.

"Your timing is good," Parkington said. "Tonight's my last night as a patrol constable. Tomorrow, I move to Scotland Yard's Detective Department. This Tempest, I suspect, will require quite a bit of investigating to sort out."

That was a bit of a lucky break.

"It's important that you do not tell anyone that I told you this, or that Fletcher and the other authors you've worked with in the past are connected to this at all—"

"You like to, at times, insinuate that I'm a simpleton, though I don't suspect you actually think that I am. I can tell you that I do know how and when to keep a secret."

"So do I," she said quietly.

He was watching her with a searching gaze again. Best to beat a hasty retreat. She dipped a quick and firm nod before crossing to the door and pulling it open. She didn't even glance back as she walked out of the room, past the cell, and out of the station entirely. The night was dark, and she knew how to disappear into the shadows.

The DPS was in danger, and, though she was loath to admit it, she couldn't keep them safe without Parkington's help.

Still, she didn't know if she had just sealed her own fate by drawing the attention of one who presented himself as a knight in shining armor but who could prove, in the end, to be a dangerous knave.

POSIE AND PRU
DETECTIVES FOR HIRE

by Chauncey Finnegan

Chapter One

Posie Poindexter was bored. Pru Dwerryhouse would have been, too, if she'd realized boredom was an option.

The two had set up house together on the occasion of Pru's seventieth birthday, Posie having already marked that milestone a year earlier, and had continued on in that arrangement for well over a year. They'd known each other from childhood and had the good fortune to have lived near each other all their lives, marrying men whose homes were in the same village. It was, in fact, in the very village of Downsford where they lived still.

The two were well known to all. Posie, with her shockingly white hair and ordinary brown eyes, stood at the height of a child but with the wrinkles of a poorly laundered shirt. And Pru, whose hair would have been as white as Posie's if not for her dedication to dying it an odd shade of dark brown using nuts and oil and other strange things, was built very much like the local church steeple, and she always wore something on her person that was blue.

Though neither of them realized as much, they had

become somewhat legendary in their tiny village. It wasn't that either was necessarily more strange than anyone else living in Downsford. Mr. Green had a pet mole he called Walter and walked about on a lead. Mrs. Brennan also had a favored color of clothing, always wearing something that was white, which somehow made her gray hair look more like snow than silver. The local vicar insisted on walking backward for at least one quarter hour every morning. The blacksmith also worked as the farrier yet was terrified of horses.

Downsford was an odd place. It was also, at the moment, a bit tiresome in the eyes of one particularly bored resident.

"I need an occupation," Posie said on a sigh, her eyes on the window and the rain running down it in rivers.

"I believe the army would think you too old. And I do not think the vicar would let you take his living." Pru did not make this observation in jest. Pru never did. Her humor was, without exception, unintentional. "Do you suppose a woman of seventy-two could take up farming?"

"Not an occupation in *that* sense." Posie looked away from the window at long last. "I need . . . a hobby."

"The blacksmith seems to enjoy his hobby," Pru suggested.

Posie shook her head. "Blacksmithing isn't his hobby; it is his occupation."

"I thought you were looking for an occupation." Pru looked up from her knitting, genuine confusion on her face.

Posie rubbed at the spot above her right eye, the bit that had ached on and off with great regularity the last year or more. She'd begun referring to it as *petite pru*, the Frenchified name making the recurring headache more elegant somehow and the one for whom the headache was named less insulted.

"Perhaps we might open a lending library." Posie would enjoy that for a time.

"Who would lend us a library?" Pru asked, her knitting needles clicking quickly and rhythmically.

"It isn't a library that is lent out but a library that lends things *to* people."

"Ooh. What sort of things?"

"It's a *library*."

Pru's look of curiosity remained.

"Books, Pru. Books."

"Where would we get the books from?" Pru's needles clicked unceasingly. "Seems we would need more than we currently have. Not too many more, though. It's a small village after all."

As was often the case with Pru, she'd stumbled upon a worthwhile insight quite by accident. Posie only owned seven books and hadn't the funds for purchasing more. Even if she came upon a literary windfall, a village of Downsford's size with its rather un-literary mindset would hardly have use for stacks and stacks of books.

"We used to look after dogs," Pru said with her usual smile. "We were good at that."

"When we were six years old. Could you imagine the two of us chasing after dogs *now*? I can hardly climb stairs any longer. You don't always remember where the stairs are."

"Well, each house and building has stairs in different places, don't they?" Pru continued knitting, clearly unconcerned about the possibility of being bored for the remainder of their lives. "Perhaps we could train dogs to find stairs for us."

"I think we can safely eliminate any potential pastimes that involve dogs, Pru."

"Oh, that is a shame. We were good at looking after dogs."

Petite pru perked up at that declaration. "There must be other things we are particularly good at," Posie said. "Some other talents we possess."

Pru smiled vaguely, not the least upended by their discussion.

"A shame I did not gain your propensity for knitwork," Posie said. "We might find some occupation involving that."

"I could knit sweaters for dogs!" Pru suggested eagerly.

"Whatever we choose," Posie said firmly, "it will have nothing to do with dogs."

Pru's silver eyebrows pulled low. "Oh, that is a shame. We were good at looking after dogs." She knitted another minute, then said, "Do you remember that time when your mother's ear baubles went missing—the ones with pearls—and we found them? That had nothing to do with dogs."

Posie did remember that. They'd gone on a very extensive search, one that included asking a great many questions of a great many people. After a time, they'd realized the jewelry had likely slipped behind a piece of furniture in Posie's mother's dressing room. They'd told her parents of their deduction, the dressing table was moved, and, much to everyone's delight, the baubles were there. It had been an exhilarating experience.

"We did solve that mystery rather expertly, didn't we?" Posie felt proud of herself, thinking back on it. "And I do recall it was not the first nor the last one we solved."

Pru nodded eagerly. "We sorted out why my knitting needles were bent."

They had, at that. They'd been all of twelve or thirteen and had followed the clues until they'd discovered that their brothers, as good of friends as the two of them were, had been using Pru's needles as swords in their reenactment of famous battles, all of which were staged in the back garden. It was, in fact, all the mud they'd found on the needles that had raised their suspicions that the boys had absconded into the garden with the needles.

"We could solve mysteries." Posie sat up straighter at the idea. "People could come to us with their puzzles, and we could discover the answers."

"We would be like the Bow Street Runners used to be: solving mysteries, being very dashing in their red waistcoats." Pru's eyes suddenly pulled wide. "Oh, I could—"

"Please do not offer to knit us red waistcoats."

"They don't have to be *red*."

Solvers of mysteries. Sorters of puzzles. There was nothing boring about any of that. "How do we let people know that we are now detectives?"

"We could tell them," Pru said over the continued needle clicking.

"If we are to be true detectives, then we need something more impressive than starting rumors about our availability."

"What if we made trade cards, like the tradesmen use in London?" Pru offered one of her rare but much appreciated useful suggestions.

Trade cards. Posie liked that idea very much, indeed. The town hadn't a printer, but they could obtain heavy paper and create their own cards by hand. That might prove a very elegant and personal touch.

In the end, it proved intriguing, at least. All around the

village, cards began appearing with hand-drawn floral borders and the words *Posie and Pru: Detectives for Hire.*

The bit of advertising paid almost immediate dividends. A mere three days later, the newly minted detectives were visited by someone in great distress.

Mary O'Reilly was employed as a housekeeper in the home of Mr. Flanagan, a local man of not insignificant wealth, who had long been known to be rather dreadful and had for two days now been quite inarguably dead.

Mrs. O'Reilly was given a cup of tea and a shortbread biscuit, both of which Pru had decided were absolutely necessary to the running of their newly opened detective service. The three women chatted about little nothings—from dogs to knitting to the weather—and once they'd reached the amount of inconsequential chatting all conversations in England were, by unspoken agreement, required to include, Posie introduced the true topic at hand.

"What is the mystery we can help you sort?" she asked.

With a deep sigh and a look of worried confusion, Mrs. O'Reilly said, "I cannot be certain, but I think Mr. Flanagan was murdered."

"Murdered?" Posie was careful not to sound excited, though she was. Her excitement was not on account of a murder having been committed but as a result of being in a position to *solve* a murder. "Have you any idea who might have committed this heinous crime?"

Mrs. O'Reilly nodded, her cap nearly sliding off her gray curls. "It might have been . . . *me.*"

CHAPTER 4

Fitz hadn't expected to spend his first day in the Detective Department asking a favor of his superiors. He'd found it best in his previous reassignments to keep his head low for a time, to not kick up dust as it were. But he knew Móirín Donnelly too well to also know that coming to *him* for help was a significant thing.

He knew she didn't actually dislike him; he didn't actually dislike her. They enjoyed needling each other and engaging in the banter of pretended animosity. But he also knew she didn't truly trust him. She'd not said as much, but he suspected she'd had difficult experiences with police constables in the past. She wasn't the only one.

It was one of the more difficult parts of his job—trying to help the people who most needed him when others of his profession had given them reason not to trust him. He'd entered this line of work to make a difference in the world, and, despite his efforts, he didn't feel he'd really managed it. Not yet.

But he had been at the bottom of the ladder, and that limited a person. The last few years had seen him climb the ranks a little, gain some influence and some leeway in where and how he spent his time. Joining the Detective Department would, in time, afford him even more of that. And he needed it. He told himself it was because he wanted to help more and do more and save more people. But he knew, even if he didn't admit it, that he needed a position of access and authority if he were to have any hope of finding out the fate of his family after nearly twenty years.

Gaining himself a reputation for being demanding was certainly not the best beginning.

"And what reason have we to believe that the one calling herself the Tempest was, indeed, the one who'd killed the Mastiff?" Sergeant Wheatley asked, clearly doubting.

Fitz couldn't simply say, "Because Móirín Donnelly told me so, and she knows what she's talking about." Neither could he say, "Because Fletcher Walker told her so, and Fletcher Walker also knows what he's talking about." He needed to take a more careful approach.

"We have heard all over London whispers about the Tempest, that a reign of terror was coming. When I arrested Claud Kincaid for the attempted murder of a member of Lord Chelmsford's staff and he was warned that the Mastiff wouldn't be very pleased with Kincaid's capture, it wasn't the Mastiff's displeasure that worried him. He said, 'The Tempest is coming.' And he said it with absolute terror."

"How is it you know the Tempest is a woman?"

"I have ears on the street, Sergeant Wheatley. They tell me things. They tell me what they're seeing and what they're hearing."

"You'll find, here in the Detective Department, that we take what we hear from the criminal element with a hefty grain of salt. Most of 'em are just trying to save their necks."

"And *you*'ll find I don't take the word of those who aren't trustworthy as gospel. But I've heard the same thing from many places. From reliable sources. From people who have nothing to gain by misleading me. The Tempest has used the name Serena as well as Clare. She has the ability to blend in with all corners of this city. And she, apparently, is wrapping her noose around a great many necks."

While the sergeant looked a bit less doubtful than he had a moment before, he did not seem to entirely believe him. Fitz set aside his frustration, reminding himself that the inspector hardly knew him and didn't yet have reason to trust his judgment. It'd take time to build a reputation in the Detective Department. Problem was, Fitz weren't at all certain he had time.

If he could start bringing in reliable information, sniffing out proof and clues, and show himself able to excel at the job he'd been hired to do, he could make strides toward having the trust and the ear of his superiors at Scotland Yard. But he'd have to do it quickly. The Tempest was already murdering people.

"I can include this in the list of matters I'm digging into."

The sergeant shook his head. "You're new to the department. We don't start new fellas on matters like this. Petty crimes, small organizations, fugitives—things like that."

Fitz hid his disappointment. He'd already pressed his luck more than he likely ought to have on his first day. "I trust you'll not have any objections if I keep my ears perked and pass along what I learn."

"I suppose not." The sergeant's attention was on his own notes on his desk. It was a dismissal, and Fitz knew it.

He nodded and walked away. He passed the tiny desk that was meant to be his in the small, shared space allotted to the department. He snatched up the packet of papers he'd been given upon his arrival that morning. He'd known he would have to prove himself, but he'd not expected to actually be bored. A quick glance at his assigned cases earlier had told him he'd likely feel precisely that way if something of more immediacy wasn't eventually given to him.

But, with time on his hands, he could wander back down to Vandon Street, where he'd once lived with his grandfather, and look again for any clues that might remain after twenty years. He could dig into papers and information about the area, things he would've missed when he was nine and had found himself entirely alone in the world. He wouldn't be doing the people of London any good while seeing to his own personal mystery, but he'd be putting to rest some of his own worries.

And he'd be sniffing out more on the Tempest, whether Sergeant Wheatley thought it worth doing or not. Fitz knew there was significance in that case, consequences that would be coming. He could feel it in his bones, and he'd learned long ago not to dismiss his intuition when it clawed at him.

The trick'd be doing it without undermining his standing in his new position.

Finesse. It was what he needed most, but it weren't one of his strengths. He tended to toss himself into things head-long—like climbing churchyard fences to capture a criminal on the run. But this was the time for tiptoeing. He wasn't one for breaking the rules entirely, but he did bend them now and then. It seemed he needed to do so again.

He crossed back toward the door, which took him past Sergeant Wheatley's desk. "I'm for the Old Bailey." Fitz tucked his envelope of cases into his coat pocket. "Testifying at a trial today."

The sergeant nodded but offered no other acknowledgment.

Fitz snatched up his hat and made his way out into the drizzle.

He'd not ever lived anywhere but London, and he was well aware that the city was likely more dreary than many locations. He'd read enough penny dreadfuls to know there were warmer climes and more daring adventures to be had elsewhere. He also knew enough penny dreadful writers to know that at least some of that was an exaggeration.

The distance from Scotland Yard to the Old Bailey was a bit more than he cared to cover in the rain, so he hailed a hackney and, after informing the jarvey of his destination, Fitz climbed inside the dry interior.

Staying dry would also allow him to do a bit of reading. He pulled his packet of papers out once more, glancing over his assigned cases. By day's end, he'd have them memorized, which would simplify things.

One case concerned the Phantom Fox, a sneak thief who, by all accounts, had never taken anything more valuable than a hairbrush or a porcelain figurine. The reports indicated even those who'd reported the thefts were indifferent about the item's return, being far more annoyed at having someone in their house uninvited than in losing the little baubles. He wouldn't exactly be a hero for solving a crime no one seemed to care about. A waste of time, really. And a frustrating one.

His other cases were equally petty crimes, including a few people the law was searching for on account of crimes committed elsewhere. He'd do what he could to solve those mysteries, all while working on the two mysteries he most wanted to sort out.

The Old Bailey was a notorious place, one that drew a crowd when a trial or execution was scheduled. And the more notorious the crime, the bigger the crowd. Claud Kincaid had attempted to murder a member of Lord Chelmsford's staff, with ample witnesses and a brazenness that added horror to the act. The former Lord Chancellor had fled his own house afterward, fearing for his safety. All of that whipped up interest, and the Old Bailey was teeming with people when Fitz arrived.

He placed himself where the witnesses were expected to sit, awaiting their time in the witness box. Nothing in the design of the room or the benches was meant to make a person comfortable, but he did his best. It could sometimes be a long time before people were called to offer testimony. Trials could last a couple of days, with no one knowing what came next. Many witnesses wandered to nearby pubs or set themselves in corridors or amongst the press of people, waiting to be summoned. Fitz preferred being present for as much of the trial as he could. He came to know people that way, those accused of crimes, those subjected to them, those charged with dispensing justice.

What few others saw in these trials were those who often tipped Fitz to the perpetrators and victims: Fletcher Walker and his fellow penny dreadful authors. They'd recently formed an official society, calling themselves the Charitable Authors League of London, but they'd been undertaking clandestine missions far longer than that organization had existed. They played a role in these trials, but always kept their part a secret.

They'd been part of uncovering the current crime, in fact. Fletcher and Dr. Milligan had captured Claud Kincaid not long after Martin Afolo, who was both a member of Lord Chelmsford's staff and a writer of penny dreadfuls, had been stabbed. Fletcher was playing least in sight, so no one knew where he was. Dr. Milligan was dead.

Claud was standing in the dock, the tall, barred sides caging him in but not obscuring anyone's view of him. During the many trials Fitz had witnessed, he'd seen the accused express many emotions: worry, indignation, anger, desperation. Claud simply looked terrified. His filthy hands, fingernails gnawed to jagged stubs, grasped the bars tightly. He watched the crowd with wide, frightened eyes, muttering to himself and visibly shaking.

Watching *the crowd*. Not the judges. Not the barrister who would be arguing for his execution. Not any of the people who held his life in their hands. No, Claud was afraid of the people who'd come to watch. There was someone in the crowd, or someone he feared was among them, who scared him even more.

That shifted Fitz's attention to the others in the gallery and pressed up against the windows. Who was inspiring such fear in a man who ought to've been far more focused on the trial that would decide his fate?

Before Fitz could search the crowd with any degree of thoroughness, the barrister addressed the judges. "We've a bit of a difficulty, I'm afraid. I've attempted to talk with this man to ask him what he says happened so I can present to you the case, since he hasn't a barrister of his own. But all he will say is 'The Tempest is coming.' Only that phrase. It never varies, never changes. I've witnesses aplenty, and we can certainly move forward, but I think we have to consider the possibility that we are trying a suspect whose mental capacity is lacking."

One of the judges addressed the prisoner. "Is this true?"

"The Tempest—"

"—is coming, yes," the judge finished for him. "We understand you have declared this already."

Claud shook his head. "The Tempest is here."

Those four words sent a wave of horror through a good

number of people in attendance. A few even rose and ran from the room.

The Tempest is here.

Did Claud mean here in the courtroom? Or did he mean the criminal mastermind and her network of fiendish helpers had seized control of the London underworld? Claud *was* a Kincaid, after all, and that family of notorious murderers and grave robbers was known to be part of that criminal ring. He'd know if the violent schemes were coming to a head.

"The Tempest is *here*," the prisoner repeated.

The judges looked on helplessly as chaos erupted. If the Tempest was, indeed, in the room, she'd never be seen or caught in the pulsing throng.

This was not the case Fitz was meant to be investigating, but it had landed in his lap. He couldn't simply ignore it.

He rose from his place and pushed against the crowd toward the dock, hoping to have a word with Claud or the barrister. He needed more information. No one stopped him when he reached for the door of the dock. Whether that was because he was recognized as a reliable member of the police force or because too much was happening that no one had noticed, he didn't know.

In the end, it didn't matter. Fitz hadn't even opened the door when Claud slumped to the ground. No word, no struggle, no indication of distress. He simply fell, sprawled on the ground in an unmoving heap, wide-eyed with terror.

Fitz pulled the door open and rushed inside. But it was obvious Claud Kincaid was dead. His skin had turned a grayish-blue, and foam dribbled from his mouth.

"This man needs help," Fitz called out, though he knew it was too late.

Screams of panic added to the chaos of the courtroom, inspiring the crowd to a near stampede of terror. That Claud had been poisoned was obvious, and his death had come moments after issuing a horrified warning about someone all of London was learning to fear.

Fitz caught sight of a marking on the dock, one made in ash. Two lines and the letter *K*: the mark of the Kincaid family, one they left to claim credit for the crimes they committed and to remind those who would oppose them that they had the power to enact retribution.

They were criminals of the lowest order yet had somehow gained access to this dock and this prisoner, murdering a member of their own family in full view of judges, barristers, witnesses, and the very public the Tempest sought to control with fear and threats—the Tempest who had long since brought this notorious family into her circle of criminals.

Fitz moved away from the dock and the body of Claud Kincaid, allowing the officers of the court to see to him. The room was nearly empty, people having fled into the streets, repeating the phrase that would soon be all over London: "The Tempest is here."

CHAPTER 5

Móirín and her brother, Brogan, had lived in the same flat for years, but the violent threat of the Tempest had forced them to abandon yet another home. Life had required that of them far too often.

"'Tisn't quite so peaceful an area of London as we'd been occupying," Brogan said, looking over the parlor. It was all but empty as they'd not been in a position to move much of their furnishings during the quick retreat from their flat. "But we've quiet enough and room enough. Almost."

"Room enough, for certain." Móirín brought a blanket to Vera, sitting near the fire her da had built. "A room for m' favorite sister-in-law that she's welcome to share with my twaddly brother if she'd like. A room for her father, who'll be happy to be living in an actual home again, I'd wager."

Mr. Sorokin had been in hiding from the Mastiff, keeping safe two children that his criminal circle had threatened. They were all together again.

"And little Olly and Licorice'll be pleased as anything to claim their own corners of the parlor," Móirín continued. "A far sight better than the doorways and hovels they've known in the past."

"Aye," Brogan said, tossing a copy of Chauncey Finnegan's latest to Olly. The children loved the penny serials, and this "new" arrival on the scene was providing both of them with a welcome distraction.

Wouldn't the entire house be shocked to know Móirín was Chauncey, and she'd been writing penny dreadfuls for half a decade under dozens of pen names?

Brogan turned to Móirín. "But you've not assigned a room to your own self. You can hardly say that's 'room enough,' for certain."

Móirín waved off his observation. She was not worried for herself. "You meant it when you said you'd be tucking yourself here and not going about for a time?" she pressed. "Not seeking out odd jobs or anything of the like?"

Brogan nodded. "'Tis too big a risk. I'll get m' chapter to m' publisher, and we'll make do with that money."

Móirín crossed to him once more, eyeing him firmly but kindly. She spoke low, so just the two of them could hear. No sense in bringing worry to everyone. "You and I both know that ain't money enough for a whole household."

"I've not had any other income these past months," Brogan said.

"But *I* have. If we've any hope of eating and heating this place and getting Vera the powders she needs to continue healing, we need more money than your stories'll bring, no matter that they're brilliant."

"You're liking m'most recent, are you?" he asked.

"Something's strange with that train in 'Terminus.' I can hardly wait to find out what."

He colored up a little, something gingers did easily. For not the first time, Móirín was grateful to have their mother's coloring: dark hair and eyes, skin that neither freckled nor reddened overly easily. "Are you standing by your insistence that coming and going from this place is too dangerous to do every day?" Móirín pressed.

"I know it is, but please don't require me to tell you how I know."

Bless him, Brogan had worked hard to keep secrets these past years, secrets he didn't know she already knew.

She couldn't risk his safety by burdening him with the enormous secret she still kept from him. The Tempest would kill to know the identity of the Dread Master. Keeping that secret tightly controlled was all Móirín could think to do.

"You'll not have money enough in a matter of days if I'm not working, Brog. And yet I can't come and go every day without riskin' everyone's safety here, which I won't do. So 'tis fine that there's not room for me here."

"We've always room for each other, Móirín. Always and without hesitation." His earnestness touched her more than he likely realized.

Making room for her, helping her, had cost him his life in Dublin. The trouble they'd found themselves in their homeland had required them to change their names more than once, a painful thing for two children still reeling from the deaths of their parents to endure. That Brogan always made room for her and cared what happened to her had given her hope in even the darkest times.

"I know a place I can go," she said. "Safe and difficult to find, where I can arrive and leave without drawing notice. I'll stay there for a time, allowing me to still work and bring in

SARAH M. EDEN

money. And, through Mr. Sorokin, I can get it to you, and he can let me know when 'tis safe for us to be together again."

"I can't be at ease knowing you're in peril, Móirín," Brogan said. "I promised our parents."

"*We* promised our parents," she reminded him. "And they knew perfectly well, even then, the stubborn person I am. They'd not be the least surprised that I'm being difficult about this. And they'd remind *you* that I'm well able to take care of m'self even in a great deal of danger."

"I don't want anything to happen to you, *mo deirfiúr.*"

Brogan almost never called her by the Irish term for sister. He was more worried than he was letting on, and she knew full well he had ample reason to be.

"*Mo dheartháir grá*"—it had been even longer since she'd addressed her beloved brother in Irish—"I'll not put any of you in danger, but I also won't let you starve nor let you grow desperate enough to steal your meals. We've done that far too many times, you and I."

"We've not ever lived apart," Brogan pleaded. "Not once in all our lives. And now, to have you who knows where with so much danger all around . . . I'd never stop worrying."

"I've not stopped worrying about you since I was nine and we buried our parents." She took his hand. "But worrying about me to the point that you let your wife suffer? That ain't you, and you know it."

He glanced at his wife, still pale and exhausted from the effort of moving house. His determination to object to Móirín's plan appeared to waver.

"Keep your family safe, Brog," Móirín said. "That's your most important job right now."

"You are my family," he said quietly.

46

"And always will be." She'd've squared her shoulders, but they were never *not* squared. Life had taught Móirín to not let her guard down. And she didn't. Ever. "I'll help get you all settled, then scamper off tonight. And I'll make certain you have the money you need and none of you is in want. And I'll be blasted careful doing it, I swear."

"I don't like it," Brogan said firmly. "There is more danger than you know, more than I can even tell you about. If you're out there gadding about, you'll get yourself killed."

"I've been gadding for ages, and no one's murdered me yet."

With the tiniest twinkle in his eyes, Brogan said dryly, "Some of us've been sorely tempted."

She laughed a little. 'Twas good to see a bit of humor from him. Perhaps he wouldn't be upset with her too long for leaving him and seeming to disregard his warnings.

Mr. Sorokin walked past them, and Móirín moved quickly to his side.

In a low voice, she said, "We need to talk before I hop the twig, but I'm needing to not be overheard."

The man simply nodded and kept walking. Móirín followed. They were soon situated in a makeshift room built onto the back of the flat by someone with more confidence than skill. Mr. Sorokin closed the door, faced her, and waited.

"*Govori, posyl'nyy golub'.*" The Russian code phrase—"Speak, messenger pigeon"—was used amongst her secret network of informants, and while Mr. Sorokin was one of her messengers, he didn't know her true identity.

He nodded his acknowledgment.

Continuing in Russian, she whispered quickly, "I learned from Gemma Milligan that you helped, years ago, a woman connected to Joseph Hunt, one of the participants in the Radlett murder. That case, for reasons our head hasn't yet identified, is the motivation for the current violence being enacted by the one who calls herself the Tempest."

"Whispers are saying she and *not* the Mastiff is the one terrorizing London." He made the observation as a statement, but his expression turned it into a question.

She nodded. "Our head needs to sort out what is pushing her to such violence and what her next move is likely to be. The Radlett murder is part of it, and we're looking for all the information we can get our hands on."

"I can't tell you much about the woman I helped, except that she was likely your age, perhaps a bit older, hovering near to thirty years. She had a child with her and was looking to escape the life she'd been forced into by poverty."

Too common a story for identifying someone based on it.

"The woman's mother worked at the inn Hunt owned before he was transported for his crimes. She wanted honest work like her mother had known, so I forged her some references."

Mr. Sorokin had fled Russia and the wrath of the tsar, finding new work in forging false documents to help desperate people in need. He was a skilled printer and a remarkably intelligent person. He was one of her most valuable sources of information, and one of the reasons she felt confident leaving her family in his care.

"Our head will insist on more than that, *tovarishch*," she said.

"Find someone who can crack a safe," Mr. Sorokin said, "and you can have more than that."

Unexpected. And intriguing.

"There is a tobacconist's shop in Southwark that used to be an old print shop. In the back is a safe that's not been opened in years. The combination has been lost, which is just as well. Inside are a great many papers, filled with sensitive information."

"About people you've helped?" she guessed.

He gave a single, quick nod. "The shop was easy to get into in the dead of night, and the safe was empty, so I 'borrowed' it. Then it got locked and no one could get in, including me. Information about the woman from the Radlett case is inside amongst the rest."

"Do you trust me enough to tell me where the safe is and let me break into it?"

His gaze narrowed. "Do you know how to crack a safe?"

"I know someone who does."

"And what would you do with the other papers you find?"

"Only I would see them," Móirín said. "And I'm silent as the grave."

"And twice as terrifying, some would say." Mr. Sorokin didn't seem to disapprove. "Could you get those papers back to me without being caught out?"

"Is this concern about *the papers* being found or *you*?"

"Both. I'd not risk these children's lives or my daughter's or your brother's, but I also am not keen to put at risk the people I've helped."

She understood. "I hope I've shown you over the past few months that I'm both reliable and capable."

"More than anyone I know," he acknowledged.

"Tell me where to find this shop, and where in the shop to find the safe, and I'll bring you the papers with no one, other than our head, the wiser."

He seemed to believe her. "Take Southwark Bridge Road past Charing Cross rail line. The shop is on that road not quite to Great Suffolk Street. You'll need to enter from a door toward the back, but a bit on the side. There's a room in the back with shelves and behind one of them, near to the ground, is the door to the safe. It'll be hidden, dusty and dinged. Hope of getting into it was abandoned ages ago, and it's all but forgotten now."

'Twas a tricky ask, but she knew a couple of people who could help her. Which, of course, would mean revealing her role to one more and lying a little to the other. When she'd first taken on the role of Dread Master, she'd figured not telling a bunch of authors that she wrote penny dreadfuls or where she got her information about poor or vulnerable people needing help would be the biggest secrets she had to keep from them.

Now it seemed keeping crushing secrets was all she did.

THE QUEEN AND THE KNAVE

by Mr. King

Installment II
in which our valiant Sentry faces a Perilous Decision!

If Reynard had harbored any doubts about the true identity of the pine marten in the queen's garden, the fact that it willingly allowed him to pick it up and carry it back to the sentry box and then sat watching him with pleading and hopeful eyes would have managed to convince him. Pine martens, as a rule, were neither tame nor cooperative. This one acted more like a sweet-tempered kitten than a wild animal.

"I confess, Your Majesty, I haven't the first idea what is to be done now." How odd it was addressing an animal as "Your Majesty," but, no matter appearances, he knew who she was. "Were I to tell anyone that you are Queen Eleanor, they not only would not believe me but I would lose my post, you would likely be tossed into the forest, and Dezmerina's declared desire for revenge would be fully and horribly realized."

Few people would have kept such a level head in the face of so strange a situation. But Reynard was no ordinary sentinel. His father had been Captain of the Guard and had raised him to be both adaptable and brave, both open-minded and focused. And, though their stations in life were very different, Reynard and Queen Eleanor had known each other from childhood and had even, when still little children, played together quite as if they were equals. They occasionally now even had very brief but friendly conversations.

He felt as if he knew her, as much as any commoner could ever know his queen. He liked the person she was. He cared what happened to her. And all that, no doubt, helped him keep his composure. Survival in a crisis seemed somehow more possible when the outcome impacted more than oneself.

Inside the sentry box was a single stool for sitting on, though the only time it might have ever been used would be when two sentries were present but only one standing at duty. Reynard had never known that to happen. He'd often inwardly scoffed at such a permanent solution to a non-existent problem, especially when the box could hardly spare the space. He was grateful for it now.

Her Majesty sat on the stool, watching him as he spoke, making their conversation less odd—as much as was possible when a conversation was being held between a person and a pine marten.

"If I don't stand at my post, the Captain of the Guard will be summoned. I'd do best not to draw his attention until I've thought of a believable explanation."

The pine marten queen tipped her head, giving him a quizzical look.

"I am not usually one for inventing stories in order to avoid the truth," he assured her. "You must admit, this is a very unique circumstance."

She dipped her head, a movement very close to a nod.

"I will stand at my post and do my utmost to look as though nothing is at all amiss, but I will also spend that time trying to sort out what ought to be done next."

Queen Eleanor curled into a ball of deep brown fur and rested her head on her tail. No matter that her features were now that of a weasel-like animal, her expression was easy to interpret. She was sorrowful, worried, but not defeated. Reynard felt certain she, too, was pondering how to thwart Dezmerina's determination to destroy the newly crowned queen.

Reynard had not the first idea how to accomplish that. He'd once known someone who could have helped. A woman who'd had magic, but who'd not used it to cause hurt or harm. She'd healed and helped and benefited everyone she could. She'd been one of the most remarkable people Reynard had ever known.

But his mother was gone now, and with her all the knowledge she'd had.

His father had passed away two years earlier, meaning Reynard answered to a Captain of the Guard who was far less likely to believe him should he present to him such an odd tale as he had to tell.

What was to be done?

So few people in the kingdom had magic. Dezmerina had spent many years hunting those who did and killing any who refused to lend their gifts to her cause. Some were forced into doing her bidding under threat against their families. Those who were most able to assist in their queen's current distress would, most certainly, be too afraid to make their abilities known.

Were he even able to find someone with magical ability, how was he to leave the palace grounds with a pine marten without drawing undue attention? Should anyone ask why he left the sentry box at the end of his shift and took with him a wild animal, he'd have great difficulty explaining it, never mind justifying having kept the creature in the sentry box.

While Reynard was trying, without success, to determine his next step, Queen Eleanor was pondering many things herself. Her form had changed to that of a woodland creature, but she was still herself, still had her own thoughts and feelings and memories. She still had her intelligence and determination to be the best queen she could be. But how could she possibly be any sort of queen at all if she remained a pine marten?

Whilst she was required to be absent during the arrival of the kingdom's barons—a fortunate bit of timing, considering her current state—she was absolutely required to offer a welcoming speech the night of the Barons' Feast. The Unification Ceremony would not occur for two more days, but failing to give the opening speech would put the feast in such jeopardy that the ceremony itself might as well be canceled.

Her father would have known what to do; she was utterly certain of it. But she hadn't his wisdom to call upon. If not for Reynard, she would have been utterly alone, struggling to feel even a modicum of hope. Though they'd not interacted nearly as much in their grown-up years as they had while still children, she trusted him as much now as she ever had. He was a good man, kind and brave, with just enough of a rogue's love for adventure to give her added confidence that he wouldn't simply abandon her in order to fulfill his duty to stand where he was and ignore all else.

Eleanor could not recall ever having heard a pine marten make noise. They must have had the ability, but she could not predict what she would hear when testing her voice. Would the sound be quiet and weak? Would there be no sound at all? Truth be told, when she spoke as her human self, she often felt weak. She couldn't deny other people thought the same.

But she needed Reynard's help. She needed him to stay with her. And she wanted to help find a solution to her problem. Being able to speak to him would facilitate that.

She hesitantly attempted to speak. What emerged was a shrill, almost catlike sound. She tried again, concentrating. The sound changed ever so slightly, but it did change. With effort, she might find her voice. She might manage to talk or to at least communicate.

Reynard stepped close once more, speaking to her whilst still facing forward, looking, to anyone glancing in his direction, as if he were doing nothing but keeping watch.

"Two palace guards are coming toward us. They will be here either to take up their position on watch or to bring a message to the sentry on duty. They will spot you the moment they arrive." He looked back at her without turning more than the smallest bit. "If you will go to the back of your garden where the weeping birch grows and hide yourself well, I will meet you there as soon as I am able."

The pine marten queen nodded, grateful she could do so.

"I will not abandon you, Your Majesty," Reynard promised.

She slipped from the sentry box and moved with the swift grace of the creature she had become, moving easily between the iron slats of the gate and into the garden, aiming for the tree Reynard had specified.

With Queen Eleanor safe from the notice of the approaching guards yet still in danger of being spotted by a gardener or gamekeeper, Reynard, feeling nervous but determined, watched his colleagues arrive.

"Her Majesty's lady's maid reports the queen has not yet returned from her walk in the garden. Have you seen the queen?"

Reynard nodded. "She did walk in the gardens earlier. The last I saw Her Majesty, she was walking in the direction of the back wall. It is likely she returned to the palace by way of the entrance there."

"Was anything amiss?"

If only Reynard knew if these two would believe him were he to tell them the truth. All the kingdom knew of magic, and all the kingdom knew of Dezmerina's violent and destructive use of it. But, somehow, their fear of her had translated into a certain stubborn refusal to believe that the harm she had caused had truly been caused by her.

The horrid sorceress had such full hold on the kingdom that she either forced cooperation or frightened into denial.

"Queen Eleanor appeared to be deep in thought," Reynard said. "I very much had the impression she did not want to be interrupted." Somehow he'd managed to offer an answer that wasn't entirely false.

The taller of the two guards, Chester, motioned with his head toward the other. "George will stand sentry in your place. I am to search the garden. The Captain has asked that you make a search of the surrounding forest in case the queen decided to wander further afield."

At last, a spot of luck.

The changing of guards was quickly accomplished.

George stood at full attention. Chester slipped into the garden. And Reynard made his way as quickly as he could without drawing their notice into the adjoining forest, following the curve of the garden wall to the place where the weeping birch stood.

He spotted the pine marten queen quickly. She climbed agilely down from a high branch to one that grew out over the wall. From there, she leapt to him, and he caught her, wincing at the piercing of her claws on his arm.

Holding her protectively and watching for signs of other searchers, wanderers, or Dezmerina herself, he rushed further into the woods. It would be dark soon; they daren't go far. But neither dare they remain within sight.

Reynard knew of a small cottage in the woods. It had belonged to his mother, and it was the place she had retreated to when Dezmerina had begun her efforts to gather or destroy those with magic. It was protected through charms and enchantments. They could be safe there. But what they would do after that, he did not know.

The sun was setting, the light disappearing quickly. The small animal in his arms grew heavier, more awkward to hold. He stopped his forward rush and set her down. As he did, the last rays of light disappeared.

And, in a twist and swirl of impossible movement, the pine marten transformed once more into Queen Eleanor.

CHAPTER 6

The Tempest is here.

That terror-filled declaration hadn't left Fitz's thoughts since he'd watched Claud Kincaid die in the dock at the Old Bailey. Claud had tied his demise to the Tempest. The mark of the Kincaid family had tied them to his death as well. The Tempest was killing people, had been all along, and Fitz refused to let it keep happening without at least trying to stop her and those who did her bidding.

Sergeant Wheatley weren't overly excited about Fitz's focus turning away from his assigned caseload, so Fitz was taking up the matter more quietly. As quietly as one could when making a call at Newgate Prison, leastwise.

There was a man held there, known as the Raven. He'd been working for the Mastiff, running a corrupt gambling ring, when he'd been arrested during a roundup of criminals. It was Fitz's involvement in the discovery of those activities that had finally seen him accepted into the Detective Department. His knowledge of the Raven's activities had come to him by way of Fletcher Walker. So much of what Fitz had accomplished was connected to the authors he'd come to know and the unseen work they did looking after London's poor.

The Raven was brought into a consulting room, where Fitz was waiting. He never knew if a prisoner would spill his budget in the hope of receiving leniency in his sentence or treatment, or if he'd simply stubbornly refuse to even look at the fellow doing the questioning. Predicting which would occur was generally impossible, but Fitz had a feeling this time. Trusting his intuition had served him well.

He dipped his head to the prisoner and received a perfectly friendly smile in return. It didn't seem the least feigned. The man also didn't seem afraid for his safety or desperate for company or smugly sure of himself. This, it seemed, had the potential to be a simple conversation, which was precisely what Fitz needed.

"What can I do for you, constable?" the Raven asked, seated comfortably.

"You can tell me what you know about the Tempest."

The Raven's mouth turned down at the corners. "Why're you hammering at that particular nail?"

"A storm's kicking up in London. Makes sense to invest in a weather vane."

"Makes more sense not to spit into the wind," the Raven replied dryly.

He was open but, it seemed, also hesitant, which made sense. The Mastiff had been shockingly powerful and violently dangerous, and he had answered to the Tempest.

"No spitting," Fitz said, keeping his posture and tone casual. "Just wondering which way the wind blows."

"Seems to me you ought to be asking the Mastiff all these questions. He answers to the Tempest, and only he knows who the fellow is."

The Raven gave no indication he was fabricating his explanation. He, then, didn't know the Mastiff was dead, or that the Tempest was a woman.

Interesting.

"Claud Kincaid attempted to kill a member of Lord Chelmsford's staff," Fitz said. "And Kincaid went up for trial a couple of days ago." He watched the Raven for any response to the subject but saw only vague interest in the man's eyes. "He died in the dock. Poisoned. I have a theory, but I don't know enough about the potential poisoner to say for certain if I'm on the right track."

"You think the person is the Mastiff?" the Raven asked, narrowing his eyes.

With a shake of his head, Fitz said, "The Kincaid family themselves, under orders from the Tempest."

"The Kincaids'd be eager to scrub out a stain on the family name, which anyone of them foolish enough to get caught would be considered. But why do you think the Tempest would dirty his hands with a minor criminal like Claud?" *There* was the smugness Fitz had been anticipating from the moment the man had walked into the room.

"Because the prisoner's last words were 'The Tempest is here.' Made me wonder if he meant it literally—that the Tempest was present at the time or the Tempest's handiwork at least."

"Like I said, the Tempest doesn't have to dirty his hands with such things. Enough do his bidding. Degrees of separation, you know." The Raven actually looked proud, as if the slipperiness of the one he ultimately answered to made him more clever by connection.

"The Kincaids ain't known for doing anyone else's bidding," Fitz pointed out. "And poison ain't their usual style."

"But it is among the calling cards of the Protector."

The Protector. Fitz knew that rough-and-tough. He helped strong-arm and blackmail business owners and working-class folks into paying protection money. Fitz had known the man to inflict beatings and burn down establishments, but this was the first he'd heard that poison was also in his arsenal.

"Would he have poisoned the fellow on the Tempest's orders?"

The Raven shrugged. "Perhaps the Tempest thought the man might squeal. No one crosses the Tempest and lives to tell the tale."

"You're telling a lot of tales right now," Fitz reminded him.

"Nothing our leader would begrudge me saying." His smile was a bit slippery, a bit stomach turning. Fitz was not leading this conversation as much as he'd thought. He was being told what he was "permitted" to know.

"The Tempest removes threats?"

"And incompetence," the Raven added. "The Kincaids don't abide that either. Likely approved of Claud's demise."

"Seems the Tempest would run out of allies eliminating so many of 'em."

"More can be recruited. Can't seem to twist the Dread Penny Society, though. People that inflexible get themselves killed."

Fitz had heard of the rumored society of authors. He'd often suspected the very writers he teamed up with from time to time were, in fact, members of that organization. He'd never asked, knowing they would never tell. Sometimes it was best not to know *every* secret.

SARAH M. EDEN

"This society is the Tempest's target, is it?"

"A mere bump in the road," the man said. "A road to far bigger and more glorious things."

"You seem to have some expectation of being part of those 'glorious things.'"

"Soon enough, there won't be a corner of this city the Tempest does not control. Not even the ones you think are safe. *Especially* the ones you think are safe." On that declaration, the man rose and walked to the door, giving it a knock.

The guard opened it, and the Raven slipped into a look of humble compliance. He was ushered out, the door left open for Fitz to make his departure as well.

"There won't be a corner of this city the Tempest does not control," Fitz mused as he left the prison. And part of her plan for doing that was eliminating the authors who'd made themselves her enemies. That realization sat heavy in his thoughts as he walked along Fleet Street. He needed to get word to them somehow.

If there was anyone who could find Fletcher Walker at a moment's notice, it was the street urchins, and they were all over London. Fitz motioned one aside, a bootblack he knew for certain was acquainted with Fletcher.

"Oi," he called to the boy. "Could you get a message to Fletcher Walker for me?"

The boy shrugged. "Ain't seen 'im in days. No one has. But I can try."

"Tell him the storm's breaking, and the literary crowd's likely to get soaked."

It was testament to how often Fletcher received odd, coded messages that the boy didn't seem the least surprised by the

62

senseless declaration. The boy simply tipped his hat and went on his way.

Fitz bought a newspaper, something he did every day. Some of his best clues had been found in those columns. He could read it on his way back to Scotland Yard, where he'd have to convince his superiors that he'd been doing the work he was supposed to be doing, rather than pulling at a thread Sergeant Wheatley hadn't been keen to see him pursue.

But he didn't get that far. A few pages in, at the bottom of a column, was a small item, one he might have easily missed if not for the subject of his recent ponderings.

Chandan Kumar, author of penny serials, reported missing by worried wife. Publisher confirms his newest serial offering will be halted awaiting his return.

Kumar was one of Fletcher's associates. One of the authors Fitz suspected was part of the Dread Penny Society. One of those who had recently formed the Charitable Authors League of London, which Fitz had begun to suspect was a front.

The Raven's words returned to Fitz's mind: "Can't seem to twist the Dread Penny Society, though. People that inflexible get themselves killed."

Killed.

CHAPTER 7

óirín had a few safe houses throughout London, hideaways where she had tucked people away when they were in grave danger. It was in one of those houses she found herself now, one large enough to include Fletcher, Elizabeth, and Barnabus and Gemma Milligan.

She and Fletcher were waiting to meet with another Dreadful, a man named Stone. After that meeting, Móirín would make every effort to convince him to place himself, if not in this safe house, in one of her others. In a short time, he would know the secret of her identity, and that required additional precautions.

Exactly on time, Stone arrived, giving the code word he'd been provided with. Móirín unlocked the door and motioned him inside. He'd've had no warning that she'd be at one of the Dread Master's safe houses, but he didn't say anything, didn't seem surprised, didn't do anything but step inside himself. Stone had never been one to ruffle easily.

He was warmly welcomed by the others, who'd've had every reason to understand why Stone had been invited. They all knew of the Dread Penny Society and knew its membership. Móirín and Fletcher had decided on an explanation for *her* knowledge of the DPS and presence in the Dread Master's safe house. The danger had grown, they'd said, and the Dread Master insisted they needed Móirín's help keeping the Dreadfuls safe, especially Brogan, as well as increasing their ability to stay a few steps ahead of the Tempest. The Dread Master could no longer justify keeping the secret of the DPS from someone who could help them as much as she could.

Lands, she was weary to her bones of lying. But lying was keeping people alive.

While everyone else was gabbing, Móirín made her way down the narrow and oddly angled corridor to the room she had claimed as her own. Fletcher would eventually bring Stone that way so they could have a bit of a jaw without being overheard.

She was grateful to be staying in a place with other people rather than entirely alone. But with them thinking they were keeping secrets from her and her needing to actually keep secrets from them, Móirín still felt isolated. Nothing new in that.

Brogan had more than once said that if he didn't love her, he would likely be terrified of her. Most people were *just* terrified. Life, as she'd known it, was as much about death and danger as happiness and connections. She'd spent a good part of her life keeping death and danger away from those whose happiness mattered to her.

Many had told her she was foolish to attempt to save lives when everyone eventually dies. Many more had laughed her to scorn upon hearing that she worked hard to save the lives of those whose lives were unlikely to be long regardless.

Móirín let them laugh. She knew who she was, and no amount of mockery would change who she intended to be.

She set some paper on the table in the corner where she did

her work. She'd managed to finish the installment for her publisher earlier that day, though it had been a struggle. Writing felt so frivolous compared to everything that was happening. But it was her only source of income now, and Brogan's family needed her support.

When Fletcher and Stone eventually came into the room, Móirín watched Stone, curious about how much he'd already pieced together. The man showed only curiosity, and even that was subdued.

Móirín closed the door, making certain it fully latched, before turning back. "How much did Fletcher tell you about this meeting?" she asked Stone.

"Only that I'd been summoned here."

Móirín nodded. Fletcher was a blasted good secret keeper. "How much additional danger are you willing to invite? That'll change how much you're told now."

"I've been in danger all my life," he said. "Courting a bit more won't sink me."

"But it might put your sweetheart in greater danger," Móirín warned.

Stone allowed the tiniest hint of a smile, which, coming from him, was the equivalent of a grin. And this particular grin was an utterly besotted one. "Celia knows how to take care of herself."

Not everyone knew Stone had a sweetheart. Either Fletcher was hiding his surprise well, or he was in on the secret. Hardly mattered, though. Their focus needed to be on the matter at hand. She'd do well to stop letting her mind wander.

"You were brought here to gab with me, specifically. And I'm here because this is one of *my* safe houses."

Stone's brows shot up as she identified herself as the Dread Master.

"The general membership doesn't know my identity because the Tempest, I suspect, is particularly keen on knowing who the Dread Master is. People can't let slip what they don't know themselves. And if they happen to be overheard talking about their mysterious leader, they'd be heard to say they haven't any idea who *he* might be."

"I wondered now and then if the ol' fellow might've been you," Stone said.

"I figured you did." It'd been difficult the last few years not to confide in him. They'd become good friends, and they trusted each other. To see that he didn't hold against her the secret she'd kept was reassuring.

"What do you need me to do?" There was a reason Stone was part of the DPS's most difficult and precarious missions in the years since he joined; he was ready for nearly anything and not easily shaken.

"You worked at a tobacconist's shop a few years back, in Southwark," she said.

He nodded.

"Did it happen to be on Southwark Bridge Road?"

His gaze, already piercing and focused, grew more so. "It was."

"At the back of that shop, tucked amongst the shelves, did you ever come across a safe?"

Stone nodded. "The man I worked for said it had been there when he opened shop in the place. No one knew the combination, and the previous businesses weren't the sort to fill a safe with money or jewels or any such thing. No one bothered trying to open it."

It was the right shop, then. "Mr. Sorokin hid some papers in that safe before it was locked tight. Among those papers are ones about a woman who's connected to the Radlett murder, which is connected to the blackmail the Tempest tried to use against Lord Chelmsford. I've some hope we'll find a clue in that safe, but Mr. Sorokin doesn't have the combination either."

"How are you intending to get into the safe?" Fletcher asked.

Stone shook his head. "Cracking safes ain't one of my skills, Móirín."

"Mine neither." Fletcher shrugged. "I can pick doors, but a safe's a different beast entirely."

"The Phantom Fox can crack a safe," Móirín said.

Looks of doubt flashed across the men's faces.

"I've seen her do it," she said, "though she doesn't know I saw." Móirín was keeping a heap of secrets.

"I ain't doubting she can break into a safe," Fletcher said, holding his hands up in a show of innocence. "I'm doubting Hollis'll be at all pleased at the idea of his beloved Ana being pulled into something so dangerous."

Hollis was one of the Dreadfuls, and the Phantom Fox was, in reality, his highborn wife. Hollis wasn't a controlling husband who lorded over his wife, demanding that she think and do and say only what he dictated or approved of. His objections would be centered around his concern for her safety.

"She helped us get papers from Lord Chelmsford's house not long ago," Móirín reminded them. "I think she'd help again. And she's not entirely unaware of the dangers her husband's group of literary friends have courted of late. I'd tell her enough about this latest mission for her to make the decision her own self."

"Do you know where to find Hollis and Ana?" Stone asked. "They're hiding with her father, but I don't know where."

"I've a pretty good idea." Móirín hadn't exactly been spying on her fellow Dreadfuls. She'd simply paid tremendously close attention, learning all she could about them. It was proving helpful now, as she felt she could predict where most had put themselves. She only hoped the Tempest hadn't been paying the same close attention.

"Assuming she'll come with us, the Phantom Fox and Stone and I'll break into the tobacconist's shop after it's closed and get into that safe. Once we have Sorokin's papers, we'll scamper in different directions and cross paths again at Southwark Cathedral before continuing on our separate ways."

Stone nodded. "One difficulty you might not have thought of. The shop next to the tobacconist's is a dealer in old clothes. Customers only come in and out during the daytime, but there's clobberers and seamstresses there at all hours, day and night, repairing and cleaning clothes to be sold. That'll make it difficult to get in and out without being heard."

Stone had told Móirín that he and Celia had met working in adjoining shops. "Does Celia still work there?" They might choose a day when she was at work and could provide a distraction.

"She don't."

A bit of bad luck, that. "Ask her, without giving away too much, what time of night we'd most likely not be found out."

Stone nodded.

"I'll write a letter from the Dread Master. Fletch, I'll give you an idea where you can find Hollis. Be blessed careful when you deliver it to him."

"It'll be good to know where he is," Fletcher said. "It's been a blame strange thing not knowing." Fletcher and Hollis had been close friends for years.

"Bring an answer back," Móirín said, then turned to Stone. "And let me know what Celia says about our best timing on this. We need to manage it sooner than later, but 'twouldn't do to get ourselves nabbed."

"Speaking of." Stone pulled from his back pocket a folded newspaper and dropped it on the table, then tapped at a small item at the bottom of a column.

Chandan Kumar, author of penny serials, reported missing by worried wife. Publisher confirms his newest serial offering will be halted awaiting his return.

"Is it possible he's thought missing because he's in hiding?" Fletcher wondered aloud.

Móirín shook her head. "He'd not go into hiding without his family. If his wife is reporting him missing, then he's full missing." *Blast it.* "Get whispers to your urchins, Fletch. We need to find out what happened to him."

"I've been wondering if the Tempest's nabbed him," Stone said.

It was a possibility Móirín knew would haunt her until she knew for certain.

POSIE AND PRU
DETECTIVES FOR HIRE

by Chauncey Finnegan

Chapter Two

Posie and Pru's very first case, unfortunately, required them to undertake a journey. The late Mr. Flanagan's home was merely down the road, but leaving the house when one required an increasing number of aids and preparations was, no matter the distance, *a journey.*

"I don't know that you need *two* shawls," Mrs. O'Reilly said to Pru. "The weather is not overly chilly."

"One is my *indoor* shawl," Pru was quick to point out. "The other is for out of doors. I must have both."

Mrs. O'Reilly eyed Posie's canes—three of them. "Indoors. Out of doors. And . . . ?"

"No, no, no." Posie held aloft her shorter, hook-topped cane. "For steep paths." She raised the slightly longer, thicker one, with the wide base. "For slick paths." She held up the third one, quite elegantly made and boasting a silver handle. "For indoors."

"Roger the cheeseman would likely let us use his pony cart," Mrs. O'Reilly suggested in tones that grew more doubtful the longer she watched Posie and Pru's preparations.

Young people, Posie said inwardly. Mrs. O'Reilly was barely fifty. What did she know of canes and shawls and such?

"We can walk there," Posie insisted.

And they did. Pru put her out-of-doors shawl on top of her indoor shawl. Posie opted for her slick-paths cane, though she kept her indoors cane hooked over one arm. And they made the almost-half-a-mile walk at quite a clip, arriving at the late Mr. Flanagan's house in forty-five minutes.

"Which door do we use, Posie?" Pru asked. "We're here as tradespeople, being detectives for hire, but we've only ever entered homes through the main door."

It was a valid question, though Posie hadn't thought of it yet. "Being detectives doesn't mean we're not still ladies. I think we'd do best to call at the front door as we would if we weren't now detectives."

"We haven't a butler," Mrs. O'Reilly said. "You'll have to wait until I am inside and can answer your knock."

Which is precisely what they did.

Posie and Pru waited under the front portico until they heard Mrs. O'Reilly call out from the other side of the door that they could knock now.

Which is precisely what they did.

At the opening of the door, Posie produced one of their cards. "Posie and Pru. Detectives for hire," she said with pride.

Mrs. O'Reilly accepted the card and motioned them inside. "May I take your . . . out-of-doors items?"

"Excellent." Posie gave the housekeeper her wide-ended cane and leaned on her silver-handled one instead.

Pru handed over her heavier shawl.

"There are knitting needles in this shawl." Mrs. O'Reilly sounded confused.

"My out-of-doors knitting needles, of course," Pru said.

Mrs. O'Reilly saw to the storing of their items in the small cloak closet before ushering them from the entryway to a small withdrawing room. "This is where Mr. Flanagan was found."

Posie hadn't been in the Flanagans' house before, but she'd heard there was a room inspired by the Hall of Mirrors at the Palace of Versailles. Seeing the half dozen mirrors hanging on the wall proved less impressive than Posie had expected. Most of the mirrors were quite small, and most of the wall was only a wall.

Perhaps Mr. Flanagan had actually died of being entirely underwhelmed by a room that had promised palatial perfection. Posie had read a great many novels in which disappointment had proven fatal.

Or, perhaps he'd caught sight of himself in a few of the mirrors at once and, thinking several people had appeared in the room without warning, was so startled that he died of surprise—another possibility she had learned of through novels.

"Had Mr. Flanagan recently been in receipt of particularly bad tidings?" Posie had also read of people who, upon being told something shocking or mournful, died of unhappy news.

"No," Mrs. O'Reilly said. "In fact, his son had only just arrived at the house for a visit. Mr. Flanagan was beside himself with happiness."

Happiness. Did people ever die of happiness?

"What was he doing in here?" Pru asked. "Other than being dead, I mean."

"One of the maids came in because she'd heard a loud crash and a shattering sound. She felt certain he had been drinking a glass of sherry."

Ah. And had likely been disappointed, surprised, or shocked to death by something.

"Might we talk with the maid?" Posie asked.

"Of course."

"And have a bit of tea and biscuits?" Pru pressed.

Mrs. O'Reilly dipped her head. "Of course."

"And have a seat?" Posie's cane was reliable, but her bones preferred resting.

"Please do," Mrs. O'Reilly said before disappearing out of the room.

"I suppose if a person has to die unexpectedly," Pru said, looking around as she shuffled toward an obliging chair, "this is not an unpleasant place to do it."

"I have three theories already, Pru, each as likely the next." Posie lowered herself into a wingback chair. She set her cane in front of her and rested both hands atop the handle. Her late husband used to assume that very pose when waxing long about something or other of significance. "We simply must determine if he was disappointed, surprised, or shocked in the moment before his death."

"Are those the only options?" Pru settled into a chair of her own.

"No, but I believe that is where we should begin."

Ten minutes passed before Mrs. O'Reilly, with the maid in tow, returned to the mirror room to find both Pru and Posie sleeping peacefully in their chairs. She was reluctant to wake them, but there was a mystery to be solved, after all, and if she was in fact a murderess, she would very much like to know.

With the two septuagenarians awake once more, the investigation could continue.

"This is Jane," Mrs. O'Reilly said, gesturing to the maid. "She's the one that found him."

"Did he look surprised?" Pru asked. "That is one of our theories."

"He didn't look surprised," Jane said. "I suspect he was, though. No one's expecting to be dead."

Posie nodded knowingly. "What else can you tell us?"

"He was lying on the floor, dead as can be. And the glass he'd been drinking from was shattered on the floor. The sound of it breaking was what brought me in. Saw him lying there. Saw Mrs. O'Reilly in the mirror. Leastwise I thought it was her. Let out a scream, I did, though on account of the sherry stain in the carpet I was going to have to scrub out. I didn't know he was dead. Once I did, I screamed on account of that."

"And did your screaming bring anyone else to the room?" Posie asked.

"Someone who might know if he'd been disappointed or surprised or shocked?" Pru pressed.

"Young Mr. Flanagan—our Mr. Flanagan's son—rushed in. He sorted out quite quickly that his father was dead." Looking as though she'd pieced something together, Jane eagerly added. "*That* Mr. Flanagan looked surprised and shocked. Might that have something to do with it?"

"I suspect he looked upset because his father was dead," Mrs. O'Reilly said.

Posie couldn't argue with that. She addressed the housekeeper. "Jane said you were in the room. What did you see?"

"I didn't know I was in the room until Jane told me later. I don't remember it."

Interesting.

"How did you know it was Mrs. O'Reilly?" Pru asked Jane.

"She was wearing her white dressing gown. It was billowy and flowing in the mirrors. Couldn't help but notice that."

"And you don't remember it?" Posie asked Mrs. O'Reilly.

"Not at all. Which is why I don't know for certain if I killed the poor man. Can't even remember being in the room. I must've been in a trance or something like that."

This was a stranger mystery than Posie had bargained for. If they could solve this, they would be legendary detectives.

"Are there any additional puzzles we might ponder?" Posie asked.

"One other," Mrs. O'Reilly said. "The young Mr. Flanagan is missing a dog."

And at that, Pru sat up straighter than she had in years.

CHAPTER 8

Any person who had a choice and a sense of self-preservation avoided Southwark at night. Móirín had both, yet that was precisely where she, Stone, and the Phantom Fox went the next night under cloak of darkness. This area of south London was home to the Kincaid family, grave robbers who didn't mind a spot of murder now and then. It was also an area that boasted criminals of every ilk. Breaking into a shop in this corner of the world was either incredibly foolish or an act of unwarranted arrogance.

Stone's experience with this exact building helped them tremendously, as he knew where to find the entrance Mr. Sorokin had suggested. Ana had warned that seldom-used doors were often the loudest, so they'd brought a small bottle of oil to help the hinges cooperate with their evening's endeavor.

Stone and Móirín tended to the hinges while Ana climbed to a window above their heads. Rushing through their efforts would almost certainly end in disaster. Yet, being in such a dangerous area of town made patience feel less like a virtue and more like a liability.

Hinges fully oiled, Móirín slowly opened the door, pushing

it just far enough for Stone to slip inside before closing it behind them. The shop was silent and dark, a sure sign the owner and workers were gone, and yet Móirín knew Ana was there. There was a reason the most famous thief in London had managed to evade capture for so long.

Just as they passed through a threshold, a dark figure dropped from a cabinet of drawers onto the ground beside them.

"The shop is empty," Ana whispered. "But there are voices in the one next door."

Celia had said there'd likely be three people at the old-clothes shop, enough that they'd jaw a bit to cover the small noises Móirín and her companions couldn't avoid, but not so many people that a heap of ears would potentially catch the tell-tale sounds of nearby thievery.

In the darkness, the sound of a match strike was followed by the tiniest flame. A thin candle was lit and set on a small candleholder with a shield to one side, offering a bit of light to the room. Ana handed it to Stone, and she and Móirín followed him into the shadows.

The shelves in the storage room were far from empty, hiding any glimpse of the safe. Stone pointed out a section. All three of them, careful and quiet, began pulling down boxes, careful to stack them in a way that they could put them back exactly as before. 'Twas crucial they not be caught out in the moment but also that their presence not be guessed at in the days to come.

They'd not cleared a single shelf when the voices on the other side of the wall grew suddenly louder. Móirín froze, as did the others, listening and breathing as shallowly as possible. The raised voices broke out in laughter, then returned to their previous volume.

The three of them resumed their work without a word or

a pause. Long minutes passed before they had the shelf clear. A rusty, dust-encrusted safe door was visible on the wall behind. It wasn't large; no one would guess it contained anything at all, which had served Mr. Sorokin well.

"Tell me where you need the light," Móirín said to Ana.

"A little to the left. Turn the shield to focus the light on the safe." Ana pulled from her well-hidden pocket a small cone, pressing the narrow end to her ear and the wider end to the safe. Slowly, she turned the dial, her eyes closed.

Seemed an odd thing wanting the light shown so precisely when Ana wasn't even looking, but Móirín'd found it best, when an expert was offering their expertise, not to question their methods.

Stone stood guard nearby, his back to them, his eyes on the doorway. He seemed particularly on the alert. She knew he was endlessly vigilant, but there was something different in his posture, something that set her on edge.

Ana continued her work, and Móirín was careful to keep the candle positioned exactly as requested, but she too was searching the sounds of the night, listening for whatever had caught Stone's attention.

Then she heard it. Footsteps. Inside the shop.

"We need to scamper," Stone whispered, stepping back to them.

"How close are you?" Móirín asked Ana in a tense whisper of her own.

"One number more," the Phantom Fox said.

They needed the papers. But giving away that the safe had been opened would make people ask too many questions. 'Twould risk Mr. Sorokin being tied back to it and that would put him and the children he guarded and Vera and Brogan in danger.

The footsteps were slow and still at a distance. No anxiousness to it. No running.

"Got it." Ana opened the door to the safe. It creaked, faintly.

Móirín snatched the twine-bound papers from the safe and slipped it into the bag she wore tied against herself. To Ana, she said, "Go. Make your way to the meeting spot. If we're not there in thirty minutes, go home."

"How will I know you're both safe?"

"You won't, but you getting home is most important." She wouldn't see yet another family in danger from their actions this night.

In one swift motion, Ana blew out the candle, snatched it up, and disappeared into the darkness.

Móirín had just buttoned her coat, hiding the bag holding the papers, when a pinpoint of light appeared in the doorway. She and Stone pressed themselves out of sight.

"I can't see you," the voice said, "but I know you're in here."

Parkington.

"I'd wager you got five minutes. Whatever jig you're dancing, sort it out, then we need to pike off."

Móirín didn't waste an instant. "Help Stone and me with the boxes," she said as she shut the safe door and spun the spindles to lock it tight.

"Should've known you'd be part of this mischief, Móirín," Parkington said.

"Just keeping you on your toes."

She, Stone, and Parkington set to putting the boxes back in their original positions.

"How'd you find us here?" Stone asked as they worked.

"Celia Ganda—who is apparently no stranger to you, Stone—heard a whisper the Kincaids were meaning to be active in Southwark tonight. She also knew you were headed this way. Figured there was a chance you'd get yourself killed crossing paths with them, and she didn't intend to sit back and let it happen."

"How'd she know to trust you?" Móirín asked.

"She'd seen me at some of the Charitable Authors League of London efforts. Figured I must've been a decent sort of fellow. Good judge of character, wouldn't you say?"

"I wouldn't go that far," Móirín muttered, grateful to have a reason to jest in a tense situation. It always helped her cope.

They'd only just set everything to rights when raised voices sounded from outside, loud enough to proclaim they didn't intend to make their arrival secret.

"Time to hop the twig," Parkington said. His candle was the only light they had. They followed it, moving swiftly.

Glass shattered in the front of the shop. The Kincaids were usually stealthy with their crimes, but stealth didn't matter when something was meant to be a warning. Catching them out, she suspected, was just that.

More glass broke in the back. They were coming in from both sides.

"Out the side entrance," Móirín ordered. "Then go in different directions. Stone, get to our meeting spot."

It was too dark to see if the men nodded in agreement, so she had to assume they did. She opened the door on silent hinges, and they slipped out, running off in opposite directions.

Though Móirín didn't know the tobacconist's shop the way Stone did, she knew the streets of London. There were few corners of it she hadn't explored, either while hunting rough-and-toughs or outrunning them. She slipped in and out of alleyways, behind buildings, not pausing to look behind to see if anyone was on her tail.

Speed was crucial. Stealth even more so.

All was quiet when she reached Southwark Cathedral. Móirín casually entered the churchyard, careful to tuck herself in the shadows against the building's mismatched nave. Being on the south side, her view was mostly of the railway bridge not sixty feet away. Even the buildings were smothered in this crowded area of London. Little wonder so many people felt suffocated and trapped.

And her Dreadfuls were tucked in even tighter than usual, hiding from the gathering storm.

Móirín set her hand against her coat, reassuring herself that the papers she'd filched were still there. There'd best be helpful information in the stack, else they'd risked a confrontation with the notorious Kincaids for nothing.

A woman walked past the iron gate leading from the street into the churchyard. As she did, three short hoots sounded. It was the signal that told Móirín the passing woman was Ana and that she was safe and on her way home. Móirín breathed a partial sigh of relief. When Stone passed by to the sound of the same owl, she breathed more fully still.

She was a little worried about Parkington. She often harassed him and enjoyed grumbling at and bantering with him, but she did like him. He was a decent sort of person, and he'd always been willing to help out when it was needed. And, she suspected, he had a pretty good idea that the authors operating publicly under the acronym CALL were in fact the secretive Dread Penny Society, but he'd never seemed the least inclined to use that against them.

And he'd saved them that night, no denying. Saved them at enormous risk to himself.

She pushed away from the cathedral wall, slowly making her way to the street. Parkington didn't know where their meeting place was, so she'd not know if he'd slipped past the Kincaids. Her network could search him out, though. She would set them on that in the morning.

As Móirín made her way along the outside of the church-yard, a figure emerged from behind a shrub. She had her knife at the ready; she *always* had her knife at the ready.

"Don't think I'm not prepared to slice you into ribbons," she warned.

"I suspect you'd do far more than that, but I don't think it'll be necessary."

Parkington. Again. Twice in one night he'd managed to sneak up on her, something no one ever did.

"I didn't know where you was intending to meet," he said, "so I did my best to follow you."

"Seems to me your best is pretty good." She lowered her knife but didn't sheath it; Southwark more than warranted keep-ing it handy.

"Was that a compliment?" His tone of pretended shock proved entertaining, which she appreciated. The night's work had left her anxious.

"Any words of praise I might've let spill were an accident, I assure you," she said with a laugh.

He chuckled and walked beside her. He, it seemed, was headed for the north side of the Thames as well. She watched every shadow and could see him doing the same. She'd've taken as much care even before the Tempest's rise. She did it doubly so now.

"I'll be thanking you for coming to warn us tonight," she said. "We'd've been strung up by the Kincaids for certain."

"If Fletcher's meaning to send any of his people out on dangerous escapades, tell him he'd do best to drop a word in my ear. I've extra eyes and ears around London. Might help keep the lot of you a bit safer."

"You're not known for breaking the law, Parky. Telling you what his people're up to would likely mean telling you about crimes we're planning to commit." She glanced at him as they walked. "That'd put you in a fair bind."

"It'd be difficult for me to be less important in the department at this point." He sounded thoroughly annoyed.

She could appreciate that. "'Tisn't easy being the new man, is it?"

"A bit too easy, and that's the rub." He shook his head. "I'm bored out of my skull being kept to petty criminals and fugitives what ain't made a peep in years."

Quiet fugitives. If only he realized he was walking alongside one.

"I'd prefer chasing the same yarn I suspect you and the ones you bide with are clawing at," he continued. "The sergeant I answer to told me to keep to what I've been assigned. I suspect he'd like a reason to toss me out, and I'm not itching to give him cause."

They stepped onto the Southwark Bridge, the Thames flowing beneath them, Southwark quiet behind them.

"I'd a job once where I answered to someone like that," Móirín said. "Thought himself rather fine because he'd the ability to make the people answering to him do what he wished by threatening to take their jobs away. Made life miserable."

Parkington nodded. "I suspect you didn't bow to his dictates without some degree of rebellion."

Oh, he didn't know the half of it. And good thing, that. Her "degree of rebellion" in that matter was the reason Parkington was, unbeknownst to him, looking for her. The "crime" she was wanted for had been committed entirely in self-defense, but the law didn't put much store by that when 'twas a poor woman defending herself against a comparatively more important man.

"We've not always got on, you and I," she said, "and I know some of your grumblings about me aren't feigned, but I'm finding myself ready to suggest we join forces."

"Partners in preventing crime?"

She shook her head. "Partners in bringing down a criminal. I make no promises about what I'll be doing in the accomplishing of it."

"Best not tell me about any of that. I'm walking a thin line as it is involving myself in this." He had his hands tucked in his pockets, but she suspected at least one of them held a weapon.

Which was good because she could hear footsteps behind them. A glance at his face told her he heard them too.

He set his arm around her shoulders and pulled her up against him as they walked. "Whoever that is'll think we're out for a midnight tryst," he whispered.

'Twas a good strategy. But his arm around her, the nearness of him, the scent of rosemary and almond that always hung about him, even the sound of him breathing, rendered her pulse a bit dodgy.

The bridge spilled them onto Queen Street. Footsteps continued behind them. Parkington pulled her into the arched doorway of Vinter's Hall, where shadow would obscure them a bit. He pulled her into an embrace that, from a distance, would look like confirmation of the impression they'd been trying to give. Up close, it *felt* rather like it as well.

He kept one arm around her and rested the fingertips of his other hand against the side of her face. Under other circumstances, it would've been a tender and affectionate gesture. But she knew why he was doing it now. Anyone passing by wouldn't be able to see her face. Not trusting blue-bottles had kept her alive for five years. Parkington certainly had a way of making it hard for her to not trust him.

"Someone's passing by," he whispered almost silently.

She pressed herself up to him, not out of fear but to make their ruse more convincing. Blast it if she didn't find some comfort in his arms, even knowing it was all an act. Loneliness did that. Or maybe 'twas something about him in particular.

His fingers brushed her cheek as he lowered his hand. "He's gone past."

"Out of sight?" she whispered back.

Parkington craned his neck, looking around the stone sides of the archway. "Out of sight." He breathed a sigh of relief. "Let's get going."

They stepped out, keeping close together but not touching as they had been. Nothing was said as they walked on, not for long minutes. She'd've liked to ask him if he'd enjoyed holding her; part of her wanted to know if he'd do it again. But she wasn't fool enough to open that particular door, considering the complications that waited beyond. Best she keep to a topic they could more safely discuss: a vicious, murdering criminal.

"Have you learned anything about the Tempest's activities?" she asked him. "Other than whispers of trouble in Southwark tonight, I mean."

He nodded, the movement illuminated by a gas streetlamp.

"I have come across a few things. But it's only a piece of the whole, which makes doing a blasted thing about it almost impossible."

She had a few pieces of that whole herself. Joining forces with a bobby wasn't her preferred path forward, but she needed to know what he knew.

"Would you be available tomorrow evening for a gab with some of us trying to claw at that yarn, as you called it?" she asked.

He nodded again. "Are you still living on Picadilly?"

"Like a lot of others, I've tucked m'self into hiding," she said. "But I can tell you how to find me. The directions are convoluted and for good reason. You might need to put them in writing but make certain no one gets hold of the paper."

"All those in the Detective Department are sharp, but only I never need to write things down after hearing or seeing them. You simply tell me, and I'll remember."

'Twasn't as reassuring as he likely thought. He didn't forget things he learned. The slightest clue about her past, and he'd be able to recall it if the matter of a certain Irish lady fugitive ever crossed his desk.

But the Tempest had to be stopped. She'd told herself that again and again over the past few days as more of her life had unraveled and more risks had needed to be taken. The Tempest had to be stopped.

They paused. There were no people nearby, but she still whispered directly into his ear the detailed instructions on how to find the safe house. One more person who knew one of her secrets, but also one more person helping her save countless lives.

The DPS needed Parkington's help, so she'd take the risk. She'd take it and hope it wouldn't be the decision that, in the end, proved her own downfall.

CHAPTER 9

Fitz hadn't asked Móirín or Stone what they'd taken from the hidden safe the night before, and that bothered him. He was now a Detective Constable. Curiosity was meant to be his most besetting sin. The fact that he'd not even thought to ask made him wonder if, perhaps, he weren't cut out to be a detective after all.

Perhaps that was why he'd not ever been able to solve the mystery of what had become of his grandfather. Even a lifetime of searching for him hadn't left Fitz with so much as a whisper.

What sort of a detective was he turning out to be?

"Made any progress?" Sergeant Wheatley stood beside Fitz's small desk, glaring as he always did, at least when talking with Fitz.

"On which matter exactly?" Fitz leaned back in his chair and watched the man, making certain he gave every impression of casual confidence.

"Any of them," Wheatley drawled. "You've not completed a single assignment since you joined us."

"The matters I've been assigned are all at least three years old. I've been a detective constable for a week. Do you expect me to solve in one week what the entire Detective Department hasn't solved in *years*?"

Nearby, Detective Toft stifled a laugh. Sergeant Cowden grinned, though he didn't make a sound. The two sergeants were more or less of equal rank, but Wheatley had seniority and, Fitz suspected, the ear of the commissioner, Sir Richard Mayne.

"What is it you *have* done?" Sergeant Wheatley asked doubtfully.

Wouldn't he be surprised if Fitz answered that he'd helped two shop breakers slip away undetected with some stolen loot? "I know a constable in L Division what worked in the Dublin police force until a few years ago. Since one of my assignments involves a fugitive from Dublin, I thought he might offer some insight."

"The information we provided you weren't enough?" Sergeant Wheatley scoffed.

Fitz didn't flinch. "Seeing as Scotland Yard ain't solved it in five years, I'll let you answer your own question."

Taking advantage of Wheatley's uncharacteristic silence, Fitz pushed onward. "I've at least a little information to go on with that one. And the answer to this'n"—he tapped the paper listing the suspected activities of the Phantom Fox—"has likely eluded the Detective Department because London's pawnbrokers ain't crawling over each other wanting to get hold of worthless porcelain figurines and combs no one but the Phantom Fox seems to want."

"So you're chucking it over already?" Wheatley looked to the others in the room, clearly expecting Fitz to be roundly condemned.

"Hardly." Fitz allowed his gaze to pass over the others as well. "I'm leaving off the approach taken thus far in trying to find the things taken. Don't make no sense to do so. Most thieves have an area of London they specialize in. Once I determine which one this Phantom Fox calls his own, I can predict where he might strike next, catch 'em in the doing of it."

Detective Toft nodded his approval.

Sergeant Cowden went a step further. "Good strategy, Parkington."

Sergeant Wheatley looked thoroughly annoyed. Let him be. Fitz was doing his job and doing it well. And he was also solving other mysteries he shouldn't've had to be addressing in secret. Eventually he might find himself with enough solved cases to his name to be given the freedom to look into other matters openly.

Sensing he would lose some of the foothold he'd gained if he bided much longer, Fitz gathered his papers and tucked them in his desk. He stood, tipped his hat, and simply walked out, not slowing until his feet took him out of the building entirely and onto the pavement.

The Thames was near enough that he could smell it. If he were in a jesting mood, he'd've said the same about the Houses of Parliament. Not a jest he would've made out loud, not with so many people around. He was on shaky footing, and it wouldn't do to make too many enemies.

He'd more than an hour before the time he'd agreed to meet with Móirín and likely Fletcher and who knew who else at the secret place she'd given him directions to. That suited him. He'd someplace he needed to see again.

Fitz assumed his formidable air, the one that kept people from asking too many questions or thinking him a juggins ready to be cheated. But he also made certain not to look threatening, as far too many were quick to take that as a challenge. While he could hold his own with his fives, he was in no mood for a street brawl.

He walked down Victoria Street. It was a rum bit of London, far finer than anyone of his ilk could've claimed as his own. He always felt like a lump of coal in a display of diamonds when making his way through this bit of Town. Turning up James Street let him breathe easier. The Quality were still within earshot, but this spot was home to folks more like himself.

At Vandon Street, he paused. It wasn't just where people *like* him made their homes. It was where *he* had made his once upon a time. Life had been promising then. He'd been an errand boy for a haberdasher, bringing in a bit of coin, living and working in a safe corner of London. And he'd had family.

Fitz stood outside his one-time home. Not much about it had changed. He'd studied it a thousand times in the last twenty years, searching for clues, searching for answers. He never found any.

Where'd you go?

He'd be a Detective Sergeant one day, maybe even an Inspector. He'd have records and information at his disposal. He might finally piece together what had happened all those years ago, and why he'd been left behind.

Fitz tucked his hands in his pockets and continued walking. It was always that way when he let himself wander to Vandon Street. He'd stop in front of his one-time home. He'd wonder at it all. Then he'd walk away.

This time, he had somewhere new to go.

With your back to Kent until the circle of the church makes Portland great, then Titchfield great, and a house to an alley. Three doors. Two stairs. One knock.

Móirín's instructions had been veiled. The place was clearly meant to be very well hidden. He'd pondered the night before where he was meant to begin. Once he'd stumbled on the answer, he'd shook his head at his own foolishness. It seemed obvious after discovery. At Park Square Gardens was a statue of the Earl of Kent, facing Portland Place.

He set his feet in that direction, maintaining his façade of a man unaffected by his surroundings, invulnerable, not wandering in the least, though he was taking a roundabout path to his beginning point. He walked for a full half an hour before his feet reached the statue. He turned, his back to the Earl of Kent, and began walking down Portland Place.

He'd told Móirín he didn't need to write anything down, that he would remember. And he did. 'Twas a talent he'd had from a young age. He reached All Souls Langham Place, a church with a tall, very round tower attached.

Until the circle of the church makes Portland great.

Following the turn of the road as it matched the turn of the building set him on Riding House, which crossed Great Portland Street.

Then Titchfield great.

One street down was Titchfield, which, he knew, led to Great Titchfield Street.

Then house to alley.

There were plenty enough houses to make that clue useless. Except, he knew Móirín was too clever to waste words nor make their meaning obvious. Back a bit on Great Titchfield was Riding House again, but a block further afield. Doubling back was a known way of confusing anyone who might be following. Sometimes a bit of a street could only be reached from one direction or the other.

Coming from the direction he was, he came upon a wide alleyway.

House to alley.

Clever, she was. Little wonder he found her so fascinating, so distracting. She crept into his thoughts when he weren't expecting, settling in like she meant to stay. And after holding her in his arms the night before, he suspected Móirín Donnelly would be a rather permanent fixture in those thoughts.

Three doors.

But on which side? She'd've given him a hint if it were right or left. He'd wager that meant it were both.

One to his right immediately. A second on the left a pace later. Almost directly across but the tiniest bit further down the alley was a third. A low door in a low wall—the sort one didn't step through if one weren't prepared to find something unpleasant. Not the sort of place he'd wish for her to call home, but a blasted good hiding place if one needed to not be found.

The door was locked, but Fitz had learned to get past that during the years he'd lived on the street after his grandfather disappeared. In a flash, he had the lock picked and the door open. He stepped through, closing it behind him, and looked around at a dilapidated courtyard and the backsides of buildings, some in dodgy condition.

Two stairs.

If the pattern held, he'd be aiming for the second set of stairs he saw. Though it was daylight, the courtyard was dim, one of those bits of London that seemed at odds with itself, broken in some indescribable way. Fitz spotted a set of iron stairs to his right, a bit worse for wear but not rickety. Around the back of the building to his left, in an even dimmer corner, was another set of stairs that could've been called rickety only on a good day. That'd be the one meant for him.

At the top was a narrow walkway, tall walls on either side, and even less light than in the courtyard. At the far end was a single door, one that looked like it hadn't been opened in ages.

One knock.

He followed instructions. A long moment passed before a slat in the door pulled sideways, revealing a small opening through which someone on the other side could see him.

"Oi?" That sounded like Fletcher.

"Parky's a right rubbish blue-bottle," he said, not bothering to hide his annoyance at the code phrase Móirín had given him. He suspected she had invented it specifically for him.

The slot in the door closed, followed by the faint sound of multiple locks and bars being undone on the other side. The door opened fully, and he stepped through.

He fully expected the space to be as ramshackle as the passageway leading to it, but it weren't at all tumbledown. The chairs pulled around the table in the center were mismatched and well-worn. The floor was bare. But the room was lit, despite the windows being boarded up and covered with fabric. That'd allow very little sound out, which told a story about this place sure enough. If he didn't know the people he was there with, he'd've suspected he'd stumbled upon a den of villainy.

While Fitz made his quick evaluation, Fletcher slid the bolts and locks back in place, securing the door. He then moved past Fitz and called out, in a voice that carried but was somehow still quiet, "We've a bobby for keeping company."

At that, people began stepping in.

Elizabeth Black, who ran a girls' school and had helped with any number of difficult situations, showing herself capable and brave.

Stone, who Fitz'd always want on his side, no matter the skirmish.

Then Dr. Barnabus Milligan and his wife, Gemma, stepped out of an adjoining room. Barnabus and Gemma—whose *funeral* he had attended a little over a week earlier. He'd seen them nailed into their coffins. He'd seen those coffins carried into a church, carried back out, buried in the ground. It was by their graves that the Mastiff had been found the morning after their internment.

"Best pop your gob closed, Parkington," Fletcher said with a laugh. "The good doctor and our dimber Gemma'll think you ain't happy to see them on this side of the ground."

"I'm pleased as plums. Confused. But pleased."

Móirín entered the room from the only corridor inside. "'Tisn't so confusing, Parky. Our Gemma's versed in the resurrectionists' art. Simply plies the trade for good instead of mischief."

"Have you tried plying your trade for good?" he tossed back.

She walked closer, something in her posture and expression more saucy than anything. "And what trade would that be?"

Oh, it was tempting to pull her into his arms as he had the night before, a moment he'd relived in his thoughts countless times since. She'd not welcome that, though.

"Trade? Bridge crossing, maybe. Doorway duckin'. Covert cuddlin'."

The corners of her very tempting mouth tipped upward. Móirín Donnelly could take a bit of jesting as well as she gave it. It were one of the things he liked most about her. He didn't have to tiptoe, though he suspected she'd hand him his head if he were ever actually unkind.

Everyone was taking seats at the table, so Fitz did too. That Móirín took a seat beside him weren't an unwelcome thing.

"Which of the Kincaids resurrected you?" Fitz asked Gemma. Her family had played a role in the courtroom murder he'd witnessed, but if one of 'em had a conscience, that'd be a helpful thing to know.

"*This* Kincaid," Gemma said. "Resurrected myself, and taught Baz to do the same."

"Yourself?" Fitz leaned back in shock. "I ain't never heard of that being done."

"As far as we know," Barnabus said, "it never has been. We need her family to think we're dead. Hiding the truth by doing something even they can't do was our best option. They'd lay waste to a whole lot of people if they knew they might find Gemma again."

"The Mastiff was found dead near your graves," he said. "Was he killed because he found out you weren't in there?"

Doc shook his head. "He was killed by the Tempest because, according to her, he was no longer useful. She sent the Kincaids to dig up the grave, knowing they would find him in one of our coffins. Without her commanding them to do so, they wouldn't have taken the risk of being found out resurrecting. There was no gain in it for them, and no reason to believe Gemma and I were anywhere but in those coffins. It's the whole reason we undertook such a risky self-resurrection: it was believed to be impossible, believed so firmly that even her family would accept we were both dead."

"But now they know you aren't," Fitz said.

"Not necessarily." Gemma looked tired and a little worried.

"They have three possibilities to chase now: that one of us ain't dead, that neither of us is, or that we *are* dead, but one of our bodies was pulled from the coffin to make room for the Mastiff. We're hoping that, knowing resurrecting oneself isn't something that's ever been done, they'll assume the last."

"How'd the Tempest get the Mastiff's body into a coffin with no one the wiser?" he wondered aloud.

"I don't know," Gemma whispered. "But the fact that she keeps managing things she shouldn't be able to is a reminder that we ought not to underestimate her."

Fitz nodded slowly, finding places in his mind to slip this new information. The Raven didn't know the Mastiff was dead or that the Tempest was a woman. The Kincaids knew that the Mastiff had been murdered, though not necessarily by whom, and didn't realize they'd been double-crossed by one of their own and her husband.

Blast it, but he was frustrated the Detective Department wouldn't let him officially pull at this thread.

With everyone settled, Fletcher addressed the group. "I've been given the nod to spill a few secrets to this group. Don't make no sense to wait."

The group's curiosity was not displayed equally on all their faces. Some of that was likely due to Stone and Móirín's ability to hide what they were thinking. But the rest, Fitz suspected, was owing to not everyone having the same level of ignorance.

"Parkington, you've helped a group of authors the last few years take on some of the rough-and-toughs of London. We recently formed the CALL, but that ain't the whole of who we are."

It was enough for Fitz to confirm what he'd suspected. "You're the Dread Penny Society, ain't you?"

Fletcher nodded, not looking at all surprised that he'd solved that mystery. No one else looked surprised either. They all knew, then.

"We've wanted to invite you to join for ages," Barnabus said, "but you have this horrible habit of not writing penny dreadfuls, and that's a requirement for membership."

As far as Fitz knew, Gemma and Móirín didn't write penny dreadfuls. Elizabeth wrote silver-fork novels, but that weren't the same thing at all. So they weren't members but knew about the society just the same.

"Is your brother a member?" Fitz asked Móirín. "I know he pens penny dreadfuls."

"He is," she said. "But he don't know I know he is." There was a warning and a request in that.

"I'll not be the one to tell him," Fitz promised.

Móirín nodded.

"Is Chandan Kumar one of yours too?"

It brought all their eyes to him.

"He's been reported missing, and it's made me wonder."

Fletcher's usual joking expression was somber. "We're trying to find him. Even the Dread Master—that's the one that runs this organization—can't sniff him out. We're trying to tell ourselves he's simply hiding like the rest of us, but . . ." Fletcher shook his head.

The tone in the room was sober. Kumar was either in danger or something horrible had happened to him.

"I was at Newgate a few days ago," Fitz said, "and gabbed a spell with one known as the Raven."

Recognition lit every face.

"He insisted, with a stomach-turning bit of smugness, that the spider at the center of the criminal web he's part of has set a specific goal of destroying the Dread Penny Society, and I don't think he meant *disbanding*."

Móirín released a quiet but tense breath. "I need to warn Brogan," she said. "If anything happens to him . . ."

Fitz set his hand on hers, hoping the gesture'd be welcome. She didn't pull away.

"I don't know if you've heard," Fitz continued, "but Claud Kincaid was murdered during trial at the Old Bailey."

"I heard poison," Fletcher said.

Fitz nodded. He looked at Gemma. "The dock had the Kincaid mark on it, in ash."

"Where was the *K*?" Her question was a bit too calm, the sort of pretended ease one summoned when trying to hide a deep worry.

"In the middle," he said.

She took a deep breath. "That's my uncle Silas's mark. It was either done under his orders or by his own hand."

"I'd've assumed the Kincaids punished him for getting caught and embarrassing the family, but he kept saying, 'The Tempest is here.' Over and over. The barrister overseeing it all said it was all Claud would say in the days leading up to the trial. Cain't help but think the murder was more than a family matter."

"And it was the Kincaids that ran you out of the tobacconist's shop last night?" Elizabeth addressed the question to Stone and Móirín.

Stone answered. "Seems that way. We were lucky Celia heard whispers and dropped a whisper of her own in Parkington's ear."

"And we're doubly lucky we got what we wanted before having to pike off." Móirín stood, pulling her hand from Fitz's, something that disappointed him more than it ought. She set on the table three papers.

"Mr. Sorokin created a set of forged documents for the woman talked about in these papers. Because making forgeries believable requires enough truth to not reveal the lie, he took vast notes about the person's actual life and abilities. Her name was Lucy Morgan. She came to him fifteen years ago, and she has a connection to the Radlett case, which is of great importance to the Tempest. But we don't yet know why nor if there's a connection between our foe and this long-ago forgery."

They all leaned over the table, eyeing the papers as best they could. The lantern light helped but also cast uncooperative shadows.

"I've seen the Tempest," Gemma said, "and I'd bet my eyeteeth she's not yet twenty-five."

"Lucy was older than that when the forgeries were made," Fitz said, pointing to a note on one of the papers. "And that was fifteen years ago. She can't be the Tempest."

Móirín shook her head. "But 'tis mentioned she had a child with her, a daughter. If the information she gave Sorokin was accurate, the girl would be about the right age to be the Tempest. It'd be a mighty helpful thing, as it simplifies our search, but I don't think we can count on it."

"Especially seeing as, when he knew her as Clare she seemed a heap younger than when we crossed paths with her as Serena." Fletcher rubbed his chin. "I suspect she's one who can make herself seem to be whatever she thinks is most useful in any given moment."

"Lucy told Mr. Sorokin she was born in Hertfordshire, but her daughter was born in London," Elizabeth pointed out. "If the daughter *is* the Tempest, then there'll be record of her somewhere in Town."

"London's a sprawling place," Fitz said. "And people in poverty don't always leave a trace."

"We've a name for Lucy Morgan now," Móirín said. "'Tis more than we had to go on before."

"I can ask Lord Chelmsford if he recalls anyone named Morgan when he was connected to the Radlett case," Fitz said.

"You know Chelmsford?" Stone asked.

Fitz nodded. "Been lookin' in on him a couple times a week since he moved to a safer place after Claud tried to kill Martin Afola." He sat up as something occurred to him. "Martin's one of your lot, i'n't he?"

"He is," Fletcher said.

That explained a few things. "I'll find out what I can from Lord Chelmsford." He turned to Móirín. "Is Sorokin hiding with your brother and sister-in-law?"

She nodded. "They're tight as bedbugs but heaps happier."

"Might be you could warn Brogan and gab a piece with Sorokin at the same time."

"I wish I could go with you," Gemma said to Móirín. "It's only been a couple of weeks since I saw Vera, but I miss her."

"I'd wager she misses you too," Móirín said. "She ain't the sort to be pleased to sit around in silence with no company."

"If you think they won't mind me knowing where they are, I'll come with you," Stone said. "Wouldn't mind an evening with friends."

Móirín's expression grew mischievous. "Would Celia enjoy an evening with newfound friends?"

"She might." Stone gave nothing away.

"She certainly showed herself reliable," Fitz interjected. "I'd think you could trust her with that secret."

Móirín's gaze turned to him. "We could trust you with it too. What do you say, Parky? Wanna take part in a lively evening of very quiet revelry?"

"Quiet?"

"On account of all of us are, to one extent or another, in hiding."

Ah. "So, Stone and his sweetheart, and Brogan and his sweetheart, would be spending the evening with me and . . . you." He let his smile turn a little roguish. "Are you trying to tell me something, Móirín?"

She shrugged. "That I'm desperate."

Fitz tossed a look of amused disbelief around the table, earning chuckles and grins in response. Returning his attention to Móirín, he was treated to a sight he knew he'd never grow weary of: her smile was soft and her gaze was warm and the tiniest hint of color touched her cheeks. It was the look of a woman not entirely displeased at the idea of an evening spent with him, and he liked that. He liked that a whole lot.

POSIE AND PRU
DETECTIVES FOR HIRE

by Chauncey Finnegan

Chapter Three

"Oh!" Pru's eyes lit with excitement. "We are very good at dogs. Posie didn't think we'd be doing any dog-related detective work, but I just knew we would. I just knew it!"

"I think we would do best to focus our efforts on the more critical matter at hand," Posie said. "The issue of the dog can wait until we have determined if Mr. Flanagan was in fact murdered and by whom."

"The young Mr. Flanagan is very fond of that dog," Mrs. O'Reilly said. "And he's heartbroken at having lost his father. It'd be a kindness to relieve him of one source of grief, though we can't relieve him of the other."

The more time Posie spent with Mrs. O'Reilly, the more convinced she was that the woman was not the sort to murder a person. Granted, Posie had not, to her knowledge, been acquainted with any murderers. She had, though, read a great many novels. And the murderers in those novels were very sneaky and very selfish and very . . . murdery.

"We are very good at dogs." Pru was even more animated than usual.

"Nonetheless," Posie said, ignoring the first whispers of *petite pru* sneaking up on her once more. "I think our wisest course of action is to speak with young Mr. Flanagan. He might know things we do not, things that would help us solve the matter of his father's death."

Posie took firm hold of the arms of her chair and slowly rose, doing her utmost to hold back the grunt that usually accompanied the effort. It was such an "elderly" thing to do, and she preferred not to feel or seem old.

"You can converse with him in his library," Mrs. O'Reilly suggested. "He does not like to spend time in this room on account of it being where his father died."

That seemed reasonable enough.

They followed Mrs. O'Reilly down the corridor. Posie had her indoor cane, which was particularly helpful. Pru's indoor shawl was proving well worth bringing also. This was why Posie knew they would be excellent detectives: they thought ahead.

That forward thinking was also why Posie reminded Mrs. O'Reilly that they never had been provided with the requested tea and biscuits. Not only did Posie anticipate being hungry in short order but she knew full well that to begin a proper conversation with Mr. Flanagan, they had to begin with tea and biscuits.

Mrs. O'Reilly provided those basics of any English welcome a mere moment before the grieving son entered the library. He eyed them with obvious confusion but also offered a genteel bow and a kind word of welcome.

"Please sit for a moment," Posie offered. She was well aware that calls required them to follow a certain protocol.

They had tea and biscuits. Now they needed to talk about unimportant things none of them truly cared about.

"How have you found the weather of late?" Pru began.

"Pleasant." Mr. Flanagan sat among them, being wonderfully polite, but seeming a bit uncomfortable. "And you?"

"Most pleasant weather," Posie said. "The sky does seem to promise rain before the day is out."

"I shall make certain to be prepared for that possibility."

Pru took a sip of tea before moving to what was usually a very insignificant topic. "Dogs are quite lovely creatures."

Mr. Flanagan's expression grew immediately somber. "I do like dogs. I have a dear little beagle. He's been with me since he was a puppy and hasn't ever run away. But I don't know where he is now. The little thing's disappeared."

"We'll find him," Pru promised. "We're very good at dogs."

"When did your dog go missing?" Posie thought it best to gather information about this less important mystery as quickly as possible so they could return to the more pressing matter.

"I cannot say precisely, but sometime during the day my father died. I realized that night that I'd not seen the little beagle in some time. The horridness of all that had happened had entirely distracted me."

And that brought them nicely back to the mystery Posie most wanted to solve. "Your father's passing is what has brought us here, in fact."

"What about his passing has so interested you?" Mr. Flanagan was being very kind, but Posie recognized the wariness that had entered his expression. He had, thus far, proven himself a more genial person than his father had ever been, which was to his credit, but they would be wise to explain and not try his patience.

"We have our suspicions regarding the manner of his death."

Something oddly like relief filled his face. "I've had similar suspicions but hadn't dared voice them. I think someone might have killed him."

Posie and Pru nodded in unison. To Posie's relief, Pru didn't say anything about Mrs. O'Reilly's potential involvement. It was best not to give away one's purpose when seeking out those who might attempt to thwart it for their own benefit.

Mrs. O'Reilly stepped inside the library a moment later. She offered a curtsey to her new employer. "Your man of business is here to see you, sir."

"Thank you, Mrs. O'Reilly. Please show him in." He looked at Posie and Pru. "As this is the most fitting room for me to conduct business, I fear I will have to be a little rude and ask if we might end this discussion early?"

"We're needing to collect clues as it is," Posie said. "We'll see to that."

"Collect clues?" Mr. Flanagan repeated with a hint of a smile. "You are dedicating yourselves to the matter, it would seem."

"We are, indeed." Posie shook a bit as she rose but proudly did not make any noises.

"Do share with me anything you might learn." Mr. Flanagan bowed to each of them.

"And we will make certain not to neglect the matter of your dog," Pru promised him.

"That is very good of you."

Mr. Flanagan's man of business was shown in as the two detectives for hire were shuffling out. The slowness of their departure meant Posie overheard a little of the conversation beginning between the men.

"I have looked over the expenses you are anticipating, Mr. Flanagan, and I do believe you can afford to make some changes in the household staff."

Once in the corridor, Mrs. O'Reilly joined them. "Have you learned anything of significance?"

"Quite a few things, in fact," Posie said. "We simply need to sort through them. Jane saw a woman in a flowing white nightdress in the many mirrors in the room where the late Mr. Flanagan died. He'd been drinking and dropped his glass before dropping himself. The young Mr. Flanagan's dog disappeared during this time, and everyone knows dogs are more aware of things unseen than people are."

"I suppose that is true," Mrs. O'Reilly acknowledged.

"I find myself growing ever more convinced that the culprit was, indeed, seen by Jane in the mirrors, but that, contrary to what she thought she saw, the woman in the flowing white nightdress was not actually you."

"Then who was it?" Mrs. O'Reilly asked.

In near perfect unison, Posie and Pru both said, "A ghost!"

CHAPTER 10

Before telling Stone or Parkington where Brogan and his family were hiding, Móirín had first asked her brother for his permission. It wasn't her decision to make, after all. Which people—and how many—knew the secret was a decision he ought to be permitted to make. She suspected he might have said no, but Vera looked so hopeful, so pleading, that it was clear she was a little lonely.

When Vera had worked in the print shop she and her father had owned, before it had been burned to the ground on the orders of the Tempest, she'd interacted with dozens upon dozens of people each day, and the significant injuries she'd sustained in that fire had left her unable to leave the house for months. Now, the prospect of company had lit her face in a way Móirín hadn't seen in some time.

"Can you bring them here by a roundabout way?" Brogan asked Móirín.

She popped her fists on her hips. "Can I bring them here by a roundabout way?" she repeated, feigning offense at his doubt. "I think you forgot just who it was you were talking to."

Brogan offered a very brotherly apology tumbled together with an ample amount of teasing.

She tucked in his hand the money she'd been paid from her publisher for the most recent installment of "Posie and Pru: Detectives for Hire" and had utterly refused to hear any of his objections.

"You'll have four of us descending on you tonight," Móirín had said. "Prepare yourselves for a wonderful time."

But, now, standing at the door of their tucked-away flat, having given Stone and Parkington separate, coded instructions on how to get there, she felt uncharacteristically unsure of herself.

Kumar was missing, and none of her many and varied contacts had been able to locate him. None of Fletcher's street urchins had heard a whisper either. She'd gone by the place where Dominique was holed up, but there'd been no sign of him there. 'Twas possible he'd simply gone elsewhere, but she couldn't quite convince herself of it.

The members of the DPS were in danger. That meant Brogan was too. They depended on the Dread Master to keep them safe, and she wasn't entirely managing it. All their lives, Brogan had depended on her to keep the two of them safe. She feared she was failing at that too.

But when Mr. Sorokin opened the door and motioned her inside, she summoned her confidence and smiled. Vera needed this night to be a happy one. If Vera was unhappy, Brogan would be too. Móirín had promised their parents more than just to keep him safe. She'd sworn to look out for him, to give him every chance of living a good and happy life. She'd promised.

"I cannot tell you how excited I am," Vera said, motioning her to come closer.

Vera wore her best dress, and Brogan had spruced himself up as well. The flat, still sparsely furnished, appeared to have been scrubbed top to bottom.

Móirín hugged her sister-in-law once the door was closed. "I daresay you're excited because, like the rest of us, you're desperate to meet Stone's secret sweetheart."

Vera smiled, a laugh in her eyes. "I am, though not as excited as Brogan is. He keeps making guesses as to what she's like, what Stone will be like in her company. Even my father, who is hardly acquainted with Stone, is intrigued."

Mr. Sorokin sat in the corner beside a small table on which was a candle. The windows were covered, though not as entirely as they were at the safe houses. It'd keep people from seeing inside but wouldn't stifle all the noise. 'Twas expected that people would live in this flat, and it'd actually draw more attention to make it seem empty.

As Brogan walked past Móirín on his way toward his wife, he paused long enough to whisper to her, "Thank you. Vera's more alive tonight than she has been in weeks."

Móirín nodded. Inwardly, she sighed with relief. It'd been difficult lately, feeling like she was failing him, feeling she was breaking the most important promise she'd ever made.

She'd only been nine—and Brogan even younger—when the two of them had walked from their home in the Irish countryside to Dublin. How they'd survived the walk or the following years when they'd lived in desperate poverty on the streets of that unforgiving city, she'd never know. There had been too many nights when she'd only been able to acquire enough food for one of them.

It was then she'd gained a knack for lying to Brogan, telling him she'd eaten her share on the way back to the hovel where they'd tucked themselves. She'd told him her shoes fit fine, though her feet'd been bleeding, because there'd been coins enough for only one pair of secondhand shoes, and he'd needed them. She'd told him so many times that she wasn't scared, wasn't hungry, wasn't falling to pieces inside. She learned to lie to him, and, heaven help her, she was doing it still.

While Brogan helped his wife prepare for the remaining guests, Móirín moved to sit beside Mr. Sorokin. "I found some things of yours." She spoke quietly but not whispering. Whispers often drew more attention than simply speaking in a soft voice.

Mr. Sorokin's eyes narrowed. "Which things?"

"Papers."

The flash of understanding in his eyes was gone almost as soon as it appeared. "Did you find the ones you were looking for?"

She nodded. "Had to skim over a few first."

"Probably learned a few things," Mr. Sorokin said. "Can I trust you to keep those things secret?"

"Even the grave don't hold as many secrets as I do."

"I feel that way myself at times," Mr. Sorokin muttered.

"Seems you and I have a few things in common," Móirín said. "Not the least among them being that in the past we've gone by different names than we're using now." She saw him pale a bit and realized how her revelation might've sounded. She patted his hand lightly. "'Tis not a threat, simply that if the name I went by at the end of m'time in Dublin were widely known *here*, it'd be m'neck. Knowing the name you had when you fled Russia, I realize the same is true for you."

His eyes darted to his daughter, full distracted in conversation with Brogan. "The Speshnev name is no longer safe."

"I should think not. Another by that name was amongst

those in the Petrashevsky Circle who were arrested and scheduled to be executed."

Mr. Sorokin nodded. "A cousin."

"I have seen a list of those in the Circle," Móirín said. "He was the only one with that surname."

"I was the keeper of the records." Both sorrow and pride entered his voice. "I kept my name off, which some would consider cowardly. In the end, it means history will not condemn me, but plenty of others do."

"Your involvement was not kept entirely secret?"

He shook his head. "I'm still sought by Russia for my role. Some from the Circle are searching for me too, and not to congratulate me on my escape."

"You're family to my brother, which means I'll do anything for you and Vera, including keeping every secret you need me to."

"Do you have the papers with you tonight?"

She nodded. "Though we'd best make the transfer now while Vera's distracted, unless you're wanting to be peppered with questions for the rest of forever."

He sighed and slumped in his chair. "Never knew a woman who could pester a person with questions like she can."

Móirín smiled, grateful for his lighter tone. "I can give you the papers now, but you'll likely have mere moments to secret them away somewhere."

He nodded.

She undid the buttons along the side seam of her skirt, behind which was a large pocket. She pulled out the twine-tied bundle and handed it over, feeling a burden lift from her shoulders. She was always willing to help, but sometimes she felt exhausted by the weight of all she carried.

"Thank you," he said, sincerity clear in his voice.

She reached up inside the hidden pocket and undid the front latch of the single suspender she'd attached over her shoulder to help counter the weight of the papers. Without it, anyone looking at her could tell something heavy was under her dress. But with that something gone, leaving the suspender attached would hitch that side of her skirt up.

Mr. Sorokin slipped from the room; no one noticed him go.

Parkington arrived next. Brogan had been surprised to hear the detective constable was on the guest list, but she'd told him that he was among the group of people helping Fletcher track down the Tempest and her co-conspirators. That had seemed explanation enough. He trusted Fletcher. He trusted her, too, but sometimes she wanted to tell him he shouldn't.

Before Móirín could toss a single jesting remark at Parkington, Stone arrived, and she swore the entire room held its collective breath.

Stone was as stoic and unreadable as ever. Beside him and holding his hand was one of the prettiest women Móirín had ever seen. Like Stone, she was Black and had eyes that spoke of intelligence and lived experience. *Unlike* Stone, she was smiling broadly and seemed eager to make new acquaintances.

No sooner had Stone introduced Celia Ganda to the rest of the lot than she took up the conversation, entirely at ease with everyone.

To Móirín's delight, Celia approached her almost immediately. "I cannot tell you how pleased I am to finally meet you." Her speech identified her as London born and raised, another difference to the man who watched her with adoration.

"And I'm right tickled to finally meet you," Móirín said. "Stone's a friend, almost a brother, and the fact that he'd not arranged for us to meet before now has been a source of annoyance, I'll tell you that."

Celia smiled. Beautifully straight teeth were a rare thing in London, but Celia could claim them. She also, Móirín discovered as the evening continued, possessed another rare trait for a Londoner: she was friendly. 'Twasn't to say all of London were a heap of grumpy misanthropes. There was simply a sheen of distrust over the vast and perilous city.

As the evening continued, Móirín returned to her seat by Mr. Sorokin.

"It's nice to have something enjoyably ordinary to do tonight, considering how difficult life has been lately," he said.

"It is at that."

Parkington approached and sat with them, which allowed Móirín to introduce a topic she'd needed since his arrival. To Mr. Sorokin, she said, "Parkington knows about our efforts to identify the Tempest, and that at one point you interacted with someone connected to the Radlett case." Both men nodded. "It'd be helpful in our efforts if we knew how old the little girl was who was with the woman you met."

Mr. Sorokin closed his eyes, his expression thoughtful. "I don't know that I can say with absolute certainty," he said. "Seven years old, perhaps. She was small, but she had the look of someone older than her stature would indicate. I don't know if she was made small by life's difficulties or if she was aged by them. There seemed no way of knowing her true age."

"That's actually quite helpful," Parkington said. "How old the Tempest is has become a point of debate. Everyone who's seen her decides something different, so for you to have had the same impression of this little girl seems too much a coincidence to actually be one."

Across the room, the two couples laughed, though Stone's "laughter" was mostly a subtle smile. He wasn't an unhappy person; he was just reserved. Truth be told, she liked that about him. He was calm in a storm. And, judging by the way Celia looked at him, she liked most everything about him. Stone was more at ease in Celia's company than Móirín had ever seen him.

Brogan, too, was more alive and joyful now that Vera was in his life than she could remember him being in years. For the first time since their parents died, there was someone who stood by Brogan with as much fierce determination and devotion as Móirín did.

They were all happy, with the promise of even more joy ahead of them. If she failed to bring down the Tempest, and the Tempest destroyed them all . . .

No. She refused to admit defeat so early in the game. She'd overcome insurmountable obstacles before. She'd do so again.

But that wasn't her only source of discouragement. She wanted her brother and her friends-who-were-like-brothers to be happy. But she envied them a little. She was a person always in hiding, always on the run. A person who kept secrets and told lies and had nothing in her future but more of the same. 'Twasn't a life a person shared with anyone. 'Twasn't a future anyone'd be clamoring to have a claim on.

"Your sister-in-law knows how to put people at ease, don't she?" Parkington said to her quietly, the sudden sound of his voice almost startling her. How was it he kept managing to do that? She was always alert, likely to an unreasonable degree. But it had kept her alive.

"Vera makes everyone feel welcome, almost without trying," Móirín said. "'Tisn't a talent of mine."

"Oi, but you're terrifying. That's a talent too, I suppose."

She grinned at him. "Do I terrify you, Parky?"

"Are you hoping you do?" There was something flirtatious in his question and in his eyes.

She leaned closer to him. "That depends on if you like being terrified."

He matched her movement, leaning toward her, their eyes meeting at a closer distance, their voices dropping because they could. "Oh, I like it very much indeed."

"And how do you like being called Parky?" She'd started doing it a few weeks earlier just to see if it riled him at all. He'd not shown himself to have a temper or to truly dislike their friendly jabs.

His smile turned undeniably beguiling. "I'd like it even more if you called me Fitz."

"Fitz." She tried the name, feeling it out. "I think I could be persuaded to call you that. But I reserve the right to call you Parky now and then."

His eyes slid over her face, seeming to study and sort her out. A blue-bottle paying too much attention was a dangerous thing, yet his scrutiny didn't make her uncomfortable. She'd not have expected that.

Through a window at the back of the room came the tiny figure of Olly, an eight-year-old urchin watched over by Mr. Sorokin ever since the Mastiff, no doubt under the direction of the Tempest, had threatened the little boy and a young girl who'd both been living with the Sorokins.

Which brought to mind something Móirín hadn't thought of yet. "Where's Licorice?" she asked Mr. Sorokin.

"She's in her room. She didn't feel like keeping company tonight, needed a bit of peace."

Móirín could appreciate that. To Olly, she called out, "Where have you been, lad?"

The boy usually had a cheeky retort. But this time, his face was pale and his expression worried. Few things scared the children of London's hardened streets. And little Olly looked utterly terrified.

Móirín was on her feet in an instant, the rest of the room only a step behind.

"What's happened?" she asked the boy.

He looked up at her, wide-eyed and growing paler by the moment. "There's a mark on the wall." His voice wavered.

"What sort of mark?" she asked.

"Made with ash. Two lines and a letter *K*."

The mark of the Kincaid family. They marked places both where they'd done their dirty work and places they intended to target, like signing a work of art, proudly claiming credit for what they'd done or meant to do. Nothing good came to a place they marked.

Móirín hunched a bit to look Olly in the eye. "Where exactly was the mark?"

The boy swallowed with difficulty. "Under Miss Vera and Mr. Brogan's window."

She could feel the shock in the room, could sense them freeze. She was not so easily felled. "Olly, fetch Licorice from her room. Tell her to bring her coat and make certain her shoes are on."

"Are we leaving, Miss Móirín?" Olly asked.

Móirín nodded. "As quick as a bird on the wing." She turned to the others. "Brogan, fetch any powders or medicines Vera needs. The two of you fetch your coats. Stone, can you get

SARAH M. EDEN

them to my safe house where Barnabus and Gemma hid before their funeral? Not the one where I'm staying, but the other one."

Stone nodded.

"You and Celia decide what you mean to do. If the mark was put there tonight, you two might be targets as well."

"We'll sort it," Stone said. "And we'll all get there safe."

Móirín turned to Mr. Sorokin as Stone and Celia helped Brogan and Vera. "Tell me what you need for you and these children to be safe. Everything I have is at your disposal."

Sorokin shook his head. "I'll not burden you with that."

"*Tovarishch*," she said firmly, "I am not a messenger; I am the Pigeoneer. Tell me what you need."

She could see the moment he understood what she was telling him. The hesitation disappeared, replaced by complete confidence.

"Is there room for us in the place where you're sending Brogan and Vera?"

She nodded. "There's no one hiding there just now. But 'tis a place that's meant to be abandoned, so the children can't be going in and out. They'd be stuck inside for I don't know how long. Can they endure that?"

"We can," Licorice said, following Olly into the room. Both children moved directly to Mr. Sorokin, tucking themselves against him. He set an arm around each of them.

"You as well?" Móirín asked Olly.

He nodded, though a bit frantically. "If the Kincaids won't find us there, I'll stay in as long as you tell me."

Móirín addressed Mr. Sorokin again. "You need to fetch some papers." Next, she turned to Fitz. "Vera can't climb out the window, which means we'll be walking right out the door and down the corridor."

Fitz didn't seem to need any more instructions than that. "I'll go ahead, make certain all's clear." He pulled on his coat and hat and left with a quick step.

Móirín positioned herself at the door as the parlor filled again, everyone in their coats and sturdy shoes, waiting for the signal to flee.

Brogan moved to stand beside her. In a quiet voice, he asked, "*Your* safe house?"

She nodded. He'd be piecing it together soon enough.

"Seems there are some things you've not told me," he said.

"Secrets have kept us alive, Brogan."

"But from each other?" He sounded hurt.

As much as she wanted to make this right, to explain and fix and plead for understanding, they hadn't time. He and his family had to get out of this dangerous place.

Fitz popped his head around the corner of the corridor and gave her a nod.

"Get your family safe, Brog," she said.

"What about you?"

"I'll watch out for m'self. Follow Parkington's lead, then Stone's. Keep a weather eye out."

He might've stayed longer, arguing with her as he sometimes did, but Stone nudged him out the door. After a moment, only Móirín remained. She locked the door, herself still inside, then made for the back, intending to crawl out the window. A locked door might buy them some time before anyone realized the flat had been abandoned.

She pulled on her coat then moved around the flat, blowing out the candles and extinguishing lanterns. In the dark, she made her way to the window Olly had climbed through. She pulled back the curtain and made a quick assessment of the best path out. An obliging tree made the descent simpler than she'd expected it would be.

Her feet hit the ground, and she made another assessment. No unexpected sounds. Nothing seemed to be lurking in the shadows or behind the shrubs. Either the Kincaids were devilishly good at keeping hidden or they'd not yet come to claim their target. She didn't mean to hang about waiting to see which it was.

Stone and Brogan were more than experienced enough to see their group safely to their destination without anyone the wiser. Mr. Sorokin had sneaked himself and his family out of Russia under the nose of the tsar. He could manage an escape as well. That was all the reassurance Móirín would have that night.

Her safe house on Whitfield Street was smaller than the one she was sharing with Fletcher, Elizabeth, Barnabus, and Gemma. And though the two locations weren't terribly far apart, there was no easy way to communicate without someone journeying between them. She'd not know until the next day if all was well on Whitfield Street.

She made her way, fast but silent, around the building to the window Olly had indicated was the site of the feared mark. It was still there, clear in the light of the nearby streetlamp. The mark of the Kincaids, a dastardly promise of the horrible fate that might have befallen them all if the little boy hadn't seen it there.

She heard footsteps and spotted Fitz walking toward her, his hat pulled low on his head. She pointed at the wall. "Not a single smudge, no dribble from the rain this morning. That's been put there recently."

"Then I'd say the two of us ought to pike off," Fitz said.

She was accustomed to facing such dangerous moments and

the aftermath alone. But there was something reassuring, almost restful, in not having to do so this time.

They made their way through and around the hedges, between dilapidated walls, making their way toward the safe house she'd called home of late. Their path was circuitous, overlapping, back and forth, dipping in and out of entirely dark places, emerging where it didn't make sense. All the while, they both watched for people following or paying too close attention. And neither of them spoke.

Even once they were inside the Riding House safe house, the door bolted behind them, she didn't say anything. But he didn't leave, didn't abandon her.

"A shame tonight didn't end as well as it began," Fitz said.

She paced. "Do you suppose they made it to the other safe house?"

"I've not a doubt. Not a person in that group don't seem capable of managing that. Even the children have those skills. They made it, mark me."

"Thank you for your help," she said, feeling tired to her very bones. "Seems like you're constantly saving us from one predicament or another."

"I *am* quite the flash cove," he said with feigned arrogance.

She was able to smile at that, though her mind wasn't at ease. "We have to stop the Tempest. People can't keep living like this."

"I'll do everything I can, though I have to do it unofficially. I'll look in on Lord Chelmsford, see what I can find out from him."

She summoned enough energy to unbutton her coat and hang it on a nail. "I hope you don't have too far to go to get home. It's late, and it's been a difficult day."

"Will I cause too much bother if I toss myself in a corner

here and grab a bit of sleep before I have to be to Scotland Yard in the morning?"

"Bother? You helped everyone get out of the flat tonight. I think a cold corner in a dark parlor is repaying you rather cheaply."

"I lost my home and family when I was nine years old," he said. "Sleeping in a cold corner *inside* a building is a heap better than what I had then."

She sighed. "I lost my home and family at the same age. And, yeah, a lot of cold places and a lot of long nights."

Fitz leaned close and brushed a brief kiss to her forehead. "I'm sorry that happened to you, Móirín."

She leaned against him, letting her guard down for just a moment. 'Twas a rare thing for her. "And I'm sorry that happened to you, Fitz."

He held her. She couldn't remember the last time someone had done that. She'd not let anyone. It didn't set her mind entirely at ease, didn't make her worries disappear, but for the briefest of moments, she felt better.

Then Fletcher stepped out and ruined it.

Fitz gave him a quick explanation of the night's events, and the two of them set about getting Fitz what he needed for the night.

Móirín dragged herself into the room she called her own. She lit the candle on her table, its light illuminating the few paragraphs she'd managed to scratch out for her publisher. She needed to work on it, but in that moment, she couldn't've summoned the light and laughing tone it required, couldn't've pretended all was the sunny laughter and ridiculousness of Posie and Pru.

She dropped onto her bed fully clothed and told herself all would be well. But she didn't entirely believe it.

CHAPTER 11

itz spent an hour the next morning at Scotland Yard pretending Sergeant Wheatley weren't ringing a peal over him. Once he felt he'd endured enough scolding to make certain the other detectives would remember he'd made a look in, Fitz told them he was off to gather information, though he didn't specify on what matter, and made his way toward Eaton Square.

It weren't a long walk from Scotland Yard, and one that, if he went by way of James Street, would take him past Buckingham Palace. He could tell himself that was the reason he took that path, despite it being a detour from his true destination. Truth be told, he went that way because it took him past Vandon Street and the home that had once been his.

But this time, he didn't stop or let his thoughts linger on what had been. He kept walking toward Eaton Square and Lord Chelmsford and the puzzle he and Móirín and the others desperately needed to piece together. His own personal puzzle could wait.

He'd looked in on Lord Chelmsford a couple of times a week since the baron had fled his London residence for this small, rented home. Claud Kincaid's attempted murder of Martin Afola at Chelmsford's home, revealed to have been the work of the Mastiff and the Tempest, had alarmed the former Lord Chancellor, and for good reason. He, himself, was being targeted, with attempts made to sully his name and reputation, specifically in connection to the Radlett case. Though this area of London hadn't been part of Fitz's patrol area, he'd connections enough in B Division to arrange to be part of keeping Lord Chelmsford safe.

No matter that he was now a detective constable with every reason to go wherever his work took him, he still felt out of place in such a rum area of London, no matter that it was near to where he'd once lived. London was like that. Corners of wealth butted right up to corners of want.

Constable Durand was out front of Chelmsford's place, leaning against a streetlamp, looking as though he were simply lazing about instead of making his patrol.

"All right-tight?" Fitz asked him.

"Peaceful as a cat's purr."

"And you ain't in bad loaf with the commissioner over this?" Fitz pressed.

"Why should he fuss over it?" Durand asked with a smug shrug. "Just keeping a weather eye out on the area. Part of my job, i'n'it?"

If Fitz ever had influence over the Detective Department, he'd pull Durand in without hesitation. The man was thorough and clever and as reliable as the sunrise.

"You mean to have a look around?" Durand asked.

"Part of my job, i'n'it?" It was, in fact, what Fitz did every time he was there. He'd walk around the outside of the place, looking for jimmied windows or people lurking about. This time, he was also looking for marks made in ash. But nothing was odd, nothing out of the ordinary.

He went next to the servants' entrance, where he was immediately recognized and quickly ushered inside.

"Anything unusual to report?" he asked the housekeeper.

"Peaceful as stars," she said.

"And Lord Chelmsford?" he asked as they made their way up the servants' stairs.

"I know he'd rather be at his own home, but he seems content." She gave Fitz a look of knowing annoyance. "Though the maids are discontented at the moment. Our mangle won't turn, and they're woefully behind with the laundering."

"I spent time in my childhood making repairs to any number of things," Fitz said. "I can give it a look."

She patted his arm, the way he suspected mothers did with their sons. "We've a man coming to look at it. But if I can't sort the thing, I'll send word to Scotland Yard and take you up on your offer."

"Please do."

They'd reached Lord Chelmsford's book room. The baron greeted him warmly.

"Constable Parkington, always a pleasure to see you."

Not something Fitz's nine-year-old self, sleeping in doorways, hungry and afraid, would've ever imagined a lord would say to him.

Lord Chelmsford clasped his hands together. "Have you learned any more about Claud's unfortunate end?"

Fitz shook his head. "We know it were the work of the Kincaid family, silencing one of their own."

Chelmsford never required him to stand through their interviews, but Fitz felt more comfortable doing so.

"And this Tempest you spoke of last time," Chelmsford said. "Is she still at large and unidentified?"

"Unfortunately." Fitz shrugged. "We're gathering what information we have. We'll find her."

"The Mastiff's blackmail was connected to the Radlett murders. But is it actually this woman who's upset about it?"

"Yes, we think she is somehow connected or feels her family was injured by the outcome of your work in representing Joseph Hunt." Fitz was grateful they'd jumped so quickly to the matter at hand. "Do you remember anyone during that time with the surname Morgan? A woman, perhaps?"

He leaned back in his chair, eyes drifting to the side as his thoughts wandered through his memory. "There was a maid at Hunt's inn by that name."

Exactly what Mr. Sorokin's notes had hinted at.

"She was furious when Hunt was sentenced to transportation and Probert went free. Furious." Fury could be a strong motivation.

"Was she angry because the inn closed?"

Chelmsford shook his head. "That was likely part, but her anger was more personal. She had an infant, not even a year old."

The inn closing was likely what eventually sent the woman to London. "Losing her job would make caring for that child difficult."

Chelmsford nodded. "I can't say with any certainty, but her frantic pleas and bone-shaking anger at Hunt's sentence made me wonder if, perhaps, the child was his."

Fitz felt a piece fall into place. If that infant *was* Lucy Morgan and she *was* Hunt's daughter, then the misery of her life, the loss of her father and potential family, could very well have been laid at Chelmsford's feet. And fury could be passed through generations, fueling Lucy's daughter to claim a new name and seek revenge for the wrongs she felt had been done to her family.

"Did this woman seem angry at anyone else?" Fitz asked. "The others who committed the crime? The other barristers?"

"The others' fates weren't what put her in such a difficult situation. It was Hunt's. She was upset with me and the courts. I have a vague recollection of her denouncing the king himself."

George IV had been sovereign then.

"I didn't take her outbursts as actual threats," Lord Chelmsford said. "She seemed as afraid as she was angry."

Angry with the monarch. As far as Fitz knew, the king hadn't been involved in the Radlett case. So why direct her fear-fueled anger at him?

"Please send word if you remember anything else about Miss Morgan," Fitz said. "I suspect she's part of the Tempest's story."

"I have a not outlandish ambition to be Lord Chancellor once more," Lord Chelmsford said. "All of this becoming widely known would likely prove detrimental to that goal. No prime minister wishes for his administration to seem weak because a member of it has been targeted and sent into hiding."

There was some truth to that. "The constables I have asked to keep a keen eye on your home and on your residence here are reliable toffs. They know how to keep their tongues in their mouths. And the people who're looking into this threat against you ain't the sort to spread word of their comings and goings. If'n we can get a step or two ahead of this Tempest, I daresay you'll weather the storm with no one the wiser."

"The Detective Department's fortunate to have you, Park-ington."

With a humorless laugh, he said, "Would you mind telling them that?"

"It is a difficult thing to not be appreciated for the work you do." Chelmsford gave a slow nod that spoke of remembered experiences and even a few regrets.

Fitz popped his hat on his head. "Keep taking the precautions you are. If fortune's on our side, you'll not need to take them much longer."

Lord Chelmsford shook his hand, something the baron had done the last couple of times Fitz had checked in with him. But it weren't a common thing for a constable, detective or otherwise, to be shown such consideration. "Please thank the others who are helping solve this mystery. And tell them I am at their disposal."

Wouldn't Móirín laugh to hear that? She was not one to accomplish things through conventional means. She'd sooner climb through a window or pick a lock or drop into a den of thieves with her trusty knife and derringer and convince them to tell her their secrets before making a formal request of Lord Chelmsford. The woman was the most fascinating and intriguing person he'd ever known, and holding her in his arms the night before had been fascinating in its own way.

"I'll come back by in a day or two," Fitz told him. "And I'll do a quick check of the house before I go."

"Thank you," Lord Chelmsford said. "Is there anything I can help you with?"

He wanted to ask the baron to have Sergeant Wheatley re-assigned somewhere very far away, but causing upheaval likely weren't the brightest idea. "You don't happen to know the whereabouts of a certain Irishwoman wanted for murder, known by the name of Maeve O'Donald?"

Lord Chelmsford's expression turned ponderous. "She is 'known by the name of'? Do you have reason to suspect this woman's actual name is different from the one you have?"

Fitz nodded. "The information from Dublin says it was likely a false name."

"I can't say I've heard anything of such a person."

"Unfortunately, neither have I." He dipped another quick bow. "But I'll sort it. That's what we in the Detective Department do."

He stepped out of the book room. Fitz knew the house well, having searched it when Chelmsford first arrived, making certain it was safe, then checking periodically in the time since.

The house wasn't large by the standards of most of Lord Chelmsford's class, but it still took Fitz another thirty minutes to look in the various rooms and make certain all was as it should be.

All was quiet in the house. Most of the staff was working belowstairs.

The servants' stairs weren't busy, and when he reached the corridor that led past the kitchen and various other workrooms, the members of Lord Chelmsford's small staff greeted him by name.

Fitz stepped around the staff as best he could, not wanting to be a disruption. But as he passed an older man, his feet stopped of their own volition. He turned about, heart somehow pounding and stopping all at the same time.

The man slipped into a side room off the corridor, offering Fitz only a glance at his profile. A fleeting bit of a face. The tiniest clue as to whether Fitz was seeing who he thought he was seeing.

He couldn't be certain. He thought he knew the man, though it had been years.

Fitz caught the eye of a passing maid. "Sally, who was that older man that just stepped in that room there?"

"White hair, carrying a workbox?"

"Oi."

"That's the man what came to fix the mangle. Started sticking something terrible, it did. We was fortunate to find someone quickly. I hear he's done fixed it up brilliant."

Fitz's landlord on Vandon Street had been quite handy, fixing things all the time. He'd been a bit younger than Grandfather, but not much. He'd be twenty years older now. About the age this odd-job man seemed to be.

"Do you know his name?" Fitz asked.

The maid shook her head. "I don't." She offered a quick, apologetic glance before hurrying along with her work.

Fitz followed the man into the side room, trying not to get his hopes up. They'd been dashed too many times for him not to anticipate it happening again.

And, of course, it absolutely happened again.

There was another exit out of the room, which the mystery man must have taken because the room was empty, with not a single clue as to whether Fitz had just seen someone from his past, someone with a connection to his grandfather's disappearance.

He stepped from the room into the corridor and stopped a passing footman. "What's the name of the man that came to fix the mangle?"

"Mr. Booth or Mr. Hook or something like that," he said. "The butler'd know. He's the one what hired him to do the job."

"Do you know where the butler is?"

"He's in with Lord Chelmsford."

Fitz had earned some of the baron's respect, but he hadn't the right to interrupt his business. But he'd be back here again. He'd learn what he could and, if fate was kind, he might cross paths with the handyman again.

THE QUEEN AND THE KNAVE

by Mr. King

Installment III
in which Clues are discerned and Hope is not lost entirely!

For a moment, neither Reynard nor Eleanor could speak a word nor take another step. What had undone the spell? What had caused the queen to resume her true form? Was it a trick? A trap?

Both must have had the same thought in the same moment as they both said in near perfect unison that they would do best to seek a place of hiding whilst they sorted what had occurred.

This was, of course, the very reason Reynard had suggested they flee into the forest. "There is a cottage," he told her, "not far distant from here that had once belonged to my mother. I believe we will be safe there."

"Will not Dezmerina find me there?" Eleanor did not seem afraid, simply cautious.

"It is protected," he said. "In fact, it is protected specifically against Dezmerina and her aims."

Eleanor was no stranger to the history of her kingdom,

allowing her to understand instantly what Reynard was saying. "The one who lives there has magic."

"*Had* magic. She is no longer among us. I am thankful, though, that she was not, in the end, destroyed by the evil sorceress. Avoiding that fate is the very reason she enchanted this cottage."

Wishing not to remain in the open much longer, they rushed in the direction of the protected cottage. They quickly lit candles, illuminating the interior and its dust-covered furnishings and supplies. A trunk of blankets allowed them to guard against the cold without needing to light a fire that might draw undue attention. The cottage protected them from Dezmerina but it would not, necessarily, prevent the palace guard or any of the barons from discovering them there.

"I cannot imagine Dezmerina's curse would be so quickly and easily dispersed," Eleanor said. "Yet, I am in my own form now. What could possibly account for it? And how long will it last?"

"I wish I knew those answers." Reynard was, indeed, frustrated not to know.

"I am meant to address the barons at the opening feast tonight." Eleanor's brow pulled in thought. "That will occur an hour after dark, which is not long from now. If I could be certain I would remain myself for any length of time, I would rush back to the palace. This week is vital to the continued peace in the kingdom. I dare not risk destroying what generations have worked to achieve."

"The wording of the curse is crucial," Reynard said. "It cannot behave in ways that are contrary to what was spoken. The difficulty comes in interpreting what is actually said as the wording is always, by design, confusing."

"You seem to know a great deal about such things." Eleanor did not sound horrified at his knowledge of magic.

"Like many in Amesby, there are some in my family who have magic—who *had* magic. I was taught that curses follow a pattern," Reynard said. "The first line indicates the circumstances under which the curse manifests, the second is how. The third line predicts the impact of the curse, while the fourth lays out the requirements for ending it."

Eleanor's mind returned to the curse once more, thinking through the wording, through the details.

> Whene'er the sun lights Amesby skies,
> Her queen will see through pine marten's eyes.
> While battles rage and chaos reigns,
> Her life will ebb whilst mine remains.

"The second line is why I transformed into a pine marten," Eleanor said, thinking aloud. "And the situation has already led to chaos. The guards and household are searching for me. I can only imagine the panic is growing as the time for the welcome speech approaches." She felt more than a small amount of that panic herself. Her first significant duty as the new monarch, and she would fail at it. "The *how* and the *impact* have, thus far, proven quite accurate."

"The first line contains the rules of the curse." Reynard thought on it as well. "'Whene'er the sun lights Amesby skies.' The sun is not lighting the sky just now. I had thought it simply meant so long as there existed a sun, which would mean forever, but that might not be the case at all."

"I am only to take the form of a pine marten during the daylight," Eleanor sorted out loud. "And it is currently not daylight."

Reynard met her eye. "And will not be again until morning."

Eleanor pulled the wool blanket more closely around her. "I could return to the palace and make the welcome speech. I'm not meant to remain at the feast, so no one will remark upon my departure. And tomorrow is the Baron's Consultation Day, when the monarch is not to be present. So long as I escape the palace before dawn, my transformation will not be seen by anyone. There would not be panic created by my current circumstances, but neither would I neglect any crucial parts of this excruciatingly crucial week."

"I can help you return to the palace," Reynard said. "And I can help you escape in the morning."

"Will not your absence be noted by the Captain of the Guard?" She knew the guardsmen were held to strict schedules, and desertion was not tolerated.

"Once we have discovered how to lift this curse, my absence will be easy to explain. Until then, the future of the kingdom depends upon our successful navigation of the difficult road Dezmerina has laid before you. The barons must be appeased. The kingdom must retain confidence in you as monarch. And the transformations the sorceress has subjected you to must be stopped."

His firmness of purpose and unwavering dedication helped to bolster Eleanor's. She was not a person of weak principles, neither was she in any sense a coward. The enormity of all that had happened was, however, a weighty and difficult burden.

"Let us return to the palace forthwith," Eleanor said, sounding more like a queen than she had in some time. "I will deliver my welcome speech, then retire to my chamber, insisting I wish to give the barons full opportunity to enjoy their feast and prepare for their work on the morrow."

"Do you wish to escape the palace tonight or shortly before sunrise tomorrow?" Reynard could not assist in her escape if he did not know when she would be undertaking it.

"Tonight, I believe. If I wait overly long, I might find myself mistaking the time of sunrise, and my maids will find a pine marten in my chambers. Heaven only knows what they would instruct the gamekeeper to do with me."

While all the kingdom knew of Dezmerina's power and nefariousness, few would believe the wild creature found in the queen's bedchamber was the queen herself. And were they faced with proof, far too many people, especially amongst the kingdom's barons, would either panic at such a fate befalling their monarch or seize upon the sudden vulnerability of the kingdom to claim power of their own.

Their only hope was to keep Eleanor's current state a secret until the means of ending the curse was discovered. A problem with a known solution, however difficult, was less terrifying than one which could not be made right.

Reynard pulled a small leather box from a high shelf. He removed from its interior a carved stone hanging from a length of leather. "This amulet will offer some protection as we journey back to the palace. Its magic is not impenetrable, and we will not be as safe as we are within these walls, but it will offer us some defense."

They each took hold of one end of the leather strap, the arrangement offering them both claim on the amulet's powers.

"Where shall I meet you after you complete your speech?" Reynard asked.

"There is a small sitting room adjacent to my bedchamber.

Inside is but one chair. It faces a window with a heavy curtain, the hem of which pools on the floor. Tuck yourself behind that curtain where it sits against the wall so you will neither be seen inside the room or through the glass of the window. I will meet you there."

Reynard nodded, committing her instructions to memory.

They rushed through the forest, both holding fast to the amulet, both grateful for the other's bravery and cleverness, both unsure of how they might thwart Dezmerina.

Once inside the castle, having entered through a door well-hidden but known to Eleanor, they were greeted with a dilemma. Eleanor needed to make her way to the great hall to deliver her address, while Reynard needed to hide himself in the small sitting room to wait for her. They could not both hold the amulet if they did not remain together.

"I will be surrounded by the barons and the household," Eleanor said. "Dezmerina's efforts are dependent, in part, on the power of uncertainty. I do not believe she will harm me whilst I am among a crowd. You, however, do not have that protection."

"Your life is more essential," he said.

She shook her head. "I feel firmly in my heart that we are both necessary to undo what the sorceress has done. I will have the protection of witnesses. You must have the protection of the amulet."

Before he could offer another objection, they both heard the approach of footsteps.

"Go," she said. "Down this passage to the winding stone steps at the end. Three revolutions, through the door, down that corridor. The third door is the one you want. Go. Quickly."

And on that declaration, Eleanor let go of the amulet and hurried in the opposite direction. How she hoped in her heart he reached his destination without incident, without harm! She had harbored such worry over her duties this week, over the speech she was about to make, yet it now seemed so insignificant compared to the obstacles in front of her.

She reached the exterior doors of the great hall just as the Master of the Royal Wardrobe arrived, flanked by dressers and servants who all looked remarkably nervous. That their concern visibly ebbed when they saw her gave Eleanor a surge of both relief and pride. She knew, logically, that their relief likely came from having feared she would not fulfill this duty rather than simple pleasure at seeing their queen, but she embraced the feeling just the same.

Gold-threaded gloves were placed on her hands. Her shoes, stained by grass and mud, were replaced with ones of silk and ribbon. A mantle of deep purple velvet and lined with ermine was fastened around her, draping at her sides and covering all but the front hem of her dress.

The royal coiffeuse quickly brushed and pinned her hair, undoing the damage of so difficult a day in an instant. The lighter of the queen's crowns was placed on her head, the one she wore when seeing to official duties while not seated upon the throne.

Queen Eleanor turned to face the doors through which she was to enter the great hall. She took a calming breath, then nodded to indicate her readiness.

Two footmen opened the large, heavy oaken doors. The din of voices inside dropped immediately to a curious hush. Chair legs scraped the ground, and the rustle of fabric indicated the barons had risen, which was required of them when their monarch entered a room.

In her brief time as queen, Eleanor had practiced this moment as well as the others she would undertake that week. She knew where to stand and what to say. She'd feared she would quake her way through the ceremonies, but to her great surprise and relief, when she stepped into the hall, she felt her legs firm beneath her, felt her pulse maintain its quiet rhythm.

She climbed atop the dais and faced the gathering.

"Barons all, you are welcomed most warmly to the royal palace to begin our week of unification." The speech was the same every time it was given, and Eleanor had long ago memorized it. "The Kingdom of Amesby is proud and dignified. There is abundance in the land and goodness in her people. You, dignified barons, are come to make ironclad once more the peace that has for generations seen us prosper and progress. In the spirit of that unity, I offer you this feast."

At that final declaration, known to all who heard it, the rearward doors flew open and servants carrying salvers of food and ale stepped inside the hall to deliver the monarch's offering to the newly arrived nobility.

"Huzzah!" the barons shouted, as was required of them. "Huzzah! Huzzah!"

As the third shout was made, Eleanor retraced the path she had taken mere moments earlier and returned to the corridor beyond the great hall. The barons were left to enjoy their feast, casually discussing over the meal what would be formally discussed among them the next day.

The week of unification had begun.

But after the Baron's Consultation Day, Eleanor would no

longer have an excuse to be absent during daylight hours. If a means of ending Dezmerina's curse was not found quickly, the Unification Ceremony would not be completed, and the chaos and battles the curse predicted would become reality.

She and Reynard had but one day.

And one day could not possibly be enough.

CHAPTER 12

Stone arrived at the Riding House safe house the afternoon following the abruptly ended party. Móirín had been frantically writing all day, both so she could get the money from her publisher to keep so many Dreadfuls and their families in her safe houses and also to distract herself from worrying about Brogan.

"All tucked in," Stone told her. "The Whitfield Street location is filled to bursting, but it'll do."

Móirín breathed an inward sigh of relief. They'd arrived safely. "How's Brogan?"

"Focused," Stone said.

"On what?"

"His wife, mostly. He's a bit protective of her."

The swift journey had likely been difficult for Vera. "Is she worse for last night's troubles?"

"Worn to a thread, but as resolute as ever." Stone didn't look worried, and he was reliable about such things. "And Sorokin and the children seemed to settle in quickly."

That accounted for almost everyone. "What about Celia?"

"She's decided to stay there. She lived in Southwark long

enough to know the Kincaids ain't a family to take lightly." He looked over at Gemma, sitting at the table beside Barnabus. "She's fair-minded and doesn't think less of you for your family connections."

"Tell her we don't think less of her for her choice of sweethearts," Barnabus tossed back with a grin.

"Speak for yourself, Barnabus," Fletcher laughed. He and Elizabeth were in the room as well.

"Are you planning to stay at the Whitfield Street safe house too?" Móirín usually joined in the jesting, but she couldn't manage it just then. "The Tempest'll know you're one of us. Makes you a target, it does."

"I'd hoped there was room for me here," he said.

"Here?" That was unexpected. "Why not stay where Celia is? Fletch is hiding *with* Elizabeth. And Barnabus *with* Gemma. Brogan *with* Vera. Ain't no reason you couldn't do the same."

"Celia ain't likely to toss herself into a living arrangement with a fella she ain't married to," Stone said.

"Are you saying *I* would?" Elizabeth tossed back. "I'll have you know that I'm living with *my husband*."

Husband? They were married? When had that happened?

Those very questions were tossed out by the others in the room. Móirín kept hers to herself, right until Fletcher dared to meet her eye.

"Could've whispered to a person," she said. "I'd've liked to have attended."

In the tiny pause that followed, she saw the acknowledgment in his eyes she was looking for. They were closer friends than most anyone knew, having secretly run the DPS together for years. Not being invited to *his wedding* was a blow.

"We decided real sudden. Didn't invite no one other than Hollis and Ana."

"At least you weren't entirely alone, then." She was grateful for that, though it didn't entirely ease the sting of being left out of that bit of his life. Doing so much of what she did in secret meant she felt closer to people than they usually felt to her. There seemed no avoiding that, not if she wanted to keep those people safe.

"Once we're on the other side of our current troubles," Fletcher said, "Elizabeth and I'll have to have another ceremony. It'll be pretend, but it'll also be necessary. Sneaking around and getting married in secret hits far too close to an elopement for the comfort of those who keep her school funded. Putting on a show for them cain't be avoided iffen she's wanting to reopen Thurloe."

"Is she wanting to?" Móirín asked.

"I think she'd like to if it proves possible."

So many people's dreams were being crushed by the Tempest.

"If the two of you've gotten hitched at last," Stone said, "seems we oughta at least have a party."

That brought shocked glances his way. Stone wasn't one to suggest frivolity.

He eyed them all dryly. "It ain't like I suggested we hold a wake."

"Had one," Barnabus said. "Don't mean to have another."

They had, indeed, held a wake for Barnabus and Gemma to help support the ruse of their demise.

Gemma seized on Stone's suggestion. "There must be something to decorate the place with. And we can set out sandwiches."

"This here's a bare-bones accommodation," Móirín reminded her, not wanting any of them to be disappointed.

"Tosh," Gemma waved that off. "We'll do it up prime, you'll see."

Soon enough, a party was being planned for the secret newlyweds, Gemma drawing up a list of makeshift decorations. She had a way of pulling people into schemes and making them glad to have been drawn in. 'Twas one of Móirín's favorite things about her.

Stone, despite having suggested the festivities, came and stood by Móirín. "I ain't working my other job, so I can't stop taking installations to my publisher. But I can't risk leading anyone back to where Celia and the others are."

Móirín nodded. "'Tis the same reason I sent Brogan there myself."

"Is there room here?"

She shrugged. "Parkington stayed last night. Tossed himself in a corner. If you're not opposed to that, we've room enough."

"When the DPS starts meeting again," Stone said, "we oughta consider letting him join, whether he decides to write or not."

"You seem confident there'll be a Dread Penny Society at the end of all this."

He eyed her with a bit of scrutiny. "Aren't you?"

"Have to be," she said. "If the DPS doesn't set things to rights again, I'll be stuck forever with *two* sets of newlyweds. A person can't go on too long surrounded by nauseating matrimony."

A brief and subtle smile answered her jest before a single knock on the door interrupted everyone. They all knew the procedure, and everyone slipped out of sight, taking the candles and lanterns with them.

Móirín moved to the door and its multiple locks. She opened the small slot that allowed for words to be exchanged without the door being opened.

"Parky's a right rubbish blue-bottle." That was Fitz.

She had the door unlocked and open in the blink of an eye, and he slipped inside. "Wasn't certain you'd be wandering back this way." But she was glad he had. She called out to the house in a low voice that still managed to carry, "'Tis only Parkington come to ruin the party."

"Thank you for that," he said, though a laugh undermined the grumpy tone he was clearly trying to strike.

As the others returned, Móirín slanted a look at Fitz. "We've only just learned that Fletcher and Elizabeth went and got themselves churched without bothering to tell anyone, and now Gemma's piecing together a party for them."

"Whether they want it or not?" Fitz's mouth tipped up at the corners.

"Compulsory parties are the very best sort."

Fitz laughed, something she'd defiantly refused to find warming or attractive over the months she'd known him. His laugh was, of course, both those things, but she didn't have to admit as much. 'Twas likely best, in fact, if she didn't.

"Did you have a party for Brogan after his wedding?"

Móirín nodded. "As much as Vera's injuries would allow. Made for a nice day, leastwise. Our parents would've been pleased."

"Family is important," he said. A look passed over his face, the sort that meant a person had suddenly remembered something. "I told you that my family disappeared when I was a boy."

She nodded.

"It were just my grandfather. All the rest were long dead and buried."

That loss must've come when he was too young to remember it well; there was no emotion clogging his words.

"When I was nine years old," he said, "I returned home to the flat where Grandfather and I lived, and the place had new people living there. And none of them had any idea what'd happened to my grandfather."

Blimey. "And you've been looking ever since?"

"As best I can. In between saving people who've broken into tobacconist's shops, that is."

Móirín grinned. "That were a lark, weren't it?"

"A lark? If the Kincaids had found you there, you'd not be smiling about it."

"Ah, but they *didn't* find us, did they?"

He hooked an eyebrow upward. Why was it that eyebrow made her heart flip? Curse him for being a fine-looking and good-company sort of fellow who was also a blasted policeman on the trail of fugitives. Made it awful hard to resist the urge to flirt beyond what was wise and impossible to forget how it felt when he'd held her the night before.

"You've confidence, Móirín Donnelly. I'll give you that."

"Confidence I've *earned*. You'd best give me that too."

Though his expression didn't turn entirely somber, it did slip back into the earnest one he'd been wearing when he'd first turned down this conversational path. "I think I saw someone today who knew me and my grandfather. Someone I ain't seen since my grandfather vanished."

"You did?"

Fitz nodded. "Couldn't catch up to him, though, which boiled a bit, I'll tell you."

"Do you think he'd know what happened to your grandfather?"

"He's the first person I've come across since I was a boy who *might*."

She took hold of his hand, knowing full well it was a more personal gesture than was likely wise. But he seemed to need some reminder that he wasn't alone at the moment. "Who was he?"

"Our landlord at the time. Never saw him after the new people moved into our old flat. I don't know if he were ignoring me when I came looking for him, or if he sold the place and simply walked away." Fitz shrugged but didn't let go of her hand.

"Where'd you see him this time?"

"Lord Chelmsford's place. He'd come to make a repair, but he left before I could talk to him."

"A shame, that. You must've been looking for your grandfather for sixty years now."

He tossed her a narrow-eyed look. "How old do you think I am?"

"*Old*," she said with emphasis. In actuality, she'd done the sum and knew he was very near to her own age. But the man was far too fun to tease for her to avoid doing it for too long.

"I suppose I'd best sit, then, before these ancient legs of mine simply buckle." He kept hold of her hand and led her to the table. "Besides needing to rest my weary bones, I also thought you'd appreciate knowing what I learned from Lord Chelmsford."

Fletcher, who sat at the table, looking a little overwhelmed at the whirl of activity Gemma was creating around them, asked, "Did you learn something useful from the baron?"

Fitz nodded. "Insightful, at least."

Useful would've been better, but Móirín would take whatever she could get.

"Said there was a woman at Hunt's inn with the surname Morgan. She was young, had an infant child, and was none too pleased with the outcome of the trial. Spat daggers at Lord Chelmsford over it, even had sharp words for the king."

"I didn't realize ol' George had any part in this," Fletcher said.

"I don't know that he did," Fitz said. "But *this* Miss Morgan seemed angry with him just the same."

"Did Lord Chelmsford know if the infant was a boy or a girl?"

"Didn't say. But he did say he'd wondered at the time if the baby was Hunt's and that might be why the woman was so upset about him being transported."

Móirín leaned back in her chair, rubbing at her mouth as she thought. If Lord Chelmsford's theory was correct, and if they were correct that the little girl Mr. Sorokin had met had grown up to be the Tempest, then Hunt was the Tempest's grandfather. At the very least, she might *think* he was.

"Hunt being sentenced to transportation didn't just cost generations of Morgan women a safe and respectable situation, it tore apart their family."

"People don't recover easily from losing their families," Fitz said knowingly.

Fletcher nodded. "And if anger was already attached to that loss, that anger might stay attached to it through the years."

"I think we might be treading the right path here, lads."

Móirín rapped her knuckles on the table. "Makes sense that the Tempest would try to destroy Lord Chelmsford by weaponizing his work on this trial if it's what destroyed her family, at least in her view."

"Why not just kill him?" Fletcher asked. "She's killed plenty of others."

"I don't know." Móirín didn't like not having the answers.

"And why was Granny Morgan angry at the king?" Fitz added.

"I don't know."

Gemma walked past in that moment. Móirín motioned her over.

"You said there was a display about the Radlett Murder at Madame Tussaud's?"

Gemma nodded. "Oi. He's in the Chamber of Horrors there, where a heap of other notorious folk have wax figures. The catalog says who they are and what they did, and the docents can tell a person heaps more about them."

Móirín looked at Fitz and Fletcher. "Either of you two care to take a stroll to Baker Street tomorrow?"

CHAPTER 13

Despite her propensity for sneaking into places she wasn't supposed to be in, Móirín actually gathered most of her information under perfectly ordinary circumstances. When she stepped into Madame Tussaud's wax museum with Fletcher the next day, they did their utmost to give the impression of two people looking to pass a pleasant afternoon rather than two people on a hunt.

Móirín obtained a catalog, continuing her impression of casual interest as she flipped through to the section detailing the Chamber of Horrors.

"There he is." Fletcher pointed at the bottom of a page. The entry spilled onto the next page but was frustratingly short.

THE GALLOWS

JOHN THURTELL, whose love for gambling led him to commit the murder of Mr. Weare, under circumstances of great atrocity. After his sentence to death he designed this gallows, on which he was executed at Hertford on the 9th January, 1824. The circumstances of the murder of Weare by the turf gambler were utilised

by the late Lord Lytton in the incident of the murder
of Sir John Tyrrell, by Thornton and Dawson, in the
novel of "Pelham."

"Fellow designed the gallows he was hung on?" Fletcher
shook his head. "A bit morbid, that."

"And not terribly helpful to our cause."

They followed the steady flow of visitors making their way
into the waxworks display; some bent over catalogs, others
gawked and pointed at the wax figures. The perusal eventually
led them to the Chamber of Horrors itself, with full-sized wax
figures of notorious people from history, as well as a display of
wax heads of people who'd lost their actual heads to Madame
Guillotine.

Thurtell was easy to find. He was on display beside the
gallows he'd designed. The platform on which the condemned
stood contained a falling-leaf trapdoor, rigged to drop the prisoner "in an instant," with the platform itself designed to hide
his body from view afterward. Above, an enormous crossbeam
sat atop two equally large uprights. The gallows were painted
entirely black, creating a harrowing effect. Thurtell himself was
almost an afterthought in the display, despite the notoriety of
his crime. Other than a plaque identifying him, there was no
further information about the man or the others involved in the
infamous murder.

"Perhaps one of the workers might come gab a spell with us
about this fellow," Fletcher suggested. "Gemma said they do that
and know a heap."

She'd've begun looking for someone who worked there, but
her attention was immediately caught by a man with a menacing

gait, the hardened expression of a callous criminal, and a hand that was missing a finger.

"We've an odd sort of companion," Móirín said, tipping her head toward the thief and murderer London knew as Four-Finger Mike.

Fletcher didn't flinch, didn't show even a moment's surprise. Under his breath, he muttered, "What's that thatch-gallows doing out of prison?"

"Apparently, touring a museum." Móirín watched out of the corner of her eye as the man drew closer, seemingly heading directly for them.

A woman stepped up next to Móirín, eyeing Thurtell. "Seems an unimpressive man, doesn't he?"

Were Móirín anyone other than her unflappable self, seeing the Tempest herself standing there as leisurely as you like might've scared her witless.

"Is it his method of murder or his low quantity of victims that doesn't impress you?" Móirín asked.

The Tempest's gaze remained on the wax figure, her expression revealing absolutely nothing of her thoughts. "I have no patience for incompetent people."

"Incompetent people *require* patience," Móirín countered.

"I do not offer people anything they do not deserve." She spoke without anger, without frustration. It was a simple statement of fact. "And lest either of you are standing there thinking *I* deserve a knife or a bullet, best give it another thought. Four-Finger Mike is not the only one in this museum, even in this room, who answers to me. And they are each of them under instructions: should anything at all happen to me, they are to choose someone in this museum at random and do what it is they do best."

Móirín met Fletcher's eye and knew he understood the consequences of the Tempest's threat. 'Twasn't merely a matter of being tried for murder themselves. People would die. And the wax museum was currently playing host to a lot of people, some of them children.

"Móirín thought of the children first, I'd wager," the Tempest said. "I always do too."

"No need threatening children," Móirín said. "There're a few of you, as you've said, and I've only a one-shot gun."

"Still, children can be useful." The Tempest looked at Fletcher. "Thank you for the two you sent to the good doctor's safe house a few weeks ago. They were terribly useful."

Fletcher stiffened, worry filling his eyes. "What did you do to them?"

A smile tugged at the woman's mouth. "Am I going to make you cry?" she mocked. "Urchins disappear all the time, Fletcher. Especially the ones who trust the wrong people."

"You mean me?" he asked through tight teeth.

"A lot of them trust you." She shrugged then looked up at the wax figure again. "Which means you should be looking for more than two."

Fletcher didn't often let his alarm show, but it did then.

"Go," Móirín said to him.

He rushed from the Chamber of Horrors. She knew he'd be checking on the street children he looked out for, accounting for everyone he could, chiding himself for believing that "Serena," as the Tempest had called herself then, had been who she'd said she was.

"They follow you without question, without hesitation," the Tempest said, watching Fletcher go. "And most of them don't even know who you are."

But the Tempest did.

The weight of that realization pressed the remaining air from Móirín's lungs. She'd been hiding her identity from the Dreadfuls these past weeks to keep that information from the Tempest. And she already knew.

She knew.

"Is there a reason you've chosen this place to have our little gab?" Móirín asked. "Can't say I'm overly fond of wax figures. Make m'nerves crawl around a bit."

A self-satisfied smile lifted the Tempest's mouth though it never fully formed. "I thought they might. Still, I didn't *choose* this spot. I simply followed you in."

"At least there's room enough for the both of us. Can't say the same for the poor fellow depicted inside the gibbet." Móirín motioned toward that display on the other side of the Chamber of Horrors. She shuddered a little. "'Twouldn't like that, m'self, being locked in a cage that way."

"We all have our limits, I suppose." The Tempest's gaze returned to Thurtell, contempt curling her lip. "His limit was a short drop with a quick stop."

"How poetic," Móirín said dryly.

"We are very alike, you and I," the Tempest said. "That's what makes this so much fun: outmaneuvering a slightly inferior version of myself."

"I'm not a thing like you," Móirín said.

"Oh, but you are. Which is why I'm going to win. I know what you'll do. It's how I knew to sit on a certain roof on King Street and watch for the mysterious 'Dread Master' to step inside by way of a back door, allowing me to discover your identity."

Nolan had, no doubt, given the woman access to the roof. Blasted traitor.

The Tempest continued. "And I know what you want, which is how I know what will break you."

"You seem very confident in whatever it is you've begun planning." Móirín didn't appreciate that confidence, truth be told.

"*Begun* planning?"

The Tempest, then, had already made vast preparations for whatever lay ahead of them. Móirín hadn't doubted it, but hearing it confirmed was helpful.

"Wouldn't our supposed similarities mean I can also predict what *you* will do and what would thwart *you*?" Móirín asked.

Again, that small, self-satisfied smile appeared. "I hope so. Otherwise, I will be forced to end this out of sheer boredom."

The Chamber of Horrors continued to be busy. People all around. Four-Finger Mike still hovered nearby. Móirín didn't imagine she had much time before her nemesis slipped away again.

"Why was your grandmother angry at George IV?" Móirín tossed the question out without preamble.

The Tempest grew very still, and her smile disappeared on the instant. For once, she did not have the upper hand.

"The king had no direct say in the outcome of this matter." Móirín motioned to the wax figure before them. "Yet she blamed him for it."

"My family is not the topic of this discussion." The Tempest was calm, but a storm was brewing.

Móirín'd be wise to make her departure sooner rather than later. But she'd learned their suspicions about the Tempest's identity were correct. She needed to learn as much as she could.

"There's a wax facsimile of George IV in the Hall of Kings,"

Móirín said. "Are you planning to tiptoe over there and spit in his eye?"

"You are so very near to the answer you are looking for that I am half tempted to tell you what you're missing." A smile. A hint of a laugh.

"Let me tell you what *I* feel I am missing," Móirín said. "Why are you fixated on the Dread Penny Society? We had nothing to do with the events you are hell-bent on avenging."

"The Dreadfuls are the reason I have not yet avenged it. That is unacceptable. Unforgiveable." The Tempest's expression turned icy. "The Dreadfuls made themselves my enemy. They chose this. *You* chose this. Nolan told me of your motto—that you do not forget, you do not relent. I do not either. I obliterate. I am the nightmare and the violence, the storm and the lightning strike. I have traps already laid because I know how to destroy an enemy."

"And how is that?"

Her eyes sparkled with a disconcerting level of enjoyment. "Cut off the head, of course."

"It seems to me you have had ample opportunities for beheading the DPS." As Móirín was that head, she was rather invested in the topic. "Why all these games? Why all this effort?"

"Because that is what one does to one's enemies: torment them." The Tempest spoke as if she were discussing the weather rather than her enjoyment of torturing people. "If you were me, would you not also go to such lengths to rid yourself of so vexing yet intriguing an enemy?"

"I am not you." Móirín was firm in her declaration, though whether to convince herself or the Tempest, she wasn't certain.

"Of course not. If you were me, you would have already sorted this. You'd know I'm collecting them."

"Collecting *who*?" Móirín pressed.

The Tempest looked over her shoulder and twitched a finger at Four-Finger Mike. "Don't spend too much time digging for information, Móirín. The tunnels are growing crowded."

Collecting them. Tunnels.

The Tempest stepped away, clearly meaning to meander out as nonchalantly as she'd entered.

"You have no interest in seeing the monarchs?" Móirín asked her.

She looked back, her expression regal. "What would be the point when the whole room is a lie? There can be only one queen."

THE QUEEN AND THE KNAVE

by Mr. King

Installment IV
in which Heartache proves itself a most painful Affliction!

Reynard kept perfectly still and perfectly quiet while waiting behind the heavy curtains in the queen's personal sitting room. To be found there would mean imprisonment, charges of trespass and treason, likely death. Though he knew Queen Eleanor would come to his defense and spare him such a fate, she could not do so during daylight hours. And if he were caught in so compromising a place and the queen was found to be missing again, the conclusions jumped to would be devastating indeed.

All had remained calm and peaceful in the residence wing of the palace, a sign, he hoped, that the welcome speech had gone as planned without disaster or misstep. He hoped that was true not merely for the sake of the kingdom but because he knew the ceremonies surrounding this week weighed on Eleanor's mind—on *the queen's* mind.

He'd found himself making that mistake of late: thinking of the queen in friendly and personal terms. They had once, when children, been friends, even using each other's given names quite freely. He'd fallen too easily back into that once-permitted indulgence, though to his relief not aloud.

Quick, quiet footsteps brushed over the carpeting of the room and, in a swift bit of movement, the curtain fluttered then fell back into place with this new arrival positioned with him behind it. He'd not lit any candles in the room nor were those in the corridor bright enough to illuminate his sudden companion. The person was near enough for Reynard to feel the warmth of them. He didn't speak, not knowing if he'd been spotted or if he was, quite by accident, sharing the space with someone who hadn't yet realized he was there.

"My speech went as it ought." The queen spoke softly, her breath tickling his face. She must have been standing very close indeed.

"I am pleased to hear that." He spoke in a whisper. "Were you chastised for your earlier disappearance?"

"There was not time. I did, though, receive a few quizzical looks." Her hand brushed his arm then settled against his chest.

There was something unexpectedly reassuring in that simple touch, one that ought to have made him take a few steps back in order to regain an appropriate distance from his monarch. But, instead, he found himself setting his hand atop hers, holding it gently above his heart.

"There are enough from the household staff still in this wing of the palace that we dare not make good our escape yet," she said softly.

"Will they not be searching for you?"

She shook her head, though he did not see the movement. "I informed my lady's maid that I was retiring early and asked that the curtains around my bed be drawn. I further insisted I not be bothered all night and that I would most likely stroll my garden in the morning for a constitutional. That should prevent my absence from being discovered to-night and offer an explanation for my disappearance in the morning."

"How late are the staff likely to be active in this area of the palace?" Reynard asked.

In a movement she gave no thought to but found entirely natural, Eleanor leaned against him. She spoke even more softly. "Another quarter hour, most likely."

Hesitantly, Reynard set his other arm about her, keeping her tucked close.

Both participants in the clandestine embrace insisted to themselves that the arrangement was entirely a matter of safety, an effort to remain undiscovered. Both firmly ig-nored the insistence of their hearts that holding each other was proving both deeply enjoyable and utterly peaceful. And both knew better than to speak a word of those feelings to the other.

The quarter hour passed as if on the back of a tortoise. They stood so near that they could hear each other breathe, that the cold of the stone wall warmed behind them, that nei-ther, for the first time in far too long, felt alone.

But neither did either of them look at each other, though the room was too dark for them to have realized as much. And as neither spoke, their thoughts were also unknown to each other.

How heartbreaking are moments of connection when those experiencing them are not free to express what they are feeling!

The residence wing outside the queen's sitting room grew

silent, most of the candles had been extinguished, and the intrepid pair were able to slip from the palace, doing so with as few words as could be managed.

They held fast to the amulet as they rushed into the forest and directly to the cottage waiting for them there and the enchantments that would protect them.

They were safe . . . for a time.

Eleanor pulled back the heavy burlap on the front window just enough to look up at the tops of the trees and the still-dark sky. "I'm dreading the coming of morning."

"Does the transformation hurt?" Reynard's voice echoed with compassion.

She shook her head. "It doesn't, oddly enough. And I don't even feel uncomfortable in the form that I take. I still think as myself. I can still understand people when they speak." She clasped her hands together and pressed them to her chin. "I tried to talk while in pine marten form. I didn't manage it, but I'm not certain if that is because doing so is impossible or if I simply need to continue practicing."

"Do keep trying," he pleaded. "If we could actually speak during the daylight hours, we would have a better chance of sorting out how to end this curse. It is too complex for either of us to remedy alone."

"I will keep trying. I swear to it."

His smile was soft and appreciative. "You are not easily defeated, Your Majesty."

Her eyebrows pulled sharply together as she shook her head. "Please don't call me that."

"But you are the queen. That is how I am meant to address you."

Misery tugged at her features as loneliness began filling her heart. "We were friends once, Reynard."

At the reminder, Reynard's posture grew rigid. "When we were children," he said with firm propriety. "When you were not yet queen. Now that you are, it would be inappropriate for me to think of you in any other terms."

He was attempting to remember his duty.

She was attempting to feel less alone in the world.

Only *he* succeeded.

Pushing from her thoughts the memory of him holding her in his arms and emptying her heart of the hope she'd allowed to grow that he might care for her, Eleanor turned away. She couldn't bear the idea of her heartbreak and misery being so obvious to him.

She took up the wool blanket she'd used when they'd last been in the cottage and wrapped it around herself once more. Dawn would come eventually, and Amesby's queen would again "see through pine marten's eyes." Even in the sorceress's curse, Eleanor had been identified only as "the queen."

That was all she was to anyone. She was the ceremonial robes she wore. The scripted words she spoke. A position but not a person. And everything depended on that continuing to be true.

Reynard's words had hurt, but they were true. And they were a needed reminder of what was required of her. When she had been crowned queen, her personal hopes and dreams and wishes had been set aside, made secondary to what the kingdom needed. She would suffer fewer disappointments if she remembered that.

Eleanor wiped away a tear, feeling foolish and weak.

Reynard watched that tear form, feeling guilty that his

words had contributed to her sorrow. He hadn't meant to hurt her.

"For what it's worth," Reynard said into the heavy silence, "I liked being your friend all those years ago. I wish that hadn't needed to change."

She didn't look at him, but kept her eyes on the window. "I'm not allowed to wish for things any longer. Not for myself. I would do best not to forget that."

Several long moments followed, and Eleanor lowered herself onto a pallet in the corner, wrapping her blanket about her. Reynard set himself in a corner, another blanket draped over him. Exhausted, discouraged, and both lost in their separate thoughts, they drifted off into equally fitful sleep, unsure and wary of what the future might hold.

CHAPTER 14

ne queen.
Collecting them.
Tunnels.
If you were me, you would have already sorted this.

Móirín moved through Marylebone, taking a very round-about path back to the safe house, her mind spinning all the while. *You would have already sorted this.* She needed to think through all the Tempest had said and find the clues in it. They were there; Móirín was certain of it. But hidden and disguised.

Queen.

Collecting.

Tunnels.

But 'twasn't those things that returned with the most force to Móirín's mind, but rather "We are very alike, you and I." Again and again, the Tempest had acted as though there were no difference between her, a murderer who was terrorizing the people of London, and Móirín, who was trying so hard to save them.

Móirín knew they weren't the same. Why, then, did the Tempest's insistence otherwise bother her so much?

She was turning off Bentinck Street onto Welbeck when a scuffle caught her attention. The briefest of glances stopped her in her tracks. Two toughs—one she knew to be the Protector— were being barely held off by two finely dressed people. And not just any people: Hollis Darby, one of the Dreadfuls, and Ana, the Phantom Fox.

Móirín didn't hesitate; she never did. She rushed forward, pulling a short shillelagh from her pocket. She tugged each end at the same time, and the stick telescoped, which she twisted until it clicked into place. A portable fighting stick of her own design.

The nearest rough had hold of Ana, his back to Móirín, and didn't see her coming. She swung her stick right at his kidneys. He doubled over, not quite crumbling, but his grip loosened. Ana pulled free. To be certain, Móirín brought her stick down on his arm.

She tossed the weapon to Ana so she'd have some means of defending herself. Móirín pulled her knife from its sheath in her boot. Hollis was putting up a fight, but the Protector was brutal and enormous. And, despite taking a blow to the kidneys, his partner was still on his feet.

How to fight off both? Why the blazes had she left her derringer at the safe house?

"You're ruining our fun, love," the man she'd already pummeled said, coming closer.

"I do that."

She brandished her knife, but while the ruffian hesitated, the Protector didn't. He landed a punch that sent Hollis sprawling.

Ana rushed toward her husband, but the Protector pointed his knife at her. "I'll cut you to ribbons, kitten."

As he struggled to his knees, Hollis said, "Get Ana out of here, Móirín."

The other rough closed in, and Ana swung the shillelagh with a fierceness that sent him back a few steps. Móirín turned her knife on the Protector just as the man dragged Hollis to his feet and pressed his own knife against Hollis's throat.

"Get Ana out of here, Móirín," the Protector repeated with a sneer. "You ain't part of our collection."

A cart pulled up behind him, the horses loudly objecting to being stopped. The Protector tossed Hollis onto the cart, then climbed in and held his captive there. The driver gave the horses their heads.

Móirín ran after the cart, Ana right on her heels, but they couldn't keep up, couldn't catch it.

"Hollis!" Ana called, her voice breathless from fear and exertion. "Hollis!"

The cart had turned too many corners. Móirín didn't even know which direction to go in. The second ruffian was gone. No clues. No chance of getting Hollis back. She and Ana stood, breathless and beaten, as people flowed in all directions, oblivious to the kidnapping.

"I told him to be careful," Ana said, sucking in sharp breaths. "So many of the Dreadfuls are disappearing. But we were running short on food." Her breaths caught. "We had to take the risk."

So many of the Dreadfuls are disappearing.

"We need to get you safe," Móirín said. Then she needed to gather up all those who hadn't *disappeared* yet.

"What are they going to do to him?" Ana asked in a small voice.

"I don't know." She also didn't know how many or which of

the people around them might be loyal to the Tempest or being forced to do her bidding. "We have to get you safe."

"What about my father and Very Merry?" Ana wasn't panicking, but the enormity of all that had happened was creeping into her voice.

"We can get them both safe," Móirín promised. "I have places to hide you all."

"Together?" Ana pressed.

Móirín nodded.

"And Hollis?"

Móirín held her gaze with a firm and determined expression. "I'll find him. I swear I will."

The feeling at the Riding House safe house when Fitz arrived that afternoon was different. Heavier. More uneasy. And the parlor was full. Ana Darby was there, as was a man he quickly discovered was her father and a little street urchin named Very Merry, whom he'd crossed paths with before.

"If you're thinking of arresting us, const'ble," the girl said, "best get to thinking about something else. Miss Móirín's in charge here, and she don't like blue-bottles."

He expected any of the other adults in the room to either make a quip of their own or come to his defense. But no one said anything, and the tension in the air didn't ease. Something'd happened.

"Where is Miss Móirín?" he asked Very Merry.

"In her room down the corridor." The girl looked rather proud to know the answer. "You ain't gonna bullyrag her, are you?"

"I ain't the sort to harass a person," he said.

Very Merry narrowed her eyes. "Best not be."

Fitz made his way to the door of Móirín's room and gave a quick knock. He heard footsteps on the other side move closer, then stop just beyond.

"Parky's a right rubbish blue-bottle," he said.

The door opened, and Móirín eyed him with annoyance. "You don't have to say that every time, you know."

"What bug've you got in your bonnet?" he tossed back.

She motioned him inside, then closed the door. "Hollis Darby was snatched up by the Protector today. At knifepoint. I think the two roughs doing the snatching would've done Ana a serious harm, if I'd not interfered."

She sat on the edge of her bed. "Fletcher and I went to Madame Tussaud's this morning to see if we could learn something more about the Radlett case, but we'd not been at Thurtell's display for more than a minute when Four-Finger Mike came sauntering in."

Four-Finger Mike? "He's in prison."

"Not anymore, apparently." She shook her head. "Then the Tempest herself stepped up beside us."

"Blimey." He sat beside her.

"It was like having a conversation with a riddle. Everything she said felt two-sided. She knows we haven't sorted her out yet and don't know how to stop her, and she loves it. Loves that she's torturing us."

Fitz took hold of Móirín's hand, concerned at how exhausted she looked and the hint of defeat in her voice.

"I did confirm that she *is* the little girl Mr. Sorokin met all those years ago and that her connection to the Radlett case is what we thought it might be." But she didn't look reassured.

"I asked why her grandmother was angry with George IV. The closest she came to answering was saying she didn't care to go gawk at the late monarch's wax figure as 'there can be only one queen.'" Móirín released a slow and tense breath. "She also said she's 'collecting them,' that 'the tunnels are getting crowded,' and that going head-to-head with me was like 'outmaneuvering a slightly inferior version' of herself."

"She sees similarities between you?"

Móirín sighed. "Said that a few times, she did. 'Twas the only thing she said that didn't sound like a puzzle."

He squeezed her hand. "Have you sorted any bits of that puzzle?"

She looked at him. "I'm not used to confiding in people, Fitz. 'Tis a strange thing for me to be doing so easily."

"Perhaps it's simply that I'm a remarkable person. Have you thought about that?"

She smiled a little, and the simple change did his heart good.

"The Protector, as he was snatching Hollis, said he didn't need Ana or me because we weren't part of the collection, which means the Tempest is 'collecting' my Dreadfuls, I think."

"Do you think they're being kept alive?"

"I can't say with complete certainty. She heavily hinted that she killed two children under Fletcher's care, but I suspect if she was murdering the Dreadfuls, she'd have said as much."

Killed two children. They were searching for a monster.

"She mentioned 'tunnels,' so I'm wondering if she's keeping the Dreadfuls she's snatching in some kind of underground cavern."

Underground cavern. A thought popped into his head. He stood and moved to the table where Móirín had papers spread about. He pulled from his coat pocket the papers he'd taken from Scotland Yard with the details of two of his cases. He dropped them on the table while he fished out a scrap of unused paper and his lead pencil.

"Did you think of something?" Móirín asked, crossing to him.

He nodded. "How many of the Dreadfuls are missing at this point?"

"Six that I know of."

He wrote that down. "And you got the impression they're being kept together?"

"It'd make sense, seeing as she's calling them a collection."

Six adults, together, in an underground cavern.

"It can't be a place easy to escape from," Móirín added, "or I suspect at least one of 'em would've done so. And it can't be a place people'd stumble across, or there's a chance one of my informers might've spotted it."

That matched what he was thinking. "On my last night at D Division, I brought in a tosher. Could be that's why my mind's running this direction, but I think we oughta consider they're being kept in the sewers."

Móirín's brows drew together, her mouth tugging downward as she thought. "There're hundreds of miles of sewers. A far sight too many for us to go about searching them all."

"Has to be a part where at least six blokes can be kept at once, with room enough for more. Has to be hard to escape but easy enough to reach since they keep tossing people in. Can't be in a part the toshers frequent, or they'd be spotted. But also can't be in a part that's too dangerous to stay in for long. That'll narrow it down."

"Would this tosher you arrested give you any tips on where we ought to be looking?" Móirín asked.

"That's what I'm hoping. The promise of a bit of leniency in his sentence might convince him to help us."

"Careful with that approach," Móirín said. "Offering a lesser sentence if a criminal is helpful can turn around and hurt a fella if that bit of leniency ain't what others think it ought to be."

That were true enough. It was proving to be the backbone of the Tempest's grudge against the world. "If Lanky Mack can give me information about where to look, I'll climb down and see what I can find."

"*We'll* climb down," Móirín said.

Fitz raised a brow. "Are you itching to have a lark in the sewers?"

"I'm always looking for an adventure." Her smile was very nearly wicked. And while her perfectly ordinary smile was enough to make his heart flutter, *this* smile clutched at all his insides, pinching his lungs and squeezing his heart in a gloriously painful bit of enjoyment.

"If you help me solve one of these other cases Wheatley is grumbling about, I'll take you on any number of adventures, Móirín."

"I've been known to solve a mystery or two." She took up the papers, flipping through them. "The Phantom Fox."

"Heard of him?" Fitz asked.

Móirín nodded. "I have. Best sneak thief London's ever known, yet never steals anything of worth."

He nodded. "I know, which makes me less inclined to try to nab the fella. If even the people he's filching things from don't care about getting them back, it seems we ought to leave well enough alone for now."

Móirín laughed lightly, another thing that did uncomfortably wonderful things to him. "I'd agree with you there, though it pains me to do so."

"One of these days, you're going to admit you like me more than you want to think you do."

"Never." She moved to the next paper in the stack, studying it.

"That one's an old case. Five years back. Maeve O'Donald is said to be in London, but from what I've learned, she likely ain't *called* Maeve O'Donald."

"That'll make it a right slippery case."

He nodded. "It is."

Móirín set down the papers. The lightness that had been in her expression had vanished. "The Tempest said she and I are very much alike. I'm doing my best not to believe it."

Fitz set a hand on her arm. "You ain't nothing like her."

"I've had plenty enough people tell me how terrifying I am for me to not believe them. And *terrifying* is the best description I can think of for our elusive enemy."

Blimey, she actually believed it. How could she?

Fitz slipped his arm around her. "Could you imagine the Tempest climbing into the sewer to save someone? Or worrying herself like you are because other people are in danger?"

"I suppose not."

He leaned closer. "Consider this. Perhaps she told you how alike you are, not just because she knew it'd upend you but because she wishes it were true."

"She wants to be me?" Móirín asked with amused doubt.

"Why wouldn't she?"

Móirín brushed the tip of her finger along his jaw. "I *am* about to kiss a constable. I can see how she'd be jealous of that."

"Are you?" he whispered, his gaze dropping to her surprisingly tempting lips.

"Are *you*?" She spoke as quietly as he had, her eyes on his mouth as well.

"Seems I oughta do it now rather than after we've had our gad about the sewers."

There was something pleading in her "Mm-hmm." Far be it from him to ignore such a request.

He wrapped his other arm around her, holding her to him. He bent closer, stopping with his lips hovering a hair's breadth from hers. "You might find that kissing a constable will prove addictive," he warned in a whisper.

She very nearly closed the minute gap between them. "I'm willing to risk it."

His mouth found hers, that mouth that had quipped and teased him for months, that now confided in him, that spoke of trust and confidence. She wrapped her arms around his neck, and he tightened his embrace. Not even a ray of light stood between them.

Everything about kissing her was even better than he could have imagined. The soft warmth of her lips. The perfectness of holding her. The way her fierce embrace sent his pulse racing.

He hadn't the strength to pull away. But she ended the moment, seeming to regret the necessity.

That kiss had solidified for him the change he'd felt coming for weeks. She'd been a bantering adversary, then a reluctant ally. But she was more than that to him now. Far more.

POSIE AND PRU
DETECTIVES FOR HIRE

by Chauncey Finnegan

Chapter Four

"A ghost?" Mrs. O'Reilly did not seem to fully grasp how likely that explanation truly was. "What has led you to think the murder was perpetrated by a ghost?"

It was simple, really. For a detective at least.

Posie smiled, eager to explain. "Janey saw a figure in the mirror dressed all in flowing white. Ghosts always dress like that. Always. And it would explain why she thought you were there when you were *not* actually there. The ghost, you see, simply looked like you. And since you have a long white nightdress, she wrongly believed the ghostly gown was your nightdress. It is well-known that people quite regularly die of being startled. What could be more startling than the sudden appearance of a ghost?"

"I suppose that does make a bit of sense." Mrs. O'Reilly began nodding.

"Further," Pru added, "dogs find ghosts particularly worrisome. And the young Mr. Flanagan lost his dog during the time this ghost was being murderous. It all fits brilliantly."

Of course Pru would find clues of a ghostly crime based on the dog's disappearance.

"Little Morris at the stable looks after the dog when young Mr. Flanagan is not around," Mrs. O'Reilly said. "You could ask Morris if the dog seemed particularly worried."

"An excellent idea." Posie pointed ahead with her inside cane before leaning on it once more. "Let us make our way to the back garden."

"I'll need my outdoor shawl," Pru said. "It's blue," she reminded Mrs. O'Reilly.

"Will you be wishing for your outdoor cane?" Mrs. O'Reilly asked Posie.

"That would be preferred, yes."

The two detectives began their slow walk toward the back of the house. Before they reached the doors leading to the back garden, Mrs. O'Reilly caught up to them with Pru's blue outdoor shawl and Posie's wide-bottomed outdoor cane.

"Do you truly think the culprit is a ghost?" Mrs. O'Reilly sounded hopeful if not entirely convinced. "I would feel extremely relieved to know for certain that *I* wasn't the guilty party."

Posie patted her hand. "While I will not discount the reality that someone might commit a crime whilst in a trance and not remember the doing of it, or perhaps suffer a blow to the head and have the memory of that crime erased, I do think it is more logical that this particular crime was the work of a specter."

Mrs. O'Reilly released a tense breath. "What a relief."

They stepped onto the back terrace, aiming for the stables at the far end of the path ahead. It would be a long walk, and it was at a bit of an angle. Posie thought perhaps she ought to have brought her steep-trail cane rather than her slick-ground cane.

Off to the side, Mrs. Brennan could be seen making her way to the stone steps leading down to the rear servants' entrance. She wore a dingy white bonnet and brown coat over a dress of blue-and-white gingham. On anyone else, it would have been a soft choice, pleasant and unobtrusive, but Mrs. Brennan somehow looked all angles and sharpness.

"I didn't realize Mrs. Brennan worked here," Posie said.

"She doesn't," Mrs. O'Reilly said, "though she had applied for positions in the past. The late Mr. Flanagan was not interested in expanding the staff."

"The young Mr. Flanagan is," Posie said. "I overheard him discussing such with his man of business."

"We *are* in need of a couple of extra maids." Mrs. O'Reilly didn't sound pleased at the possibility. "Do you wish me to accompany you to the stables?" She looked very much as if she hoped they would decline her offer.

"We can make our way there on our own," Posie assured her.

They'd only gone half the length of the walk when Morris skipped up to them. His name was simply Morris, as no one knew his surname, not even Morris. He'd arrived in the village a year earlier at only six years old and had worked as the stable boy at Mr. Flanagan's house ever since. Mr. Flanagan was not known for his kindness, but he'd shown a rare bit of compassion in the matter of Morris the stable boy.

"Good day to you, Morris," Posie said.

"We're looking for a lost dog," Pru added. "We're detectives now, and we are very good at dogs."

"The dog *is* missing," Morris said, eyes wide and earnest. "Ran at the house the day Mr. Flanagan died. Frantic and loud and acting like he'd . . . well, like he'd seen—"

"A ghost?" Posie pressed, feeling certain she knew the answer.

"Could be," Morris answered. "But I were going to say like he'd seen a villain, someone terrible."

"Ghosts can be terrible," Pru said.

Morris shrugged. "The little dog gets on with most people. Only them who most people don't like seem to upset him."

"People like whom?" Posie pressed.

"He didn't like old Mr. Flanagan much," Morris said. "Don't like the blacksmith, but most of us don't. He thinks Mrs. Brennan oughtn't be allowed to come anywhere near the house. And young Mr. Flanagan said there's a man in London the dog don't like none."

"The dog doesn't like Mrs. Brennan?" Pru asked.

"Not a bit. But then none of us does, do we?"

There was truth to that.

"Perhaps the dog simply doesn't like the color white." Pru shrugged. "I have tried to tell Mrs. Brennan that if she is to choose a color to wear at all times it ought to be an actual color. White, I think, doesn't really count."

Posie tapped her finger to her lips, musing on the clues they had uncovered so far.

The dog barked at something—or someone—it didn't like.

The murderer, seen in the mirror, was wearing white and bore a resemblance to Mrs. O'Reilly.

Mrs. Brennan had wanted a position, but Mr. Flanagan

wouldn't give it to her, yet young Mr. Flanagan seemed more inclined to expand the staff.

"Oh, dear, Pru," Posie said. "I think we might have to *unsolve* this crime."

CHAPTER 15

There was an unofficial uniform for descending into London's sewers. Going into the sewers without permission was illegal, yet those who did it regularly wore clothes that gave them away. It was either arrogance or necessity. She opted to believe the toshers knew they were about. She and Fitz donned clothes that matched those that'd be worn by the others traversing the great underground tunnels.

A long coat, greasy from years of use, with enormous pockets. Canvas trousers—Móirín wore hers under an old dress she wouldn't mind burning after that night's work. Shoes they'd obtained for next to nothing at an old clothes' shop. A canvas apron. A dark lantern strapped to their front, just beneath the right shoulder. The shutters focused the light so it'd illuminate their path or the ground depending on how upright they were standing. A pole, longer than either of them was tall, with an iron hoe at one end.

It was an odd outfit, but somehow it didn't render Fitz any less annoyingly handsome. Unfair of him, really, being so dimber *and* showing himself a devilishly good kisser.

He was more than just a constable—which had made him

dangerous enough when they'd first met—he was now a detective assigned to find her, though he didn't know it. Seeing the details of all she'd been accused of doing written so plainly on that paper under the name she'd used at the Guinness Factory had drained what little fight had been left in her the night before.

Then he'd kissed her, and she'd been wide awake the rest of the night, shifting from pleased with the memory and panicking with the misstep she'd made.

Soft hearts get broken. And *tendres* get distracting. She couldn't afford either.

"Ready for a romp in a veritable Garden of Eden?" Móirín asked Fitz, adopting her teasingly annoyed tone.

"Always ready for a romp," Fitz said with a very regal bow. "Milady."

"As much as I like that, I think I'd prefer 'Your Highness' or 'Your Majesty.'"

His smile tipped with mischief. "Oi, but I ain't always good at doing what I'm told."

"A bit of a knave, are you?"

"I aim to be far more than that." He was pulling her interest in all the right ways, which was a shame, really. She couldn't let things move in that direction.

"At the moment, I'd say you're aiming to be a sewer explorer," she said.

Fitz laughed and pulled a paper from one of the enormous pockets in his coat. "This is from Lanky Mack, our friendly tosher. He gave me detailed instructions."

"If they're half so detailed as his description of what we're meant to wear, I'm surprised he managed it on one sheet of paper." She eyed the pole and hoe. "What do you suppose this jigamaree is for?"

"Are you certain you want to know?"

"I'd thought it might be to dig valuables out of the muck," Móirín said. "But the way you said that makes me think it's somethin' far worse."

"*Can* be used for digging. But it's far more useful for doing battle with the rats."

"Garden of Eden, indeed," she said wryly.

"Lanky Mack warned me the rats are not to be taken lightly. They're the reason toshers don't go into the sewers alone."

This was growing worse by the minute. "Do you suppose they've given my Dreadfuls something to fight off the rats with?"

"I think the Tempest wants them alive, wants you to be racing the clock to find them. That means *not* letting the rats eat them."

They climbed down the banks of the Thames where an outpouring of a sewage tunnel allowed toshers to enter the vast system. Fitz shined his lantern on the paper he held. "Once inside, we'll turn down the first tunnel we come to on our left."

"You're certain Lanky Mack gave you reliable instructions?" Móirín pressed.

"If I don't return, there'll be no one to speak up for him when it's time for his sentencing. He needs me to find my way back out of the sewer."

Móirín studied the paper. 'Twas a combination of written instructions and a rough map of the tunnel system. She was standing quite close to Fitz. Almond and rosemary—that enticing scent that always hung around him. By the time the day's work was completed, neither of them would smell the least that pleasant.

"You ain't even looking at the paper, Móirín," Fitz laughed.

"I'm distracted by your stench, Fitzy."

He laughed even harder. 'Twas one thing she'd discovered about this odd blue-bottle: he'd a fine sense of humor.

"Remind me to remark on *your* sweet smell when we've finished this mission of ours," Fitz said.

Dry as could be, Móirín said, "I suspect I won't have to remind you."

"If you're wanting to kiss me again, you'd likely best do so now."

"*You* kissed *me*." She turned enough to look at him, intending to remind him—and herself—that they'd important work to do and needed to keep their focus. But he was so close, and his eyes were so brown, and his mouth was so shockingly tempting that for the tiniest moment, her mind refused to recall what the business at hand actually was. But only for a moment.

She plucked the paper from his hands and stepped back.

"This here's the cavern where we're most likely to find our missing Dreadfuls?" She indicated a spot on the hand-drawn map with the words "Look here."

"Oi." Fitz ran his finger along the tunnels they'd take to get there. "These are passable, and Lanky Mack said no one's dropped dead in them, so they ought to be safe."

"Are some of these tunnels plagued with people dropping off dead?"

"They are. Air that ain't always safe is the theory. Of course, some tunnels in the older parts have a miserable tendency to collapse. We'll avoid those too."

"I'd hope so." Móirín folded the paper and tucked it in the bag tied against her chest. "Let's go wade through the refuse."

"I'm voting we avoid that as well," Fitz said. "There'll be no escaping the smell, but—"

"But the company'll be brilliant, I'm sure you're meaning to say next."

"I'll confess, I ain't unhappy with the company."

Oh, that pleased her more than it should've.

Fitz tossed her a smile. "In we go, love."

Love. She knew people tossed out that endearment without thinking. She wouldn't let herself believe it was anything more than that.

Other people were slipping in the tunnel, so they followed. Safety in numbers, as it were. Especially, apparently, when avoiding murderous rats. The smell was shocking, but they were meant to seem like regular toshers making a nightly journey into the sewers, and showing they weren't accustomed to the stench would undermine that.

So Móirín did what she'd learned to do as a child: she lied. She pretended. She acted.

A narrow foothold ran along the sides of the tunnel, just above the flow of putrid fluid. She and Fitz followed the others, walking where they did and, using their own long-handled spear, plunged down into the muck, to keep their balance.

"Fine thing the tide ain't in, i'n'it?" someone said in the group.

The tide. The rats. The stench. To think her Dreadfuls might be trapped here tore at her heart.

Some in the group took the first left tunnel. That'd help with the rat issue. It'd also help Fitz and Móirín not get lost.

Sludge and slime left the bricks beneath their feet slippery. The toshers moved with a sure-footedness Móirín could hardly believe. The lanterns they all wore offered some light, but not enough.

A rat brushed past her foot, but she kept her head. Panicking would likely only see her fall into the stream of refuse.

The path shifted upward, stairs built into the brick bottom, but just as slick as the rest of the tunnel.

"Be green, hen," Fitz called back to her, letting his Cockney colors fly more than he usually did. "Ground's slippery as an eel."

Another rat ran over the toe of her shoe. She whacked the creature off with the handle of her hoe. The stench of the sewer became more than a smell the deeper they went. It became a flavor that wrapped itself in her mouth, a weight that settled in her lungs. The map Lanky Mack had drawn made the cavern seem close to the entrance of the Thames. She hoped that proved right.

At the top of the climb, the tunnel forked. They needed the path on the right. The narrower one.

No one else was headed that way. Only their two lanterns illuminated the path. The going was slower. She leaned heavily on her hoe, needing it to help her keep her balance. A step ahead of her, Fitz did the same.

Then the tunnel widened a bit, revealing a platform built into the side of the tunnel, wide enough and tall enough for ten or twelve people to sit.

But no one was there.

Not a single person.

"They ain't here." Fitz's frustration echoed in the dank tunnel. "I don't know whether to be relieved or irritated that we still don't know where they are."

"I'm choosing the relieved approach," Móirín said. "I'd rather they weren't stuck in a place like this."

"Lanky Mack didn't think there were another place that fit what we was looking for," Fitz said. "If they ain't here, they likely ain't being kept in the sewers at all."

"I think even the rats'd be grateful to hear that."

"Means we need to think of another 'tunnel,'" Fitz said.

"Let's think of another one up-top where there's fresh air."

"You'll hear no arguments from me." Fitz turned enough for his lantern to shine on the far side of the platform, and he pointed to a ladder. "We can go up from here. We'll have to be quiet about it, since it's easier to get caught here than at the sewer outflow."

"I'd be willing to get tossed in jail if it meant being free of this place."

He climbed onto the platform, then turned back and helped her up. "I do know a constable who's sometimes willing to do a favor for people who wander around in the sewers."

"He sounds like a saint," Móirín said.

"He don't currently smell like one."

"No, he don't." She couldn't see his face—he was already climbing up the ladder—but she felt certain he smiled. She wasn't doing a very good job of maintaining her indifference to the man.

This sewer tunnel wasn't far beneath the surface. They reached the top of the ladder relatively quickly. With some effort, Fitz moved the iron manhole cover, and they both emerged in the fresh air above.

Móirín blew out her lantern's flame, all the while filling her lungs with as much sewer-free air as they could hold. Fitz pushed the iron cover back into place. Both of them abandoned their stench-encrusted coats and aprons. The shoes they'd keep on until they got closer to the safe house, then abandon them so they'd not bring the smell or the sludge inside.

While Fitz was tucking their tosher clothes behind an obliging hedge, Móirín caught sight of someone up the road, just passing under a streetlamp. Someone she knew. Someone she owed a bit of a beating.

"How would your prickly Sergeant Wheatley feel about his newest Detective Constable nabbing one of London's most-wanted criminals?" Móirín asked.

"He'd die of shock, I'd wager."

"Either way, it'd fix things nicely for you." She pointed with her long-handled hoe toward the man she was watching closely. "The one they call the Protector—yours for the plucking, Fitz. And I'll have you know, I'm handy in a scuffle."

"That don't surprise me in the least." Fitz popped his knuckles, before taking up his tosher tool again. "Let's catch ourselves a criminal."

Quick as lightning and quiet as the moonbeams, they positioned themselves. Móirín stepped in front of the Protector, her back to him so he'd not recognize her. Without warning, she bent down as if to get a pebble out of her shoe, forcing him to stop for just an instant. That instant was all Fitz needed.

He snatched the man's arm and spun him around. "Oi, oi, bully boy."

The Protector cocked back his free arm, clearly meaning to belt Fitz.

But he clearly hadn't planned on Móirín.

She set the corner of the iron hoe at the back of his neck, pressing enough for him to know it weren't a small thing.

"I ain't constrained by a vow of allegiance to the law," she warned. "It'd be simple and enjoyable to end your reign of 'protection' in this city."

"A woman ain't gonna—"

"Best not end that thought, nocky," Fitz warned. "That woman's holding one of the biggest blades I've ever seen."

"And I'm well-versed in blades," Móirín added.

Fitz took advantage of the Protector's distraction. He spun the long wooden handle, hitting the man in the middle, sending him doubling over. Fitz tossed his hoe into the hedge, then snatched up the Protector's hands and tied them with his own handkerchief.

"You . . . stink . . ." The Protector's sneer was undermined by his breathlessness from being hit in the stomach.

"Let's go for a walk," Fitz said, pulling his prisoner upright and pushing him onward.

Móirín followed but kept out of sight. She, too, abandoned the tosher's hoe, trading it for the welcome familiarity of her knife.

"We ain't a half bad team, you and I," Fitz said to her.

"Don't get used to it," she said. "I ain't one to make a chum out of a blue-bottle."

CHAPTER 16

Fitz had been part of three divisions of the Metropolitan Police before joining the Detective Department, so he knew the location of nearly every police station in the metropolis. Finding one within a short distance of where they'd nabbed the Protector was an easy enough thing to manage.

He dragged his prisoner inside with a nod to the officers. "Detective Constable Parkington," he identified himself. "This here's the man you'll know as the Protector."

That they looked both impressed and a bit intimidated told Fitz they were well aware of the enormity of this arrest.

"This'n'll be processed over to Newgate," he said. "Someone'll collect him in the morning."

That seemed to give the Protector pause. Good.

"The detective smells of the sewers," the Protector said, finding his voice again. "Seems he oughta explain that."

"Gladly," Fitz said. "I found a heap of tosher's clothes and implements cast into a hedge. Been trying to sort out who it belongs to."

That came near enough to the truth without tripping him up with it. Directing a constable or two to the spot where he and Móirín had dropped their disguises and hoes would bolster his claim.

To the constable nearest the holding cell, Fitz said, "Open the cell. I ain't meaning to stand here all night."

The man snapped to it, while the other constable watched in awe.

Móirín, Fitz noticed, kept to the shadows in the corner, entirely silent. She had no love for policemen in general; he'd known that about her from the beginning. Though she'd warmed to him—his lips tingled at the memory of some of that "warmth"—he didn't imagine she was happy to be surrounded by others plying his particular trade.

Soon enough the Protector was in a cell, locked and secured, and Fitz returned to the table at the front.

"Fetch me a paper," he told the officer. "I need to write out a report."

He'd done this so often, he hardly needed to think about the necessary steps. And he'd interacted with enough constables in enough stations to know that the two working here were greener than he'd prefer. Simply telling them what needed doing would be the best use of his time.

Fitz scribbled out a quick recounting of the Protector's apprehension, though instinct told him not to name Móirín in the report. He certainly weren't going to include the bit where he'd only just crawled out of a sewer when he spotted the criminal. He weren't overly keen to gab with Wheatley, but he looked forward to that man learning that Fitz had nabbed someone as infamous and elusive as the Protector. Bringing in such a significant prisoner, and doing so without much of a struggle, was impressive. Even Wheatley would have to admit that.

"Don't sign that off too quick-like," the Protector shouted

from his cell. "Might be you'd like to offer a bit of clemency when you hear what it is I know."

Fitz usually ignored the prisoners when they said such things. It generally came to nothing, and there was always plenty of time to listen to what they had to offer once they were settled in and feeling a bit more trapped. But this prisoner was connected to the Tempest. If he had anything helpful about *that* criminal, Fitz wanted to know.

He set his report where he knew it was meant to be, then casually turned toward the cell. It weren't a large station; he didn't need to walk anywhere.

"I know who killed Claud Kincaid," the Protector said. "And I know how."

Fitz didn't let his interest show. "So do I." In truth, he only knew it were someone connected to the Kincaid family and that the method was poison, but getting a fellow to spill more was often helped by making him think a small spill wouldn't do him no good.

"Silas. Himself."

Gemma hadn't known if the murder had been the direct handiwork of one of the ruling brothers of the family or done under their instructions. Knowing Silas had done the deed himself *was* a new bit of insight, though Fitz didn't change his expression.

"Bumped into Claud as he were being brought to the dock. Spread the poison on his hand. Silas knew Claud'd touch his mouth. Had taken to chewing at his nails on account of being afraid of the Tempest. From his hands to his mouth—all it took."

"I was there when he died, mate," Fitz said with a shrug. "You ain't telling me anything I ain't already twigged." That was a lie, but the man was spilling secrets without securing any promises. Seemed wise to let him keep on spilling.

The Protector paused, clearly trying to find a new tidbit of information to trade. "I know something I know you don't." He sounded confident this time. "If'n you did, you'd be the hero of the detectives."

The man had his attention now. Still, Fitz offered no promises. He suspected he didn't need to. After a short breath, the prisoner proved him right.

"There's a fugitive the police've been searching for, both here and in Ireland. Has evaded capture for five years now. No one even knows her name for sure and certain. But I do."

The Maeve O'Donald case.

"Why should I believe you?" Fitz asked.

"Because I ain't keen to go to Newgate, but she's even less so. Seems a good trade to me."

Fitz folded his arms and eyed the man with an eyebrow raised in doubt.

"Killed a man in Dublin, she did," the Protector said. "Came here straight after and been hiding ever since, using a different name."

Yes. That was the case he thought it might be.

"It's whispered about on the streets. People've pieced it together, but she's made herself a reg'lar guardian angel to them poor and sickly folks. All the food she gets 'em and medicines and new places to live if'n they's being harassed. The lugs has won their silence by making 'erself their champion."

That sounded like—

"Móirín Donnelly," the Protector said. "Toss out that other name she were using. It's her. Always has been."

Without a thought, without hesitation, Fitz said, "Whoever

told you that load of lies oughta be put on your list of people you ain't gonna trust. I've known the Donnellys from the time they arrived here from Ireland more than *six* years ago. Cain't kill a fella in a country a person ain't in herself."

The Protector looked flummoxed, which was to Fitz's advantage.

Fitz turned and spoke to the constable at the desk. "This man's facing almost certain execution. I suspect he'll tell you a heap more useless things and outright lies to try to save his neck."

The constable nodded solemnly. That'd help a bit, though now Fitz needed to make certain whoever processed the man over to Newgate was told a heap of lies *by Fitz*. Blast it all, he weren't fond of telling falsehoods.

"I'm itching for a bit of air," Fitz said. "Reckon you can keep this fella on that side of them bars for a minute or two?"

"We sure can," came the firm promise.

As Fitz passed Móirín, still tucked in the corner, he motioned for her to follow him out. Once on the pavement and out of earshot, he spoke quickly and quietly.

"How long've you and Brogan *actually* been in London?"

"Five years," she answered in the same low tone.

"Have you ever used a name other than Móirín Donnelly?"

"I have." Those two words were even quieter than the previous ones.

"And when you looked at m' papers for the two cases I'm supposed to be solving, was the Phantom Fox the only one you thought familiar?"

"It weren't."

Blast it all. "Is what that royster said true, then?"

"Enough of it."

Gumblimey. "Why didn't you tell me? Did you think I'd

just hand you over?" He wouldn't've. Leastwise, not without hearing the whys and hows. He'd come to know Móirín too well to ever believe she was a cold-blooded murderer.

Keeping very still, she said, "I'd rather you not be needing to lie."

"I told a right rapper just now."

For the first time, she actually looked up at him. The night weren't a bright one, and the blue lantern outside the station didn't offer much help, but he thought she looked . . . doubtful. Doubtful in him? In herself? "I thought, when you put the lie to his words so quickly, that you'd already sorted it out. You didn't seem at all surprised."

"Turns out, I'm a good liar but a 'right rubbish blue-bottle.'" Blast it all. How was it he'd been made a detective but still missed the clues that'd been right in front of him?

"You're not rubbish, Fi—Detective Constable Parkington. And I'm sorry you had to fib for me. I will tell you this much, though—there's a great deal in the report that ain't at all true. You might've eventually caught 'Maeve O'Donald,' but you'd've been doing it without knowing the whole truth."

She might've told him more, might've spilled a bit of that "whole truth" if not for the approach of footsteps, footsteps that proved to belong to another constable, come to begin his shift.

Like a shadow, Móirín disappeared in the dark, taking with her a surprisingly large piece of Fitz's heart.

THE QUEEN AND THE KNAVE

by Mr. King

Installment V
in which Help is sought and Danger is courted!

Reynard awoke to find soft sunlight peeking around the makeshift burlap curtains hanging in the windows. Morning had come. And looking at the pallet where Eleanor—*Queen Eleanor*—had been sleeping, he saw she had transformed once more. A deep-brown pine marten lay curled in precisely the way it had in the sentry box the day before.

She'd said the transformation didn't hurt. He hoped that continued to be true.

Reynard rose, stretching out the tension that had built in his body after he'd slept in so odd a position. He was not required to stand sentry today. Everyone amongst the palace guards was permitted two days in each month away from their duties. He'd chosen these days weeks ago, having wanted to attend the feats of skill and strength that were held during the week of the Unification Ceremony. That had proven fortuitous.

It is too complex for either of us to remedy alone.

His own words from the night before had returned to him

again and again in his dreams. This could not be addressed by only the two of them. They needed others. Others who had magic. Others who might be willing to take a stand against Dezmerina.

And Reynard knew where to find them.

He changed from his sentry uniform, which he'd been wearing for far too long, and into a set of clothing that had once belonged to his father. If ever he needed his parents' wisdom to reach him from beyond, it was then. His mother would have understood the curse without difficulty. His father would have known how to safeguard the queen. Reynard was struggling to manage just one of those tasks.

He set a hat on his head and pulled a knapsack over one shoulder. He intended to awaken the pine marten queen before departing, but she woke on her own. Queen Eleanor had told him she could understand him when he spoke, that she still thought as her human self. So he addressed her as such.

"I know of people who will help us," he said. "People who can be trusted. They were associates of my mother, who built and enchanted this cottage. And while she was here, she was safe. You'll be safe here as well. I am going to see if I can find us help."

She hopped off the pallet and moved swiftly to the wall near the door. Stretching to her full length, she reached up on the wall, her paw nearly touching the amulet hanging from a nail. She looked back at him, then back at the amulet a few times in succession.

He understood. "I'll wear the amulet while I am out. It will protect me, and this cottage will protect you."

She dipped her head in a way that made him think of a nod.

He knotted the amulet's two leather straps and placed it around his neck. "Please be safe," he said. "I will return as soon as I can."

Reynard slipped from the cottage, closing the door firmly behind him. He paused for a moment, concerned for Queen Eleanor, unsure of his ability to complete his task successfully. But being in his mother's cottage had made him feel she was close. She had always believed in him. She would have insisted he forge ahead with confidence.

He moved with swift feet through the forest toward the vast field where the competition of skill and strength was to be held. It had been many years since he'd spoken with his mother's friends, but he remembered them, and he hoped they would remember him.

Spectator benches had been placed in neat rows on the hillside overlooking the field of competition, but the press and pull of so many eager to watch gave the neat layout a decidedly chaotic feel. That suited Reynard's purposes brilliantly. No one would take note of him wandering about, having conversations. He'd be able to learn what he needed and make his pleas for help without adding to the danger of the situation.

I'm not allowed to wish for things any longer. Not for myself.

He'd seen for himself how hard Eleanor tried to be the best queen she could be, doing what the kingdom needed her to do. Was she truly required to lose so much of herself in fulfilling her duties? It seemed terribly unfair.

"Reynard!" Marwen, an older man, one known to him from childhood, called out and waved him over. "How fare ye?" It was the greeting used by those with magic when encountering each other or each other's families.

"I am as I have ever been, though not all know the how or when." That was the reply used when one needed assistance from those with magic. Dezmerina was the reason they were all in hiding; she was the source of nearly all their difficulties.

Marwen walked with Reynard to where a woman sat, awaiting the start of the competition. Her name was Gerhilde, and she had been one of Reynard's mother's dearest friends.

"Reynard," she greeted. "How fare ye?"

"I am as I have ever been, though not all know the how or when."

"Tell us of both."

He sat between them, and all three set their gazes on the field below, giving every impression of chatting casually whilst enjoying the day's offering.

Keeping his voice low, Reynard said, "Our mutual adversary has set a curse."

"Upon what or whom?" Marwen asked.

"To one known as Eleanor."

There was a pause, a silent gasp.

Gerhilde pressed for greater clarity. "Known to us all?"

"Known to us all," Reynard confirmed.

"And what has been done to her?" Marwen's concern filled his soft voice.

"She has been transformed into an animal, but only in the daylight."

"What are the four patterns?" Gerhilde asked.

"The manifestation is while the sun is in the sky. The 'how' is that Eleanor is transformed into a pine marten. The impact is battles and chaos. The ending I cannot truly sort out."

"Tell us the fourth line," Marwen said. "We will help you sort it."

"'Her life will ebb whilst mine remains,'" he quoted. "I have my fears about what that means."

"Your fears are likely well-founded," Gerhilde said. "While the curse is in place, the one it is placed on will slowly die."

"But that is impact, not requirements for ending." Reynard shook his head. "Unless the only way to end the curse is for—" He couldn't bring himself to finish the thought.

"The curse will end when Eleanor's life has been drained," Gerhilde said. "Or—"

"I like the possibility of 'or.'" Reynard liked it very much, in fact.

"Or when the caster of the spell has died," Gerhilde finished.

Whilst mine remains. If Dezmerina's life no longer remained, that would end the curse too.

"But no one has been able to defeat her since she began her reign," Reynard said. "Indeed, many have been lost in the attempt."

"So much so that you will have difficulty finding those willing to join you in your fight," Marwen said.

"And how did you know I intended to attempt a recruitment?"

"Because you know better than most that a single person, or even two, are not enough to stop one as powerful as she."

Gerhilde nodded in agreement.

"But if this curse is not lifted, chaos and battles will tear this kingdom asunder. That must not be permitted to happen," Reynard said.

"She knows how to cause fear," Gerhilde said. "Fear is a powerful thing."

"Then we need to find something more powerful," Reynard said firmly.

But before they could imagine what that something might be, the competition below quite suddenly stopped.

Everything stopped.

An explosion of sparks and a whirlwind of color split the scene, revealing the sudden presence of Dezmerina.

"Where is your queen?" she demanded in a carrying voice, echoing in the silence around her. "She is not at the palace. She is not here."

No one spoke, but eyes were darting about, searching for answers in the faces around them.

Below, Dezmerina cackled. "Your barons are consulting. Tomorrow the Unification Ceremony will be held. But where is your queen? She has failed you. She has flown. War will descend, and chaos will reign in her stead, and I alone will maintain power enough to protect those who choose me."

The already silent air grew heavier with worry and uncertainty.

"You have the night to choose your side. Once the ceremony begins, there will be no changing loyalties." She held her hands to the sky, clouds roiling and spinning above her. "You have the night."

And in a flash of lightning, the sorceress disappeared.

CHAPTER 17

So many locks and bolts were on the inside of the safe house door that no one could let themselves in. Móirín gave a single knock and waited. She heard the slot in the door open, but no light emerged from the other side.

"I've a knife in my pocket, and I've not stabbed anyone all day." Fletcher had invented that code phrase for her. She'd not muttered it with quite as much frustration as she did then.

The slot slid closed, scraping as it did. Locks clicked open. Móirín breathed out, pushing from her mind her swirling thoughts about Fitz and focusing instead on formulating her next plan for finding her Dreadfuls and ridding the world of the Tempest. She refused to think of Fitz and the disapproval in his tone as he'd spoken of her past and his need to lie for her. She refused to admit she'd fallen in love with him a bit.

Perhaps more than *a bit*.

The door cracked open, just enough for her to slip inside. She closed the door behind her. Stone stood nearby, holding a lit candle.

"Sorry you were needing to wait up so long," she said.

He shook his head. "Most of us're up."

Around the room a few matches struck, and the shutters on dark lanterns opened, illuminating the space. And it was packed full of people. Those who made their home there at the Riding House safe house were present, but so were Celia, Brogan and Vera, Mr. Sorokin, Licorice, and Olly.

Worry twisted Móirín's insides. "Did something happen at the Whitfield Street safe house?" There was no point whispering. Everyone present knew where they'd come from.

"Four-Finger Mike was seen hanging about the area. Bit too close for comfort," Stone said.

Everything lately was too close for comfort. "And the move was made without being seen?"

Stone nodded. "Even safeguarded two little urchins at the same time."

Móirín turned to Fletcher, knowing he'd know precisely which urchins they'd rescued.

"The two children the Tempest said were hers," he clarified.

At last, a spot of good news. "You found 'em." She sighed in relief.

"You smell like the Thames on a hot day," Stone said. "You made your drop into the sewers."

That she and Fitz were meaning to make the underground search hadn't been kept a secret from either safe house. Ana, in particular, looked heartbreakingly hopeful.

"They weren't there," Móirín said. "We nabbed the Protector, though. Some information might be wrestled out of him."

"We still don't know where Hollis is?" Ana sounded almost desperate.

Móirín didn't often grow emotional, but the failures and revelations of that night's work had her perilously close to doing so. "I'm not meaning to stop looking. While I can't promise you that he's safe, I am full certain he's alive. And I'm proper certain we'll find him."

That didn't bring much relief to the room.

"You'll all be excusing me," she said. "I'm needing to change out of these clothes that, I'm told, stink of the Thames on a hot day."

She made her way through the press of people toward the corridor. A few lighthearted comments were made about her odor. She did her best to respond in kind, not wanting to weigh them down when they'd already been through plenty of difficulty.

She lit a candle in her room and closed the door. A couple of bedrolls were stretched out, which made sense. They'd all be sharing space with so many people under one roof. Her mind spun as she took off every layer of sewer-infused clothing. Had the other safe house actually been found, or had Four-Finger Mike simply stumbled onto the area? Would the Protector spill any secrets other than hers? What price would Fitz pay when his lies on her behalf were discovered? Where in the blasted blazes were her missing Dreadfuls?

The water in the washbowl was frigid, but she didn't overly care. The smell of sewage needed to be dealt with. She soaped and washed every inch of her, then set to addressing her hair. She'd be miserably cold the rest of the night with her hair damp, but it was a far sight better than continuing to smell like she did.

She was in her nightdress, tying her sewer clothes up in a canvas bag, when a light rap sounded on her door.

"Are you done addressing the sewer smell?" Brogan asked from the other side.

"I am, sure enough. Let yourself in."

Brogan entered and immediately closed the door. He'd something private to discuss, it seemed. She had far too many possible topics to guess at which one he'd broach first.

So she picked one. "Who'll be staying in here?"

"We'd reckoned on Vera and Licorice and Very Merry."

She nodded. "Vera'll need the bed. She'd be in too much pain if she sleeps on the floor."

"'Twas one of the things I wanted to talk with you about, ask you if you'd mind giving it over to her."

"You don't even need to ask, Brog. She's a sister to me; I'd never leave her to suffer." She tossed the canvas bag and its contents against the wall near the door.

"Do you think you'll ever rid those of the smell?" Brogan asked, motioning to the bag.

She shook her head. "I suspect they'll have to be burned."

"Good thing they're ugly."

Móirín tossed him the annoyed-older-sister look she'd been using since they were children. "Good thing *you're* ugly."

He bumped her shoulder with his, something *he'd* done since they were children. But it wasn't as lighthearted and teasing as usual. There was a heaviness to him she couldn't ignore.

"You'll crush yourself under whatever it is that's weighing on you," she said. "Best spill it."

Brogan tucked his hands in his trouser pockets, eyeing her with hesitation.

"We've been telling each other everything all our lives," she said. "No point stopping now."

"Have we, though?" He shook his head. "I was tying myself in knots, trying not to lie to you about my work with the DPS, drowning in guilt that I was hiding something so significant from you. And then I discover, only because we were in danger, that you've been hiding from me the fact that you knew all along I was in the DPS, that 'twas a sticky point for me that I couldn't tell you, and that you were the blasted Dread Master the whole time. Why didn't you tell me?"

He sounded hurt. Deeply hurt. Not terribly unlike Fitz had.

"I was already asking you to carry a heavy secret, Brogan. I couldn't ask you to carry another. I promised our parents I'd look out for you."

"I made the same promise, Móirín. And you're making it terribly hard for me to keep it."

"Only Fletcher ever knew my role in the DPS," Móirín reminded him.

"The night we fled from the Kincaid's mark, Stone didn't seem at all surprised when you more or less confessed you were running the show. I'd wager you told him. My father-in-law looked as though he'd pieced together a few things he'd already known, so he likely knew more than I did. Even Parkington wasn't shocked."

She hadn't told Fitz, but, thinking back, he had seemed to know she was more than a mere messenger or informant for the DPS. He'd been privy to enough things the past few weeks to've sorted it out. More than Brogan had been.

"I was trying to keep you safe," she said. "And, in the end, you weren't. 'Tis another thing I got wrong."

"You're not yourself tonight, Móirín." He set his hands on her arms, studying her. "What's knocked your feet out from under you?"

"A few too many missteps."

"Considering you were traversing the sewers, *missteps* would be no small thing." The attempt at humor was appreciated.

"While I'm making confessions," she said, "I should tell you my income hasn't come just from cleaning these past years. I've also been writing penny dreadfuls under a few different names."

He smiled. "I twigged that you're Chauncey Finnegan."

"Twigged?" She actually managed a laugh. "You've been spending too much time with a certain woman from Southwark. She's making you sound like a South Londoner."

"If I told Vera that people think I sound like a Londoner, she'd laugh both of us right back across the Irish Sea."

"And that wouldn't end well, would it?"

He shook his head. "'Twouldn't at that." Brogan sat on her bed and motioned her over. "I'm enjoying 'Posie and Pru.' I'd not have realized it was yours if you hadn't named half the characters after people we knew in Ireland. O'Reilly. Flanagan. Brennan. Even our friend Morris from our days living on the Dublin streets."

She didn't realize she'd done that. "I've been rushed on this one. Didn't have time to *twig* more creative names." She sat on the bed, her legs tucked up next to her. "I should tell you that Parkington knows I'm a fugitive. He's been assigned the Maeve O'Donald case and, tonight, pieced together that I'm her."

"What's he mean to do about it?" Brogan asked.

"He said he weren't going to turn me in. He even told a bouncer to keep another constable from knowing who I was. But he's in a tight spot now. If any of the other detectives sorts out what he has, he'll be in the same sort of trouble you will: helping a criminal hide from the law."

"You two seemed chummy the night you had supper with us. Vera wondered if perhaps . . ." Brogan let the sentence dangle, but she knew what he'd left unsaid.

"I think there was some of that starting," she confessed. "But it couldn't ever come to anything. He's the law, and I'm running from it. Add to that the fact that I have a criminal mastermind dedicated to destroying me and anyone connected to me; this is no time for falling in love."

"Aye, but the heart doesn't pay much heed to a person's calendar, does it? Simply does what it wants to do whenever it wants to do it."

In yet another show of emotion she didn't usually allow herself, Móirín reached over and squeezed her brother's hand. "Have I told you how happy I am that you and Vera found each other? That your hearts did what they wanted when they wanted and that you're happy? Have I told you how much that means to me?"

His familiar and reassuring smile eased some of her ever-present tension. "You have."

"And are you meaning to be angry with me forever over the secrets I've kept from you?"

He gave her shoulder a shove. "Where's the fun in not being angry with m'sister when I've a good reason to be?"

Brogan had always had a knack for lifting her spirits. Heaven knew she needed it just then.

"Will you swear to me you'll stay in here where it's safe, until we can sort out where the Tempest is hiding the people she's snatching? Until I can stop her?"

"If you were asking only for me, I'd tell you to go to the devil and do whatever I wanted." He smiled tenderly. "But I won't put Vera in danger. I'll stay in here with her until it's safe again."

"And will you do me another favor?" Móirín asked.

"If you'll do me one."

Curse her emotions that were refusing to stay entirely tucked away. "Brogan Donnelly, I'd do anything in the world for you."

"I know," he said without his usual teasing. "You're the best of sisters. The very best."

"Will you think really hard about where these blasted 'tunnels' are that the Tempest is filling up with our Dreadfuls? I *have* to find them, but I fear I've lost what was a partner-in-stopping-crime."

"Parkington?" Brogan guessed.

"Everything went so wrong." She sighed. "I probably should've told him sooner who I was, but I think I always knew it'd end like this."

"That brings me to the favor I'm asking of you." Brogan hopped off the bed, keeping his gaze on her. "Direct some of your famous Irish stubbornness at that blue-bottle and don't give up on him. I've not ever seen anyone look at a person the way he looked at you and there not be something in it."

"What do you mean?"

He shook his head. "You're not thick. You know the answer." On that declaration, he left the room, abandoning her to her heavy heart and spinning thoughts.

CHAPTER 18

Fitz dreamed about Móirín Donnelly. Or, rather, he had a nightmare. He dreamed she was snatched up by the Tempest, tossed into the sewers, and he couldn't get to her no matter what he tried.

That feeling of horrified helplessness dogged his heels all the way to Scotland Yard. Knowing she was wanted by both the Dublin and London police, and that she was chasing the most dangerous criminal either city had ever known, he couldn't convince himself the threat had been left behind when he'd awoken.

"There's a great deal in the report that ain't at all true. You might've eventually caught 'Maeve O'Donald,' but you'd've been doing it without knowing the whole truth."

Móirín's final declaration the night before hadn't left his thoughts. But she'd piked off before explaining what that "whole truth" might be. Before explaining why she'd not told him sooner.

He could understand why she'd kept the secret when they'd first known each other. But the past few weeks, he'd thought things had changed between them.

"Parkington. There you are." Sergeant Cowden somehow

sounded both pleased and annoyed to see him. Odd. Wheatley was usually the grumbletonian in the group.

"I know I'm arriving later in the morning than usual." Fitz couldn't think of any other complaint Cowden might have. "But I were out blasted late following a trail. I'd argue that earns me a bit of sleep this morning."

"I'm not concerned about your schedule," Cowden said firmly. "Did you nab the Protector last night?"

"Oi. I were out following whispers that the toshers were active. My path crossed his in a lucky accident."

"When did you leave the station where he was being held?" Cowden seemed more than casually interested in the answer.

"About three o'clock this morning. Why're you so curious?"

Detective Toft was in the room as well, listening with interest.

"The Protector never arrived at Newgate," Cowden said.

"Is he still at the station?"

Cowden shook his head. "Wheatley went to collect him and make the transfer, but he weren't there. Constables said he'd already been moved. But Newgate never got him."

"He's gone?"

"Escaped, but he clearly had help."

Dash it. "Wheatley said he'd already been taken? Have we accounted for the person who moved him?"

With a pointed look, Cowden said, "We have *now*."

There was no point denying what was being implied. "The prisoner was still in the cell when I left the station at three this morning. The constables on duty had specific instructions to send word here and request a sergeant or inspector make the transfer."

"That request arrived. Wheatley volunteered. The Protector weren't there when he arrived."

It didn't make the least sense. "It'd be the same constables who were there when I left last night. Let's ask them who it was that moved the prisoner. I can say for sure and certain they'll tell you it weren't me."

"But Wheatley said—" Toft began.

"I don't give a toss what Wheatley said. He's made it clear these last weeks that he'd do anything to see me in the suds. I suspect that includes lying. We don't have long before the Protector's trail goes cold. We can stand here arguing about whether I'd let the vermin escape after risking my neck to bring him in, or we can find out the truth and try to catch him before he disappears for good."

"Wheatley does seem to have a chalk against you," Toft said.

"Oi." Fitz looked at Cowden. "You've heard him rail against me without reason."

Acknowledgment tugged at the man's face.

"Has Newgate confirmed, independent of Wheatley, that the Protector never arrived?" Fitz asked.

Cowden nodded.

"Then there're only a few possibilities." Fitz kept his anger from his voice, knowing Cowden responded better to reason and logic than emotion. "Someone else claimed the prisoner, and the constables, who've no reason to do so, lied about who. Or Wheatley, who has ample reason, lied about who. Or, and I'm hoping this ain't the case, Wheatley *did* claim the prisoner but didn't deliver him to Newgate like he was meant to and invented a story about what happened to him."

When neither Cowden nor Toft immediately denied the possibility that Wheatley'd been lying through his teeth, or even that he might've let a prisoner escape, Fitz felt his suspicions weren't entirely baseless.

"Has Wheatley come back here?" Fitz asked.

Cowden shook his head. "He sent word that he's on his way to meet with Sir Richard Mayne."

Blimey. "He's meeting with the commissioner?"

"And likely telling him these same whiskers," Toft said. "He'll likely be believed, too."

"Seems he's after more than getting you tossed out of Scotland Yard. If Sir Richard believes him, you'll likely be the one headed to Newgate," Cowden added.

Deuce take it all. "I need to get to that station and get the actual story."

"I'll go," Toft said. "If Wheatley's already turned Sir Richard's opinion, you'll be watched for there."

"It'll be past noon before we get there," Cowden said. "The constables who were there this morning when Wheatley would've gone by won't be there. Their shift'll be up. But we need to find them. They might be in danger."

"I do think the Protector'll play least in sight for now," Fitz said.

"Oi," Cowden spoke tightly, "but I don't know that the Raven will."

"The Raven? What's that scaly cove going to do from inside Newgate?"

Cowden hooked an eyebrow. "He escaped. This morning."

"From Newgate? That ain't likely to happen without help."

"Oi, and you are known to have visited him in recent weeks." Cowden's words were less an accusation and more of a warning.

"Wheatley might very well be lying to Sir Richard about me having something to do with the Raven's escape too." Fitz rubbed at his face. The situation was growing worse. "What if the commissioner believes him?"

Cowden turned to Toft. "I'm sending you to find the constables on duty last night. Their addresses should be on record here at Scotland Yard. Find those men. Find out what happened this morning. But remember, they might be under threat, and lying because of that."

Toft nodded. "I'll sniff it out."

Cowden turned to Fitz. "Stay out of sight for a bit. Toft and I will dig into this."

"I've a place I can tuck myself." He pushed out a breath. "I'm well-known to most of the constables in the divisions this side of the Thames. If you need anyone else digging through this, any number of 'em will help you." Never before had he been more grateful for the connections he'd fostered between divisions while working additional shifts throughout London.

With almost as much stealth as he'd needed to get Brogan and Vera and their guests to safety the night of the dinner party, Fitz slipped from Scotland Yard. He needed to get out of sight. But first, he needed to warn Lord Chelmsford. The Raven and the Protector were both associates of the Tempest. And if she also had a sergeant in the Detective Department in her pocket, then the baron needed to be on alert.

He took quieter roads all the way to Eaton Square, not even stopping to have a look at his former house. A constable was outside Lord Chelmsford's place, as always. This time it was Evered, a reliable, keen-eyed fellow.

Fitz skipped past asking for a report. Time weren't on his side. "Two monstrous criminals escaped this morning, and both are connected to the trouble that sent Lord Chelmsford from his home. Be devilish careful."

"Which criminals?"

"The Raven and the Protector."

"I ain't heard of the Raven, but I know about the Protector. If they're birds of a feather, then we're in a bad loaf, sure as you're standing there."

"And there's reason to believe someone in our ranks is working with them." Fitz didn't think he needed to say who just yet, seeing as he didn't know for certain if Wheatley was anything more than vindictive. "Guard up, Evered."

"We'll stay alert," he promised. "But if you came to drop a word in the baron's ear, you should know he ain't here."

Nervousness tiptoed over him. "Where'd he go?"

"Had a meeting of some sort. Said it were too important to miss." Evered held up a hand to hold off Fitz's next question. "Durand went with him."

"Did anyone see him leave, do you suppose?" Fitz asked.

"Likely not. They piked off by way of the servants' door."

That was wise. "At the back or the side?"

"Back," Evered said. "Housekeeper said the side entrance is poky. Don't hardly ever use it."

"Keep an eye on that door," Fitz said. "Rarely used doors are often the ones criminals choose."

Evered nodded.

"This person among us who's working both sides of the coin," Fitz said, "he's doing all he can to smear me with his sludge."

"*You?*" Evered snorted. "No one who knows you at all would believe that."

"I hope you're right. But keep your ears open on that score as well."

"Will do, guv." Evered nodded firmly.

It was all Fitz could do at the moment. The baron weren't

home, and hanging about only increased the risk Fitz'd be seen by Wheatley or someone sent by Sir Richard. He didn't dare go back to his flat for clothes and such; that'd be one of the first places he was looked for.

He was about to walk away when a man emerged from the side of the house, a box of tools under his arm.

"Repairman?" Fitz asked, jutting his chin in the man's direction.

"Mangle was giving the servants trouble again."

The mangle? The man came into better view, and Fitz knew it was him, his one-time landlord.

He followed the man's path, catching up to him in front of the next house and walking alongside him. "Mr. Cook?"

The repairman slowed as he looked at Fitz. "Do I know you?" He had the smack-gums diction of one without teeth left. A common thing amongst those his age. And his breath rattled, common among far too many ages in London.

"You do, though you might not remember. My grandfather and I lived on Vandon Street. You were our landlord."

Mr. Cook shook his head. "I ain't owned that building in years."

"Twenty, in fact," Fitz said.

The man kept walking; so did Fitz. He needed to get himself into hiding, but he couldn't miss this chance to learn the truth about his grandfather.

"If it were up to me," the man said, "I'd still be doing that work rather'n dragging this bag of aching bones all over. Would be, too, but I had a tenant what didn't pay his rent. I ought to've tossed him out, but I felt bad for him. He kept saying he'd have it in a few days. Said that for weeks, and I do think he were trying."

"He never paid?"

Mr. Cook shook his head. "Couldn't pay my own bills because of it. Lost the building. The bloke what snatched it up intended to toss the man out that same day, already had new tenants lined up, but when he went to evict him, the man had already hopped the twig."

Tossed him out that same day, right when Mr. Cook had left as well. Blimey, but that was too much of a coincidence. "What was that man's name? The one what didn't pay his rent?"

"Parkington," Mr. Cook said.

Grandfather had never said he were having money troubles. And he'd not have piked off without saying a word. He wouldn't have.

"The ol' toast seemed a decent enough fellow, but . . ."

Fitz wasn't certain he wanted to know how Mr. Cook would've finished the sentence, but he knew he needed to. "But *what?*"

"But he ruined my life. Makes it difficult to have good thoughts for the man."

In many ways, Grandfather had ruined Fitz's life too. But he didn't struggle to think well of him. Fitz loved him. Yet it sounded like he'd run from his debts with no thought for his grandson.

Why was it people were always doing that to him? Running off and leaving him to pick up the pieces? Even Móirín had in a way. He'd realized what she'd been keeping from him, but rather than staying and explaining and helping him sort it out, she'd left.

Mr. Cook kept walking, his pace brisk despite his shuffling steps.

Fitz shoved his hands in his pockets and turned down an obliging alleyway.

Grandfather had shabbed off. He'd filched on his rent,

broken his promises, then left Fitz to pick up the pieces. Twenty years of searching, and this was what he'd found. Disappointment. Disillusionment. Discouragement.

His mind hardly made an accounting of where his feet took him. He was paying attention enough to know he weren't being followed, and no one he passed was someone he ought to be wary of. But he was all the way to Móirín's safe house before realizing where he'd gone.

Was as good a spot as any to tuck himself away, he supposed. That was, of course, assuming he'd be welcome.

He went through the usual steps. A single knock. Said "Parky's a right rubbish blue-bottle" when the slot slid open. Stepped inside and waited for the locks to be turned before candles and lanterns were relit around the room.

It was full. People he knew had been kept elsewhere appeared to be making their home here now. Hang being welcome, there might not be space.

In the midst of all the people, he spotted Móirín. She stood at the head of the corridor that led to her room. And she was watching him with as much uncertainty as he felt.

He set his hat and coat on a nail already in use—there weren't any empty ones—and made his way through the crowd. She watched his approach, but he couldn't read her expression for anything.

Fitz stopped in front of her. "Have you got room here for another?"

Slowly, a smile spread over her face, and her eyes lit. But rather than simply answering, she did something far more shocking: she threw her arms around him.

POSIE AND PRU
DETECTIVES FOR HIRE

by Chauncey Finnegan

Chapter Five

"Morris, rush to Mrs. Brennan's house and see if the poor little dog is there," Posie said. "I suspect it will be."

Morris didn't hesitate. Posie and Pru would do best not to as well.

"To the house, Pru!" Posie pointed the way with her out-side cane, and the two of them hobbled at their fastest pace—somewhere between a slow stroll and a moderate walk—back toward the house. Being a detective was exhausting. Who knew there would be so much rushing about!

"Do you truly think Mrs. Brennan stole young Mr. Flanagan's dog? What a horrible thing to do." Pru shook her head. "Which, come to think of it, is rather fitting. She's not a very pleasant person."

"I suspect she didn't steal the dog so much as she took it with her so it wouldn't give her away."

"Give her away for *what*, Posie?"

"For murdering Mr. Flanagan, of course."

Pru emitted a little "Oooh" sound of realization. "Solving

the bit about the dog really did help solve the bit about the murder."

"I suppose it did."

They reached the house and found the terrace unlocked. They went through the doors and down the corridor. Unfortunately, no one was there to change their outside shawl and cane for those meant for the indoors. If not for the urgency of their errand, they might have sat down and waited for someone to sort all that out.

By the time they reached the library, where Posie hoped young Mr. Flanagan would still be, they were both a touch out of breath and more than a touch exhausted. Their entrance pulled the attention of the three people in the room: the master of the house, Mrs. O'Reilly, and Mrs. Brennan, whose presence was extremely helpful. They'd not need to go running about the house yet again attempting to find her.

Posie held up a hand to stave off any questions as she hadn't breath enough to answer. Pru had already dropped into an obliging chair. Posie lowered herself slowly; she hadn't her indoor cane, after all.

"Mr. Flan—" No. She still hadn't breath enough yet.

Pru seemed to have regained some of hers. "We think we found your dog."

"Truly?" The poor man looked as though he might grow emotional. "I've been so worried."

"That's not—" Heavens, Posie wasn't fit enough for running about being a detective. "—not the most significant—" Another deep breath. "—most significant thing we've learned."

"Can this wait?" Mrs. Brennan asked. "I was here before you, seeing to business of my own."

"Our business involves you." Posie stood, though her cane was the wrong one for doing so. "Mr. Flanagan, you shouldn't hire Mrs. Brennan to be on your household staff."

"Why on earth not?" Mrs. Brennan demanded.

"Because she stole your dog!" Pru said.

"Again, Pru," Posie said, "this is not the most pressing matter."

"Oh, yes. I forgot." Pru grinned at the room in general. "Because she murdered Mr. Flanagan."

Posie shook her head. "You haven't the first idea how to build a moment."

"I was meant to be more mysterious, wasn't I?"

"It would have been difficult to be *less*."

"Begging your pardons," Mr. Flanagan said calmly but earnestly, "please return to the topic of my father's death and your belief that this woman is connected to it."

"I take exception to—" Mrs. Brennan objected but was shushed by Mrs. O'Reilly and cut off by a wave of Mr. Flanagan's hand.

To Mrs. O'Reilly, knowing she would understand the significance, Posie said, "The person in the mirror was wearing white."

"Oh." Mrs. O'Reilly's mouth remained in a perfect *O* long after the sound dissipated.

"And people have said for years that you and Mrs. Brennan look alike," Pru said.

Mr. Flanagan eyed the two women and nodded his agreement.

"The late Mr. Flanagan wouldn't hire her, which she clearly very much wanted. Having a new master of the house would mean she could try again." Posie warmed to the subject. "And hiding in the room as she did would startle anyone—and being startled has been known to kill people."

"But it was the crash of the goblet that brought Jane into the room," Pru said. "Maybe the crash was what startled him so entirely."

"I think he dropped the goblet *because* he was startled," Posie insisted. "If you saw Mrs. Brennan unexpectedly hanging about the corners of a room, you would drop everything you were holding."

"And then die." Pru nodded emphatically.

"I do not scare people to death," Mrs. Brennan insisted.

"Startle," Posie corrected. "You *startle* them to death. There is a subtle but important difference."

"Oh, yes," Pru said. "If you scared them to death, that would likely mean you were doing something frightening. But you can startle a person simply by being something they aren't expecting, like emerging from a shadow or talking suddenly into the silence or being odd looking."

"I didn't kill him by being ugly," Mrs. Brennan said sharply.

"Then how did you kill him?" Mr. Flanagan asked quickly and casually, though he was watching her very closely.

"Poison in—" She clamped her mouth shut.

Poison in the goblet. Oh. That did make more sense than startling him to death. But Posie took pride in having identified the correct murderer and giving Mrs. O'Reilly the peace of mind that comes from knowing she *wasn't* the murderer.

It was in the very next moment that Morris rushed into the room, holding tight to Mr. Flanagan's missing dog. "He were tied up at Mrs. Brennan's, just like Mrs. Poindexter and Mrs. Dwerryhouse said he'd be."

The dog caught sight of Mrs. Brennan, and he immediately began barking and growling.

"The dog doesn't like her," Pru said. "And he was barking quite a lot at knowing she was inside the house startling people."

"*Murdering* people, Pru."

"Yes." Pru nodded. "That, too."

"Morris, take the poor thing out into the garden," Mr. Flanagan said. "Mrs. O'Reilly, have someone fetch the squire."

Realizing their work was done, and done well, Posie and Pru made to take their leave as well. Mr. Flanagan stopped them, still keeping an eye on the murderer.

"How can I thank you for managing to sort this out, and to do so in such a short time?"

"Simple enough, Mr. Flanagan. Should you hear of anyone else in need of the services of two very fine detectives, send them our way," Posie said.

"I will."

"And tell them we are very good at dogs," Pru added.

CHAPTER 19

óirín hadn't the first idea what possessed her to toss her arms around Fitzgerald Parkington. Last she'd seen him, he'd been miffed with her over a few key things she'd not told him. He'd also been in the process of locking up a criminal with all the authority of a blue-bottle who'd earned the respect of his peers. Keeping her distance from him was best; she knew it was. And yet . . .

"This is a friendlier welcome than I was anticipating," Fitz said, his arms as fully wrapped around her as hers were around him. "I'll not deny I'm needing it just now."

"You looked like you did," she said, drawing in the scent of almond and rosemary. "And you smell a fair bit better than you did when last I saw you."

"So do you, love."

Love. She was creating trouble for herself, trouble she'd pay for soon enough. But hearing him call her that again, while his arms held fast to her, fitting her so perfectly against him . . . Life hadn't offered her many perfect moments. She meant to relish this one a bit longer.

But the crowded room had other ideas. A cacophony of

quiet "ooh"s and "hey"s were tossed in Móirín and Fitz's direction.

Brogan even added, "I'd tell you to unhand m'sister, but I think this here's brilliant." He sat with his hand in Vera's.

Fletcher had an arm around Elizabeth. Celia sat with Stone, leaning against his shoulder. Gemma and Barnabus looked awful cozy. But it was the sight of Ana, alone and heartbroken, that reminded Móirín she hadn't time for dreaming of what the others had. People were missing and in danger. That had to be her priority.

She slipped her arms back, taking a step away. Fitz winked at her, which immediately brought heat to her cheeks. Blast him. She did enjoy it, though.

"If you're needing a safe place and don't mind being packed in, you're welcome to stay here," she told him.

"Why're there so many now?" He looked around the crowded room.

"The safe house they were at was compromised."

Concern entered his eyes. "Everyone got out?"

She nodded. "And they're all relieved that the Protector is locked up. Now to get Four-Finger Mike in the same situation."

He dropped his voice and said, "We've a problem on that score, Móirín."

There was no mistaking his tone. Something had happened. She took his hand and pulled him into the heart of the parlor with the others. If there was a problem, everyone in this house needed to know.

"Ears perked, all," she said. "We have trouble."

"Is that what you're calling Parkington now?" Fletcher tossed back with a laugh.

"You should hear what I'm calling *you* now," she answered.

Elizabeth, ever the voice of reason, chimed in. "Why is it you need to hide, Parkington?"

"The Protector escaped while being transferred from a local station to Newgate."

Blast it.

"And the Raven escaped Newgate itself this morning as well."

"The Raven escaped?" Ana's eyes widened.

Fitz wouldn't understand her reaction, but Móirín knew. Ana and Hollis had helped capture the Raven. They were the primary reason he'd landed in Newgate to begin with.

"We're absolutely certain both the Protector and the Raven were helped by someone in the Metropolitan Police," Fitz continued. "There's a sergeant in the Detective Department who's been gnawing at me since my first day. I assumed he just weren't best pleased to have a new arrival, though his hostility was too sharp for that. I told him from the beginning I meant to search out the Tempest. Realizing now he is working *for* the Tempest, his treatment of me ain't such a mystery."

How were they supposed to bring down a criminal who had allies in the Metropolitan Police?

"Are you being ensnared by this fella?" Stone asked.

"Oi. He was meeting with the commissioner this morning and, I've no doubt, laid all this trouble at my feet. There're some among the detectives and constables who're investigating it on my behalf. But until we can root it all out, it's best I not be easily found for a while."

"Then you've come to the right place," Brogan said.

Ana'd gone horribly pale. Celia had clearly noticed; she moved to Ana's side and put an arm around her shoulders.

"Put your minds to tunnels," Móirín told the room. "We're

looking for something that could be described that way, accessible to the public but well hidden, large enough for keeping several people inside." She looked over the group. "Between all of us, I don't think there's a corner of London we don't know, which means between all of us, we know every place the Tempest could be talking about. Make a list." Móirín held Ana's gaze. "We're going to find them. I swear to you."

Ana nodded. Celia squeezed her shoulders. Bless Celia.

Móirín turned to Fitz. "Down the corridor for a minute."

"Best go," Fletcher said to him. "She'll start calling you something other than 'Trouble.'"

Fitz didn't seem to need the push. He walked at her side, even took her hand before they'd reached her room at the end of the corridor.

With the door closed, she dropped his hand and turned to face him fully. "Let me explain what happened in Dublin five years ago."

He shook his head. "You don't have to."

"I know, but I *need* to. I need you to know all of it so when we've taken down the Tempest you can decide what needs to happen next."

He watched her closely but didn't give away his thoughts.

"I worked at the Guinness factory like a lot of people in Dublin. I gave a false name because I'd been working at Jameson and wasn't certain they wouldn't look askance at someone switching breweries like that."

"The name you gave was Maeve O'Donald?" Fitz guessed.

She nodded. "There was one overseer at Guinness who felt himself entitled to a lot of things, mostly to whatever it was he wanted from the women he oversaw. Those who refused, he fired."

Fitz nodded, apparently knowing the sort of man they were discussing without Móirín needing to explain in more detail.

"I managed to outmaneuver him enough that I didn't lose m'job and he didn't get what he demanded. That only made him angrier, and the anger made him more violent. One day, he decided he was going to get what he felt he was owed, or he was going to kill me, and he didn't seem to care overly much which one it was. I suspect he meant to kill me either way. I fought back, and in the fight that ensued, I killed him, though that hadn't been my aim. It was, however, the literal only way to survive. My only option."

"And the Peelers too often don't care about that," Fitz nodded. "Especially when it's a woman without a groat to her name."

He understood. She released a tense breath. "I ain't a killer, not in the way they paint me. Far too many people are more upset at the inconvenience of acknowledging the woman who had to fight for her life than they are at the man whose horrific behavior required her to fight in the first place. If we can be dismissed or painted as villains or told we need to be more accommodating or more forgiving, then people don't have to do anything and can still keep thinking of themselves as compassionate. If there's no one in need of protecting, it's easy to paint oneself as a hero."

Fitz stepped away from the closed door and closer to her, holding her hand tenderly to his chest. "I'm beginning to understand why you kept me at arm's length for so long."

"And the Dread Penny Society's actions haven't always been entirely legal," she added.

"Oi, but I knew that already."

"You didn't know my role in the group, though. Few people did. Few people do now."

He kissed her hand. "You're their leader, their Dread Master."

She nodded. "A criminal leading a group of criminals. Seems the Tempest wasn't so wrong saying we were more or less the same person, she and I. Anytime I let m'self think on it, I find more proof that she's right, and I hate it."

"The Tempest is trying to destroy people." He clearly meant it as a defense of her.

"And *I* am trying to destroy her and those who work with her."

"But they're criminals."

"So am I."

"She's a murderer."

Móirín gave him a dry look.

"I don't consider you one," he said, "so you can tuck that expression away. Defending yourself ain't the same as killing people because they weren't useful, which is the reason she gave for killing the Mastiff. Very different, Móirín."

"I wish I could feel like it was."

He slipped his other arm around her. "Then set your mind to this: the Tempest is doing all she can to destroy the Dreadfuls, while *you* are doing all you can to protect them."

"Some protection." She leaned into him, and he held her close. "They're disappearing, Fitz. And I can't find them."

He released a slow, deep breath.

"What're you sighing for, then?" she asked.

"It's good hearing you call me Fitz again. Last night I was 'Detective Constable Parkington.'"

"Well, last night *I* was Maeve O'Donald, which made things awkward between us."

"If you'd stayed a bit longer, we could've sorted it out," he said.

She looked up at him, resting her hand against his cheek. She wasn't usually an affectionate person but touching him was reassuring. "I won't put you in that bind again."

He turned his head enough to kiss her fingers. "For what it's worth, I'm enjoying *this* bind. Though I do have another question."

"What's that?" She couldn't stop the smile on her face.

"Being a Dreadful means writing penny serials, and I've my suspicions you're doing so as Chauncey Finnegan."

She nodded.

"As you're currently writing a story about detectives, I have to ask if either of them women is meant to be like me?"

"To sort that out you'd have to ask yourself a very important question." She spoke in a husky whisper, tilting her head enough to be within a breath of his lips.

"What question is that?" His tone matched hers.

"How do you feel about dogs?"

A knock sounded at the door. That's what came of being in a flat full to bursting with people.

Fitz stepped away enough to open the door but not entirely release his hold on her. Celia stood on the other side.

"Bricklayers Arms station in Southwark," Celia said. "It's a goods station now, no passengers, and there're plenty of train tunnels and dim corridors."

"It can be reached by anyone, but no one gads about the place," Fitz said, looking at Móirín. "Seems worth checking."

"Who knows Southwark best?" Móirín asked.

Celia shrugged. "Stone and I do. Gemma does, but she's supposed to be dead."

"Best not have her wandering about," Móirín agreed.

"Ana, I suspect, will refuse to be left behind," Celia said.

"Fletcher and Elizabeth as well, I'd wager," Fitz said.

"You think Elizabeth'll go?" Móirín didn't think Elizabeth had done much to make it obvious she was more adventurous than her Society facade would indicate.

"She and Ana might've been born fine ladies, but they've shown themselves unwilling to be left out when the time comes to do the difficult work," Fitz said. "I don't think we'll be able to leave either of them behind."

"*We?*" Móirín repeated. "Aren't you supposed to be staying out of sight?"

"We all are," he said. "Don't mean any of us are giving up the chase."

"Promise you'll undertake that chase safely?" Móirín asked.

His smile turned mischievous. "I make no promises."

She shrugged and walked past him to the door. "Then neither do I."

THE QUEEN AND THE KNAVE

by Mr. King

Installment VI
in which the Queen discovers things
of a most Distressing nature!

Though oblivious to all that had occurred at the feats of skill and strength competition, Eleanor was hardly idle whilst Reynard was away. She felt unequal to the weight of being queen and suspected others also took little comfort in the idea of her on the throne. She wanted them to have confidence in her. She wanted the kingdom to feel safe and well looked after. Discovering their monarch was a three-foot weasel-like creature during daylight hours would only add to their doubts.

The week of the Unification Ceremony was always precarious, with all the kingdom holding its collective breath, praying peace would hold. She could not risk that failing. She would not.

It took doing and a great deal of patience, but she was eventually able to pull out and open a book entitled *On the Creation, Implementation, and Elimination of Spells, Curses, and*

Enchantments she found amongst the stacks of jars and pots and other household things.

Eleanor was pleased to discover her assumption on the matter of her literacy was correct. Because she still thought and experienced life as herself, she felt certain she would still be able to read. She'd not felt as energetic today as she had the day before in pine marten form. She was weaker, more worn down. It was the result of worry and the strain of transformations, she didn't doubt. She had energy enough, though, to search the book Reynard's mother had kept in her enchanted cottage. In it, she hoped to find answers and solutions.

Turning the pages proved rather difficult. Her arms were so different in this form than in her natural one. And though she could retract her pine marten claws, she couldn't do so entirely, and she didn't want to damage the book. That slowed her search but did not thwart it entirely.

The book, she discovered, was organized in the same manner Reynard had explained the curse placed on her. Explanations and information regarding manifestations in the first section, how the magic manifested in the second. The third section discussed the impact of the magic. The fourth was dedicated to the wording of endings and what that meant for lifting a curse, ending an enchantment, or countering a spell.

Though she wanted to know how to end the curse placed upon her, Eleanor began with the first section of the book, searching each page until she found a heading that read quite familiarly.

Spells, Curses, and Enchantments Beginning with Variations upon "When the sun lights the sky"

It is a common misunderstanding that the manifestation of magic invoked with these words will be in place during daylight hours regardless of conditions in the sky. While that is generally true, there are notable exceptions.

Exceptions were precisely what she needed. She skimmed over the text devoted to wording that substituted "if" for "when" or included additional specifics such as "when the sun would normally" or "whenever the sun lights the sky, however dimly."

At last her pine marten eyes settled upon the paragraph delineating limitations to curses that used precisely the wording Dezmerina had chosen.

Should magic be implemented with the manifestation declaration of "whenever the sun lights the sky," even should the portion of the sky in which the sun's location be specified, there are rare instances when the magic will not manifest during what would, by all estimations, be deemed daylight hours. A combination of thick clouds and heavy smoke can block out enough of the sun to trick the magic into relinquishing its hold for a time. Locations with particularly high mountains to the east will see the magic delayed until the sun is higher than the mountaintops. Likewise, locations with mountains to the west will see the magic lose its grip once the sun has sunk below those mountaintops, making it last a shorter time than it would in a place without such mountains.

Neither of those things really applied in Eleanor's case. Amesby's mountains were to the north. And she could not imagine, even if clouds rolled in, there would be a fire of such enormous proportions as to block out the sun. It would be far too great a coincidence, and a tragic one at that.

This manifestation of magic can also be temporarily tricked into releasing its grip when a shadow crosses the sun, blocking its light and dimming the world. The sun still lights the sky, but the heart of the sun is covered, and the magic will believe the sun has fled.

A solar eclipse. But it would only lift the curse temporarily.

She needed to know how to end it entirely. That would be found in the fourth section of the book.

Her agility with her clawed paws was improving, but her energy was ebbing. Did pine martens always grow tired so quickly? She didn't think so. They were hunters, after all, needing to capture prey. Feeling as lethargic as she did would make her future efforts virtually impossible.

She searched through various wordings for final lines of curses and enchantments and spells until she found what she was looking for.

Spells, Curses, and Enchantments Ending with Declarations Regarding the Life of Those Involved

The curse had specifically mentioned life: both hers and Dezmerina's.

Several entries below the heading, Eleanor came upon the entry most closely resembling the curse she was living with.

Curses, spells, and enchantments which specify, in their
fourth line, the ebbing of a life rather than the ending of
one will still be lifted upon the death of the person referred
to. The difference is, that person will begin dying as a re-
sult of that magic and will, in time, succumb to it. That
death will end the curse, spell, or enchantment.

Her death would end the curse. But that death would not occur by accident or as the result of normal aging. The spell, itself, was killing her. It was likely why she was tired today, why she felt as though she was struggling more than usual.

She was dying.

There had to be another way to end the curse and save the kingdom that didn't require her death. And not merely because she didn't particularly want to die. There was no clear successor to the throne. The battles and chaos the curse, itself, would cause, would not end with the curse being lifted. Her death would not save her kingdom.

It was in the midst of this discouraging discovery that Reynard returned. He looked as disheartened as she felt. If only she'd also found a means of speaking while in this frustrating form she was forced to assume.

He spotted her on the floor of the cottage. "My mother's book. I hadn't even thought of it. Brilliant."

She didn't always feel brilliant. That he thought she was, even if only in that moment, was a wonderful thing. That she was dying was not nearly as wonderful.

Eleanor tapped her paw against the page directly atop the bit she'd been reading. Reynard's eyes slid over the page as he read.

He looked more saddened than surprised. "I consulted

with two people who are wise in the ways of magic. They said the same thing."

Eleanor leaned against his leg. She was both tired and discouraged and needed the momentary support.

"They did say that the last bit of the fourth line means Dezmerina's death would end the curse as well. But only her death or yours can accomplish it."

People had been trying for years on end to stop Dezmerina. As near as anyone knew, it was impossible. She was too powerful to kill and too feared for others to gather in anything approaching the numbers needed to have any chance of success against her.

Unable to simply tell Reynard what else she had discovered, Eleanor pawed the pages back, stopping when she reached the first entry she'd read. Once more, she pointed with her paw to the bit she needed him to read. And, once more, he did so without hesitation.

"An eclipse. You would temporarily transform back into yourself, long enough to address the barons and the people, to show them that Dezmerina's powers are not infallible, that there are gaps in what she can do, flaws in the spells she can cast. If they feel that defeating her is possible, they'll be more likely to try."

Eleanor nodded, knowing full well the movement looked odd in her current state.

"My mother did not study the sky. There will not be anything in this cottage that will allow us to predict when an eclipse might occur, or if one will happen before—"

He didn't finish the sentence. He didn't have to. They both knew full well that the curse was actively killing her.

Each day that passed, each moment, drew her closer to death, speeding her to her untimely demise.

But she hadn't time for dwelling on that. She knew of someone who could, with accuracy, determine the movement of celestial bodies, and who had, while her father was still alive, accurately predicted more than one eclipse. But curse her pine marten's voice, she could not speak to Reynard.

Eleanor turned pleading eyes on Reynard, tapping her leg anxiously, hoping to communicate with him.

Bless him, he understood rather quickly. "Do you know of someone familiar with the skies?"

She gave her best nod.

"Where do we find him?"

That was not a question she could answer with a nod or a shake of her pine marten head, which he realized quickly.

"At the palace?" he asked.

She shook her head.

"The village?"

She nodded.

"Let us go there, then. But I must warn you, fear has already taken hold of the kingdom. Dezmerina disrupted the competition today, issuing a warning to all. She declared that war is on the horizon, the queen has fled, and only those who side with Dezmerina will be protected by her. Once the Unification Ceremony begins tomorrow, she will allow no changing loyalties."

And, because no queen would arrive at the ceremony—at least not a queen in human form as the ceremony occurred during the day—that would be seen as confirmation of Dezmerina's declaration. It would usher in the start of the chaos and battles her curse promised.

The sorceress had, it seemed, thought of every aspect of her sordid spell.

What chance did a pine marten queen and a sentry guard truly have of defeating her?

CHAPTER 20

The terminus at Bricklayers Arms hadn't been used as a passenger station in the past fourteen years on account of the area being filled with people who hadn't money enough to take advantage of it. It sat quiet as a churchyard at night. Fortunately, the crowd of people who'd come along to search it were also nearly silent as they moved stealthily into the train yard.

Fitz hadn't expected Ana and Celia to be as furtive as they were proving. As far as he knew, they hadn't any prior experience with clandestine missions. But people often proved surprising.

They'd sorted out their approach before making the trek to Southwark. Stone and Celia would start in the northernmost goods shed, while Fitz and Móirín would begin in the southernmost, and they'd work their way to each other. Ana, Fletcher, and Elizabeth would check the corridors of the goods depot building. Corridors and train sheds weren't exactly tunnels, but they were similarly shaped, and the Tempest often spoke in riddles.

Moving in the dark, Fitz slipped into the largest of the depot sheds alongside Móirín. They tucked themselves beside the wall. Fitz opened a shutter on his dark lantern, creating a narrow beam of light unlikely to be seen by anyone mucking about outside. He aimed it along the side of the shed.

"This place is enormous," Móirín said quietly.

She weren't wrong. The area was one vast open building with a high ceiling and columns throughout holding up the roof. There were no doorways or smaller areas branching off.

"How the blazes would you hide people in here?" Móirín asked, echoing his thoughts exactly. "The workers'd see them the moment they arrived."

"Let's walk the perimeter," he said. "Maybe we ain't seeing something."

Crates sat alongside the tracks, empty and waiting for whatever would be unloaded the next day. Windows sat at regular intervals, arched at the top, but not even a shallow alcove hid within the walls. Everything was open and visible.

"'Tis looking more like a bad lead, this." Móirín slipped her hand in his as she glanced back at the shed they'd searched. "I'd guess the other sheds aren't much different than this'n."

"The depot building's still promising." Fitz adjusted his hand and threaded his fingers through hers. "'Tunnels' could refer to 'corridors.'"

"I don't know how much longer Ana can endure not knowing what happened to Hollis before she falls to bits." Móirín sounded unusually defeated.

"How much longer until *you* fall to bits?"

She turned a surprised gaze on him, one that quickly turned insulted. "I have never fallen to bits a day in my life, Parky."

"Parky?" He smiled at her. "I must be in trouble again."

"You're teasing me."

He shrugged. "I suppose."

Though she was attempting to maintain her annoyance, he saw amusement in her expression. It was fleeting, though, her gaze returning to the empty shed.

"She's so certain no one can outwit her. I'm beginning to think she might be right about that."

"She might not stop thinking, but you ain't one to stop looking."

"We're pitting her brains against my stubbornness, are we?"

"I know who I'd bet on in that battle." He let go of her hand and popped the shutters of the dark lantern closed. "Let's check the next shed."

But it proved more of the same, if a little smaller. Stone and Celia met them at the next shed and reported the same findings. Móirín walked ahead with Stone toward the depot building, talking quietly about strategy and the missing Dreadfuls.

"Móirín seems discouraged," Celia said to Fitz as they walked behind them.

"You've a knack for reading people. Maybe you ought to be a detective."

"I suspect I'd not be overly welcome at Scotland Yard."

It were a real shame how accurate that was. "Now that you know what Stone's neck-deep in when he's not writing his tales, do you mean to toss yourself into the adventures as well? Assuming we stop the Tempest, of course."

"We'll stop her," Celia said with conviction. "I refuse to believe anything different."

"Make certain Móirín sees your confidence, if you don't mind. I get the impression she's giving up."

"Do you actually think so?" Celia sounded doubtful. "Discouragement is different from surrender, i'n'it?"

Discouragement. That did fit what he was seeing in Móirín.

"How long do you think the Tempest'll hold on to her captives before growing tired of the game?" Celia asked.

"Let's hope a bit longer."

They met Fletcher, Elizabeth, and Ana in the shadows behind the depot building.

"Nothin'," Fletcher said. "Fewer hiding spots than an open field, and none of those held anything but dust and broken bits of crates. They ain't here, and it don't look like they ever was."

There weren't enough light to see how Ana was taking the disappointment. He could guess at Móirín's reaction. Frustrated, oi. But determined.

"Let's get back to the safe house," she said. "And be thinking of the next place to check. They're somewhere in this city, and we're going to find them."

"Don't sound like 'giving up' to me," Celia said as she walked past Fitz to Stone.

The group split as they left the rail yard, making their way back to Marylebone by different routes. Móirín and Fitz were making the trek together, taking a longer path than the others.

"We've a difficulty, Fitz."

"What's that?"

She moved closer to him as they walked. "We were checking corridors tonight because it made sense. But adding corridors to our search makes it impossible. Every house, every building has them. We've no means of searching them all."

"Wouldn't be a game to the Tempest if there were no chance of you discovering the hiding spot. I'd twig it ain't a randomly chosen 'tunnel.'"

Discouragement is different from surrender. She wasn't giving up, and that were worth a lot. And it told him not to get entirely discouraged either in the matter of so many things.

They walked on quietly, the cold night wind snatching at them.

"You remember that bloke I saw a couple weeks back, the landlord from when I still lived with my grandfather?"

"He was fixing something at Lord Chelmsford's," Móirín said.

"That's the fellow. I saw him again today. Talked to him, even."

"You did?" She looked up at him as they passed under a streetlamp.

"He said my grandfather weren't paying his rent. He lost the building, and my grandfather ran out on his debts."

"Who lost the building? Not your grandfather."

He shook his head. "Mr. Cook."

"Cook?" She repeated the name as if it were shocking.

Her interest in the name piqued his. "Oi."

"Flat-jawed smile? Wispy white hair only on the sides but a tuft in the middle? Heavy eyelids? Breath that wheezes?"

Fitz nodded. "Oi."

"First name Nolan?"

"I think that was his name." Blimey. "How do you know him?"

"I've been looking for him ever since we realized the Tempest was running London's criminal underbelly. The butler and caretaker at DPS headquarters, a man named Nolan Cook, disappeared that night after it was discovered he had been feeding her information all along."

"'Pon my sivvy." Fitz picked up his pace. "He has access to Lord Chelmsford's house. Even the constables I've stationed there know him as a trusted odd-job man. He can come and go as he pleases."

"Deuce take it."

They went from a swift walk to very nearly a run.

"Chelmsford's or the safe house first?" Fitz asked as they rushed.

"Safe house. We'd be fools to go alone to a place we know the Tempest has some control over."

Wise. "My constables are watching all entrances, even the ones that ain't never used. If Mr.— If Nolan tries bringing anyone else in, they'll be noticed."

"Have they been watching the never-used ones?" she asked.

"I mentioned it today."

"Why ain't it ever used?" Móirín asked.

"On account of the corridor's poky."

Móirín stopped, frozen in place. "Dark, narrow corridor, seldom used, but easily accessible by the right people."

He met her eye. "And it being at Lord Chelmsford's hideaway connects it to the Tempest." His pulse pounded in his neck. His mind focused on the realization. "I think we've found 'em."

"We need everyone at the safe house who can help to go with us." Móirín began rushing again.

His own feet were lighter knowing they'd at last found the hiding place they'd been searching for. They'd been *almost* running before; they were sprinting now.

All the way to Marylebone. To Riding House. The alley. The low door. The stairs. To the safe house door—

Left open.

The furniture inside had been splintered into pieces and scattered across the room.

"Blimey," Móirín whispered.

The others who'd been searching at Bricklayers Arms were

there, standing in shocked silence. But no one else was. No one else.

Móirín crossed to Fletcher. "Was it this way when you arrived?"

He nodded. "Arrived only a minute ago. They're all gone. All of them."

"Maybe they left because the place was being watched," Ana said. "Like the other safe house."

Fitz's gaze fell on a piece of paper, skewered on a coat nail on the wall. "Móirín," he called to her without looking away. "Come see this."

She was at his side in an instant. "From Madame Tussaud's catalog."

Fitz nodded. "And there's writing on it."

He heard her take a tense breath before reading it out loud. "The Tempest was here."

Gumblimey.

Móirín's pallor disappeared in an instant. She snatched the paper off the wall, folding it with sharp movements as she turned to face the room. "We're for Lord Chelmsford's house. There's a corridor there, dark and narrow and never used. *Tunnel* like."

They were all watching her, silent and focused.

"And Nolan's been posing as an odd-job man there."

Eyes pulled wide.

"He has access to the house and isn't suspected of anything by the constables watching it," Móirín continued. "The place being the baron's house connects it to the Tempest and to us, which means she has reason to think we could eventually guess at it."

"We oughta assume it's a trap," Fletcher said.

Móirín shot him a dry look. "Do you not already assume everything is a trap?" She shook her head. "How have you survived this long?"

"There were six up until tonight," Elizabeth chimed in. "Nine were snatched tonight, and the two Dreadfuls will most certainly be put with the others. All nine might. That many people are not likely to go unnoticed by the staff, no matter how dark and disused the corridor is, which means the servants are in danger too."

"As is Lord Chelmsford," Celia added.

"And whichever constable is watching the place." Fitz knew all of them on that rotation and knew they wouldn't ignore anything suspicious. That meant they'd become obstacles, and everyone knew what the Tempest did with obstacles.

"The Tempest's people will be watching all the doors," Stone said.

That was true enough, and something of a difficulty.

But, in a calm, matter-of-fact voice, Ana said, "Then we'll go in through a window. The ground-floor windows will also be watched, so we'll need a spot above that." She looked to Fitz. "You know the house better than any of us. We'll need a high window, with at least a two-inch ledge, tucked in shadow or not easily seen."

That was shockingly specific, and very quickly thought of. Odd coming from Ana Darby, a music instructor and lady born to Society. But, other than Fitz, only Celia seemed surprised to hear Ana provide a list of house-breaking necessities.

"Ana, in through the window," Móirín said. "Once inside, we need you to make noise to pull people away from the rear servants' entrance. Can you do that without getting caught?"

"With my eyes shut," Ana said.

Móirín gave a single nod, her attention already shifting to Elizabeth. "Have you been practicing with the knife like I showed you?"

"Every day." Elizabeth's answer didn't seem to surprise Fletcher. There was far more to this group than most people would guess.

To Fletcher, Móirín said, "On our way there, any chance you'll come across one of your urchins who can get whispers flying about who it is we're looking for?"

"Every chance in the world," he assured her. "I can have whispers all over London before the words are out of your mouth."

"They're already out of m' mouth." She hooked her thumb over her shoulder. "Go now so you've time to start those whispers. We'll meet you at Chelmsford's, but approach with caution." Móirín turned to Celia as Fletcher and Elizabeth rushed from the safe house. "Weapon of choice?"

"I'm handy with a knife as well," Celia said.

"Have you got one?"

"Oi."

Móirín looked to Stone, who silently held up his hands, curled in fists. She nodded, then turned to Fitz. "You armed?"

"Always."

Móirín held up the paper she'd ripped from the wall. "Into the eye of the storm, friends." As they stepped from the house, Móirín tucked the folded page into her pocket.

"Any details I ought to know about our strategy moving forward?" Fitz asked.

"'Tis a simple enough plan. She took my brother, now I'm going to end her."

THE QUEEN AND THE KNAVE

by Mr. King

Installment VII
in which the Queen and her Knavish
Guard seek the Help they require!

The day was growing late as Reynard Atteberry rushed to the village that abutted the palace. He held the pine marten fast in his arms, both of them encircled by the leather straps of the late Mrs. Atteberry's amulet.

Eleanor used her snout to point Reynard in the direction they needed to go. Her father's one-time astrological advisor made his home above the pub, making him both easy to find and, in that moment, impossible to visit undetected.

All the village had gathered in the public house. There was no mistaking the topic they were discussing. Neither was there any chance of missing the fear they felt.

Gerhilde and Marwen were present and spotted Reynard upon his arrival. They rose and joined him, both asking with their expressions alone what his business in the village might be.

"There is a man here who knows the movements of the sky. Unfortunately, our friend"—he indicated the pine marten in his arms—"is unable to tell me precisely where or the person's name."

"This is the unfortunate creature we spoke of earlier?" Gerhilde asked.

"Yes, and she is able to understand us."

"I believe," Marwen said to Eleanor, "the man you seek is Orestes."

She nodded.

"Follow us." Marwen led the way up the stairs to the landing above.

A second, narrower, darker stairwell led to a second, darker landing with but one door. At that door, they knocked, and waited.

A man, hair whiter than snow, answered their summons. His was the face of a friendly man who did not suffer fools gladly, a decidedly interesting combination. No one took time to contemplate the contradiction; far too much needed to be accomplished.

"We come with urgent business on behalf of Her Majesty, the Queen," Reynard said.

Orestes found them believable enough to let them in. He closed the door quickly behind them, a sure sign the old man knew that life in the village had that very day grown perilous.

"Her Majesty's inquiry is rather simple," Reynard said. "She wishes to know when the kingdom might expect to experience an eclipse of the sun."

"Soon, actually," Orestes said. "Quite soon."

Eleanor perked up, wishing yet again she could speak.

"One will occur tomorrow. The first time, to my knowledge, that an eclipse will occur during a Unification Ceremony. I do not yet know if that is a good omen or bad."

Eleanor turned about in Reynard's arms, looking up at him.

He met her eyes. "You will be present for the Unification Ceremony. That will undermine Dezmerina's predicted dissolution of the kingdom."

But it was more than that. She could address both the barons and the people. She could tell them what had happened and do so in a way they could not deny it. They would know she had not abandoned them, and that Dezmerina's goal was to destroy their dedication to one another.

This was hope.

"The sun is nearly below the horizon," Gerhilde said, watching at the window.

Reynard set Eleanor on the floor, giving her space to make her transformation.

Orestes watched them with curiosity, his mind sharp enough that he pieced together the situation in the moment before the spinning and twisting caused by the curse transformed Eleanor once more.

She had told Reynard the transformation was not painful. And though that was still true, she was finding that each change was more exhausting than the last.

This time, she couldn't remain on her feet. As she, now in human form, crumpled, Reynard leapt to catch her, saving her from a painful collision with the floor.

"I don't know how many more times I can do this, Reynard," she said, sighing as she leaned against him.

"It seems at least two more," he answered. "Can you endure two more?"

She tried to be brave, tried to be reassuring. But her nod and smile were found lacking by all present. They knew, to a one, she might be nearer to the curse's completion than any of them would like.

"Your Majesty," Orestes said with a bow when Eleanor had regained her feet. "It was my honor serving your father as his Royal Astronomer. I am pleased to have served you as well."

"Thank you, Orestes. Thanks to your help, we might yet save the kingdom."

"Begging your pardon, Your Majesty," Marwen said. "I believe, if we are to have a hope of that, it is your help we need most in this moment."

She wasn't certain what he meant.

He continued. "Below us, so many in this village are quaking with fear over what tomorrow will hold. They are debating what is to be done with someone as powerful as Dezmerina, who has both threatened them and promised to protect them. Their current predicament will soon spread through the entire kingdom, and all because our foe told them their queen had deserted them."

"But I haven't," Eleanor said.

"They need to know that." Reynard stood with a supportive arm still around her. "And now, until the sun rises again, you are able to tell them."

"I have never possessed a knack for grand speeches." The very thought overset her. And yet . . . "If their courage can hold, then mine certainly can. It must."

How brave was their queen! How worthy! If only she truly realized how beloved she was.

"Come." Gerhilde motioned the queen and her errant palace guard to follow her back down the narrow stairs, all the way to the public room below, where the voices were louder than they had been and the atmosphere had grown tense with wariness.

Gerhilde flung her arms out and upward, sending sparks high into the air.

"Dezmerina can sense the use of magic," Eleanor whispered, frantic.

"The magic Gerhilde is casting now will protect this pub," Marwen quietly assured her. "The enchantment will not last long, but it will keep Dezmerina at bay long enough for you to offer those here some reassurance."

Eleanor held tight to Reynard's hand. He knew it was not appropriate, that he ought to pull back and keep the distance required of a palace guard when interacting with the monarch. To allow this closeness was the act of a knave. Yet, he felt certain she needed the touch, needed the connection. He needed it too.

Those gathered at the pub had grown quiet, all watching Gerhilde.

"Let your minds rest, my friends," she said. "I bring you reassurance." She turned toward Eleanor. "Your Majesty."

Eleanor kept hold of Reynard's hand, bringing him with her as she stepped into the center of the room. Whispers bounced through the crowd as people bowed and curtsied to their queen.

"Good people." Her voice wavered, but anyone looking at her would know she was sincere in wanting to be heard. "I know the threats and promises Dezmerina made today, but I also know the lies she told you. She said I had fled, had abandoned you. But, in truth, she cast a spell on me which rendered me unable to be seen during the day. She used that curse to convince you that I am dishonorable, that you have been left alone, that the kingdom is vulnerable to the very chaos that tomorrow's ceremony was created to prevent."

As she took a quick but deep breath, Reynard squeezed her hand. Gerhilde, Marwen, and Orestes offered nods of encouragement.

"She must not be allowed to destroy our peace. She must not be permitted to steal from us our future, our hopes, or our freedom from her tyranny. Those here with me are determined to do all we can to thwart her. But, good people all, we cannot manage it alone. We need you. *I* need you."

"The sorceress will kill us if we defy her," someone in the crowd replied. "She has done so before."

"I know," Eleanor said. "And I will not require anyone to court that danger. But if you are willing to help, please do. Please."

Reynard stepped forward, addressing them himself. "You all know me. My father was born in this village, as was I. My mother had magic, like others in this room." He wouldn't name them, as doing so would put them in additional danger. "Many like my mother were killed by Dezmerina for defying her. I know perfectly well what you would be risking. But it is also why I am taking that very risk. My father dedicated his life to safeguarding this kingdom. My mother gave her life in protecting all of us from the very person who threatens us now."

"For the sake of those who have fought this battle before," Eleanor said, "please consider helping us. Our stand must happen at the Unification Ceremony tomorrow."

"Consider," Reynard said.

Murmurs began amongst those they had addressed. They all had a difficult, seemingly impossible choice to make.

Offering them privacy in which to do it seemed the kindest thing.

Reynard and Eleanor held fast to either end of the amulet that had, thus far, protected them from the sorceress who meant to destroy the kingdom and rebuild it as her own. They rushed, unspeaking, away from the village and into the forest, back to the cottage that had sheltered them.

Only once inside, with the door closed and the window coverings drawn, did they at last fully breathe. But though Reynard felt a sense of relief, Eleanor crumpled, her strength nearly spent.

"Eleanor!" He knelt beside her, wrapping his arms around her, studying her face, needing to know he'd not lost her already. "Eleanor?"

She leaned into him, her eyes closed. "I truly think I am dying, Reynard. Ebbing, just as the curse said. A slow siphoning of life."

"Do not lose hope," he pleaded.

"It is not hope I fear I'll lose, but strength." She curled a bit, not entirely unlike the position her pine marten form took when sleeping. "I have to transform at least twice more. I'm not certain I have the fortitude."

Reynard lifted her from the floor and carried her gently in his arms to the pallet, where he laid her down before pulling a blanket up to her shoulders. "Rest, Eleanor. Save your strength. And know you're not alone."

"Reynard?"

"Yes?"

"Will you promise to keep calling me Eleanor?" How she wanted him to!

How well he knew that he oughtn't! "I would be a very presumptuous and insolent sentry if I did."

She forced her eyes open, though it drained nearly all her remaining strength. "I have sentries aplenty," she whispered. "I need you to be more than that."

He wanted to be. He truly did.

CHAPTER 21

The Tempest had Brogan. Móirín would tear London apart to get him back.

They reached Eaton Square, moving as swiftly but unobtrusively as three men and four women could be when approaching an elegant townhouse in the black of night while wearing working-class clothes and not the fine togs usually seen in this rum area of town.

"Durand's supposed to be here," Fitz said, looking down the road and up the crossing one. "He ain't one to abandon his post."

That night watchman was missing. Further proof there was more happening at Lord Chelmsford's than it seemed.

"Back this way is the mews road," Fitz said. "We can reach the back and side of the house that way."

They followed, carefully but swiftly. The road leading to the backs of the houses and mews wasn't lit like the street was, but that served their purposes quite well.

"You've had the journey over to decide," Móirín said to Fitz. "Which window do we send Ana through?"

"At the back, above the terrace doors. There's a few feet of wide brick and a rainspout then a thick stone ledge beneath the window."

Ana nodded. "That'll do."

"The window'll be locked," Fitz warned.

"That won't be a problem," Ana said.

The tiniest sliver of moonlight lit the back wall. Fitz had picked a good window; 'twas decidedly climbable.

To Ana, Móirín said in a whisper, "I could make that climb, though not as swiftly or quietly as you. But you'd be dropping yourself in to a place infiltrated by thieves and nappers and murderers. A heap of a risk."

"I've spent years doing exactly this to reclaim what was mine," Ana said. "These blackguards have taken my Hollis, and I'm going in after him."

Móirín glanced at Fitz. He was whip-smart. Ana's skills wouldn't go unnoticed by him. He'd piece it together.

"I know the risk in that direction too." Ana's gaze had followed hers. "I'm willing to take it."

But Ana hadn't made a single step toward the house when Celia called out to them in a low voice, "There's someone here."

A figure was lying on the cobbles, half-hidden by a shrub.

Stone set himself a few paces back toward the street, watching for anyone's approach. Fitz and Elizabeth moved toward Celia.

"It's Durand," Fitz said.

"He's alive," Celia said. "Beaten a bit, but alive."

"Durand?" Fitz asked. "Are you with us enough to tell us what happened?"

He moaned.

"Most of us can bust into a place and hold our own in a

tussle," Móirín said, "but does anyone have Good Samaritan skills?"

"I can tend to him," Elizabeth said, taking Celia's place by the constable's side.

"Let's tuck him into the shadows," Fletcher said. "It'll be safer if you two can't be seen."

Fitz and Fletcher carefully moved the man.

Móirín and Ana returned to the climbing spot. Before beginning her ascent, Ana said quietly, "If you find Hollis and I'm not there, keep him safe. Tell him I'm coming for him."

"I will. I swear to you."

As graceful as a dancer, Ana pulled herself up the side of the house, toes finding purchase in the gaps between bricks, the rainspout offering fingerholds. The narrow ledge would be difficult for a bird to use for anything but perching, but it was sufficient for the Phantom Fox. Quick as anything, Ana had the window open and climbed inside.

"She's surprisingly good at that," Fitz said.

"She is," Móirín acknowledged. "But that's not my story to tell. I suspect she'll tell you herself if we get out of this house."

Fletcher and Celia moved to stand next to them.

"Durand and Elizabeth tucked out of sight?" Móirín asked.

Fletcher nodded. "He was awake enough for her to give him some water. She'll look out for him until we can get him to a doctor."

"She has her knife?" Móirín asked.

"She does." While that seemed to offer Fletcher some reassurance, he still sounded worried. Well he might be. Elizabeth was putting herself in danger staying behind like this.

"Think that's time enough for Ana to have made some ruckus inside?" Celia asked.

Likely was.

"We'll need to pick the lock," Móirín said.

Fletcher, Celia, and Fitz all volunteered in unison to do it, but Móirín was closest. She picked it quickly, but before opening the door, she let out a quick owl hoot, which brought Stone over.

"Stone, you and Celia check the perimeter of the house. The door we want is a bit to the side, below ground level. We need it unguarded if we're to get back out that way."

"We'll find it," he said.

"Be careful," Móirín said, though she knew it weren't necessary.

The two disappeared into the shadows. Móirín pulled the terrace door open.

Fletcher slowed as he stepped past her and whispered, "Like old times, i'n'it?"

They'd undertaken a few scrappy street brawls in the time before forming the DPS.

Fitz passed next. Then Móirín stepped through the doors and pulled them closed. Above their heads, a floorboard squeaked. A moment later, a door creaked open. Ana was moving about, providing a distraction.

Móirín pulled a candle and a candlestick from the bag tied against her body. With a quick strike of a Lucifer match, she lit the wick and handed it to Fitz. "Lead the way."

They followed him through the dark house, the occasional sound from Ana on the floor above them. Otherwise, everything was dark and silent. No movement. No candle flickered beyond the one Fitz held.

They reached the servants' stairs and slowly descended.

"I ain't never heard it so silent down here," Fitz whispered.

"If not for Durand's condition, I'd assume it were just that it's night."

Móirín would've pulled out her pocket pistol, but there wasn't enough light for firing it safely. She took out her telescoping shillelagh instead, pulling it to its full length and twisting it to lock in place. With it in her left hand, she pulled out her knife with her right.

Each room they passed, they glanced into.

Each room was empty.

"The tunnel corridor is a bit further," Fitz said over his shoulder.

The next room was dark, but Móirín heard something rustling.

"Bring the candle over, Fitz." She couldn't see anything in the room.

Fitz held it aloft in the doorway, illuminating a dry larder—and Lord Chelmsford, tied to a chair and gagged.

"Blimey." Fitz rushed past her. He set his candle on a crate, then pulled a knife from his boot and began sawing at the ropes.

Fletcher snagged a candle from the narrow worktable and lit it from Fitz's flame, then set to untying the gag in the baron's mouth.

Móirín kept an eye on the doorway.

The moment Lord Chelmsford's mouth was free, he gasped out, "The corridor just past the scullery."

"The others are being held there?" Fitz guessed.

Lord Chelmsford nodded. They were on the right trail, then.

"There are people in the house," Lord Chelmsford said. "They're watching."

"That's why we're here," Fletcher said, working at the ropes binding Chelmsford's legs.

Móirín heard movement outside the door. She tightened her grip on her weapons and stepped to the side of the door. If someone was coming, she wanted the element of surprise on her side.

The footsteps grew louder. The three men looked up, apparently hearing it. Móirín motioned for them to keep quiet and not give her away.

A wide, stocky man stepped into the doorway. "What've we here? A rescue team?"

He hadn't spoken loudly enough to alert anyone else. Best not allow him to do so.

Móirín slammed her shillelagh to his middle, then crashed it down on his back. He dropped to the stone floor, breaking his fall with his arms. She let him push his chest up off the floor, then used his own momentum to flip him on his back.

She pressed her knee to his chest and her knife to his neck. "One sound," she said, "just one, and I'll test how sharp this shivvy is."

The man's eyes pulled wide.

Before he could speak, Móirín said, "Fletch, you have a gag handy, I believe."

"So happens, I do." He came over to her side and gagged the man just as the baron had been.

"Any of those ropes still long enough for doing their job?" Móirín asked.

"Surely are," Fitz said.

Fletcher and Fitz dragged the man to the chair Lord Chelmsford had been tied to and set to work tying the scoundrel to it instead.

Lord Chelmsford rubbed at his wrists as he walked toward her. "You brought that man down as if it were nothing."

"Tells you how I spent m'days at the age when Society misses are dancing at balls."

"There are at least three others like this man roaming the house," Lord Chelmsford said. "Can you 'dance' with them too?"

She nodded firmly. "Everyone here with me can hold their own. We'll free the house."

"I'm not much use in a fight," Lord Chelmsford admitted, "but I'll do what I can."

"Start by taking up one of the candles and leading us to where the others are."

Fitz walked beside Lord Chelmsford, alert and armed. Móirín and Fletcher took up the rear, watching for movement and listening for sounds.

"*Exactly* like old times," Fletcher whispered, a grin in his tone.

"I hope we're better at it now than we were that night in Tavistock Square." They'd been attempting to get a bit of coin to a scullery maid who'd desperately needed powders from the apothecary but whose employer had refused to pay for them, and they'd been caught sneaking in. Blimey, they'd been pummeled a bit by a couple of burly footmen before managing their escape.

Lord Chelmsford stopped and turned, holding his candle up. He pointed to their right.

Móirín sped her steps. The poky corridor. Tunnel-like for certain. She saw two clumps of people there, tied in groups of four or five, gagged. No one was guarding them, which was odd.

"Untie them," she said, "but keep a weather eye out."

Móirín wove around, offering them all reassurances, while making her way to the door at the end of the poky corridor. It had a narrow window, barred, but she could still glimpse the rough-looking man watching the perimeter. The exit was guarded, at least until Celia and Stone could do something about it.

She turned back, watching each face as the candles illuminated them. She didn't recognize any of them. They must be servants in Lord Chelmsford's household.

Where were the Dreadfuls? Where was Brogan?

Light from Lord Chelmsford's candle flickered on a familiar face: Vera.

Móirín rushed to her and quickly untied the gag in her mouth. Tears fell from Vera's eyes, but not from fear. She was in pain.

"Get the rope cut as quick as you can," Móirín called to Fitz. "She's not healed enough to be in this position for so long."

Despite the agony of her unhealed body being twisted and bound, Vera spoke firmly and clearly once her gag was off. "Ana's father and mine are in this group. The children are in the scullery. Brogan and Barnabus were taken somewhere else."

Blast it. "Do you know where?"

Vera shook her head, a silent tear cutting another track down her cheek. "The Kincaids took Gemma."

Móirín met Fitz's eye, both knowing how dangerous that was.

"The Tempest didn't come here," Vera said. "She said she has 'a dethroning to attend.'"

A dethroning.

Fitz cut through the last rope holding Vera's group captive.

Móirín carefully helped her lay on the floor. Mr. Sorokin arrived at her side in the next moment, having been untied as well.

Móirín turned to Fletcher. "Get the children from the scullery. Go!"

He was gone before she'd even finished speaking.

Lord Chelmsford was seeing to the captives, helping them and reassuring them.

Móirín waved Fitz over. "Door's being watched, but I'd wager so's the rest of the house. Getting everyone out'll be difficult."

"With them free, though, we've numbers on our side."

That was true. But it weren't their only difficulty to overcome. "The Tempest said she's attending a dethroning tonight. She ain't here, and wherever she is, she ain't being an angel, I guarantee that."

"A 'dethroning'?" He shook his head. "She said something to you at the waxworks about there only being one queen, yeah?"

"When I mentioned the Hall of Kings." She pulled from her pocket the catalog page that had been left on the wall of the safe house. It was a page listing displays in that very room. A page that included George IV, who the Tempest's grandmother blamed for Joseph Hunt's transportation, the monarch being the head of the government that had authorized the sentence. A page that also included Queen Victoria.

There can be only one queen.

"She motioned to herself when she said that. She thinks of herself as the queen."

"But there is *another* queen," Fitz said. "And she's in London now."

"The Tempest would want whatever 'dethroning' she's

planning to be very public, done in a way that no one feels safe. I'd wager she's planning to intercept a royal carriage traveling to or from the palace."

"There's to be a quiet gathering at Kensington tonight," Mr. Sorokin said. The man had always proven a source of shockingly precise information.

"I'd wager the Tempest'll be waiting for Her Majesty's carriage as it leaves for the night." Móirín didn't feel any relief at sorting the question; there were still too many others remaining unanswered.

Very Merry rushed into the corridor. "I'm s'pposed to tell you the men what dragged all us here took Doc and Mr. Brogan somewhere else."

Móirín nodded; Vera had told them that.

"Said that getting Doc and Mr. Brogan to the tunnels would fill 'em up," Very Merry spoke quickly.

"They said they were taking them to the tunnels?" Móirín pressed.

Very Merry nodded. "Said they'd give those in the tunnels the night, then they'd start ending it. Sounded like they was getting ready to start doing people in."

"This isn't the tunnel we're needing to find. She fooled us. Again." Móirín met Fitz's eye. "The Tempest's people mean to start killing the Dreadfuls in the morning."

"The Tempest means to kill Queen Victoria tonight, sounds like."

"The people here ain't out of danger yet," Móirín said. "*And the Kincaids have Gemma.*" Curse 'em. "Four tragedies unfolding in four different places. I don't doubt the Tempest made certain I'd hear about all of them. Daring me to stop them all, knowing I can't. I have to choose who to save."

I know what will break you. The Tempest had said that at the waxworks. She'd been planning for this night even then. She knew forcing Móirín to choose who to save would tear at her very soul.

"I know this house," Fitz said. "Stone and Celia are here. We'll end the threat here and save these people."

"If you fail, you'll die."

"So we won't fail," he said.

"Fletch and Ana must set their minds to where the Dreadfuls might be," Móirín said. "Tell them to go the moment they think they know. Don't hesitate. We only have until morning."

"You mean to go save the queen?" Fitz asked.

Murder was enough of a tragedy on its own. The death of the monarch would send the kingdom into chaos. "Or die trying."

"Don't die," Fitz said firmly.

Móirín turned to Mr. Sorokin. "Get Vera and Mr. Newport out and safe." Mr. Newport was Ana's father.

"I can help," Vera insisted.

"I need you to," Móirín said. "You know the Kincaids from your years in Southwark. They have Gemma somewhere, and we need to sort that out. Think on where we ought to look."

"I can do more than think about things." Vera looked nearly frantic. "Let me help look for my husband. Please."

"I swore to Brogan I'd keep you safe," Móirín said. "I won't break that promise to him. I feel like I've broken every other one, but I'm keeping this one."

"The children need looking after, *kotik*," Mr. Sorokin said. "We can do that while sorting out where Gemma might be. We can do that while they save all the others."

All the others. The Tempest called herself "the violence" and "the storm." This was what she meant. Chaos. Overwhelming threats from all directions.

I know what will break you.

That was where the Tempest was wrong. Móirín Donnelly was the Dread Master, and she did not break.

She took a breath of resolve and spoke to Fitz. "Tell Fletcher I am depending on him to find my brother."

"I will."

"And don't get yourself killed."

"Same, love." He kissed her, quick but fierce.

Then Móirín ran.

THE QUEEN AND THE KNAVE

by Mr. King

Installment VIII
in which Choices must be made and Consequences faced!

All the barons were on the palace grounds for the Unification Ceremony, gathered in neat rows according to the ancientness of their various titles. Beyond them, the people of the kingdom stood, sat, and waited with interest for the ceremony to begin. On the dais was a perfectly round table with the three-wicked candle and ceremonial wreath upon it. The bejeweled crown lay atop a velvet pillow, awaiting the arrival of the queen.

But she was already there.

Tucked behind the tapestry table covering, Eleanor, in pine marten form, assured herself of two very crucial things: that Orestes's prediction of a full eclipse would prove accurate and that her pleas at the pub the night before had convinced at least some of the people present to stand up to Dezmerina when she inevitably arrived in fury and nefariousness.

At Reynard's insistence, Eleanor was wearing the protective amulet. She was, after all, alone on the dais and would continue to be even after the eclipse allowed her to transform

267

into her true form once more. She was weaker than she'd ever been and had every expectation of being weaker still after the next transformation. If she had any hope of thwarting Dezmerina, she needed all the help and protection she could call upon.

As often as the gathered people's eyes watched the dais, they also turned them upward to the sky. The eclipse had begun, the encroaching shadow covering more than a third of the orb. The sun's heart had to be covered in order to fool the magic. That would not happen until the eclipse was nearly at its height.

Reynard was amongst the palace guards, recruiting them to the cause, rallying their support, and calling upon their sense of duty and desire to safeguard their kingdom and their queen.

Gerhilde and Marwen had sent whispers out amongst the others with magic, reminding them of those they had lost, encouraging them to stand with those who ought to have support.

Orestes wandered amongst the villagers and other people of the kingdom, speaking of the violence Dezmerina was known for and of the impossibility of one person—even the queen herself—defeating a villain like that if she was required to do so alone.

The time for the ceremony arrived. Word had spread from the pub all the way to the barons of the curse placed on the queen, one that made her unable to be seen in the daylight. Her absence, therefore, was not entirely unexpected, but neither was it reassuring. This ceremony had been the backbone of the kingdom's peace and tranquility for generations. No matter that their monarch was not neglecting it out of indifference or even choice, to not complete the ritual would take them into uncharted waters.

Above their heads, the dark shadow passed farther over the sun, enough so that the sky itself was rendered dim.

From her place hidden behind the tapestry-covered table, Eleanor could feel an odd pulling and twisting. It was similar to what she felt when transforming, but it seemed to be shifting back and forth at the same time. Parts of her attempted to become human, while other parts firmly remained pine marten. In the middle of a transition, her becoming-human-limbs would transform to animal paws again.

It was, without question, the worst transformation she'd experienced. The others, as she'd assured Reynard, had not been painful: exhausting and uncomfortable, yes, but not agonizing.

This one was.

The murmurs from the crowd grew louder. The ceremony was late.

Eleanor silently pleaded with the eclipse to speed its path, to cover the heart of the sun, to grant her both relief from the agony of this broken transformation and the time she needed to address her people as herself. As if fate had chosen to be kind to her, the pine marten fur and clawed paws gave way to her own skin and clothes, to her own hands and fingers.

Drawing on every bit of strength she had left, and there was precious little, she rose and stood, leaning against the tapestried table. A gasp rose from the barons and gathered villagers alike.

"My people," she said quickly, attempting to keep her

voice loud enough to be heard, even as she could feel herself fading. "Dezmerina will arrive at any moment, I have no doubt. She has done all she can to stop this moment, to destroy this kingdom. We must not allow her to do so."

Eleanor lit the ceremonial candle and placed the wreath around it with shaking hands. A speech was usually given, pledges both given and received from the monarchy and the barons to live in peace, but it was the lighting of the candle and the placing of the wreath that was the crux of the ceremony. After that, the crown was to be placed atop the monarch's head, a symbol that the royal reign would continue in harmony with the nobility, the merchants, the people, and the kingdom as a whole.

A crash of thunder announced Dezmerina's arrival on the dais before Eleanor's crown was put in place. Some in the gathering ran for their very lives. They could hardly be blamed. Dezmerina did not make idle threats.

"Your time is up," the sorceress declared to them all. "This kingdom will soon be claimed by me, to be ruled as I see fit. Make your loyalties known."

"Queen Eleanor!" The shout went up from amongst the guards. Reynard had convinced them, securing their loyalties.

The guards' declaration seemed to give courage to the barons, who added their voices. The people gathered did so next.

Dezmerina's look of confusion was unlikely to last long. She would be angry soon enough.

"You cannot control them with fear," Eleanor whispered. "They are determined to be free."

Dezmerina flung her arms in a circle, and a pack of unnaturally enormous wolves appeared, lined up along the edges of the dais, keeping the would-be defenders of the throne at bay. Anger having seized her expression, the sorceress looked at Eleanor at last.

"It is daytime. Why are you not as you were cursed to be?"

"Your magic cannot see the heart of the sun." Eleanor's legs shook beneath her, but she stood tall.

"The eclipse," Dezmerina muttered. "No matter. It will pass soon enough, and you will be helpless and hopeless. You cannot survive another transformation. And even if you did, you would never escape my wolves. They are very fond of the taste of pine marten."

The dais was surrounded by those eager to defend their queen and their kingdom. The wolves might have been fond of pine marten, but Eleanor suspected they would not object to a meal made of those they were currently holding at bay.

Her eyes fell on Reynard. She could not bear the thought of him being killed in this fray, of his life, so precious to her, being lost. But what could be done but fight?

Whene'er the sun lights Amesby skies,
Her queen will see through pine marten's eyes.

Soon enough, the eclipse would pass, and Eleanor would be transformed. She was the queen, and that was the curse.

Except the recrowning of the monarch was part of the Unification Ceremony.

Eleanor was the queen. But if someone else was crowned as part of the ceremony, by one who had the authority to do so—which Eleanor did—that person would, symbolically, at least, be the monarch. And the curse did not specify that

Eleanor was to be transformed, but rather that the *queen* was.

"Will you let them live?" Eleanor asked, rushing her words, hoping to outlast the eclipse enough to prevent her transformation. "If I place this crown on your head rather than mine, will you let them live?"

Dezmerina's eyes narrowed. "I would consider it."

"No, Eleanor!" Reynard called out from amongst the crowd. "Do not believe her."

She looked out at the faces of those who were ready to defend her. "I am certain this will be for the best." How she prayed they believed her!

Her insides were beginning to twist again, a sure sign her time was running short. Eleanor took up the crown but didn't move hastily. She needed Dezmerina to be crowned without enough time to return the favor once she realized what the ceremony would do to her. The pain increased, the tearing apart of her body from within as it struggled to know what form it was meant to take.

Eleanor set the crown on the sorceress's head.

"I am queen," Dezmerina said with satisfaction.

"Whene'er the sun lights Amesby skies," Eleanor repeated, feeling her strength return swiftly, "the queen will see through pine marten's eyes."

The shadow slipped off the sun above.

Dezmerina's body spun and twisted, the crown falling from her head, but the curse had taken hold. Her shrieks of anger turned the heads of her wolves. Their curiosity turned to unmistakable hunger as the sorceress took the shape of the one creature her pack craved the most.

In a dart of fur, the pine marten ran from the dais, the

wolves after her. With the canine guards on the chase, some people they'd been holding back ran to the dais, while others rushed around it, following the pack to determine the fate of the one who had hurt them for so long.

CHAPTER 22

"You truly think this Tempest will attempt to assassinate Her Majesty?" Lord Chelmsford asked.

Fitz didn't have a sure answer. The Tempest felt she had a righteous vendetta, justifying her punishment of people connected to her family's troubles, including the head of the government that she felt betrayed Joseph Hunt. London's most violent villain would certainly feel herself entitled to assassinate the reigning queen. And yet, something felt amiss in the plot.

"How do we get out of here?" one of the maids asked. "Those men are still watching."

"We've other people in the house," Fitz said. "We ain't doin' this alone."

"Someone's outside *that* door," Mr. Sorokin said.

Fitz nodded. "I'm hoping we can go out the front servants' entrance. That'll spill us onto the street, and there's a lamp right out front. Safer than the shadows at the back."

Olly and Licorice rushed into the corridor and directly toward Mr. Sorokin.

Fletcher was right behind them. "Talked with Stone through

a window in the scullery. He and Celia say there are two fellas at the front of the house, guarding the exits. He thinks he and Celia can deal with them if they've a spot of help."

"Stay here with this lot," Fitz said. "I'll climb out and assist."

Fletcher accepted the trade, and Fitz hurried to the scullery. He looked out the window and saw Stone hunched there, waiting for him.

Fitz pushed a chair to the window and climbed out. They were toward the front of the house, in a small alcove between it and the adjoining house.

"Just up and around to the front," Stone whispered. "A couple of fellas standing guard. The three of us could likely bring them down in a scuffle, but they'd likely raise the warning to others, which'd make trouble for the people being held inside."

Celia nodded. "We need a battle plan."

Fitz inched to the corner of the wall and peeked around. A thug waited a few steps away; another was only a few steps beyond him. Even if Fitz had been the sort to shoot people without warning—which he weren't—firing would only raise that alarm sooner.

Fitz eyed the area, ensuring there were only two they needed to engage. Then his eyes settled on something that nearly pulled an audible sigh of relief from him. On a ledge, above the guard farthest from them, a lone figure walked quietly but confidently.

Ana. *The Phantom Fox.*

Blasted good timing.

"You likely know who she is," Celia whispered. "She don't deserve to be tossed in jail."

"Scotland Yard and I ain't chummy just now. I'll not be tossing anyone in jail anytime soon."

From her perch, Ana looked in their direction. Fitz motioned toward her and then the guard just below. Then he hooked a thumb behind him and at himself, then pointed at the guard nearest them.

She nodded her understanding.

If they could tackle the guard closest to them in the same moment she knocked over the other from above, they'd clear the front servants' entrance without alerting anyone else in the house.

Ana stepped with a surefootedness that a cat would envy until she was directly above her quarry. It'd be a fair drop, but Fitz trusted the legendary Phantom Fox to judge what she could manage.

Fitz stepped quietly from his spot and pulled his short cudgel from where it was strapped to his thigh. Stone and Celia were directly behind him.

Fitz watched Ana so they could time their efforts. In the instant she dropped from the building, Fitz thumped his thug hard at the back of the neck, then swung the cudgel at his knees. At the same time, Stone ran past him to assist Ana in silencing the second guard.

Celia pulled a handkerchief around the mouth of the guard Fitz had brought down, gagging him. No noise emerged from Ana and Stone's direction, so they must've managed a silent assault as well.

"Stone, Celia, go through the front servants' entrance— carefully—and let out the people being held there. We'll toss these'ns in there instead and let 'em wait until the constabulary comes looking."

His guard gurgled in wordless objection as Stone and Celia left to see to the release of prisoners.

"Give me a reason not to toss you in there," Fitz said, "and I might take pity on you."

The man growled again, but the gag made his words impossible to understand.

"Sorry, mate. That don't convince me." He looked over at Ana.

Stone had tied the guard's hands behind his back with his neckerchief. Ana stood over him with a fighting stick aimed at the back of his neck.

"Well done," Fitz said to her.

"Did we find who we were looking for?" she asked. The hope in her voice broke his heart; he didn't have good news for her.

"We found some of who we was looking for," Fitz said. "But not all."

Again, the man he'd tackled made muffled objections and moaned a bit.

Fitz looked down at the guard. He didn't doubt the man was in pain. If there'd been a way to manage this without hurting the bloke, he'd've done it. But this was not a situation to be managed with velvet gloves. Of course, a bit of cooperation from the man might answer a few lingering questions. The bloke seemed anxious not to be imprisoned. Might be Fitz could use that as leverage.

"I'll lower your gag, cuffin, but if you give me *any* reason to think you'll raise the alarm, I'll knock all your teeth in."

The man grew very still. The threat had done the trick.

Fitz pulled the gag down but kept it close in case the man tried anything.

"The Tempest threatened my family if I didn't stand guard here," he said, his voice pleading.

That was likely true; it was a known tactic of hers.

"The man that shoved me here said to another one that the Tempest set this all up, that, the Tempest said, 'No one'll be left to die here alone; she'll follow the trail by herself.' This here's a distraction. But if we didn't do what she said, she'd kill our families. She's done such things before. We all know she has."

"The Tempest arranged a misdirection," Ana said, stepping closer. "And we went right along."

No one'll be left to die here alone; she'll follow the trail by herself.

The "she" didn't refer to the Tempest; the Tempest was the one being quoted.

Móirín had followed the trail to Kensington. By herself. So no one here would be alone. The Tempest expected her to leave Eaton Square on her own, but where did she expect her to go? To find Gemma? The Dreadfuls? To save the queen?

The Tempest was clearly intent on making Móirín put her own life on the line to choose who lived and who died. And one of those choices would bring the two of them face-to-face.

"Please, detective," the unwilling guard said. "My family's in danger. So's this other bloke's. The ones in the house are the Tempest's coves."

In the next moment, the servants' door opened, and Lord Chelmsford's staff rushed out, followed by those who'd followed Móirín there and those they'd come to rescue. Fitz relayed the situation to his comrades.

"Fletcher," he said, "figure out how to save these blokes' families, get my constable to a doctor, send someone to wherever Vera thinks Gemma might be, and, by criminy, sort out where the Dreadfuls are being held. We're still looking for something like a tunnel."

"And you?" Fletcher asked.

"The Tempest is counting on Móirín being alone and unsupported. I ain't gonna let that happen."

CHAPTER 23

The street outside Kensington Palace was empty and quiet. Móirín'd had her fill of empty, quiet places.

An assassination could easily occur anywhere along the route from Kensington Palace to Her Majesty's residence. But the Tempest would not wish for the act to be ascribed to random crime or become whispers branching in dozens of directions. She would want it to occur in a place of importance and significance. She needed the attack to be not only on the monarch herself but on the very seats of power and influence.

Móirín remained in the shadows, eyeing her surroundings, watching every movement of shrubbery, every gust of wind. She was the only one who could stop this. The Tempest knew she would come. The Tempest understood Móirín better than she ought.

"We are very alike, you and I."

Móirín hated that she couldn't entirely disagree. They'd both endured family tragedy, both lived on the wrong side of the law. They both had, in different ways, an army at their disposal. Though it made Móirín sound vain, she knew they were both very intelligent and very capable.

"If you were me, you would have already sorted this."

How often those words, tossed at her with self-assured laughter, had repeated in Móirín's mind. The Tempest knew Móirín was clever, but she also felt certain there was no one so clever as herself.

If we are so alike, then I can guess what you'll do.

Móirín surveyed the area once more. Where would she place an assassin if she were the one planning it?

Hidden, that much was certain. But with a clear view of the palace gate and the road the carriage would travel. Móirín was full sure it'd happen at the gate as the royal carriage left for the night. There'd likely be other guests watching the departure who would be terrorized by the crime, left afraid and on edge.

It would occur in close proximity to the guards, which would make everyone feel less safe. And it would make the palace itself a symbol of death and chaos and anarchy. But the killing would likely technically happen on the streets of London and not within the palace grounds, as that would make everyone afraid of every other corner of the city.

It would happen here, as the queen left.

Móirín would have one chance to stop it.

Only one.

On the other side of the gate, she heard the rumble of wheels, distant and quiet, but approaching. Whatever was going to happen would be happening soon.

Two guards walked to the center of the gate, standing on the palace side rather than the street side where Móirín was, and pulled it open.

Where was the assassin? Was there more than one?

Time was growing short. She could hear the carriage more clearly now. It was drawing near.

Tall trees grew on either side of the gate, their branches extending far past the wall, but at a height beyond reach even if one climbed the wall. But they did create deep, dark shadows. Móirín was hiding in one of them herself. It seemed the likeliest place for the assassin to attack from.

As the crunch of gravel from the approaching carriage grew louder, a figure emerged from behind a dip in the wall.

A woman.

The Tempest?

The figure stepped closer to the gate; her steps rigid yet hesitant. The Tempest didn't move like that. She was a good actress, but there'd be no reason to pretend timidity in that moment. This woman wasn't Móirín's foe.

But the glint of a streetlamp on the barrel of a gun in her hand told Móirín the woman *was* the one who'd come to kill the queen.

Another step placed the woman in a better view and a greater spill of light.

Gemma.

No. Gemma wouldn't do this. Not willingly, at least.

The Kincaids had stolen her. For this, it seemed.

The carriage was near enough that Móirín could make out its dark shape.

The Tempest was forcing Gemma to kill the queen, which would force Móirín to kill her friend.

The turn of the wheels. The creak of the carriage.

Móirín pulled her derringer from her pocket, holding it ready to fire.

The carriage was within view.

Gemma didn't raise her weapon. There was a determined set to her shoulders. A defiance.

Defiance.

Someone was forcing her. Someone near enough to do her

harm in the moment if she failed. Someone armed and watching. Someone bearing the name Kincaid, no doubt.

The carriage was mere feet from the gate.

Gemma's head turned, only slightly, only momentarily, to the other side of the street.

Móirín saw a man there. A man with a gun.

The royal coachman called out to his horses as the carriage approached from the gate.

The Kincaid lying in wait raised his gun, but at the carriage or Gemma, Móirín couldn't tell.

Hers was a single-shot weapon. She had to be right. And she had to hit her mark the first time.

The carriage was at the gate.

Móirín aimed, praying she was right, then cocked the gun and squeezed the trigger.

The sound sent the horses into a frenzy. The coachman, experienced and steady-handed, kept them in check. The footman riding beside the driver met her eye.

She pointed across the street at the unnamed Kincaid, now lying on the ground.

The footman whispered something to the driver, who tetched the horses to a faster clip and hurried his royal passenger out of danger.

The guards at the gate rushed out into the dust and gravel kicked up by the speeding carriage.

"That man had his gun aimed at Her Majesty's carriage," Móirín said. "He meant to see her shot."

"His name's Arlo Kincaid," Gemma said as she rushed over, no sign of the gun she'd been forced to carry. "He's a known murderer and resurrection man. No-good blighter, he is. Anyone'll tell you. This woman saved the queen, no doubting it. Saved her for sure and certain."

"I saw the no-good lulling about the past while," one of the guards said. "Thought he was just gawking, but he seemed a bit too keen on what was happening."

"I saw him raise his gun," the other guard said. "But it happened in a flash. One minute, his gun is up, the next *he's* down."

The sound of running footsteps interrupted whatever might've been said next. More guards were approaching, more groomsmen and stablehands. It'd be chaos in a moment.

"Best make certain he ain't getting up," Gemma said.

"And that he's not able to reach his weapon," Móirín added.

The guards' focus shifted to across the street, so Móirín took hold of Gemma's arm and pulled her out of view and into the tree-shaped shadows.

"They were positive you were going to shoot me," Gemma said, releasing a tense breath.

"Because far too many people think I'm a dolt." Móirín kept an eye on the area. Stopping a royal assassination shouldn't have been this easy.

"They said they'd kill Baz if I didn't agree to come here," Gemma said. "And Uncle Arlo said he'd shoot me if I didn't take my shot at the carriage."

"And if you didn't shoot at the queen, he was going to." Móirín was certain of that. "But I think you'd've taken the bullet rather than shooting one yourself. I was counting on it."

Despite the activity around them, a sense of calm settled over the two women. An earnestness. A focus.

"Please tell me you've found Baz," Gemma whispered.

Móirín shook her head. "Not yet, but we did find some of the others. The Tempest is taunting us."

"She couldn't be certain you'd come here tonight," Gemma said. "I heard her tell Arlo as much. He said it weren't no bother to him. He'd enjoy seeing to the queen and wouldn't mind spilling more of my blood as well."

"More?" Móirín didn't like the sound of that.

"The Kincaids like to take credit for the crimes they perpetrate."

Móirín's heart sank. "They've cut their mark into you."

"No matter. They didn't succeed tonight. At least not in this."

"Is Arlo the only one of 'em here?"

Gemma nodded. "My other uncle's with the Tempest."

Wherever she was.

More people were rushing to the scene. The whole area would be awake and in chaos soon enough. And in the midst of it, someone rushed directly toward her. She pulled out her knife, not having had time to reload her derringer.

"It's Fitz," the man said the moment he came near enough to be heard.

Relief flooded through Móirín.

"Have you found Baz?" Gemma asked.

"Not yet."

One of the palace guards approached the trio. "To whom does the queen owe her life?"

Having her name whispered about was a dangerous thing. "I'd say she owes her life to the expert driving of her coachman," Móirín said. On that declaration, she hooked arms with Fitz and Gemma and walked away, hoping no one pressed the matter further.

"You don't mean to take credit for what you just did?" Gemma asked.

Móirín shook her head. "The Tempest wasn't here for any of this," she told Fitz. "We've freed her prisoners, rescued Gemma, and saved the queen. That means the Tempest is with the missing Dreadfuls. She has to be."

"That's the crime she most wants to be present for, apparently," Fitz said.

"But she wasn't present for all their kidnappings," Gemma said. "Hollis, at least, was nabbed by other people."

"'Tis the crime that comes next that she's most interested in." Móirín took a breath, forcing herself to remain calm. "And we learned tonight she means to see it done before morning."

"We have to find them," Gemma whispered, urgent and worried.

"It don't make sense," Fitz said. "She said she was attending a dethroning, but she weren't here for any of this."

"This, then, ain't the dethroning she was talking about." Móirín was growing tired of riddles.

"That's what makes this so much fun: outmaneuvering a slightly inferior version of myself."

The Tempest was, no doubt, enjoying it all thoroughly.

"A dethroning," Gemma repeated. "Do you twig there's another monarch visiting London she might be going after? The Kincaids marked the Russian ambassador's house weeks back on her orders."

Fitz shook his head. "I'm certain that was tied to her blackmail attempts to destroy Lord Chelmsford."

In a flash so sudden Móirín wasn't certain how the idea even formed, she knew the answer. She knew it.

"Nolan let her inside DPS headquarters while he was still there." It was how the Tempest had accessed the roof, after all. "She was inside likely months before we closed it up, so she knows the chair Fletcher sits in while running the DPS meetings is jokingly called his *throne.*"

"Blimey," Gemma whispered.

It was all suddenly falling into place. "The house is filled with passages, secret ones tucked behind walls and under the house. *Tunnels.* 'Tis a perfect description. She's had access for ages without us knowing and likely has discovered nearly all its secrets. Now she's turned our house against us."

The answer had been so obvious, yet she'd missed it.

"*You are so very near to the answer you are looking for.*"

The Tempest had hidden the Dreadfuls right under Móirín's nose. She was outmaneuvering Móirín at every turn, and she knew it.

"She'll be waiting for us," Móirín warned. "She'll know we're coming, and she'll be ready."

"Baz is there," Gemma said. "I'm not giving him up without a fight."

"That's a good thing, Gemma, because a fight is exactly what we are going to have on our hands." She squared her shoulders. "Are you more comfortable with the gun your uncle forced you to take, or would you rather wield something else?"

"I'm better with a cudgel."

"Do you have one?" Móirín asked.

"Not on me, no."

Móirín pulled her collapsible shillelagh from its hiding spot and twisted it to lock it into its full size. "I'll trade you. I've used my shot and would rather not have to reload."

The exchange was made. A hackney was hailed.

In the length of a breath, they were on their way to King Street, Covent Garden, directly into a trap they'd no real hope of escaping.

CHAPTER 24

They hadn't an hour to spare to make the trip to King Street on foot. But neither did they dare take a hackney all the way to the site of a coming battle. Móirín gave the driver instructions to put them down at Trafalgar Square, and during the ride there, she gave Gemma very specific instructions.

"Take St. Martin's Lane. Between the third and fourth buildings is an alleyway called Brydges Place. Narrowest, darkest, longest alley. Couldn't fit two abreast. And so tall on either side, there'll not even be starlight making it through. You'll feel like you're walking into a pit of vipers."

"Will I be?" Gemma asked.

"Aye, if you go farther than you're meant to. The first door you come across will be a splintered wreck of a thing, hardly filling the doorway. Beyond that is an abandoned, gaping room. It'll be filled with urchins. They make their home there at night. You need to ask for Henry Bootblack. Tell him the Pigeoneer sent you." She pulled an etched penny from her bag and set it in Gemma's hand. "Tell him exactly this: 'Rush a whisper to our friend's ear: time to come home.' He'll know what to do."

Gemma didn't hesitate when they reached their destination.

They all alighted. Gemma ran toward St. Martin's. Móirín and Fitz ran toward King Street.

"You're sending Fletcher's urchins to warn him?" Fitz guessed as they ran.

"To summon him. We've no hope of besting the Tempest and her army without an army of our own."

At King Street, they slowed their steps, caution being more necessary than speed. A pass-through several doors down from headquarters led to a back garden behind the building abutting theirs. That sidewall in that back garden had a gap that allowed access to the back of headquarters. The Dreadfuls sometimes came in that way when wishing not to draw attention by arriving in droves for a meeting. But not one of them knew that the shed built against the back had a false wall or that through that wall was a narrow set of steep stairs that led to a well-disguised door through which Móirín accessed her hidden Dread Master's office.

It was her and Fitz's best chance for entering headquarters without being seen. She led the way, letting them both in through the heavily bolted door. The air inside was heavy and musty, a good sign that at least this part of the headquarters had not been breached.

The room was entirely dark, but she knew her way around the space too well to be hampered by that. She quickly found the candles, set two in holders, and lit them.

The room appeared very nearly as she'd left it, with everything seemingly untouched, except the wall of weapons. The Tempest was always several steps ahead, leaving Móirín to sort out what steps to follow and what traps to avoid.

Frustration wouldn't do her any good, so she firmed her resolve. Again. Life had taught her the knack of that. She grumbled about unfairness and frustration, but she always pulled herself together again. Always.

"There are eight hidden passages in this house. One begins here. Another in the butler's room. The kitchen. The corridor to the right of the first-floor landing. Behind the pub."

"There's a pub?" Fitz asked.

Móirín finished the list. "The back of the cloakroom. The library. And the dry larder." He needed to know all the possibilities, and she was depending on him to remember everything and help Stone and Fletcher search when they arrived. "I don't know how many of those Nolan discovered while he was here, but the Dreadfuls'll be in one of them. We may have to search them all."

"While being hunted by the would-be queen, most likely," Fitz said.

"She's undertaking a dethroning, and the chair the Dreadfuls think of as a throne is in the room at the end of the passageway leading from here."

"Do you think she'll be waiting there?"

Móirín shook her head. "It'd be too easy. The hunt is as important to her as the kill."

"Again, I'd like to make it clear that I'm requesting that you not die." He spoke with a bit of a laugh, though Móirín knew he wasn't taking their situation lightly.

She couldn't join in the jest though. The Tempest had said there could be only *one* queen. She'd said this hunt was against "a slightly inferior version" of herself, and since she considered herself queen, the dethroning was aimed at Móirín. She was the ultimate target and, she suspected, the Tempest did not intend to allow her to escape that night's struggle alive.

"The Tempest took most of the weapons that were in here, and she'll know exactly what we were left with. But I think they're worth taking with us." She crossed to the weaponry and pulled down what few items remained. "After we get through the passage from this room, we'll split and search on our own. We'll cover twice as much ground that way."

"The Tempest wants you to be alone." Fitz accepted the knife she handed him. "She'll be counting on it. She's been a step ahead of us this whole time because she thinks she can predict what you'll do. Seems we'd toss her plans into disarray if you did something unpredictable."

It was actually rather genius. Móirín slipped an extra knife into the sheath she'd sewn into the side of her boot. "I can predict what *she* will do because she has planned according to what *I* am most likely to do. Acting a bit out-of-character would disrupt that."

Fitz nodded. "So, where do we start?"

Móirín grabbed a shillelagh and slipped it in a loop on her dress she'd added specifically for such things. "The Tempest would expect me to begin looking in the tunnels I'm certain Nolan discovered since she would know that I would realize he introduced her to them."

"Still can hardly believe your butler-on-the-run was my landlord when Grandfather disappeared. London ain't that small a place."

That had bothered Móirín too. Not that Fitz had found an odd connection to the DPS, but that a seemingly ordinary landlord had dived so deeply into the world of crime. People did change. Falling on hard times hardened people. But it still felt too coincidental.

"There's a passage in the room he used—the butler's room—that hadn't been touched at all in the time he was here. At least that's how it looks." Móirín took up a candle. "If she hid the Dreadfuls there, it'd be a terribly obvious choice."

"And she'd've twigged that you'd realize as much."

Móirín nodded. "And that I'd start somewhere else. Which means, I ought to start there."

"Unless she's twigged that you'd twig that she—"

"We could chase our tail endlessly on this." Móirín handed the other candle to him. "I'd not've thought to begin in the tunnel off Nolan's room if we'd not had this discussion, so I think starting there is our best chance of doing something she won't expect. Can't guarantee it, mind, but a chance."

She led the way out of her one-time office and into the narrow, dark passage beyond. They kept a close eye on every shadow, every corner. Their footsteps echoed. Always did in this tunnel. She'd been able to hear Fletcher's approach every time he'd made the walk.

They climbed the winding stairs. She knew without looking where the lever was to open the door. From the other side it looked exactly like the wall. No one knew it was there except for Fletcher and herself. And now Fitz.

The Parliamentary Room, where they were now, where the empty throne sat awaiting another meeting of the DPS, was silent and dark and still. They made their way by candlelight to the sliding door that led to the entryway. It was open only an inch, but it was enough to show that the entryway beyond was brightly lit.

They stepped out. On the table where the Dreadfuls would leave their etched penny upon arrival at headquarters was a teapot, two teacups, and a small slip of stationery with the word "Welcome" written in a tidy, unfamiliar hand.

"That's my Dread Master's stationery," Móirín said.

"That's—That's my grandfather's teapot." Fitz sounded and looked shocked.

Though Móirín was surprised, she'd learned not to underestimate the lengths the Tempest could and would go to in this game of cat and mouse.

"How? I've not seen any of his things in twenty years." Fitz stared, mouth agape.

"Perhaps Nolan relinquished the building *after* your grandfather disappeared and not *before*."

"He stole it," Fitz muttered. He set his hand on the side of the teapot. "It's still warm."

"Which means they likely know we're in the house." Móirín motioned him toward the servants' stairs. "Keep a weapon in hand."

Móirín wasn't used to being repeatedly outsmarted. Though the Tempest had said with utter confidence that the only person who could keep pace with the Tempest's intellect was the Tempest herself. That intellect wouldn't be so dangerous if the one wielding it weren't so violent.

Fitz followed Móirín down the narrow servants' stairs. The headquarters was just as quiet as Lord Chelmsford's house had been. The belowstairs was just as still. Móirín didn't doubt the place was full of people, but where, exactly, the Tempest and her associates were lying in wait remained to be seen.

Móirín led Fitz to Nolan's room. She set her lantern on the bureau, wanting both her hands free. The footprints she and Fletcher had left in the thick dust weeks ago were still visible. And they were the only ones. At the time, she'd stepped into the room, moved around a bit, and left. She traced her footprints as she recounted those brief minutes when she'd been searching for a clue.

Nothing appeared to have changed. Nothing appeared to be different.

"Someone's been in here," Fitz said. "Two someones based on the footprints."

"Fletcher and me," she said. "The night of Barnabus and Gemma's funeral."

"There's hardly any dust in the prints. Do you suppose there ought to be more by now?"

'Twas possible. Still, there were only two sets. If more people had been inside since the time Móirín had been here, there'd be a mess of prints. But if these were *newer* than they seemed . . .

She followed the path she'd taken in this room, watching to see if the footprints matched. She'd gone to the bureau first that day, just as she had now. Then she'd walked around the room. There'd been a noise in the corridor, and she'd tucked herself behind the door, heels against the wall.

But the footprints in the dust didn't do that. She'd stood there for a while and had left prints. She knew she had. But there were none there with heels against the wall.

Curious, Móirín set her foot in the dust directly beside one of the prints meant to be hers. She was wearing the same shoes as she had before. The print she left now didn't match.

"These are new footprints," she said. "Someone's gone to pains to make them seem like the originals. If I'd not noticed the ones missing behind the door, I'd not have ever thought to check if they matched my shoes."

"And a quick glance would've suggested the room hadn't been disturbed," Fitz said. "You'd not guess that eight of your Dreadfuls had been dragged through here and into the adjoining tunnel."

Dragged. "They'd not have gone willingly or peaceably. They'd have left the original footprints a right mess."

Fitz nodded. "So the Tempest swept away the tracks they left, added more dust to the floor, and recreated the footprints you and Fletcher left, trying to trick you, or at least slow you down."

He was bang on the mark. Móirín crossed to the bed. "Bed has to be moved to open the door to the hidden passage behind it. I'd wager the redusting covered the evidence that the bed's been moved a few times."

"That's where we need to go then," Fitz said.

They moved the bed, and Móirín hunched low. She located the scratch on the wall that marked where the hidden lever could be found. She pressed the bottom edge of the baseboard, and with a bit of a grinding sound, a section of the wall slid out of sight. Candlelight flickered beyond.

Either the Tempest knew they'd find this spot and had lit the candles in anticipation, or they were lit because people were being hidden there.

Oh, please let it be Brogan. The Tempest hurt people through their families. That put Brogan in extra danger. She had to find him before the Tempest's countdown reached its conclusion.

She blew out the candle on the bureau. The passageway was lit, and she'd rather have two free hands. Fitz seemed to come to the same conclusion.

They crossed the threshold and stepped into the dimness beyond. The air felt different. Not merely colder and more damp. Tension popped and arced all around. A warning. A threat.

This passageway led to a large subterranean room. The passage from the kitchen led to it as well, but that door had proven unreliable, sticking at times and making a great deal of noise.

She had, at one time, considered the room they were heading toward for her Dread Master's office. It was too difficult to get to, but that made it a convenient place to put hostages.

The closer they got to their destination, the more candles were lit around them. It was possible the Tempest had lit the area for her accomplices' benefit, but Móirín was beginning to doubt that.

"I think she knows we're coming," she said as the door to the underground room came into view. It was already open.

"I think you're right." Fitz adjusted his grip on the large knife in his hand, wearing the most focused expression she'd ever seen him wear.

How had her well-meaning efforts to help the vulnerable of London led to this? A terror-filled walk through a labyrinth she'd long ago claimed as her own to face down a criminal who could outthink the sharpest minds, who lacked any sort of conscience, and who was capable of nearly anything.

Móirín had only wanted to help; now people were getting hurt because of her.

"You do realize, Parky, if you get killed, I'll be cross with you forever."

"Back to Parky, am I?"

"Grumbling at you is helping me keep m'head."

"When I told you that I'd prefer *you* not get killed, you didn't tease me back or offer any kind of answer. That had me a bit nervous, I'll tell you."

She took a breath. "I've sorted out how this is likely to end. I ain't going to pretend I don't know who it is our foe wants to 'dethrone' or what that ultimately means."

"Móirín."

She pointed up ahead and spoke over whatever objections

he meant to make about her fate. "This is the room we're aiming for."

Móirín slipped her cudgel from its loop. A gun would be more effective at range, but the one she had traded Gemma for, like the one Móirín had used outside Kensington Palace, had only one shot. She'd not use it unless it was necessary. A knife and cudgel could accomplish a lot of things, as she well knew.

They stepped into what had once been an empty room.

In the silence, Fitz whispered, "What in the blazes?"

CHAPTER 25

"Are they all wax figures, do you think?" Fitz had been to Madame Tussaud's and hadn't found the displays disturbing. But being in an underground room, lit by flickering candelabras, with at least a dozen wax figures all facing the doorway, was unsettling in the extreme. Especially since they looked like people he knew. The people he and Móirín were searching for.

"I told the Tempest I found wax figures unnerving. Seems she was paying attention." Móirín approached the one who looked like Martin Afola, a young writer who'd nearly been killed by Claud Kincaid. He'd gone missing in recent days. "This one's wax." She poked the figure's shoulder. Then poked a little harder. "But only the head. The body's stuffed, with hay it feels like." She looked over at the figure of Kumar. "This one as well."

Fitz eyed Irving and Dominique, two of the older penny dreadful authors, and Hollis Darby. All three had wax heads. "You don't suppose Madame Tussaud is working with the Tempest, do you?"

"Unlikely. The woman's been dead for at least fifteen years. But that day at the waxworks, the Tempest said she had people there who answered to her. Looking around, I'd say those people were craftsmen and sculptors."

"She had them making all these." Fitz had encountered his share of criminals whose fixation on some wrong or another pushed them to extremes. The Tempest went beyond any of that. She wasn't content to simply kill her enemy; she wanted nothing short of agonizing annihilation. "This has to have been in the works for months."

"All planned far ahead of time." Móirín motioned with her knife toward a wax figurine bearing an unnerving resemblance to Barnabus Milligan. "They snatched Doc *tonight* but had this ready and waiting."

Standing apart from the others was another figure: Brogan. "This'n as well," Fitz said quietly.

Móirín moved to stand in front of the likeness of her brother. She didn't look truly shaken—Móirín never really did—but there was worry in her eyes. "They'd not all be facing the doorway if the Tempest hadn't known I'd check this spot through the passageway I took." She shook her head. "Seems we didn't think our way around her plans after all."

"What do you twig's in the travel trunk?" He motioned toward a large, battered chest set against the opposite wall.

"I can't say I'm overly anxious to know." But she moved to it anyway.

Fitz'd learned a great many things about Móirín Donnelly in the time he'd known her, and he admired her grit as much as her intelligence and beauty.

The trunk wasn't locked. She opened the lid.

Fitz leaned closer, giving himself a look at the contents lit by flickering candlelight.

Wax heads. Fletcher. Elizabeth. Stone. And himself. It was enough to turn his stomach.

"She'd aimed to abduct you too," Móirín said.

"But not you, apparently."

"She's angry with the Dreadfuls, blames them for saving Lord Chelmsford and delaying the justice she feels she's owed. I don't think she'd mind much hurting or even killing a few. But 'you cut off the head'—that's what she told me about destroying an enemy." Móirín stood and closed the lid. "You and the Dreadfuls were always bait."

"That makes you the fish and her the fisherwoman."

Móirín nodded as she looked back at the figurines, lifeless and inanimate, haunting and disquieting. "The night's getting away from us, Parky. We need to find them before it's too late."

"You said you know how this is going to end." A chill washed over him at the memory. He'd known what she meant, but he didn't want to believe it. "You can't have given up."

She met his eyes, and the fierceness he saw there eased some of his uncertainty. "If I'd given up, I wouldn't be here. But there's always a price to pay." She glanced at the wax figure of her brother. "The Tempest knows I'll pay it."

He cupped her face with his free hand. "I refuse to believe it'll come to that."

"You keep believing that for the both of us."

He leaned in, wanting to kiss her, needing to reassure the both of them. But she pulled back and stepped around him. "We need to find more than wax figures. The passage on this side leads to the kitchen."

"What do you suppose will be waiting for us in there?"

She glanced at him over her shoulder. "'Twouldn't be a terrible thing if it were a sandwich."

He recognized the shaky attempt at humor for what it was and offered a quick smile.

She took a lantern off a table near the door. "We should blow out the other lights. No point having the place burn down around us."

They did precisely that until only the light of her lantern and the candlelight spilling in from the other passage broke the darkness. It turned the wax figures into ominous silhouettes.

"What about the candles in the passage that brought us here?" Fitz asked.

"We need to extinguish those too. Do you want to take this passageway or the one that brought us here?"

He shook his head. "Splitting up is precisely what the Tempest wants us to do."

"And she has shown herself to delight in burning places to the ground with people inside. Best not make it too easy for her to do that again."

Blast it all, she was right. "I'll meet you in the kitchen."

"In the servants' corridor," she said. "That's halfway between our destinations."

"Be careful," he pleaded.

Móirín nodded and held her lantern higher, directing the light toward where he needed to go. He'd only taken a single step when she said his name. He turned back. She'd moved toward him and stood so close he could feel the heat from her body.

"You be careful too," she whispered.

He kissed her quickly, just as he'd done in the moment before she'd run for Kensington Palace. The faster he was, the sooner he'd be at her side again, watching out for danger and helping keep her safe during this dangerous hunt.

Fitz snatched up the first candle in the corridor, using it to light his path as he blew out the candles in the sconces all the way back to the door of Nolan's room. It was still ajar, and the lanterns they'd left on the bureau still sat there. He lit one with his candle, then traded them out.

The corridor was entirely silent. Fitz knew the Tempest wouldn't be alone in the house; she'd have at least some part of her army with her. Yet, the house was so quiet there was no way to guess where they might be.

"Where's Móirín?"

Only years of practice kept him from jumping at the sudden whisper directly beside him.

Ana Darby. She moved so stealthily and agilely that he knew he was right about her; she was the Phantom Fox.

"Kitchen," he whispered back. "But she means to meet up with me in this corridor."

"There's movement upstairs." That was Stone.

Fitz was so focused on helping Móirín that he wasn't keeping on top of his surroundings. He turned his lantern enough to illuminate them both.

"You sorted out that this house was the Tempest's hiding place?" Fitz asked.

Stone shook his head. "We got Móirín's message through the urchins."

Gemma'd been successful then.

"Celia's watching the front servants' entrance. Gemma's watching the back. Fletcher and Elizabeth are on their way."

Ana twitched her head toward the kitchens. "So is Móirín."

She was, indeed, coming their way. Her expression was set, focused, determined.

"Fearsome, ain't she?" Fitz said.

"It's a bit ridiculous we didn't sort out she was the Dread Master." Stone shook his head. "Seems obvious now."

"The Tempest twigged it. Móirín's the one she's after. It's the reason she hasn't simply killed the people she's snatched."

"They're bait," Ana said in a tone of realization.

"The Tempest enjoys causing fear and suffering." Stone was as stalwart as ever. "I ain't certain she planned on the rest of us being unswayable as well."

"That's what we need to be." Fitz knew Móirín had come to this place expecting not to leave alive. If he had the least to say about it, the outcome would be entirely different. "Find the Dreadfuls. Stop the Tempest. Don't abandon Móirín."

"That's the plan," Stone said.

Móirín reached them, but she didn't pause for greetings or explanations. "Stone, Ana, check the passage from the dry larder. On the back wall, you'll find a stone that's almost perfectly circular. Press it hard; it'll open a secret door to the passage. Fitz, you and I'll go check the passage at the back of the pub." Hers was not a tone that allowed for questions or opposition.

Fitz handed Ana his lantern. "The above stairs is lit," he explained. Then he held his pistol out to Stone. "Móirín has a firearm. Now the two of you will as well. Stay safe."

Stone accepted the weapon, then he and Ana made their way down the servants' corridor. Fitz and Móirín made for the stairs.

The ground floor of the house was as light as it had been when they'd first rushed through it. And the table in the entryway still held the welcome note and the stolen teapot.

"Pub's up the stairs," Móirín said. No extra words. No teasing. It was a change for her, one that drove home the gravity of it all.

Halfway up the stairs, a voice from below stopped them. "She said you'd come, Fitzgerald."

He looked back. "Mr. Cook."

"You've thrown your lot in with the losing side," Nolan said.

Fitz shook his head. "I don't side with criminals."

"You're currently siding with a murderer."

"Pot and kettle."

Móirín continued up the stairs, undeterred. But he didn't dare leave her to face yet more danger alone. Fitz made to follow.

"I know where your grandfather is," Nolan called out. "I've always known. I can take you to him. You can be together."

Heaven help him, he hesitated. He halted.

"It's how I knew where to get his kettle," Nolan continued. "You'd be done searchin'. Done lookin'."

He'd be with his grandfather again. His family.

Another figure appeared on the floor above just as Móirín reached it. Fitz knew him, had confronted him with Móirín weeks ago when the resurrectionist had been attempting to kidnap Gemma Milligan: the second of the Kincaid brothers, Silas.

"Where's my brother, girl?" the man growled.

He was a known murderer, among other heinous crimes, but Móirín didn't flinch.

"Where's *mine*?" she demanded.

"No one thwarts the Kincaids," Silas shouted. "No one."

Without warning, he lunged at Móirín. Before she could react, before Fitz could take a single step toward her, she stumbled backward. Light glinted off the knife in Silas's hand. But Móirín hadn't fallen. Hadn't dropped. Had he missed?

Fitz rushed to her, reaching her just as a voice, calm but carrying, brought everything to a halt.

"You oughtn't to have done that, Silas." The Tempest rose

from a chair in the far corner of the large first-floor landing and slowly approached.

"Did he get you?" Fitz whispered to Móirín, praying the answer was no.

She took in a sharp breath, one tinged with pain. That were answer enough.

"I told you, Silas, no one hurts her but me. I *told* you." She spoke like he was a very young child, almost pityingly. "Why is it you don't do what you're told? You force me to do things I don't want to do." She looked into the open door of a room not more than a few steps away. The Protector and the Raven stood there, watching. Nolan was still halfway up the stairs, eyes on all that was happening above.

"My friends," the Tempest said, "this one doesn't listen. I'm afraid I no longer require him."

She snapped her fingers, and the two thugs emerged, grabbing Silas by the scruff and dragging him down the stairs. He shouted profane objections all the way down. Spat on Nolan as he passed.

The Tempest watched the display with a look of annoyance. "I ask so little of them. Only that they help me and do the simple things I ask." Her steely gaze turned to Móirín. "What do you do when your lackeys make life difficult for you? Punish them? Their families? People oughtn't put their families in danger by being uncooperative."

Fitz put an arm around Móirín's back. She was standing steady, but she'd already grown more pale.

A few more of the Tempest's roughs stepped from the room where the Protector and the Raven had been. They looked fierce and dangerous, but also afraid. When their eyes darted to the Tempest, that fear turned to terror.

The Tempest hadn't looked away from Móirín. "Has that adorable Fletcher Walker and 'Mr. King' and the Phantom Fox arrived yet to search for your pathetic little Dreadfuls? They will find them, of course. I always intended them to. The only thing in question was whether or not they'd find them in time."

"By morning," Fitz repeated what they'd been told.

"Handsome *and* clever." She looked him up and down. "I can see why our Dread Master keeps you around." The Tempest was surrounded by people Fitz knew would protect her, though whether out of loyalty or under threat of punishment, he didn't know. She looked past them, down the stairs. "Did you convince him, Nolan? Dangle that promise in front of him?"

"He weren't convinced."

The Tempest clicked her tongue. "But he can tell you where your grandfather is, Detective Constable Parkington. He knows, I can assure you of that."

His hand at Móirín's side was growing wet, and he feared he knew with what. If he abandoned her now, it would all end.

"Do you know how he knows?" the Tempest said, an unnerving glint of satisfaction entering her piercing gaze. "Because he's the one who killed him."

Fitz pulled in a sharp breath.

"He told you your grandfather owed him money, didn't he?" Again, the Tempest used that tone of horribly tried patience. "Quite the other way around, I'm afraid. And when you became a constable a few years back, the poor man had quite a dilemma on his hands. You might piece it all together and bring the law down on him. But who could possibly tie up loose ends that were nearly twenty years old? Who could find any and every person who could provide you with a clue and take care of the problem?" She smiled sweetly.

"Why not do *me* in and 'take care of the problem'?"

"Oh, sweeting, because Nolan needed to know I could whisper the truth of it to you at any moment. That kept him *very* obedient these past few years." She looked pleased. "I helped him with that spot of trouble so he would help me here, in this house, with these . . . people." The word seemed to sit sour in her mouth. She looked to Móirín again. "They're all here, Móirín. But they aren't all together. One among the lot is far too valuable to waste on a little side chase, don't you think?"

"Brogan," Móirín whispered.

Fitz didn't like how weak her voice sounded—or the clear note of pain beneath it.

"Leave off the hangdog look, Detective Constable. She's too tough a bird to die from a prick in the side." The Tempest looked utterly annoyed at him for being concerned about another human being. "Besides, she has to live long enough to save a very important life. Don't you, Móirín? A life you promised to safeguard and, yet, somehow haven't. How very disappointed your parents would be, if they weren't dead, that is. Somehow it is our dead family members whose opinions seem to matter the most." The Tempest looked to Fitz. "But you know that."

Dead family members. Dead for twenty years. For all the time Fitz had been searching for him.

"I grow weary of this." She addressed her guards. "The new arrivals will soon find and free the busybodies who usually occupy this ridiculous house. Find them and make certain they do not leave here alive. They die, or the people you're here protecting die. Your choice." Móirín was the focus of the Tempest's disconcerting glare again. "You still haven't found what I've hidden from you, and time is running short."

"I'll help you find Brogan," Fitz said to Móirín.

The Tempest shook her head. "It's only fun if she goes alone. Don't ruin it, or I'll be forced to end the game early."

He wouldn't be permitted to help, and Móirín, already injured, would be on her own.

The Tempest looked him over again. "I will allow you a head start before releasing my hordes. That should make it more of a challenge for them." She made a shooing motion. "Run along, little Parkington. Run before they do. Find the others and begin your search."

"Pub's down the corridor to the left," Móirín whispered. "Check that tunnel."

"You're wasting time," the Tempest said, her words a bit singsong.

"Go," Móirín told Fitz, quick and firm. "Go save my Dreadfuls."

"Who will save you?"

She flashed a smile. "*I* will."

"I grow weary of this." The Tempest looked utterly bored. "I can kill your brother from here, Móirín. Don't tempt me."

Móirín's eyes pulled wide in a look that spoke of sudden understanding. She turned and rushed down the corridor behind her.

"Go save her Dreadfuls, little Parkington. It was her last request."

Last request. He refused to believe that. He would find and rally the other Dreadfuls, and they would provide Móirín with enough support to have some hope of emerging victorious. But first, *he* needed to find them before the gathering storm crushed them all.

CHAPTER 26

I *can kill your brother from here."*

Móirín didn't know if the Tempest had meant that to be a clue, but it had told her on the instant where Brogan was being kept.

There was a hidden room on the other side of the wall from where the Tempest had been standing. It was too wide to be called a closet but too narrow to function as a real room. The door leading to it was tucked around a corner and blended in perfectly with the wall. The secret areas of the house were well hidden, but this one had eluded even Móirín for the first few years.

She pried open the hidden door, clutching the spot between the wall paneling where the latch was. The passage beyond was not lit, but there was light at the other end. She moved quickly and carefully.

"I can kill your brother from here."

The sooner Móirín reached him and helped him escape, the more likely he would survive. But the wound she'd sustained, and the blood that was soaking her dress, left her weaker and slower than she'd prefer.

She knew the room she was headed to. It was large and open and unencumbered. 'Twas also easily escaped. Either there'd been a change made to hold him there, or it was heavily guarded. Móirín had her trusty knife in hand, doing her best to prepare for every possibility.

And yet, when she reached the doorway, she was not at all prepared for what she found.

A gibbet cage, not unlike the one she had spoken with the Tempest about at Madame Tussaud's, sat in the corner, a chain connecting it to the ceiling, though it was not swinging in the air.

Brogan sat on the ground outside the cage, his back to her, facing the wall. As fast as her injury would allow, she rushed to his side. She knelt next to him, wincing at the pull on her wound.

"Ah, Brogan. I've been worried about what the Tempest might've done to you. Are you injured?"

"'Tis a trap, Móirín," he said. A blindfold covered his eyes. "I've not sorted exactly what, but 'tis a trap."

"Of course it is." She pulled the cloth from his eyes. His wrists were cuffed, and the irons were connected by chains to the gibbet. Brogan's feet were also shackled and connected to a chain padlocked to the wall.

"They took Vera," he said hoarsely.

Móirín set a hand on his shoulder. "We found her at Lord Chelmsford's. Her father's with her, and they're both safe."

The sigh that escaped him shook with emotion. "You swear she is?"

"I swear to it."

"You need to help the Dreadfuls get out," he said, "then get yourself safe."

Móirín shook her head. "Even if I was such a horrible and cowardly sister as all that, your jailer would never allow it. Things happen the way she intends, or she rains down punishments. If I left, she'd kill you for certain."

That he showed no surprise or shock told Móirín he'd come to understand his fate already.

"How much can you move with all these chains?"

He shook his head. "The ones at m'feet don't allow me to stand. The ones on m'hands make it too painful to move much."

Both sets of chains were held in place by heavy padlocks out of his reach. "You've not spotted any keys have you?"

He shook his head. "I've been blindfolded since before I was brought into this room."

The heavy chain connecting the gibbet to the ceiling was not the only chain threaded through eyebolts installed above their heads. This was put here by the Tempest, which meant every bit of it would have a purpose.

Móirín traced the path of the chains connected to Brogan's wrists. They passed through the uppermost row of bars and inside the gibbet. She could make out a padlock amongst the spiderweb of chains interwoven at the top of the gibbet.

She looked back at him. He looked decidedly worse for the evening's altercations. Though the corner was dim enough that she might be seeing shadows rather than the bruises she suspected were there, she didn't doubt the Tempest's people hadn't been gentle when they'd snatched him from the safe house. This was why she'd kept her role in the DPS a secret. Her brother had been targeted more closely and more fiercely than the others *because* of his connection to her.

"I'm going to get you out of here, Brog." She pressed her

hand to her throbbing side, her dress sticky and wet. "But I suspect I can only manage it from inside the gibbet."

"She's probably rigged it somehow."

"I know." She grabbed hold of the nearest iron crossbar. Knowing it'd hurt quite a lot to pull herself to her feet, she took a moment to build up the will to do it.

"You move like you're hurting," he said.

"Silas Kincaid mistook my ribs for a knife sheath." She shrugged. "Absent-minded of him, to be sure."

He tried to turn toward her, but the cuffs and chains prevented him. "How bad did he get you, Móirín? Don't lie to me."

Don't lie to me. She'd told him a heap too many falsehoods. She'd give him the truth now. "It's bad. I'm not likely to die from it, at least not quickly, but 'tis making things more of a struggle than I'd like."

"If the light were better, would I see blood?" He clearly wasn't satisfied with her answer.

"You would, and plenty of it." She'd seen it herself, and she could feel it in the heavy stickiness of her clothing clinging to her side.

"'Not likely to die'? Are you underplaying the matter?"

She hadn't the heart to tell him that, even if the stab wound didn't kill her, the Tempest fully intended to. And the woman was more than capable of it. "I've ample strength for sorting this puzzle of chains and bars. We'll have you free in a moment."

Móirín pulled herself to her feet. That small effort cost her a bit of strength. Heaven help them both if she didn't have enough remaining endurance to save her brother.

She placed herself directly in front of the open door of the gibbet but couldn't bring herself to step inside. It was a trap, just as Brogan had warned, just as she'd realized the moment she'd seen the cage. She'd told the Tempest that being locked in a cage would be unbearable. Another thing the woman had noted and not forgotten.

Though she couldn't yet identify how the mechanism worked, Móirín knew that once she stepped inside, she would not be stepping back out.

She took a quick breath. To her much-grieved parents, she silently said, *I've looked after him as I promised I would. And I'll do so right to the very end.*

Then she stepped inside.

Nothing happened, which wasn't surprising. The Tempest took too much delight in torturing people to bring the *anticipation* of suffering to an end too quickly.

Now that she was inside, Móirín could see the mechanisms above with greater clarity. A lantern hung high on the nearest wall—the wall the gibbet was touching on one side—and the light made all the difference.

The chains holding Brogan's hands were padlocked to another chain that ran directly up to the ceiling where it connected with two other chains. One threaded through a nearby eyebolt in the ceiling. At the end of it were four keys—one for each padlock, and one for the manacles and shackles binding Brogan.

"I found the keys we were looking for," she told Brogan.

"Can you reach them?"

"Maybe if I climbed the gibbet. Maybe."

"Can you, though? Being stabbed as you are?"

"If it meant getting you free, Brog, I'd climb the Tower of London."

She set her foot on the crossbar just above the base of the gibbet. With one hand holding her throbbing side and the other grasping a vertical bar of the cage, she pulled herself up to stand on the crossbar. She'd climb the whole thing if she needed to—despite her pain, despite her light-headedness—but studying the ring and clasp holding the keys to the chain above, she knew climbing up to it wouldn't do any good. The pointed top of the cage angled away from the keys. She'd need one hand to keep her balance on the cage, but she'd need *both* hands to work the clasp and thread the ring to free the keys.

If climbing wasn't the answer, perhaps the keys could be lowered.

She traced the path of the chain leading in the opposite direction toward the wall through more eyebolts and down the wall to a lever.

Móirín lowered herself to the floor. Merciful heavens, she was in pain. She took the single step needed to reach the other side—gibbets weren't known for being roomy—and pressed the side of her face to the side of the cage, getting a better look at the lever.

It was a winch.

Operating it would certainly lower the keys and the padlock holding Brogan in place. She could remove the keys and free her brother.

But this was the work of the Tempest. It could not be that simple. Though installing a gibbet and threading chains and fastening a winch to a wall was a great deal more effort than simply ambushing Móirín on the street, it wasn't a terribly complicated thing. All of this could easily have been put in place in the weeks since the DPS had abandoned their headquarters.

So what was she missing? What *else* would operating the winch do?

"Have you found anything else?" Brogan asked.

"She's left me a puzzle, and it's taking me a moment to sort."

Beneath the winch, less visible in the shadows, was another chain. It ran down the wall, through another eyebolt in the floor, and across to the gibbet door.

The door.

And in a flash, she knew. Operating the winch would lower the keys and padlock, but it would also close the door. And the door, without a doubt, would lock shut. She could free Brogan, but she would be trapped.

This was who the Tempest was. This was the sort of torture she inflicted on people, requiring them to sacrifice themselves to save their family members from horrible fates.

There's always a price to be paid, and she knows I'll pay it.

She took a step to where Brogan's back was pressed to the outside of the gibbet and lowered herself to her knees. She pressed her hand against the growing pain and wetness at her side.

"I can get the keys down and the padlock opened."

He was able to turn his head to look at her. "Without having to climb the Tower of London, I'm assuming." He smiled.

She couldn't smile back. "You know I love you, right? You know I'd do anything in the world for you, and that I couldn't have hoped for a better brother than you?"

"Móirín?" Her name slipped from him in a worried whisper.

"I need you to tell me that you know I love you. And, maybe, that you forgive me for having lied to you about being the Dread Master."

"I know why you lied," he said. "And I'm not sore about that."

Relief trickled through her despite the horror that awaited.

"And, yeah, I know you love me," he said. "I love you too.

You're the best sister a person could hope for. And one of the best people I could ever imagine knowing."

The relief began to tiptoe toward something almost like peace.

She pulled herself to her feet and turned to face the lever. Upon closer inspection, she recognized it as the handle from the Guinness tap in the pub. Whether the Tempest meant it to be as a vindictive reference to Brogan's hand in creating a pub inside the house or to Móirín's fight for her life at the Guinness factory wasn't entirely clear. Likely both.

Móirín wiped the fresh blood from her hand onto the side of her skirt. She took the lever in both hands and pulled downward. The squeal of metal on metal drowned out her involuntary groan of agony. The winch snapped upward once more. She pulled the lever down again, the same noises accompanying the repeated movement.

A quick glance upward showed the chain holding the keys was, indeed, lowering. And a look at the door showed it was closing as well.

She pulled the lever again.

This time, Brogan noticed. "Móirín, the door's closing."

"I know it." She pulled the lever once more.

The keys and padlock were lower, though still out of reach. The door was nearly closed but not entirely.

"Can you put something in the hole to prevent the latch from sliding into place?" Brogan asked. He was able to turn his head, so he could see her slowly being closed in.

"Not a bad idea."

What did she have at her disposal? The shillelagh she'd taken from her Dread Master's office wouldn't fit in the small hole. The gun she had traded Gemma for wouldn't either. She had the clothes she was wearing and her shoes, but the shoes were too big. She could try a sock, but even if she could manage to fit it into the hole, the latches of gibbets were notoriously strong. The cage was meant to be inescapable; a bit of fabric was unlikely to thwart its purpose.

"I don't have anything that'd work." She looked through the gaps in the gibbet bars, scanning the room for anything that was the size, shape, and strength that she needed. But other than the two of them, the gibbet and chains, and the lanterns on hooks around the room, it was entirely empty.

"Could you pull the lever until the door isn't quite closed, then snatch the keys?" Brogan said.

'Twas worth trying. But another pull of the lever brought the door within an inch of closing, and the keys were still out of reach. "Won't do, Brogan. The only way to get the keys is to close the door."

Before she could lose her nerve or Brogan could plead otherwise, she pulled a final time. The crash of the gibbet door echoed in the room. The Guinness-handle lever snapped upward, and the chains above her dropped until they ran out of chain. She could reach the keys with no trouble and open the padlock holding Brogan hostage.

She was in so much pain, and so desperately tired, but she couldn't stop. She worked at the ring and clasp holding the keys to the chain. After a frustrating few tries, she got them free.

She breathed through the pain in her side and blinked away the splotches in her vision. The first key she tried in the padlock didn't turn, but the next one did. She freed the chains, letting them drop to the floor in a cacophony of sound.

Brogan was able to move more and twisted in her direction.

She set the two remaining keys in his hand. "One'll be for the other padlock, the others for your manacles and shackles."

Brogan unlocked the manacles at his wrist and slipped free. He scooted to the padlock at the other end of his ankle chains.

Móirín leaned against the side of the gibbet, attempting to regain her strength. She summoned what she did have and attempted to open the gibbet door, already knowing it wouldn't budge. And it didn't.

"Any chance this last one is for the gibbet rather than the shackles?" Brogan asked, holding up the final key.

She shook her head. "'Twas all part of the plan. A trap, like we both knew 'twould be."

"You can't get out," he whispered.

"But *you* can." She pushed down the emotion rising in her chest. He would mistake it for hesitation rather than her feeling overwhelmed at the thought of finally being able to do for him what he had done for her. He'd fled Dublin with her, left behind the life he'd built and loved there. He'd given up so much for her safety, and she had never felt deserving of it or equal to that sacrifice. To finally put that right gave her a measure of peace she hadn't felt in five years.

The Tempest, no doubt, expected her to look on the decision Móirín had made and the cell she'd knowingly locked herself into with horror and terror, but she felt calm. She knew this was what she needed to do. She knew it.

Brogan tried the key in his shackles. They opened without objection. He looked up and met her eyes, emotion visible even in the dim light.

"I'll bring someone back here for you." Brogan reached through the bars and cupped her face. "As soon as I can, I'll bring someone back, and we'll figure out how to get you free of this."

She fought back her tears, reaching between the bars and touching his face as well. 'Twas an old gesture between them, a way of comforting each other in their darkest times. "I promised Vera and our parents that you'd be safe. I've told too many lies in my life, Brog. Don't add another to 'em."

"We'll be back for you." He offered that firm and final promise before rushing from the room, his footsteps echoing softer and softer as he moved farther away.

Panting with exhaustion, she dropped to the floor, bracing herself against the surge in pain that movement caused.

Brogan was free.

Fletcher, Stone, and Fitz wouldn't rest until they found the Dreadfuls.

There'd be a battle, one she'd not be there to fight.

After five years of running from the Peelers to avoid being locked away, she was in a cell. Brogan had given up everything to keep her out of one. Now she'd chosen this to save him.

She didn't doubt the Tempest would come visiting, and soon. And, even in her pain and agony, even knowing her foe was likely a dozen steps ahead of her, Móirín smiled.

CHAPTER 27

The pub was easy to find. But it wasn't empty when Fitz walked in. Stone and Ana were at an opening in the back wall.

"How'd you get here without passing the mob?" Fitz asked, rushing to them.

"There's a mob?"

"The Tempest's army. She means to unleash them any minute now."

"Close this door," Ana said to Fitz. "That'll buy us a bit of time."

The passage beyond was narrow, but lit.

"Snatch up the candles as we pass," Ana said. "The darkness might slow them down."

They did precisely that, following the passage downward.

"Where's Móirín?" Stone asked.

"Thinks she's twigged where Brogan's being kept," Fitz said. "She rushed off that way and sent me here."

"And is that blood on your hand yours or hers?" Ana asked.

"Hers." He didn't stop walking. He needed help if they'd

any chance of standing with Móirín against the Tempest, and he knew he hadn't much time to secure it.

The passage led to a small room, half the size of the one they'd found beneath Nolan's. This time, though, the occupants weren't glassy-eyed wax figures.

A row of captives were tied to iron rings bolted into the wall.

"Hollis!" Ana's cry sounded before anyone could say a word. She leapt over nearby legs all the way to where her husband sat and tossed herself against him, throwing her arms around him.

In perfect synchrony, Fitz and Stone took knives to the ropes.

"The Tempest is nearby with thugs and toughs, and they'll be on our heels in a heartbeat." Fitz had Irving free. The ropes weren't overly thick, a sign the Tempest meant them to be freed. But to what end? "Móirín's in trouble. The Tempest's been targeting her all along and means to kill her tonight. We can't let that happen."

"Gemma?" Barnabus asked as Stone cut through the rope holding him.

"She's in the house," Fitz said. "Móirín rescued her from her uncle."

"Only one uncle?" He didn't sound relieved.

Fitz had Martin free. "The other was killed on orders of the Tempest. But we can't help Gemma or anyone else if we're all stuck in here."

Irving helped Martin to his feet. The younger man had been stabbed by Claud Kincaid not many weeks back, a wound so bad it weren't clear at the time if he'd live or die. He'd be in no condition to undertake a battle.

"Anyone know if there's another way out of here?" Fitz asked, continuing to cut ropes.

"I was brought in first," Kumar said, "but not through the pub like the others. There's another exit past here that'll drop us in the Parliamentary Room."

To Irving, Fitz said, "There's a passage from the Parliamentary Room that leads down to Móirín's office. And that room leads outside. Get Martin out."

Irving nodded.

Voices sounded from the dark passage behind them.

"Onward," Stone instructed them all.

Everyone was free, and everyone moved without hesitation, following Kumar's lead.

The passageway out was shorter than the one leading in, so they arrived at the fully lit Parliamentary Room in a matter of moments. Stone and Barnabus pushed a heavy sideboard across the hidden doorway, hopefully buying them a bit of time.

Fitz led Irving and Martin to the escape tunnel behind the throne. "Take care of him."

"Like he was my own son," Irving said.

These Dreadfuls really were family to each other. It was little wonder Móirín felt as strongly about them as she did.

"I can't promise we won't be outnumbered." Stone's authoritative voice sounded among them. He stood firm and stalwart, larger-than-life, as always. A source of calm, courage, and confidence. "But we do not relent. We do not forget."

"We are the Dread Penny Society." Fletcher's voice pulled all their eyes to the actual doorway of the room. "And, this time, we ain't alone."

A shout went up behind him.

The Dreadfuls, along with Fitz and Ana, stepped out into the entryway.

The front door stood wide open, and people were pouring inside.

On the landing above, the Tempest's voice cut through the cacophony. "You all know the consequences of defying me."

She'd controlled London's most vulnerable—and the new arrivals appeared to be precisely that—through threats and violence for years. Her very voice stopped the rush of people in an instant.

Fletcher hopped up a few stairs, then turned and faced them all. "We all know you know her, know the pain she causes. We know she promises to end that pain only if you do her bidding, bidding that causes more pain. We know that. We know her.

"But you know us. Stone, who has rescued your children. Dr. Milligan, who has helped your daughters and sisters and dear friends escape the clutches of the madams and macks this monster controls. Hollis Darby, who fights for the learning that offers your children more opportunities. Brogan and Móirín Donnelly are in this house too, fighting for you as they always have. They, who give tirelessly and ask nothing in return."

He looked up at the Tempest and raised his voice almost to a shout. "Many of you are here because she threatened you or your families, twisting you into fighting for her, when everything in you screams that you fight for the freedom she's stolen from you. She'll never stop hurting you. Not ever. Not even if you kill everyone here on her command. She will still torture you, still hurt your families."

"Silence him," the Tempest commanded. People behind her began moving to fulfill her command.

"You call yourself the violence, the storm, the unstoppable

SARAH M. EDEN

force," Fitz said to the Tempest. "But you have heard the battle
cry of these people, and there is fear in your eyes. They've
learned what Mr. King's latest offering promises: there are more
of us than there are of you."

The army Fletcher had brought sent up another shout.

To the Dreadfuls, Fletcher said quickly, "Draw the battle
into the street. There are hundreds more out there who are ready
to be free of her."

"Hundreds?" Stone said.

"Elizabeth and the urchins and I have been rallying them.
The battle has begun."

Chaos descended in the next instant. Clashes and shouts
and the clang of weapons. In the midst of it all, the Tempest
disappeared. And Fitz knew where she'd gone as surely as Móirín
had known that the final confrontation would be between the
two of them.

In such quick succession that Fitz couldn't be certain which
happened first, a gunshot exploded in the air and the rush of
people pressed in all directions. The chaos was too extreme, the
fear too palpable for Fitz to keep tabs on where everyone was,
who'd fired the weapon, if anyone was hurt, if they were whole.
But the crowd *was* flooding out of the house, and not in a pan-
icked flight. They were fighting still.

Fitz turned toward the stairs, not empty but passable. He'd
last seen Móirín on the floor above. But he hadn't taken more
than two steps when a voice called his name.

"Parkington! Parkington!" Brogan Donnelly.

"Did she find you?" Fitz ran to him. "Blimey, man, you've
blood on your face."

"It's Móirín's. Please, you have to help."

He followed Brogan at a run. The shouting and clamoring and chaos grew more muffled as they turned down the corridor.

Fitz tried not to let himself wonder how hurt Móirín was, how dire her situation might be, whether they would arrive only to find the Tempest had already "dethroned" the woman she saw as her rival.

A door disguised as part of the wall stood ajar. They rushed through it and into a narrow room, lit by lanterns but no windows. In the far corner was a gibbet cage. And inside that cage, sitting on the floor, eyes closed, was Móirín.

"Love." Fitz dropped onto the floor just on the other side of where she sat. He reached his arm through the bars, touching her cheek. Her skin was not chilled but truly cold.

Then she opened her eyes. She was still alive.

She was pale and clearly weakened, but even in the dim lantern light he could see the fierceness in her expression that he'd grown so familiar with over the months he'd known her.

"This ain't no time to fall to pieces, Parky," she spoke softly, her voice shaking a little. "I've not been able to sort a way out of here yet. But I've lost a heap of blood, and m'mind's not clear anymore."

A horrible sign, that.

"I'd hoped Ana might somehow find me here." She was breathing slowly and with great effort. "I think she could manage to get up to the top of the gate and see if anything can be done to get this door open again, even a little, maybe . . . enough for me to . . . wriggle out."

"I'll find her," Brogan said. "Don't die while I'm gone."

Móirín silently closed her eyes.

In a flash, Brogan was gone. Back into the fray. Back into danger.

Did Móirín have any idea how loyal so many people were to her? Fitz's appeal to the blackmailed horde held as much weight as it did in large part because of her. There weren't a struggling corner of London what didn't know her name and hadn't been seen through hard times by the Donnelly siblings.

Móirín released a wavering, difficult breath. "I didn't want him to know how bad things are." Her voice had lost all the strength that had been there moments before.

"Can you scoot any closer, love?" Fitz reached both his arms between the metal bars, hoping to hold her, to offer some support.

She moved slowly and with pain. "I'm terribly cold. So, so cold."

"It *is* cold here." He was able to get his arms somewhat around her, but the bars made it impossible to truly hold her. He was able to kiss her cheek and rest his forehead against the bars directly beside hers. "We found the Dreadfuls—all of 'em. We'll get Doc to see to you, put you to rights."

"He can see me all he wants. But there ain't no way to put blood back in a body."

"He'd know how to control the bleeding," Fitz insisted. "With rest, you'd recover if the bleeding stopped."

She sat, breath shallow, not speaking, not teasing him.

"I shouldn't have let myself be distracted," Fitz said. "I should've stayed right beside you, watching for threats. Nolan's promises weren't— I should've known—"

"Do me a favor, Fitz."

"Anything," he whispered.

"Shut up." The tiniest flicker of a smile appeared on her face, before her expression slacked into one of utter exhaustion.

"We'll get you out of here, then you can make sure I shut my gob using whatever tactics you deem necessary."

"Do you always flirt in life-and-death situations?"

He didn't like how quiet her voice was. Footsteps moved in the passageway behind him. Finally, a bit of luck. Brogan had found Ana.

But it wasn't Brogan who stepped into the room.

It was the Tempest.

CHAPTER 28

F inally.

Móirín had known from the moment she'd realized the moving metal gates were going to form a cage that the Tempest would eventually make some kind of dramatic entrance in what she anticipated as their final showdown. The high-polished gun in the woman's hand and the head-to-toe red *was* dramatic. But taking time in the middle of a battle to change her attire was a step too far. Móirín would have been absolutely infuriated if she'd bled to death waiting for the Tempest to finally arrive.

Fitz shifted his position, so he was facing their foe and making it harder for the woman to shoot Móirín.

"Isn't this touching?" Beneath the mockery in the Tempest's voice was frustration.

Móirín would wager the battle raging beyond this cell was not going the way the Tempest wished. The Dreadfuls, no doubt, had surprised her, showing themselves to be as scrappy and brave as Móirín knew them to be.

"All these weeks, I'd assumed your brother was the one I

ought to torture you with. Who would've guessed the fugitive would fall in love with a copper?"

"I did try not to." Móirín breathed shallowly through the pain. "Parky here is just impossible to resist."

"You're going to make me vomit." The Tempest's weapon didn't shake, didn't shift.

"Promise?" Móirín asked dryly.

"I don't have my pistol," Fitz whispered to her, worried.

"The others will find us," Móirín whispered back.

"But in time?"

"No," the Tempest said simply and calmly. "Now, Detective Constable, step away."

He faced their foe once more. "You'll have to shoot me first."

"Oh, I am going to shoot you. And making this ridiculous stand won't save either of you. Nor will it grant you any additional time for your dreamed-of deliverers to arrive. I'll simply kill you both now."

"Best do as she says," Móirín said.

"I won't—" Fitz started to say.

"We tried thinking steps ahead of her, but she's always steps beyond that." Móirín weakly pushed his arm back, urging him to move away. "Antagonizing her's not going to help us."

He moved, reluctantly, head swiveling between her and the Tempest.

"Did you see my collection?" the Tempest asked Móirín. "Well, my *secondary* collection. Wax versions are far less interesting than the originals but also far more cooperative. And I know how very . . . fond you are of them."

"You did all that for me?" Móirín clicked her tongue. "You shouldn't have, dearie."

"You are trying my patience."

"At least you've acknowledged that I'm trying."

"Stand up," the Tempest demanded.

"I'm not certain I can."

"This ends with you facing me," the Tempest said. "That is always how this was going to end."

"Too bad you didn't tell Silas Kincaid that." Móirín struggled to her feet.

"He's already paid for that mistake. Now, get to your feet."

Móirín's legs wobbled. "Or what? Your years of planning revenge against Lord Chelmsford and the Crown prove to be only one of your failures? This part of your plan crumbles, ending not in triumph but with shooting a dying woman in a cage? How utterly cowardly."

"You really don't think ahead of me, do you?" The Tempest sighed with clear annoyance. "This was never going to *end* with you in a cage. I simply wanted to add to the experience—make your time here tonight more personal. Hearing you so foolishly confess at the waxworks that being confined in a cage is a fear of yours made this part of it inevitable. Really shouldn't have told me that."

"Believe me, if I'd known you were listening so closely . . ." She tried to shrug but didn't entirely manage it.

"Enough blathering," the Tempest snapped. "You'll die looking me in the eye." She pointed her pistol at Fitz. "All the way to the other side of the room, Detective. That's a good boy." Then she tossed an iron key into the gibbet. "Open the door," she instructed Móirín.

"This would've been far easier if you'd tossed the key inside while I was still seated," Móirín said as she bent down to pick it up. Pain pulsed through her whole body. The room spun as she stood upright once more. She leaned against the gibbet and slid her arm between the bars, bending her wrist back to slide the key into the lock and turn. It scraped as it inched open.

"Come, face me."

Móirín pressed her hand to her side, near to her bleeding wound but not atop it. With shuffling steps, she stepped out of the gibbet and moved to stand before the Tempest.

She motioned with her hand from the angry red stain on her side to the Tempest's red dress. "How quaint: we match."

"Shut up." The Tempest was allowing more emotion than usual.

Good.

"I could have destroyed Chelmsford, could have avenged my family. They *deserve* to be avenged. Then you and your pathetic society interfered. They—"

"Will this speech take much longer?" Móirín pressed harder against her side. "I'll need something to lean against."

Out of the corner of her eye, she saw Fitz step toward her.

"Don't move," the Tempest snapped at him. To Móirín, she said, "Lean against the wall or the gibbet cage if you're so pathetic."

Móirín shuffled to the wall. Her hand slipped from its position, trying to hold back the pain of her stab wound. Encroaching weakness would see it sliding, limp, into her pocket. She leaned her shoulder against the wall and returned her attention to the Tempest.

"You're better lit now," Móirín said. "That should please you."

With the lantern light spilling more directly on the Tempest, Móirín could see the flare of her nostrils. She was upended. The

Tempest had always been so emotionally even, but this anger was precisely what Móirín was hoping for.

"Your ridiculous inability to stop talking has made this moment easier in some ways," the Tempest said. "You told me that your gun is a one-shot pistol. And you used that shot to kill Arlo Kincaid."

"Part of the plan?" Móirín asked.

"Of course. And I heard the little detective here tell you he was out of shots as well. Which means, I outsmarted you to the very end. I win." She straightened to her full height, glaring at Móirín almost regally. "Have you any final words?"

Móirín nodded slowly, swaying.

After a moment of silence, the Tempest growled, "Your final words."

A cough. A slow blink. Her hand slipping into her pocket.

"Long live the queen." She pulled Gemma's pistol from her pocket, aimed, and shot.

The Tempest stumbled backward, her weapon flying from her hand as she tumbled to the floor.

"That won't have killed her," Móirín said to Fitz. "Snatch her gun."

Fitz had already begun moving to do precisely that. "You were pretending?"

"Exaggerating." Móirín winced as she moved, crossing to the Tempest. "I do need Doc to sew me up, or I likely *will* die in here, just not as fast as I needed her to believe I would."

Fitz stood guard over the scarlet-clad woman, pointing her own weapon at her, but still speaking to Móirín. "You planned this?"

"*She* planned this, just as I'd hoped she would." Móirín leaned fully against the wall. "The plot against the queen was too ridiculous to actually succeed and would always have ended with me shooting Arlo and using up the one shot she knew I had."

"Which is why you convinced Gemma to give you her gun."

"I offered our friend a few breadcrumbs along the way so I could know what path she was walking down." For a moment, the room spun. Maybe her exaggeration about her injury had been closer to the truth than she'd realized. "Once I saw the wax figures in the basement, I knew there'd be a cage at some point. And I can shoot as well from inside a cage as out, though she wouldn't know that."

"You poor dear," Fitz said to the Tempest. "You thought you were being so clever."

She moved herself into a sitting position, anger clear on her face.

"She not only let me out, she willingly put herself in enough lamplight for me to hit her with hardly any effort. And she thought leaning a shoulder against a wall for support was pathetic." Móirín tsked. "The poor, dead would-be-queen."

"I'm not dead," the Tempest snapped.

"Proof enough we aren't as alike as you've always insisted," Móirín said. "You take delight in killing people, and I take great pains to avoid killing 'em."

The Tempest tossed a particularly vile curse at Móirín and started to get to her feet.

"Best not, dearie," Fitz said, waggling the Tempest's own gun at her. "That bullet might've hit more than your shoulder."

Another curse, this time at Fitz. In the next moment, a rush of people entered the room. Móirín was worse off than she'd realized; she couldn't at first tell who any of them were or even how many.

"I found Ana," Brogan's voice said from just beyond where she could focus. "And Doc."

"The battle below?" Móirín pressed.

"Still going, but not for long. Those she's threatened have turned on her."

Móirín nodded. "Make certain our guest in red isn't going to bleed to death."

"I'd rather make certain *you* aren't," Doc said. "There's a lot of blood on your clothes." He crossed to her. "Look me in the eye, Móirín."

She did, though her vision was blurry.

"Lift your arm so I can see the wound."

She obeyed, and he peeled back the sliced remnant of the side of her dress. The mixture of dried and fresh blood nearly glued the fabric to her skin. Everything pulled with the movement of her dress. She sucked in a tense breath.

"This'll need stitching," he said.

"Later," she insisted.

Doc frowned, clearly frustrated by her stubbornness. "At least let me bind it to slow the bleeding."

"Tear a strip off my petticoat and use that."

She winced as he wrapped the strip of fabric around her middle. When he tied it off tight against her side, she sucked in a breath through her teeth.

"Will I live now, Doc?" she asked dryly.

"I'd say you've a sporting chance."

She *was* less dizzy than she'd been, which she appreciated. "The Drizzle—I decided to call her that from now on, seeing as she proved such a pathetic tempest—is very fond of cells. I'd like her to have the opportunity to spend ample time in one."

Brogan tied the woman's hands with a grubby handkerchief

while Ana checked her for hidden weapons. Fitz still had her gun in his hand, and his focus hadn't shifted. The Tempest, however, wasn't watching anyone but Móirín. A glare. White-hot anger.

Good doctor and good person that he was, Barnabus thoroughly checked their enemy's wound. "Slug didn't exit the back. It's still in there somewhere."

"What'll it take to get her to Newgate still breathing?" Fitz asked.

Móirín didn't think the woman was actually that close to breathing her last.

"Care to donate an additional makeshift bandage?" Barnabus asked.

"Considering how much she'll hate that, I would love to," Móirín said.

Brogan took up the task of tearing another strip of fabric from her petticoat. Móirín kept watching the Tempest, seeing the woman's anger and distaste grow. This was not at all the woman's plan, and it was eating away at her. Móirín shouldn't've enjoyed seeing it as much as she did.

Once Barnabus had her bandaged well enough to be moved, he and Brogan pulled the Tempest to her feet.

Móirín rose as well.

"You've lost a heap of blood, Móirín," Barnabus warned.

She straightened her shoulders, though the movement made her side burn. "I'm escorting this trespasser out of our home. That"—she met the Tempest's glare once more—"was *always* the plan."

Fitz stepped to her side. She expected him to object as Barnabus had, but Fitz simply nodded and smiled. "Lead the way, Your Majesty."

"Your Majesty." Móirín repeated the words with a smile. "I could grow accustomed to that."

He walked beside her, keeping to her slower and belabored pace. Behind them, Brogan and Barnabus forcibly brought the Tempest along. Ana had been given the Tempest's gun and was bringing up the rear.

They stepped out of the room through the hidden door and out into the narrow corridor. The house beyond wasn't silent, but it wasn't pulsating with the sound of war either.

Fitz's hand brushed against hers, then his fingers threaded through her fingers. She held fast to his hand as she walked, slowly and with some effort, but with her head held high. The landing was empty. The floor below was a scene of peaceful chaos. Furniture was toppled, some broken, but the fighting had stopped.

Many of her Dreadfuls were there, looking up as she slowly and carefully descended the stairs.

Stone emerged from among the crowd and pointed to the Tempest. "Is that her?"

Móirín nodded. "Her cohorts?"

"Have met various fates." Celia stepped up next to Stone, watching the descent of the captive and her captors. "Word's been sent to Scotland Yard."

Móirín's gaze shifted to the open front door, realizing for the first time that it was light outside. They'd reached morning. Morning, and her Dreadfuls were free, her brother was alive, and the Tempest's reign had ended.

Gemma stepped inside the room, Kumar and Dominique close on her heels. They froze, and she could imagine what they were seeing: the descent of their common enemy, captured and flanked by others of the DPS, led by a blood-soaked woman they knew to be an ally of the Dreadfuls, and a constable who'd risked his life and career for all of them.

The procession continued out the blue door, now hanging from its hinges, and onto King Street, where the aftermath of chaos couldn't have been more obvious. The Dreadfuls inside joined the guards around the Tempest.

On the street, the Raven, the Protector, and many others who'd happily and violently done the Tempest's bidding were being held by both members of the DPS and many of those the Tempest's cohorts had terrorized throughout London. At least three people were lying face down, guarded by more of the Tempest's victims.

Vera walked out of the crowd, placing herself beside Brogan. Hollis joined Ana.

Elizabeth and Fletcher silently placed themselves on the pavement beside Móirín and Fitz.

Looking Móirín over, Fletcher said, "Hate to tell you, but you look like purgatory itself chewed you up and spit you out."

She shrugged. "Stabbed me too." A bit of emotion surfaced without warning. "Did we lose any Dreadfuls?" she asked in a strangled whisper.

"Not a one."

Móirín couldn't stop the tear that dropped, but she held back the rest. "And those who fought alongside?"

"Injuries aplenty, but none lost."

A miracle. An actual, shocking miracle.

"You, though . . ." Fletcher eyed her. "You ain't got a drop of color in your face."

"Been a long night, Fletch."

"But a successful one, i'n'it?" Fletcher tossed out one of his signature grins, that of a now-grown street urchin still itching for an adventure.

Hooves clomped on the cobblestones, drawing all eyes in that direction. A police patrol wagon approached, and the ragtag crowd, many sporting bloodied noses and bruised bodies, parted along the street as it came to a stop directly in front of the scene of an entire night's battle.

Fitz squeezed Móirín's hand once before stepping away to give direction and information to his newly arrived comrades. That he was listened to and shown respect told her the lies being hurled at him had not taken in the way those looking to destroy him had planned.

One man amongst the constables stepped forward—a *gentleman* it seemed to her—and Fitz brought him to where they all stood guard around the Tempest.

"This mort's the one, Sir Richard." Fitz pointed at the Tempest. "Needs to be kept away from the others at Newgate, under full watch."

Sir Richard *Mayne*? The commissioner of police?

He nodded his understanding, and four constables took possession of the Tempest, replacing the handkerchief ties with proper wrist cuffs. Her legs were shackled as well. Móirín glanced at Brogan and saw that he was as satisfied by the turn of events as she was.

The woman didn't look away from Móirín. "You must realize I'm going to tell them who you really are."

Móirín didn't flinch, didn't look away. She stood silent, stalwart, unmoved.

Fitz helped his fellow constables get the fully secured prisoners in the patrol wagon. He got in as well, to ride beside the driver, but turned enough to keep an eye on the back.

Móirín watched him go, her heart sinking. He'd lied for her, and now that lie would catch up to him. After all they'd been through, all they'd fought for, that act of compassion would destroy everything. There was only one way to save him from that.

She'd always known there would be a price to pay for ending the Tempest's reign. And she'd always known she would pay it. She'd known.

And now the reckoning had come due.

THE QUEEN
AND THE KNAVE

by Mr. King

Installment IX
in which the Queen, at last, is free!

Reynard was at Eleanor's side the instant after she outwitted Dezmerina. He wrapped his arms around her, his words of inquiry rendered inaudible in the chaos. But Eleanor did not need to hear what he said; his love and concern for her was etched in her heart already. She tucked her head against him, knowing by the sound of snarls and growls from the magical pack and the shouts of celebratory relief from the crowd who had followed that Dezmerina was no more.

Directly into her ear, so she could hear him, Reynard said, "You've lost your throne, my dear Eleanor."

"She had to be queen in some way when the sun returned. If that meant I would no longer be, it was well worth it. The kingdom will, at last, be free."

That kingdom celebrated for three days following Dezmerina's demise. The wolf pack was returned to the realm of magic by the efforts of those who'd once been forced to hide their gift.

The people sang the praises of their brave queen, not knowing if she would be their queen again.

The barons undertook two days of consultation, something that had never occurred before. But then, a monarch crowning someone else during the Unification Ceremony had also never happened before.

And thus it was, during this state of uncertainty, that the ball was held which always marked the end of this most important of weeks. All the barons and their families were present. Reynard, having been elevated by the Captain of the Guard to be the second-in-command, was eligible to attend the ball inside the palace.

The rest of the guards and the people of the kingdom gathered on the grounds for a party of their own. The celebration had seldom been so jovial. Yet, underneath the joy, was uncertainty. They had seen for themselves the bravery of their one-time queen. But what was to become of her now?

Into the gathering of glittering gowns and flickering candles, Eleanor stepped, her head held high despite the precariousness of her situation. She had not been lying when she'd told Reynard that her kingdom being free of Dezmerina had been her most important goal. But she was at loose ends and, until the question of her position was settled, she would continue to be so.

She paused at the top of the grand stairs leading into the ballroom. From there, arrivals were to be announced. But how to announce her?

Silence followed, and all eyes watched as the highest-ranking of the barons approached the base of the stairs and climbed them, one by one, to the top.

He turned and looked out at the ballroom. "Barons,

gentlemen, ladies, and guests. By decree of the royal barons, I present to you—Queen Eleanor of Amesby."

The cheer that rose shook the crystal chandeliers. The cheer that followed as word reached those outside the palace shook the very trees.

Their queen was theirs once more. As brave and good and loyal a queen as any kingdom had ever known.

And, in the years that would follow, a prince consort—as brave and good and loyal as any queen had ever known—would stand at her side, loving her, loving the people, loving the kingdom.

They were free from the tyranny of one who had ruled with fear and threats. Free from the violence with which that queen would have reigned. Free because they'd chosen to stand together. Because they'd been as brave and good and loyal as any people could hope to be.

CHAPTER 29

There'd been something in Móirín's eyes as the patrol wagon left King Street that worried Fitz. It hadn't been exhaustion from the endless weeks of searching and fighting. Hadn't been the weakness of blood loss. Not relief. Not triumph.

She'd looked almost like she was on the verge of crying, and not tears of happiness.

Something was dreadfully wrong, and he hadn't the first idea what. Worse still, he weren't able to go find out. Wheatley had been proven to be a traitor, and Toft had appointed Fitz to oversee the gathering of all information connected to the Tempest.

He'd spent all day doing precisely that, despite having been up the entire night doing battle. And he'd hardly scratched the surface. The Tempest's trial would, he didn't doubt, make all previous high-profile trials seem minuscule in comparison. Her fate mattered to a lot of people because her crimes had hurt so many. If Fitz were a betting man, he'd wager those who had willingly done her bidding in exchange for power would prove turncoats if they'd any hope, however fleeting and empty, of saving their own necks. And she, no doubt, would be defiant through it all.

After making absolutely certain the Raven, the Protector, and all the prisoners connected to that criminal web were accounted for, guarded thoroughly, and unable to manipulate any other prisoners, Fitz took his leave of Scotland Yard, but he weren't entirely certain where to go from there.

Would Móirín be at the Riding House safe house where she'd taken refuge the last month? Would she and her brother have returned to their one-time home on Picadilly? Would she still be at the Dread Penny Society's headquarters?

Fortunately, they were all in the same general direction from Scotland Yard. He'd ample time to decide before needing to choose a more specific path.

He'd always had friendly interactions with most of the people in London he looked out for, but the number who greeted him, who thanked him, who stopped him to give his hand a firm shake and ask him to thank the Dread Penny Society for putting an end to the Tempest's tortures was near to overwhelming.

And he'd have thoroughly enjoyed the experience, if not for Móirín's heavy expression continually returning to his thoughts.

Many of the Dreadfuls were likely putting their meeting place to rights. Brogan, Vera, and Mr. Sorokin, along with the two little'ns they looked after, were likely at their former residence, getting themselves settled again. The safe house they'd been snatched from would be empty, more or less, and, he suddenly knew that was why Móirín would be found *there*.

Riding House to the alley. Third door. Second staircase. All the way to the door he'd knocked on so many times the past weeks. He did so again, then held his breath.

The peeking panel slid open. He'd guessed right. She was there.

"Parky's a right rubbish blue-bottle."

The door opened an instant later. Móirín motioned him inside, but didn't say anything, an odd thing for her. The interior was better lit than it had been in all the time they'd been hiding there. The windows were no longer heavily covered. Made sense, really. It weren't a hidden place any longer. The Tempest and her people had found it. But those criminals were all either behind bars or no longer on this side of the grave.

His attention didn't stay on the room for long. The last he'd seen Móirín, she'd been covered in her own blood, looking unexpectedly defeated. She'd changed her clothes, and her coloring was a far sight better. But she still weren't smiling or lighthearted.

"Did Doc sew you up?" he asked.

Móirín nodded. "He said I've a couple weeks or so of feeling sore ahead of me, but there shouldn't be anything worrisome."

"Why don't you seem overly happy about that?"

"Oh, I'm pleased as pudding, I assure you." But she didn't look it.

"Why is it you aren't on Picadilly helping Brogan and that group?"

She shrugged, walking to the table where a messy stack of papers sat next to a carpetbag. "What would I do there? I'd set m'self bleeding again if I tried carrying things around. And Brogan'd just start arguing with me about how I ought to make m'home with them and how there's room enough, despite there certainly not being any."

She straightened the papers and set them inside the carpetbag.

An unpleasant suspicion began creeping over him. "And where is it you mean to make your home?"

"I ain't certain yet, but it'll be far enough away to not make trouble for you. I might even try to get to America."

His suspicion became something far too close to confirmation for his peace of mind. "You're leaving?"

"I've not a doubt the Tempest'll offer up proof aplenty of who I am and how I ended my time in Dublin. The lies you told for me'll come back for you. Brogan helping me hide'll catch up to him. If I'm far away, that'll keep things simple for everyone."

"I've always known there'd be a price to pay." He'd not truly understood how deep her conviction on that score ran. She'd given up so much and was willing to make even more sacrifices for the sake of others.

Fitz set an arm around her, then the other, tucking her up close to him. "I ain't looking for 'simple,' Móirín Donnelly."

"Please don't make this harder, Fitz," she whispered.

"I'm sure as all-fire going to make it harder for you to do the wrong thing."

He expected her to pull away, but she leaned into him and put her arms around him. "I won't ruin your life, Fitz. I won't see you tossed in prison because of me."

"You've spent all your life sacrificing for others, love. It's time you claimed it, instead." He kissed her head and held her ever closer, being careful of her wound. "Sir Richard is already speaking about clemency for the Dreadfuls so they can testify without fear of punishment for the things they did in pursuing the Tempest."

"But my time in Dublin had nothing to do with her."

"I know it, but you'd have a bit of time before having to decide what's to be done about that. You'd have time here, time with your brother, time with me. Cain't you wait that long before leaving? Long enough to see the Tempest fully brought to heel? Long enough for *us* to decide what comes next?"

She didn't say anything for the length of a long breath. Then, in a whisper, said simply, "Us."

There was hope in that. "Us," he repeated. "You could wait long enough to give 'us' a chance."

"What if we wait too long? What if you lose everything?"

He tipped her head upward, meeting her eyes. "If I lose you, Móirín Donnelly, I will have lost everything. Don't take that away already."

"For what it's worth, leaving you is proving the most difficult leaving I've ever done."

Leaving you. She spoke of it in the present, in the now, not as something she'd been contemplating but had changed her mind about.

"I spent nearly twenty years of my life searching for my grandfather, not knowing what happened to him, wondering if he'd left me behind because he hadn't cared enough about me to even say goodbye. You weren't going to do that to me, were you, love?"

She set a hand against his cheek. "I'd meant to go by your place and make m'farewell."

"You know where I live?" He'd not ever told her that.

"Of course I do." A mischievous, self-assured smile played on her lips, the one that always set his pulse pumping. "I know people who tell me things."

"Will you trust me when I remind you that I know people too? People who can make things right-tight for you?"

"Why would they?" She seemed to take some comfort in his

embrace, but the tension he could feel in her shoulders meant she still held doubts about escaping the trap life had set for her.

He brushed a breath of a kiss over her lips. "Because fate owes you."

She copied his tender gesture. "And you mean to fight for me?"

"*Alongside* you, Your Majesty. This right-rubbish knave means to fight at your side for all his days."

POSIE AND PRU
DETECTIVES FOR HIRE

by Chauncey Finnegan

Epilogue

Posie Poindexter was delighted. Pru Dwerryhouse was *always* delighted.

The two sat in their cottage, perfectly pleased with life. Pru was knitting, an enormous ball of red yarn on the floor beside her, and singing softly to herself a song about dogs. Posie was watching rain run down the window in rivers, a common occurrence in the English countryside.

Their first endeavor as detectives had not merely been successful, it had been very quickly successful. They were, by any estimation, proper detectives.

"What do you suppose our next detective undertaking will be?" Posie mused aloud.

"I hope it's to do with dogs," Pru answered.

Dogs. Of course.

"For my part," Posie said, "I hope we eventually have a case that involves an actual ghost. That would be brilliant."

"A ghost dog," Pru suggested with a slow and emphatic nod.

It was on that unsurprising declaration that Mr. Green,

a man from the village, entered the cottage with hat in hand. "Hello, ladies. Are you still acting as detectives?"

"Indeed, we are." Posie sat up tall. "Posie and Pru—detectives for hire."

"Well, then, I have a case for you."

Posie and Pru exchanged grinning glances. "Excellent!"

CHAPTER 30

Móirín was standing in front of the Queen. The *literal* one.

Her Majesty sat in a very regal chair in a spill of light from a tall window in the grandly appointed drawing room. Near her chair, at a small writing table, sat Princess Louise.

Lord Chelmsford and Sir Richard Maynes stood to the queen's left, facing her from a deferential distance. Fitz stood beside Moirin, a bit to the queen's right and at a further distance still.

He dressed to handsome perfection. Móirín had donned her best dress, but that wasn't saying much.

"Detective Constable Parkington," Her Majesty said, eyeing Fitz with an air so regal and royal it was nearly palpable. "I understand you were instrumental in the capture of a criminal responsible for offenses too numerous to list."

Fitz dipped his head.

"And I understand you pursued the case despite the objection and obstruction of your superior in Scotland Yard's Detective Department."

Again, Fitz dipped his head.

"Lord Chelmsford has told me that you, personally, saw to his security whilst it was under threat, and did so without requiring renumeration or even credit for your efforts."

Another nod.

To the commissioner, Queen Victoria said, "Detective Constable Parkington is precisely the sort of man who ought to be a trusted Detective Inspector, not relegated to insignificant work."

The commissioner nodded, eyes lowered. "It will be done."

How tempted Móirín was to break with protocol and offer a whoop of excitement for Fitz's promotion. Instead, she kept still and silent.

Then Her Majesty turned to Móirín. "I understand, Miss Donnelly, that you killed a man outside of Kensington Palace mere days ago as the royal carriage passed through the gates. And, further, you did so even knowing that it would draw the attention of the police force to you and your location, which constituted a significant personal risk."

"I did, Your Majesty," Móirín said.

"Why?"

Móirín was not one to shrink under a demanding gaze, royal or otherwise. "Because he meant to kill you. I stopped him despite the risk because it was the right thing. When someone is in danger, I do not shrink or hesitate or relent. It is not in my nature."

"It *does* seem to be in your nature to speak very casually to your queen."

Móirín could not tell if Her Majesty was amused at that or annoyed. Likely a bit of both.

"I am too often inclined to speak my mind when I ought to keep my peace," Móirín acknowledged. "Your Majesty."

Queen Victoria watched her for a moment, one long enough that many would likely have squirmed under it. Móirín just waited. Her Majesty looked away first, though not in an expression of defeat or embarrassment. Nothing flustered their queen.

Queen Victoria turned to her daughter, Princess Louise, who had, since the marriage of her older sister, acted as the queen's personal secretary. "This woman has, as of this moment, received a full royal pardon for whatever she might stand accused of having done. See to it that this is recorded and reported to the necessary people."

Full royal pardon. Only with effort did Móirín keep her mouth from dropping agape. *Full royal pardon.* Her eyes darted to Fitz. He stood perfectly calm and perfectly composed, but she saw the tiniest upward twitch of his lips.

He'd told her to trust that fate would, at last, do her a good turn. Had he known then? Or merely hoped?

Queen Victoria looked back to Sir Richard. "I expect you will see to it that Miss Donnelly is not harassed by the police force over past . . . disagreements."

"It will be done, Your Majesty."

Grinning was likely a breach of etiquette when in audience with the monarch. Móirín didn't bother hiding hers though.

The queen looked at her once more, a single eyebrow lifted in anticipation.

"Thank you, ma'am," Móirín said.

"Having seen the danger that comes with opposing forces such as those you battled against, do you mean to stop fighting on behalf of the vulnerable of this kingdom?"

Knowing her grin likely appeared overconfident, she answered, "I couldn't stop if I tried."

The queen nodded. "See to it that you don't, and that those who have fought alongside you know the importance of what they've done."

"They know," Móirín said firmly, "but I will tell them again, and as often as I need to so they don't doubt it. They don't forget."

"Neither will I." On that, Her Majesty dismissed them.

Lord Chelmsford walked faster than Sir Richard and reached the corridor at the same time Móirín and Fitz did. He offered them both a dip of the head.

"Thank you, Lord Chelmsford," Fitz said, shaking the man's hand. "Without your advocacy, that could not have happened."

Lord Chelmsford had argued on her behalf?

The baron turned to Móirín. "You saved my life, Miss Donnelly, and countless others. That is not something I will forget."

We do not forget. That bit of the DPS pledge had always felt a little double-edged. Móirín knew that long memories were not always beneficial for the vulnerable. For the Dreadfuls, it was meant to be a promise not to forget those whose suffering was too often quickly forgotten, whose plight was easily brushed aside. To hear Lord Chelmsford and Her Majesty, the Queen, both promise not to forget the good the Dreadfuls had done was a balm to a wound that had remained unhealed for years.

Fitz and Móirín walked from the royal residence and out to the street without speaking. Only once inside a hackney charged with taking them to King Street did Fitz finally break the silence.

"That was a pleasant interview."

"Which bit, Parky? An audience with the queen, her knowledge of so much of what we did, your promotion, or my pardon?"

"Yes." He took her hand and raised it to his lips, kissing it slowly, lingeringly. "In case I haven't said it yet, thank you for not dying in that cage two weeks ago."

"You've said it."

He leaned close and whispered, "Then why haven't you said 'You're welcome'?"

"Because when you ask me that, half the time you end up kissing me." She ran a finger along his lapel. "I like those odds."

"And I like kissing you." Which he then proceeded to do.

All the way to King Street.

The hackney made a jarring stop, and the sudden lurch jolted through her not-entirely-healed wound. She couldn't prevent a quick gasp of pain. Fitz helped her out of the carriage, watching her closely. Heavens, she'd be grateful when she wasn't still healing.

They stopped outside the blue door. So often during her years of secrecy, she'd imagined walking into the DPS headquarters like a regular member, participating fully and directly. Now that she was about to do precisely that, her courage wavered. That made her feel almost as ridiculous as the continued pain in her ribs.

Fitz opened the door and motioned her inside.

"Does this mean you are finally going to start writing penny dreadfuls?" she asked him.

"Seems I'd better."

"I would suggest writing about seventy-year-old detectives. All the greatest writers do."

As she stepped past him, he kissed her quickly, then he

closed the door behind them. Headquarters had more or less been put to rights, though not all the broken furniture had been replaced. It'd likely be quite some time before everything had been mended.

Nolan was, of course, no longer the entryway fixture he'd once been. Indeed, he'd slipped away during the fighting. Fitz declared he meant to find out what had become of the man, and Móirín knew better than to doubt him.

The Dreadfuls' etched pennies were set, not on the table as they'd once been—as it had been smashed into splinters during the fray—but on the lip of the wainscoting.

Móirín spun her penny between her fingers before balancing it there amongst the others.

The door to the Parliamentary Room was open, the space where so many plans had been made, so many decisions, so many things she'd been connected to but left out of. She'd be among the Dreadfuls now, but she wasn't sure quite how they'd feel about it.

She stepped inside, and silence descended upon the entire room. All the Dreadfuls were there. So were Ana, Vera, Mr. Sorokin, and Gemma. The Dread Penny Society was growing and changing, though at its heart they were the same fearless defenders of the vulnerable.

Fletch stood in front of the throne-like chair he'd always used when acting as the head of the DPS. He offered a laughing grin to Móirín as she stepped up to him. "Cain't say I'm sad handing this over."

"What, you aren't paid enough, is that it?"

"I'd rather putter about than be respons'ble, truth be told." He pointed toward the chair. "All yours now, Dread Master. It's time and past you took your place among us."

She turned to face them all. The bruises hadn't entirely faded, and the scuffs and cuts were still healing. But they were all still there, still standing, still dedicated to the cause they'd pledged themselves to.

"With me, Dreadfuls," she said, leading them for the first time in the oath she had written five years earlier.

"For the poor and infirm, the voiceless and hopeless, we do not relent. We do not forget. We are the Dread Penny Society."

ACKNOWLEDGMENTS

I could not possibly have written this book with any degree of accuracy without the preservation of and access to

- *The Criminal Prisons of London, and Scenes of Prison Life*, written by John Binny and the reform-minded journalist Henry Mayhew in 1862.
- *The Reform of the Sewers*, by George Rochfort Clarke in 1860.
- a preserved copy of the 1866 edition of "Biographical and Descriptive Sketches of the Distinguished Characters which Compose the Unrivaled Exhibition and Historical Gallery of Madame Tussaud and Sons," the guide published for those visiting Madame Tussaud's wax museum in London. The excerpt Móirín and Fletcher read while at Madame Tussaud's is taken verbatim from this source.
- *Notable British Trials: The Trial of Thurtell and Hunt*, compiled by Eric T. Watson in 1920.
- *Passing English of the Victorian Era: A Dictionary of Heterodox English, Slang and Phrase* by James Redding Ware, published 1909.

ACKNOWLEDGMENTS

- The (modernly published) invaluable works of lexicographer Susie Dent.
- Stephen Fry's *Victorian Secrets* podcast.

I further owe many thanks to

- Jolene Perry, who has convinced me many times not to give up on this series.
- Esther Hatch, for checking my use of Russian.
- Annette Lyon, Luisa Perkins, and Sammie Trinidad for encouragement and writing sprints.
- Jesse Perry and Ginny Miller, for being proofreading lifesavers.
- Liz Swick and Jonathan Eden, for invaluable assistance juggling all of this.
- Pam Pho for continuing to offer guidance, support, and encouragement.
- Paul Eden for *everything*.

DISCUSSION QUESTIONS

1. A detective constable and a fugitive from the law wouldn't seem likely to be a good match. What makes Móirín and Fitz so well-suited to each other?

2. Losing his grandfather and his home at a young age changed the trajectory of Fitz's life. Do you think he would have still become a detective if he'd not endured that tragedy?

3. Móirín wants so desperately to believe she and the Tempest are nothing alike when, in actuality, they have a lot in common. What traits do they share? How have they chosen to use those traits differently?

4. The Tempest began her reign of terror with the goal of avenging her family. In the end, her efforts are focused almost solely on the Dread Penny Society, with Móirín most firmly in her crosshairs. Why do you think she changed her aim so significantly?

5. The Tempest brags repeatedly that she is always a step ahead of Móirín. At what point do you think Móirín sorted out the various aspects of what the Tempest had planned?

6. How do you think the Dread Penny Society will be different moving forward now that their identities, headquarters, and activities are known?

About the Author

SARAH M. EDEN is a *USA Today* best-selling author of witty and charming historical romances, including 2019's Foreword Reviews INDIE Awards Gold Winner for Romance, *The Lady and the Highwayman*, and 2020 Holt Medallion finalist, *Healing Hearts*. She is a two-time "Best of State" Gold Medal winner for fiction and a three-time Whitney Award winner.

Combining her obsession with history and her affinity for tender love stories, Sarah loves crafting deep characters and heartfelt romances set against rich historical backdrops. She holds a bachelor's degree in research and happily spends hours perusing the reference shelves of her local library.

Read more adventures from

THE DREAD PENNY SOCIETY

BY SARAH M. EDEN

Includes three new, never-before-published penny
dreadfuls by Mr. King, Stone, and Brogan Donnelly!

Available wherever books are sold

SHADOW
MOUNTAIN